vintage death

Geo Gosling

VD: Vintage Death

Published by Wheatmark®
1760 East River Road, Suite 145,
Tucson, Arizona 85718 USA
www.wheatmark.com

ISBN: 978-1-62787-305-5 (paperback)
ISBN: 978-1-62787-306-2 (ebook)
LCCN: 2015944533

rev201501

"Two things are infinite: the universe and human stupidity; and I'm not sure about the universe."
— *Albert Einstein*

"No, I don't go to that restaurant anymore. No body goes there. It's too crowded."
— *Yogi Berra*

"In politics, stupidity is not a handicap."
— *Napoléon Bonaparte*

Acknowledgments

I don't acknowledge anyone – I did this whole effing thing
myself. Well, it was somewhat edited by
Cookie, Bruce Frank, and Jill Davis

Special Thanks

I do however, give special thanks to Al Gore
for inventing the Internet

Dedicated to

No one in particular

Disclaimer and instructions...
I guess

I have no training and don't consider myself a writer. I have a B.S. degree in winemaking from the University of California, at Davis. In 1995 I sustained a severe TBI in a bicycle (me) vs. pick-up truck collision (I was wearing a helmet and it is the only reason I was not DOA.) In the following years, I have not only read a lot of books, but I have written a couple also. The two books I wrote are not novels. Oh, how I wish they were! Those two books are: *TBI Hell—A Traumatic Brain Injury Really Sucks* followed by: *TBI Purgatory—Comes After Being In TBI Hell*.

This book however, is a novel. So, even though my noggin does not function quite right anymore, it did come from my imagination and therefore, is *not* real. If anything sounds like someone or something you know, it's pure coinkydink.

There is one aspect of *all* the novels I have read that I find quite annoying: Often, at a critical juncture a word, words, or a phrase is used that I don't know the meaning of. I've decided that authors intentionally use words and phrases that the "average Joe" has no clue about because it makes them feel more intelligent than everyone else or maybe it's because they have some sort of insecurity issue...but don't quote me on that.

In my younger, wilder days I would have just skipped over any unknown word or phrase and never given it a second thought. But now, I can't seem to do that. *Are they confused or clear on the matter? Are they upset because of what just happened? Maybe they are relieved? I bet that word would clue me in. I better look it up to make sure I know what's going on. Now, where the hell did I put my dictionary?*

Out of my perturbation[1] (I would have had to look up that word) over this, I decided that in my novel I would define, using footnotes at the bottom of the page, some words and concepts I use. Now, I *could* have just used words that everyone knows, or should know, but that would have been to pedestrian[2] of me. Since I'm trying to be an author, I have to follow suit of all authors on the planet and use words that only people who want to be seen as quite intelligent use. If, by some chance, you know what the word, phrase, or concept means just ignore the footnote. If you become annoyed with the footnotes or lose your place on the page that you are reading while looking at them, again: just ignore them. I tried to make them amusing because even I realize no one wants to read footnotes that define words. It would be like reading a dictionary. The footnotes are certainly not essential to the story, but they do add to it and you could learn something.

While reading, when you encounter three dots following some text followed by more text (some text...more text) that means you should pause for a moment after reading the "some" text and before continuing with the "more" text.

In dialogue, if you encounter some text followed by three dots (some text...) that means the speaker's, or thinker's, voice, or thought trails off.

As a young whippersnapper I hated every English, literature, English-Literature, writing, grammar, composition, or any similar class that I ever took in junior high school, high school, and on into college. This book is not to be judged, or even taken

---

1 Anxiety; mental uneasiness.

2 Lacking inspiration or excitement; dull. I would have had to look-up that word to because I wouldn't have been able to see how me walking down the street had anything to do with the story.

seriously, in terms of structure, form, genre, writing rules, composition, or any other writing terms you can think of that one would learn in those types of classes; mainly because I don't know, or care to know, any of that stuff.

I never knew when to say, or write, "who" or "whom," and "whoever" or "whomever." I also never knew when to use "to" or "too." I looked up the rules online and saw explanations using words and phrases such as: "subjects," "subjects of verbs," "objects," "looking inside the clause," "versatile preposition," "past participle," (that one brought back some awful memories) "dependent clauses," etc. It was too confusing for me and *way* too much for someone with an injured brain who doesn't really care if it is "who" or "whom," or "to" or "too," as long as the point and/or idea comes across. Besides, 94.7 percent of the people who read this book aren't going to know either, so... what's the point in stressing over it? I like to think of this book as the "anti-book."

Death Número Uno

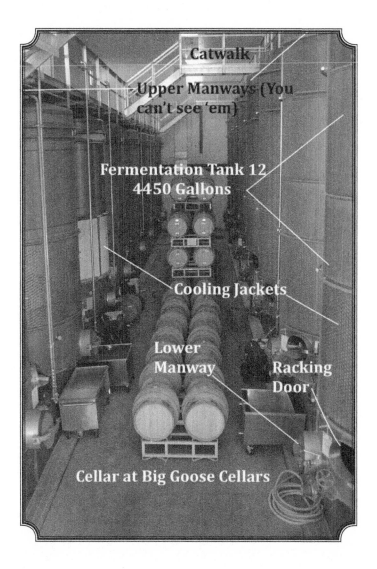

Catwalk

Upper Manways (You can't see 'em)

Fermentation Tank 12
4450 Gallons

Cooling Jackets

Lower Manway

Racking Door

Cellar at Big Goose Cellars

Chapter 1

Frank in Tank

He could not find Frank. He looked all through the cellar but he was nowhere to be found. "Frank! Hey Frank! Where the hell are ya?" Tim shouted, but received no reply. "Damn it! Where is that mule's patootie? We need to do a pump-over[1] on Tank 12. Now where the hell is that guy?" *He's probably sucking down a Coors Light and stuffing his face with Cheetos.* Finally, Tim Tauscher gave up looking for Frank and climbed the stainless steel staircase and walked along the stainless steel catwalk towards the top of Tank 12. He would do the pump-over himself, because it had to be done.

The pump-over needed to be done for a couple of reasons: One is that spraying the fermenting juice, or "must," over the layer, or "cap," of stems, pulp, skins, and possibly seeds that forms on top of the "must" during fermentation, enables the extraction of color, flavor, and tannins from the grape components. The other reason is that a pump-over ensures the fermentation "cap" stays moist and so won't develop unwanted mold or bacteria.

The aforementioned cap is formed when the carbon dioxide (CO_2) emitted by the yeast during fermentation, rises to the surface of the juice and carries solid material with it. The steady rise of CO_2 keeps the solids at the surface, thereby forming a "cap."

---

1 To circulate fermenting juice of red wines from the bottom of the tank over the skin cap that forms during fermentation to ensure optimal extraction and prevent bacterial spoilage. They are the bane of cellar workers everywhere. Then "bane" means: a cause of great distress or annoyance.

Frequent pump-overs was one of the myriad of reasons Big Goose Cellars wine often scored so high in the *Wine Watcher*. That high score, in turn, meant the price of a bottle of wine could be high enough to make even the dorkiest cork dork[2] think he, or she, was getting a something special.

As Tim neared the top of Tank 12, he noticed the upper manway was open. As he got closer to the manway, he noticed Frank's sweatshirt on the railing. He also noted that there were a couple of stainless steel valves and clamps resting on top of the tank along with some rubber gaskets and hoses that were on the catwalk—this was all equipment needed for doing a pump-over. *Well I'll be, Frank is getting the job done.* Yet, Frank Finnegan was nowhere to be seen. *Where the...?* Tim reached the top of the 4000-gallon tank and looked inside, through the open manway, expecting to just see the cap formed during the fermentation process.

Tim did see the cap but he also saw the soles of two rubber work boots. *Boots? What the hell are those doing in there? The cab will have "rubbery" overtones and that won't be good.* Tim reached down to grab the boots and remove them but he couldn't because the boots still had feet in them. He then realized the feet were attached to a body. *Holy frijole!* Tim grabbed the boots more tightly, braced himself, and gave the boots a big pull. The boots came loose easily and Tim fell over backwards. As Tim righted himself, he looked at the boots and recognized them as Franks; of course the fact that Frank had written his name on the soles with a Sharpie didn't hurt matters. *My God these boots stink! So, the feet must stink also and*

---

2 "cork dork" – A person who talks about wine too seriously. A "cork dork" uses adjectives such as "sexy," "attractive," "complicated," and "temperamental" to describe wine. Those words are used because they don't really tell you anything and you can't be wrong if you use them.

"Stinky feet is not a characteristic I want in this wine. I better get them out of there!" Holding the two empty boots, Tim looked back into the open manway and saw Frank's feet sticking out of the fermentation cap. Tim grabbed Frank's feet and gave a big pull but he was unable to lift them because they were attached to the rest of Frank's body.

Tim hoped he was hallucinating this whole ordeal but, in the back of his mind, he knew that he wasn't. Tim had not hallucinated since that night in college when he and his fraternity pledges had taken something, along with too much Jägermeister,[3] and ended-up naked on the pitcher's mound of the baseball stadium. He hadn't known what to do then and he didn't know what to do now. All he knew was that all of Frank's problems were solved, but his had just begun.

Tim thought about just turning a blind eye to the whole mess because he figured the wine, which would have a rather acidic pH of around 3.56 in a couple of days, would eventually dissolve Frank, and the problem would go away. It might even be beneficial because the Cab would have some unique, complex, characteristics and maybe get a score of 100 in the *Wine Watcher*. If that happened, Big Goose Cellars could sell the wine for $150 a bottle and *that* would make William Strong, the owner, a lot of money and awfully happy. Tim liked happy bosses; they tended to pay more. *Would Frank dissolve? Would he just decompose into nothing? Yeah I'm sure he would...at least I think he would.*

Tim felt a splitting headache coming on because he couldn't quite deal with what was going on. He had just found Frank dead inside a tank of fermenting grape juice and he, the

---

3   A German 70-proof digestif made with 56 herbs and spices. Jägermeister tastes like shit unless it has been in the freezer for a few hours prior to drinking. Fortunately, after a couple of drinks, you don't mind the taste.

winemaker, was contemplating just leaving him in there to disintegrate and then hopefully yield an award winning wine.

After quite a few minutes of contemplating just leaving Frank in the tank, Tim's common sense took hold. *Okay, I guess I do have to get the body out of the tank because he ain't just gonna dissolve in there.* So, Tim walked back to the stainless steel staircase, descended it to the cellar floor, and began to look for Roberto, the other cellar worker. Tim found Roberto Rodriguez whistling a tune on top of some barrels while topping them with wine to remove any headspace, or ullage.[4]

He yelled, "Roberto! The Frank is dead! The Frank is dead! (Think *Wizard of Oz*) Get down from there! Now! We have to get him out!"

"Que? Que? What you say?" asked Roberto. "Frank dead? What you mean, muertos? Out where? Where Frank?" *Frank cannot be dead*—he thought this Spanish, of course. Roberto did not think he had understood Tim correctly. He climbed down from the barrels and joined Tim on the cellar floor.

Tim said to Roberto, "Frank is in Tank 12. He's dead...muerto. We have to pump the wine out. All the stuff needed is already out there, just grab a couple more hoses."

"Tank 12? What Frank in there for?" asked Roberto.

"I don't know. I guess he really likes the wine," answered Tim. "We'll drain the tank and yank out Frank. Gee, I'm poet and didn't even know it," chuckled Tim.

"What hose?" asked Roberto. "I no want use wrong hose again," said Roberto with a whimper. He didn't understand winemaking, but he knew that not all hoses were the same. He

---

4   The space between the wine and the top of the container it is in. "Topping up," refers to filling this space with wine to remove any oxygen and avoid any problems it may cause...which are many.

had been reprimanded the prior harvest for using hoses that were contaminated with Malolactic Bacteria[5] to move some wine that shouldn't come into contact with the bacteria.

"Oh hell, I don't really care, whatever hoses are closest," answered Tim. Roberto grabbed the nearest hoses, hoping they were the right ones, while Tim grabbed some additional clamps, valves, and gaskets. Then they both ran out to the tank pad even though Roberto still wasn't sure what was going on. Roberto and Tim hurredly hooked-up the pump and hoses to Tank 12 in order to empty it. "Where pump to?" asked Roberto.

"Just go to tank...uh...15," answered Tim.

"But that full," said Roberto.

Oh man. That's right. "Well, go to 16 then," demanded Tim.

"But that no clean," replied Roberto.

"Oh hell," muttered Tim. *It will take ten or twenty minutes to clean that tank.* Tim wasn't about to spend time cleaning a tank, plus he didn't want to get himself all wet and dirty, so he decided to risk the wine getting contaminated with some bacteria, mold, or whatever else was living in Tank 16. Chances were the wine could eventually be "fixed" if it became contaminated with some really small critter. Besides, all Tim could actually think about was the dinner date he had that evening with a "mature" but extremely attractive, extremely rich, and recently-widowed woman.

Tim instructed Roberto to go ahead and use Tank 16. So, Roberto hooked hoses from Tank 12 to Tank 16 and turned on the pump. Soon, all the liquid had been transferred to Tank 16

---

5   Bacteria used for Malolactic Fermentation. It is a process in winemaking in which tart-tasting malic acid naturally present in grapes, is converted to softer-tasting lactic acid. That sounds pretty scientific and you can impress your friends by saying it. Not all wines go through Malolactic fermentation.

and all that remained in Tank 12 were the lees[6] and a dense pile of grape skins, seeds, pulp, and a few stems. Oh, and Frank was in there too. Tim opened the lower manway door on Tank 12 but all he could see were crushed grape remains and those pesky lees. *Oh yeah...duh, I forgot about all that crap.*

"Hey Roberto, I forgot about the grapes and lees. We will need a couple of shovels to remove them, unless you want to do it by hand." Apparently Roberto did not, because he was already standing behind Tim holding two large shovels. *Aww... you stupid American, of course I don't want to do it by hand.*

So, Tim and Roberto went about removing the crushed grapes remains and lees that remained in Tank 12. The lower manway was only big enough to allow one shovel in at a time, so Tim and Roberto were alternately grabbing crushed grape remains with their shovel, pulling them out the lower manway, and throwing them on the ground. After quite a few minutes, enough solids had been removed so that Tim was able to see a hand buried amongst the crushed grape remnants that remained.

"Okay Roberto, I see Frank's hand. I suppose we should be a little more careful now, dontchya think?"

"Why? He no get more dead," said Roberto.

Tim gave Roberto a malevolent[7] look and threw his shovel on the ground. He then poked his head into the manway of Tank 12 and immediately began coughing violently because his lungs began to burn as if a torch was burning in his chest. Roberto saw this, tossed his shovel aside, grabbed Tim's shirt collar, and yanked him back.

---

6   Dead yeast, deposits of yeast, and other solids formed during fermentation. It eventually smells like crap.

7   Having or showing a wish to do evil to others. It's a pretty common look among cellar workers at the height of harvest.

"You can no breathe in tank. Might die. I get fan," said Roberto. *What are you doing? You are a stupid white man.* He ran into the cellar and returned with a portable fan which he took to the top of the tank and placed over the upper manway. He then turned it on in order to blow out all of the CO_2 that had accumulated in the tank during the fermentation process. Nothing could be done for a few minutes while the CO_2 was being replaced with lung-friendly oxygen. So, Tim and Roberto just stood amongst all the moist, discarded lees, the crushed grape remains on the ground, and stared at each other with dumbfounded expressions.

"What happen?" asked Roberto.

"Beats me. I was going to ask you the same thing." answered Tim.

"I on barrels. I not know nothing," replied Roberto. "He fall in?" *Silly American. I bet he did just fall in.*

"I have no idea. I guess he did just fall in," answered Tim. *I know Frank's bicycle had no pedals and his helmet had no strap but...*

"No. Frank no fall in. He no that stupid," said Roberto. *Well... yes he was just like all you stupid crackers.*[8]

"Well Roberto, there is someone in the tank and whoever it is, and however they got there, they *are* wearing Frank's boots and Frank is nowhere to be found so..." stated Tim.

All of this activity caused quit a bit of commotion and William Strong, the owner of the winery, noticed it, came out of his office, and ambled over to Roberto and Tim.

"What's all the ruckus?" asked William.

"Well Bill," said Tim, "we've got a slight problem."

---

8   That is a ubiquitous sentiment amongst Mexican workers in the wine industry. Then ubiquitous means: present or found everywhere. I hate it when I have to look-up words in the definition. It pisses me off.

"A problem? Really?" said William. "What is it and how big? And what's it going to cost me?"

"Well, it's pretty big and there is no price tag," answered Tim.

"Aww come on," said William. "Everything has a price tag. Anything can be bought and money can fix anything. So tell me, what's this *big problem*?" said William as he made quotation marks with his fingers and opened his eyes really wide.

"Well Bill, there's a body in Tank 12 and we are ninety–nine-point-nine-nine percent sure that it's Frank."

"What the hell would Frank be doing in Tank 12 and why aren't you 100 percent sure? Isn't Tank 12 my Cabernet...and what the hell is this mess all over the ground?" asked William as he gestured to the lees that had been removed from the tank.

"Well Bill, I haven't actually *seen* the whole body, just the feet and the boots...which *are* Frank's, by the way. So, it's possible that it *is* just some gangbanger in there that just happened to be wearing Frank's boots, but I don't think that is too likely. He is not doing much in there because he's dead. And yes, Tank 12 is, or was I should say, Cabernet. But it's empty now because that Cab is now in Tank 16. Oh, and this mess on the ground? That's the lees and grape remains from Tank 12. We were trying to get Frank out of the tank but we had to stop for a while to let the CO_2 dissipate," said Tim.

"Aw come on Tim, don't give me any of your crap. What's really going on? Do you seriously think it's Frank in there?"

"I'm not giving you any crap, Bill. There really *is* a body in Tank 12. I think it's Frank because I told him to do a pump-over on Tank 12, his sweatshirt is on the catwalk railing near the top of the tank and, as I said, the boots I was able to pull off the dudes feet belong to Frank. Come over here and look at this," said Tim.

He led William around all of the discarded material on the ground and over to Tank 12. Tim then had William look into the tank through the lower manway, and as he pointed to the remains in the tank he said, "Look. Look in there. What do you see? Besides grape remains, I mean. Do you see anything unusual? Can you see anything without your glasses?"

"Uh, I can see. I don't need my glasses, but what should... oh wow! Holy frijole! Is that a hand?" shouted William in utter disbelief.

"Yes it is, and I believe it's Frank's hand. *That* is what all the ruckus was about. We were emptying the tank to get him out when you showed-up."

"Well, what were you planning on doing after you got him out? Hosing him off? Putting a cork in him?" said William with a slight snigger.[9]

"Uh, well I hadn't really thought that far ahead. I don't really know what I was going to do, but I certainly would not have 'put a cork in him' as you so elegantly put it. I've never dealt with a dead body before; just dead yeast. There's a big difference," said Tim, "in more ways than one."

"Well, I guess we really shouldn't touch anything else," said William in all seriousness, "let the cops do that. But I do have a group of six coming in a couple of hours and they can't see any of this. That would not be good for business. We've at least got to get this mess off the ground and I guess we can just close the tank door for now to hide Frank, so he's no problem.

"Roberto, grab a hose and start hosing this pad off. Make it look real nice," instructed William. "I'll call the police and tell

---

9 A smothered or half-suppressed laugh. I could have used "snicker" but this word sounds much more un-PC. That is why I used it and probably why no one else does.

them to get their butts over here and do whatever they need to do as fast as possible."

With that, William went back to his office and called the police department in the town of Birchwood, which is a small, hoity-toity California town of about 5000 inhabitants and is surrounded by vineyards and wineries that produce world-class wines. The majority of its residents are *extremely* financially secure and rather dull. Being a cop in Birchwood is considered to be one of the best jobs in the state because the pay is good and there is little illegal activity. Unfortunately for anyone young and single, Like a certain Officer Kendry, there is little activity of *any* kind.

William explained that there was a dead body in one of his tanks, and he had some wealthy tourists coming in a couple of hours, so they needed to do whatever they needed to do soon, and in a hurry.

The police told William to leave everything the way it is and they would send someone right over. William hung-up the phone and then quickly explained to Maria, the receptionist/secretary, what was going on and then proceeded back out to the tank pad.

William sauntered up to Tim and said, "Okay, start from the beginning. Tell me everything."

Tim proceeded to tell William how he had earlier instructed Frank to do a pump-over on Tank 12. When he later went out to check on Frank's progress, he couldn't find him anywhere; and the pump-over had not been done. He figured he would have to do the pump-over himself, but when he went to the top of the tank to set-up, he saw evidence that Frank *was* preparing to do the pump-over. However, there was no Frank. So, while setting-up to do the pump-over himself, Tim looked into the tank, through the upper manway, and saw the soles of two boots sticking out of the cap.

Tim then related to William how he had sat down to collect himself, as he was becoming rather uncollected, and then went to get Roberto in order to help him remove Frank from the tank. He continued by explaining how he and Roberto had drained Tank 12 into Tank 16.

"We were in the process of removing the crushed grape remains and lees as fast as we could, but we had to stop to allow the CO_2 to dissipate from Tank 12," continued Tim. "That's when you showed up, Bill."

"Hmm. Well I'll be damned," said William. "I called the cops and they're sending someone right out. They said not to touch *anything*. I also told Maria what was going on and she did not take it very well. Typical female. Have you ever seen a Mexican woman get hysterical? It's kind of amusing, actually."

A police car then drove up the wineries entryway and parked on the tank pad next to William and Tim. Two officers got out of the car and one of them asked, "Is one of you William Strong?"

"Yes, that would be me," said William.

"We understand you may have a dead body in one of your tanks. Is that correct?" asked the officer.

"Well...that's not entirely correct. We *do*, in fact, have a body in one of our tanks, and it is *definitely* dead; there is no 'may' about it. Come on and look in here, officer...uh...?"

"That would be McMillan, and this is my partner Officer Kendry."

William then motioned for the two officers to come over to where he was standing by the open lower manway of Tank 12. When they arrived, William had the two officers look into the

13

tank, through the manway, and he pointed to the hand that was buried in all of the fermentation remains.

William said, "See there? That is a hand. Frank was supposed to be doing a pump-over on this tank, but he was, and still is, nowhere to be found; unless of course, that's Frank's hand. If it is well, then we have found him, part of him anyway. Timmy here, also found Frank's sweatshirt on the railing near the top of Tank 12. And Those boots you see there," William said as he pointed to the boots lying on the cement, "are Frank's and they came off the body in the tank. So we, meaning Tim and I, are assuming that Frank is in the tank, and that's whose hand we're looking at."

"We never assume *anything*," stated Officer McMillan flatly and sternly. "It's bad for business."

"Plus," chimed in Officer Kendry, "it makes an ass out of u and me. Get it? An *ass* out of *u* and *me*, that's how you spell assume." *Boy, I sure am witty today.*

"We will have to remove the body and positively identify the victim," said Officer McMillan as he gave Officer Kendry a disgusted look.

William thought Officer McMillan was a little to into "cop speak," so he asked, "Has anyone ever negatively identified a victim? And wouldn't that just mean you didn't know who the victim was? I would imagine that would be pretty bad for business as well."

"No, we don't negatively identify victims. That makes absolutely no sense," responded Officer Kendry haughtily.[10] "That would be silly."

Officer Kendry and Officer McMillan were both rookie officers who had been on the force for less than a year. Officer McMillan

---

10 Arrogantly superior and disdainful. Then disdainful means "showing contempt or lack of respect" – Most small town cops act haughty.

was attempting to exude confidence, sureness, professionalism, and competency, while Officer Kendry just wanted to carry a gun, look important, and meet chics. Normally, rookie officers don't work together, but because of budget cuts they were not able to be partnered with a veteran officer.

"Now, just who is this 'Frank'?" asked Officer McMillan.

"He is the Cellar Master, or at least he was. He had been here for years," answered Tim. "We were in the process of removing his body when Bill, or William as you know him, told us not to touch anything and said he would call you guys."

"That certainly was the right thing to do," said Officer McMillan. "When there is a death involved...you just never know. The slightest...uh...*anything*, for lack of a better word, can make a huge difference in solving the case."

Officer Kendry, who had returned from the squad car after retrieving a camera, started taking photographs of the manway, the manway door, the tank, the crushed grape remains in the tank, the hand in the grapes, everything on the ground, and even the shovels. He then took some pictures of the vineyards, the winery, and a good-looking, well-endowed, brunette tourist who came out of the tasting room. When he was through, he climbed the stairs to the top of the tank and took more photographs. Finally satisfied, he returned to the tank pad and set his camera aside and said, "There. I captured this Kodak moment from every angle."

"Okay good. The first thing we do now is remove the body and make a positive, *not* a negative ID on the victim," said Officer McMillan as he gave William a miffed look.

"Okay, so how should we go about getting ol' Frank out of the tank?" asked Officer Kendry.

Tim answered, "Well, I guess we'll have to dig him out of the stuff in the tank and pull him out." He then turned to Roberto and said, "Go get that bin on wheels. We'll throw the rest of the stuff in there oh, and grab our shovels to."

"Sí señor," said Roberto as he walked away. He returned shortly with the shovels and the large, empty bin on wheels, which he rolled under the lower manway of Tank 12. He and Tim then began to remove the remaining grape skins, seeds, stems, leaves, pulp and anything else in the tank except Frank. They had to be much more careful removing all these components, to what could have been an award winning wine, because they did not want to put any kind of mark on Frank's body. They figured any marks they put on Frank might hinder the investigation. After a few minutes, they had removed enough crushed grape remains so that someone could climb through the manway and into the tank to help get Frank out. Roberto stuck his head in through the manway to determine if enough CO_2 had dissipated for him to breathe in the tank.

"Is okay now. I breathe okay," he said, "I go in now."

Roberto climbed into Tank 12 and began to carefully remove, by hand, the crushed grape remains that surrounded Frank. After a few minutes, Roberto was able to make a positive ID on the victim and it was Frank. However, he was so firmly stuck in crushed grape remains that he was proving difficult to move. *The silly gringo is stuck in the mud.*

After an hour of brute force by Roberto, Frank was free of the crushed grape remains and able to be moved. Roberto maneuvered Frank into a horizontal position, not at all carefully mind you, because he wasn't worried about hindering any kind of investigation and he never really liked Frank to begin with. He pushed Frank, head-first, to the lower manway door.

Outside the tank Tim, William, Officer McMillan, and Officer Kendry grabbed Frank's head and shoulders and not so gently pulled Frank through the manway door. Once Frank was completely extricated from the tank, he was gently laid on the cold, concrete of the tank pad. Officer McMillan stood there and looked at Frank. *Well now what the hell do we do? I never thought I would have to deal with a murder, if that's what this is, in this town.*

"We should probably get some sort of investigator," said Officer Kendry.

"Yeah, we should. Why don't you call headquarters and tell them to send someone over," responded Officer McMillan. Officer Kendry ambled back to the squad car, got on the radio, and called the station.

Chapter 2

Frank out of Tank

"Joanie, it's me, Carl," said Officer Kendry, "Can I speak with the Chief?"

"He's not here. He's at the fire station talking with the new volunteers."

"Hmm. Well can you send an investigator out here to Big Goose Cellars? Right away."

Laughing, Joanie said, "An investigator? You gotta be kiddin' me. We don't have anyone like that here, we don't need one."

"Are you serious? I thought every town had an investigator," said Officer Kendry dubiously.

"Not this one. The only crimes this town needs investigating are whose dog is barking after midnight. Is there some unknown dog that won't shut-up?" asked Joanie sarcastically.

"No, I wish. Now, where the hell is the nearest investigator? Homicide Investigator that is."

"Homicide Investigator? Homicide is murder, right? You're saying there has been a murder at Big Goose Cellars? Don't mess with me today, Carl. I'm not in the mood for it." *He is just trying to impress me, the big oaf. No one was murdered at Big Goose Cellars.*

"I am serious, damn it! There has been a homicide and we need a Homicide Investigator, *now!*" said Carl. He was trying to be a tough, no-nonsense cop to impress Joanie.

"Well okay. Gee. Sorry. Is it that time of the month again for you already, Carl? Try and relax. Give me a couple of minutes."

Joanie disconnected the call with Carl and went about locating the nearest investigator. She still did not believe that a Homocide Investigator was needed, not in Birchwood anyway, but Officer Kendry requested one and she needed this job, so... Joanie knew that the Birchwood PD did not have any kind of investigator, but maybe the Elviño County Sheriff's Office did, so she contacted them.

While Carl awaited word from Joanie, he sat in the squad car and tried to remember all of his training from the law enforcement classes he had taken in order to get his badge. He didn't have much luck. All he could remember was how to respond to loud noises coming from next door. Soon, the car radio squawked.

"Carl? You there?"

"Yeah. Go ahead Joanie. What did you find out?"

"Uh, well the nearest Homicide Invesigator is actually a detective with the county Sheriff's Office. Do you want me to I contact him?"

"Yeah, of course, and ASAP. Do you know who the investigator...er...uh...detective is?"

"His name is David Knight. I guess he is pretty good. Now, what the hell does ASAP mean?"

"Oh, come on Joanie. You can't be serious. You don't know what ASAP means?"

"I am totally serious. What's it mean?"

"It stands for, 'As Soon As Possible.' You've really never heard that before?" asked Officer Kendry in disbelief. *Boy, she really is a dumb blonde. Great set of party bags[11] but not much upstairs.*

---

11 "Party bags" – Crude name for female breasts; but certainly more amusing than "tits."

"I've heard it, but never knew what it meant. Well anyway... I'll call the Sherrif's Office right now."

Joanie got ahold of David Knight and informed him of the situation at Big Goose Cellars. Within 45 minutes, Detective Knight was standing next to Officers Kendry and McMillan on the tank pad of Big Goose Cellars. Also on the tank pad were Tim Tauscher, William Strong, and Roberto Rodriguez. The two officers brought Detective Knight up to speed on everything they knew regarding the death of Frank Finnegan.

"Well, I guess Frank won't...uh *can't*, age too well anymore. But this vintage of your Cab may have a special, undefineable quality and complexity to it and could score 100 points in the *Wine Watcher*," quipped Detective Knight. "It will be $200 a bottle Cab." He then looked at the three Big Goose Cellar people and asked, "Did any of you actually *see* Frank at the top of the tank and what he was doing up there?"

"No, I did not actually *see* him up there. I had been in my office catching-up on some paperwork and Roberto was on top of some barrels in the cellar. Frank was setting-up to do a pump-over and I decided to check on his progress, that's when I found him."

"And you are...?"

"I'm Tim Tauscher, the winemaker. This is William Strong, the owner, and that there is Roberto Rodriguez, the cellar hand," he said as he pointed to the other two people on the tank pad.

"How about you, Mr. Strong? Did you see anything?" asked Detective Knight.

"No. I just heard some commotion, came out to see what all the ruckus was, and found out Frank was in the tank," answered William.

Detective Knight then turned to talk with Roberto, but he was no where to be seen. "Now where the hell did he go? No one is to leave here until I say so!"

Just then Roberto came out of the cellar carrying a blanket. He was going to cover Frank because that's what he saw done in the movies and on TV. He went to cover Frank but Detective Knight grabbed him and yelled, "No! Do not touch him!"

"Why no?" a surprised Roberto asked.

"Yeah, why not?" asked Tim.

"Yeah, why not?" asked William. Detective Knight looked to be only about 23 or 24 years old and William was not at all confident that he knew what he was doing. He didn't look old enough to have anything to do with the law, unless he was flirting with ideas for breaking it with his drinking buddies.

"Yeah, why not?" asked Officers Kendry and McMillan in unison.

"Well," said Detective Knight, "covering the victim with a blanket, or anything else for that matter, disturbs the position of minute pieces of evidence, may move the body, and may absorb fluids needed for analysis."

"But he has been in a tank full of wine and we already had to move him to get him out of the tank," said Tim.

Detective Knight stood there with a blank stare for a long moment and then said, "Yes, that was unfortunate. Didn't these officers tell you not to touch anything?"

"No, actually these officers helped us get him out," replied Tim.

Detective Knight turned towards the two officers, gave them a look of total disbelief and said, "What!? Tell me you didn't!"

"Well, we could tell you, but we would be lying, and my mother taught me to never tell a lie," said Officer Kendry.

"Didn't you guys learn anything at the Academy?" asked

21

Detective Knight. *Leave it to cops in a small tourist town. They've been watching too much "Cops" on TV.* He stared glaringly at the two rookie cops, took some deep breath's, went to his "Happy Place," and said, "Well, there's nothing we can do about it now. Okay Roberto, go ahead and cover him with the blanket."

When that was done, Detective Knight asked Tim and Roberto to show him where the body was, when found, and how they had moved it. Tim and Roberto spent the next few minutes explaining to Detective Knight how Frank was positioned in the tank, how they had moved the wine to another tank, how they had shoveled the crushed grape-remains out of the tank, and finally, how they had removed Frank from the tank. During this explanation, Officer Kendry went and grabbed his camera and brought it over to Detective Knight and said, "Not all is lost. I took two rolls of photos when we first got here, which was *before* all the crushed grapes were removed and *before* the body was extricated from the tank "

"But no photos were taken *before* the tank was drained of the wine?" asked Detective Knight.

"Well no, of course not. How the hell could I take pictures before I got here?" asked Officer Kendry. "You'd have to ask Tim or Roberto about that."

So, Detective Knight turned to Tim and Roberto and said, "So, how about it? Did either of you happen to take photos before you drained the tank?"

You can't be serious thought Tim as he took a deep, slow breath and said, "No, I did not take any pictures. I wasn't exactly thinking about capturing this for posterity. Taking photos was the farthest thing from my mind...well, maybe not the farthest thing."

"Okay. Okay," said Detective Knight as he put up his hands. "I had to ask.

22

Was anyone else here at the time...anyone at all?" asked Detective Knight.

"Yes, Maria. She is my secretary, but she was at her desk all morning," chimed in William. "She's still there actually."

"I would like to speak with her right now. Is that possible?" asked Detective Knight as he turned toward William.

"Certainly, follow me," said William. He motioned for Detective Knight to follow him as he began walking back to his office. When they arrived, William said, "Maria, this is Detective Knight. He would like to ask you a few questions."

Maria sat down behind her desk and said, "Sí. Bueno. Okay. Ask me."

Detective Knight took out a notebook and pen, and walked up to Maria's desk. *Ooh la la, she's one hot tamale. I wonder if there is a burrito in her cama* (bed) *keeping her warm at night. I'm gonna like questioning her.* He then proceeded to ask Maria all the standard questions: Did you see anyone here this morning? Did you leave your desk for any length of time today? Did you notice any strange people around the winery recently? Did Frank have any gambling debts or maybe a drug problem that you are aware of? Did you receive any unusual phone calls in the last couple of days? Are you married? Are you free tonight? Maria answered in the negative for all the questions except the last two, which were answered in the positive. *Oh crap!* thought David. *Well, maybe the marriage is on the rocks...wouldn't that be nice?*

"Okay thank you, Maria. If you think of anything, don't hesitate to get in touch with me." *Because I sure wouldn't hesitate to get in touch with you...anywhere and everywhere.*

Detective Knight gave Maria a Sheriff's Office card with his name and number on it. He then left the winery office and returned to the tank pad. He retrieved all his evidence-gathering equipment from his automobile, a dark green Toyota 4Runner, and then went about gathering evidence. *Gee, It's a good thing I gather evidence with evidence-gathering equipement, otherwise I'd be totally lost.*

He got samples of the crushed grape remains that were thrown on the ground, of the crushed grape remains and lees that were still in the tank, and of lees that were still stuck on and *in* Frank. (I'm referring to his nostriles, mouth, belly button, and ears...nowhere else. You should be ashamed of yourself, dear reader if you're thinking about any other of Frank's orifices). He also got samples of the wine (to drink later) that had been drained from Tank 12. He then took his own photographs of the assumed crime scene. It was "assumed" because it was possible that Frank had simply fallen in the tank and suffocated from all the CO_2 present or had drowned. Unlikely, but certainly possible, as cellar workers in the region had died in both of those ways in the past.

He then dusted for fingerprints (David Knight figured that's what detective's always did) on top of the tank, on the manway, on the manway door, and along the railing of the catwalk leading to the top of Tank 12. He got some good fingerprints, he thought, but needed to run them though his database to see who they belonged to. He knelt down next to Frank's body and made a closer, more thorough visual inspection of it. He didn't learn much, except that Frank probably spent too much time on the couch eating chips, drinking beer, and watching TV.

When done, he then found Tim Tauscher and said, "Well, I am all done here. I contacted the coroner to remove the body. He'll be here shortly. I am going to go back to the Sheriff's Office Crime Lab to begin examining all the evidence I've collected. I'll be in touch but don't hesitate to contact me if anything new comes to light."

"Evidence? Crime Lab? So you do agree with Roberto. You don't think Frank just fell in. Good. Neither do I," said Tim, "and I'll certainly contact you if something new comes to light, or dark...or even heavy. Thank you very much detective."

Detective Knight then put all of the gathered evidence, along with his evidence-gathering equipment, into his 4Runner, got behind the wheel, and drove off.

Death Número Dos

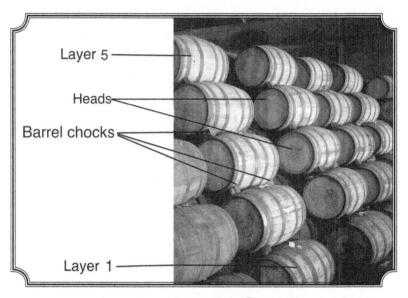

Layer 5

Heads

Barrel chocks

Layer 1

Barrel Stacks at Big Goose Cellars

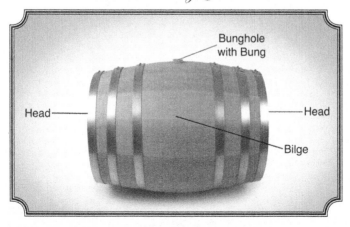

Bunghole
with Bung

Head

Head

Bilge

New Barrel at Big Goose Cellars

Chapter 3

Mark Is Mashed

Months had passed since the death of Frank Finnegan. There had been no progress in the attempt to find his killer if, in fact, he had been killed. Detective Knight had laboriously checked every fingerprint he had found, with no luck. All the fingerprints he had collected belonged to either Tim Tauscher, William Strong, Roberto Rodriguez, or Frank Finnegan himself.

Detective Knight had tracked-down every lead, which were few, to no avail. There were no witnesses to interview because there had been no one around. Big Goose Cellars was at the end of Chardonnay Lane and there was nothing within a half-mile of the winery except vineyards, irrigation ponds, and rose bushes...and they don't see or talk much. Detective Knight read the autopsy report and it stated that Frank Finnegan had died of Hypercapnia. *Hypercapnia? Gee guys, that sounds impressive but what the hell is that? Why use words that only you know?*

Detective Knight looked up Hypercapnia in a medical dictionary he just happened to have lying around and it told him that Hypercapnia was CO_2 poisoning. Detective Knight's stance on people using technical and scientific words that were specific to their profession was that they added needless confusion to any, and all, situations. *Why not use more familiar words and just say Frank had died of CO_2 poisoning? Are they trying to show how much smarter they are than the typical gumshoe?*[12]

---

12 A detective. Detectives and PIs in the late 1800s wore shoes with gum rubber soles. Thus the word 'gumshoe." The rubber soles allowed the investigator to move quietly and avoid detection. That was theory, anyway.

Still, some irksome questions remained. How did Frank get into Tank 12? How did he get into the must so deeply that only his boots were showing? He certainly couldn't have gotten that way by himself unless he was going for a swim and just dove in. And if he had dove in (for whatever reason) why hadn't he taken his boots off first? Was he so soused that he had just simply fallen in? Then that begs the question: How did he get so soused? Was he pushed? If so, by who and why? The autopsy report obviously did not, could not, answer those questions. The report did say that his body showed no signs of a struggle. There were no scratches, bumps, bruises, or marks of any kind. Nothing. Frank was clean as a whistle, except for the grape skins and seeds stuck in his nose, ears, and some other body orifices.

This was all causing Detective Knight to become increasingly frustrated because his instincts told him that Frank hadn't simply fallen into Tank 12, and Detective Knight trusted his intincts, well his investigative instincts anyway. His instincts when it came to women were a whole 'nother story.

Tangent[13] – Here is that other story in a nutshell: David Knight never just "knew" if a particular girl liked him or was even remotely interested in him. He did not pick-up on any type of flirt, hint, clue, or signal that women often employed in social situations. He just *didn't* get it. He was totally clueless. He had come to the agonizing conclusion that he was the first male Homo sapiens that was "opposite gender challenged." On *many* more than one occassion, David had appoached a woman in a bar because his instincts told him she had the "hots" for him, only to be brutally shot down after buying her quite a few drinks. So much for instincts.

---

13 A completely different line of thought or action. It's also a mathematical term and makes me sound intelligent when I use it.

However, this seemed to be the first time in his career that his *investigative* instincts were failing him. There seemed to be no evidence to support the feeling in his gut about the Frank Finnegan death, or murder as he believed it to be. It seemed this case was closed because it was never open to begin with. But try as he might, David couldn't shake the thought that Frank had been murdered, and *that* would mean there *was* a case.

Despite all this, David Knight had resolved to ignore his instincts and he convinced himself that the Frank Finnegan case was closed because there was no case. That's when Joanie from the police department called.

"David, this is Joanie. Uh, there's another dead body at Big Goose Cellars. They need you there again...ASAP."

What the...? Another one? Something strange is afoot at the Circle K. (That's a line from the movie *Bill and Ted's Excellent Adventure*.) "Okey-dokey. I'll be right there. I'm on my way." Three quarters of an hour later and with a steaming-hot mocha, Detective David Knight was once again standing on the tank pad of Big Goose Cellars with Tim Tauscher, Roberto Rodriguez, and William Strong along with Officer's McMillan and Kendry.

"Another dead body?" asked Detective Knight, "What kind of a Mickey Mouse operation are you running here William?"

"Apparently a deadly one. If OSHA, not to mention any lawyer in the state, finds out about this, I'll be totally screwed. At least then I'd be getting some sort of action...but that's a whole 'nother story." William paused and looked at Detective Knight hoping for a reaction, none came. "Anyway, follow me. This one is in the cellar barrel room and this one will cost me loads of moola. It already has."

Detective Knight, along with Roberto and the two police

31

officers, followed Tim into the cellar barrel room. Inside, they found a mess. An extremely nice smelling mess, but a mess nonetheless. There was a haphazard stack of butts,[14] all of which were profusely leaking a butt-load[15] of a previous years vintage of Cabernet Sauvignon onto the cellar floor and into the drain. Protruding out from underneath the haphazard stack of leaking barrels was a pair of rubber work boots.

"Look. See there?" said William, "I've lost *another* employee. I don't know what the hell is going on. They're dropping like flys."

"Yeah, that can't be good for...anything, and it certainly looks pretty nasty, but your wine does have a nice bouquet," said Detective Knight.

"Yeah, I thought so too," said William, "but it's all going down the damn drain now and all my employees are going to the big 'wine tasting in the sky.'"

Officer McMillan then sheepishly approached Detective Knight and said, "We did not touch or move *anything* this time and Officer Kendry took photographs of the entire scene as soon as we arrived."

"Good. You boys are learning. So what do you know for sure?" asked Detective Knight.

"Well, not a whole hell of a lot," said Officer McMillan. "That there under the barrels is Mark Madson, or *was* Mark Madson I should say. He's definitely cured of everything now. He was hired to replace poor ol' Frank Finnegan just a few weeks ago, according to Mr. Tim Tauscher, anyway."

---

14 A cask – typically used for wine, ale, or water. If you were thinking anything else, you have "sexual issues."

15 The smallest unit of measuring anything. It's both metric and English. It's 1/10 of a s***load and 1/100 of a f***load and it's 1/10000 of a mother f***ing s***load. I'm just saying that the barrels (butts) were emptying.

"Okay, fine. What about you, Roberto? What do you know?" asked Detective Knight.

"No mucho,"[16] said Roberto. "I on tank pad this morning spraying off ground when I hear big noise in here. I run in and see barrels no stack-up anymore. I see Mark boots underneath. That all I know."

Detective Knight then slowly made his way around the fallen stack of once full but rapidly becoming less full barrels of wine. He then asked, to no one in particular, while standing in a puddle of red wine, "How much wine does each barrel hold and how much does each one weigh?"

"They are 59 gallon barrels that weigh approximately 110 to 120 pounds when empty and new," answered Tim Tauscher quickly.

"When new? Does a new barrel weigh different than an old barrel? I've never heard that," stated Detective Knight.

"Sure. A used, empty barrel will weigh slightly more than a new, empty barrel due to the wine that has soaked into the wood. When a new barrel is full of wine it weighs approximately 600 pounds," Tim explained.

"Well, I see that only about six or seven barrels from the stack have been displaced. Am I missing any?" asked Detective Knight.

"Nah," said Tim. "That's it."

Detective David Knight then raised his left wrist in order to access the calculator on his 1983 Casio wristwatch that he had gotten from his grandmother when he graduated from junior high school. It still worked. It had "taken a lickin' and kept on tickin," even though it was not a Timex and was battery operated. He held his wrist close to his face, squinted, punched a few buttons with

---

16   Not much. Roberto didn't know much about...anything.

his fingertip, and announced proudly, "That would mean Mark *could* have had, at some point, about 3600 to 4200 pounds on top of him...or falling on top of him I should say. That's gotta hurt."

"Yeah I'll say its gotta, and those numbers do sound about right," agreed Tim.

"And you, William, did you see or hear anything unusual?" asked Detective Knight.

"Nothing unusual...I don't think," answered William.

"What do you mean, 'you don't think'?" queried Detective Knight.

"Well, I was in my office and I heard a truck engine revving up, you know, like it was working hard. So I came out here to see what was going on. As I was coming out of my office, I heard some tires squeel and when I looked out the window I saw a truck tearing down the driveway dragging a couple of ropes, or chains, or something. I had no idea what was going on, so I asked Maria if she knew what was going on. She said she heard the truck but did not see it and just thought it was a couple of the vineyard guys messing around because it's Friday. It all seemed pretty innocuous[17] to her. So, I don't know if it was unusual or not, I did not think it was at the time," said William.

"How often do you see the vineyard guys?" asked David.

"Oh, we see them all the time. They are always driving by the winery," answered William.

Big Goose Cellars made all of their wine from grapes that came from vineyards they owned therefore, all of their wine was "Estate Bottled." This required them to employ a number of workers to tend the vineyards, many of whom were young, energetic, Spanish-speaking males.

---

17   Not harmful or offensive.

"Okay. I'd like to speak with Maria when I'm done out here. Will she still be around?" asked David Knight.

"Of course," answered William.

"Okay. No one is to leave here for the time being," stated Detective Knight with great authority. He then started collecting evidence. He dusted the barrels for fingerprints. He didn't really know why, he wasn't going to get anything useful from the wooden staves but he thought he might get some useful prints off the metal rings around the staves. Plus, he wanted to look like he knew what he was doing. He also took a large sample of wine from a leaking barrel for two reasons: 1) It looked like something a detective should do in order to get some answers and, 2) Big Goose Cellars Cabernet Sauvignon went great with steak, which is what Detective Knight was having for dinner that evening.

He also took photographs and while doing so, noticed a barrel-topping set-up, which consisted of a cylinder containing pressurized nitrogen, a gas hose running from the pressurized cylinder to a stainless steel keg, and a wine hose with a filling wand attached to the end that ran from the pressurized keg to the deadly barrel stack. There was also a working flashlight nearby.

"Okay Tim, I'm trying to picture how this could happen, the barrels falling I mean. Full barrels don't just randomnly fall over, do they? I mean, they each weigh more than Oprah Winfrey and Kirstie Allie put together. Well, maybe not that much, but the point is: They would have needed some external force acting on them. In other words, they would have to be pushed, or pulled, over...correct?"

"Yeah, as far as I know anyway. Maybe some aliens came in, got drunk, and knocked them over, but I doubt it," answered William before Tim could say anything.

"Okay, now explain to me, if you could," demanded Detective Knight, "how someone goes about topping barrels when they are stacked in the manner you stack them." Detective Knight gave William a look of contempt because he seemed to think this whole thing was a joke.

Tim Tauscher quickly stepped-in and said, "Okay. I'll show you how Mark Madson would do it. He would fill one of these stainless steel kegs with whatever wine was to be used for the topping. In this case he was using some Cabernet Sauvignon we had left over from filling the barrels. He would then pressurize the keg with a tank of compressed Nitrogen, the one you see over there," Tim said as he pointed to the pressurized cylinder of Nitrogen (N_2) that was standing near the fallen barrels. He then continued, "A hose with a filling wand attached runs from the keg to whomever is topping barrels which, in this case, was Mark Madson.

"Mark would remove the bung from the barrel, peer into the bung-hole with his flashlight, and use the wand to top the barrel with wine, thus removing any headspace and oxygen. To peer into the bung-hole of a barrel on the fourth layer and then top that barrel, Mark would stand on the first layer of barrels, or possibly kneel on the second."

As Detective Knight was digesting this information and trying, but failing, not to laugh at the phrase "peer into the bung-hole," he looked around the barrel room and noticed, some distance away, a couple of barrel chocks used for the stacking of barrels. David Knight walked over, retrieved the chocks, and brought them over to Tim.

"Are these the barrel chocks that were used in this stack here?" Detective Knight asked as he pointed to the stack which had fallen.

"Sure looks like it. Where did you get them? Right here?" asked Tim as both he and Detective Knight examined them.

"No. I noticed them over there against that wall with the large set of doors," Detective Knight said as he pointed across the barrel room to the large entrance that was used for shipping and receiving. Both Tim and David made a closer inspection of the chocks and David asked, "Are these marks typically on your barrel chocks?" He was pointing at marks that ran the length of the chocks and looked as though they had been made by something being pulled across them.

"Hmm...no. I've never seen marks quite like that before," answered Tim.

"Interesting. I see. Well, I'll certainly keep these then, if that's okay with you."

"Yeah, sure. Why not? We have plenty of other ones."

Detective Knight then asked, "What year is the Cab that *was* in these barrels?

"It's 2012 which *was* going to be bottled in a few weeks."

"Do you happen to have any empty bottles around?"

"Yes, there are some empty bottles in my office. Why? What could you need empty bottles for?" asked Tim.

Ooh awesome! That will surely impress her. "Uhh well, to be honest there Tim, I'm going out with an older woman tonight, she's hot and I thought I would impress her with some wine that came right from a barrel. Chic's dig that sort of stuff, ya know. I'll just fill up some empties from these leaking barrels and bring 'em along, if that's cool with you."

"Yeah that's cool," said Tim with a wink. "You can take some empty bottles from my office, but don't get carried away, and *don't* let Bill see you because for every drop that's wasted, Bill gets quite irate." (A Monty Python reference from *The Meaning of Life*.)

"Hey, if things work out right, not even half a drop will have gone to waste," said David with a wink.

As Tim and Detective Knight were talking, Roberto was gathering any bucket, keg, carboy, or any other container that he could get his hands on in order to save as much wine from the leaking barrels as possible and, more imporantly, make himself look good to the boss.

Also, the barrels needed to be emptied in order to move them so that Mark could be retrieved as no one had bothered to get him out from under the barrels, as of yet. Roberto siphoned as much wine as he could from the leaking barrels into all of the containers he had collected. Then he, Tim, David, and even William went about moving the barrels. When they had freed Mark, he turned out to not be a pretty sight.

Full, six hundred pound barrels that had fallen from either the second, third, or fourth layer in the barrel stack, had crushed Mark's head. They had to have fallen from those three layers because barrels on the first layer (that would be the bottom layer) can't fall.

They also saw, amongst the remains of Marks noggin, a pair of earphones that were attached to an iPod that did not appear to be in working order right about now. Roberto and Tim managed to get Mark out of the cellar through the large shipping and receiving doors and only had to stop once to puke.

Once Mark Madson was out of the cellar barrel room, Detective Knight stood over him (they didn't bother calling the Birchwood PD this time) and said, "Well, the cause of death looks pretty apparent, but we'll let the Coroner make it official by using some fancy words and showing us how smart and educated he is.

"So Tim, I guess you and Roberto are free to go, unless, of course, there is anything else you want to tell me." Dead silence. Detective Knight was secretly hoping that Tim or Roberto knew more than they were letting on and would just spill the beans, thereby making his job infinitely easier.

"Oh hallelujah!" said Tim sarcastically. "This place is becoming a health hazard. Two guys I have been working with are now dead, they were murdered if you ask me, and I don't want to be here any longer than is necessary, because I could be next. Every minute I work here, might be my last." Tim paused, looked to the sky, and said, "Of course, a raise might make me a little braver...and the bigger the raise, the braver I'd be." Then he looked straight at William with a big grin and said, "Did you get that William?"

"Yeah, I'd like a raise too," said William sarcastically. "The old lady keeps bugging me about a new pool, and they ain't cheap."

With that, Tim turned around and called for Roberto because he often gave him a ride as he passed right by Roberto's house on his way home, but Roberto had disappeared.

Under his breath Tim said, "Now where did that damn hombre get to?"

At that moment, Roberto came out of the cellar through the large doors they had just dragged Mark through, holding three bottles of wine. He walked up to Detective Knight and said, "You want wine from barrel? Here. I just fill these."

"Ahh, muchas gracias mi amigo," said Detective Knight. *I'll get some action tonight for sure!*

Detective Knight then returned to his 4Runner and put all

his collected evidence, along with his newly-filled bottles of 2012 Big Goose Cellars Cabernet Sauvignon on the backseat. He then went into the winery office to speak with Maria, as he had forgotten about her.

"Maria," he said as he extended his hand, "Detective Knight. It's nice to see you again. I would like to ask you some questions regarding the events that occurred earlier today." *Damn she's good looking! Look at those nice firm...*uh, well you get the picture...I hope.

"Sí. Sí. Ask all you want."

"Okay, I will. Bill, or William as you call him, said that you heard a truck outside earlier. Is that correct?"

"Oh yeah, sí, sí. I hear a big truck leaving. It sound like it going múy rápido. I figure it vineyard workers. They go múy loco on Friday afternoon. I no give it no um...uh...how you say... segundo pensamiento...second thought?"

"Okay right. You didn't think anything of it. Did you hear anything coming from inside the winery before you saw the truck?" asked David.

"No, no. I hear nothing in winery."

"Did you see or hear *anything* unusual prior to seeing the truck leave in a hurry?"

"Oh no, no. I see nothing. I hear nothing. It múy tranquilo around here before I hear truck. It always múy tranquilo around here. "

"Okay Maria. Thank you. And again, if you think of anything, or hear anything, be sure to contact me." *I'd sure love to get in contact with you* thought David as he gave Maria a Sheriff's Office card with his name and number on it.

"Okay. I do that. Goodbye señor."

Detective Knight then left the winery office, went back to his 4Runner, and drove to the Sheriff's Office Crime Lab. Once at the lab, he unloaded all the collected evidence but paid special attention to the wine he had collected, as he was planning on using it to help with his wooing[18] of his date later that night. He was sort of careful with the barrel chocks he had collected as they *might* tell him something useful, as far as this crime was concerned anyway.

To possibly solve the crime before his date, David examined all three of the chocks and noticed each one had a groove in it that did not look like it could have been made by any machine or operation that took place in a winery, at least none that David Knight was familiar with.

He had grown-up in this area, and had worked the harvest at a few different wineries when he was younger. David had helped stack, and un-stack many a barrel during his time working the harvest. He had seen hundreds, if not thousands of barrel chocks but he had never seen any that looked quite like the ones he was now holding. *Where did these marks come from? They look like they came from ropes or something being pulled across the chock. Maybe there were ropes around the barrels? But why would there be rope marks on the chocks? Maybe Big Goose Cellars was doing some new trendy European thing or was using some sort of European machine that used ropes for...what? Maybe this new "trendy thing" would result in having barrel chocks that were marked in this fashion.* David Knight had all these thoughts while cursing himself for not looking at some barrel chocks from a stack that had not fallen over. Comparing

---

18 Try to gain the love of someone, typically a woman, especially with a hope of marriage. In David's case however, it was with a hope of getting some...um hot action. Even lukewarm action would have been welcome.

objects from a crime scene with similar objects *not* from a crime scene and noticing the differences, no matter how subtle, could provide invaluable clues to solving a crime or mystery.

So, Detective Knight made the huge leap in thought that he should return to Big Goose Cellars and look at some barrel chocks that had not been in the stack that had fallen on Mark Madson. Plus, it would give him another chance to see Maria, and that would be worth the trip. Detective Knight got into his gas-guzzling, pollution-enhancing, contributing-to-global-warming-and-cooling, ozone-depleting, small-children-killing, SUV and drove to Big Goose Cellars. When he arrived, he went straight to the winery office hoping Maria was there. She was.

"Hey there, Maria. How's it going?" asked Detective Knight. He didn't wait for an answer because asking that question is just a social convention; an answer is not necessary. He then asked, "You didn't by any chance happen to hear or remember any pertinent information regarding Mark Madson's death, did you?"

"Perti...what? What word mean? I no understand," replied Maria.

"Oh never mind. Don't worry about it. I need to see Tim about barrel chocks. Is he around?" asked David.

"Sí. He in cellar. Want me page him?" said Maria.

"No. I'll just go down there and find him." With that, Detective David Knight left the winery office and headed for the cellar to find the winemaker. *Man, I love the way Maria talks; it's so damn cute. Half Spanish – half English, It totally turns me on.* Of course, there was a long list of things that turned David on.

Detective Knight reached the cellar and found Tim Tauscher pulling wine samples from a stack of barrels containing Merlot.

"Hey there, Detective Knight. What can I do ya for?" asked Tim.

"Well, I need a couple of barrel chocks from one of your barrel stacks that didn't fall over. I want to compare them with the chocks I took from the stack that fell on Mark."

"Sure. Be my guest. There should be a few over there near the door to my office. They were used for a stack of Cab we just bottled last week. I've been thinking about them actually; the chocks from the stack that fell over I mean. It's the damndest thing."

"It is? Why do you say that?" asked Detective Knight.

"Well, I *have* seen marks like that before, not on barrel chocks, but somewhere, and I couldn't remember where. Then it hit me. My father used to have an old wooden Hollywood boat and he would tow it behind his pick-up truck using ropes to secure it to the trailer. The ropes made marks on the edge of his boat that looked just like the marks on edges of those chocks from the killer barrel stack."

"They did? Are you sure?" asked David incredulously.[19]

"Well, it's been a long time since I've seen his boat; he no longer has it. He sold it on eBay but never got paid. Anyway, I never really paid much attention to the marks, but I'm telling you, the marks on those chocks looked exactly like the marks on the edge of my Dad's boat, but smaller, of course," explained Tim.

"Hmm, interesting," said David in a thoughtful tone. "Now, about those chocks..."

"Oh yeah. Just take those ones in that box next to my office door. Take whatever you need and do what you gotta do," said Tim.

Tim took the whole box of chocks and then returned to the Sheriff's Office Crime Lab in order to compare them to the

---

19   Unwilling or unable to believe something – Louis L'Amour uses this word way too often.

chocks from the barrel stack that had turned on Mark. Just as he had seen upon first glance at the chocks in the box, there were absolutely no marks on them, except some red wine stains. Whereas, the chocks from the deadly barrel stack had marks all over them, and they certainly weren't red wine stains. To Detective Knight, Mark's death was beginning to look more like a murder than the first one, and the first one looked a lot like a murder. *So, now I am looking at two homicides? Holy cow! There is definitely something strange afoot at the Circle K.* He was not going to even try and ignore his instincts now.

David began looking at all the samples and evidence he had collected. As expected, he didn't get any useful fingerprints. He reviewed his notes and inferred that no one had seen or heard anything that could even be potentially useful. He looked at all of the photographs that he and Officer Kendry had taken, nothing...except way too much red-eye.

He then analyzed the wine sample he had taken for analysis and it showed that the wine was just that...wine. The wine tasted good, except it needed more oak and had too much *Brettanomyces.*[20] David glanced at his watch as he was "re-analyzing" the wine sample. *Holy fecal[21] matter! It's seven o'clock! Man, I have a date with...uh...um...oh man...what the hell was her name? Oh yeah...Rebecca, that's right. I hope this wine works.*

---

20   Brettanomyces is a yeast that is a common defect in wine. Some people like it (prefer it, actually) in small amounts. I know I do.

21   Waste matter discharged from the bowels after food has been digested. So, "fecal matter" is just shit, crap, poo, excrement, bowel movement, number 2, etc.

Chapter 4

...And They All Fell Down

David awoke with a splitting headache. The wine straight from the barrel had not worked as he had hoped. All David Knight got out of his date was a splitting headache, but his date got a nice free meal and some good wine; maybe that was her plan all along. To help maintain his image as a Lothario,[22] at least in his own mind and among his friends, David chalked his lack of success with Rebecca up to Frank Finnegan and Mark Madson.

Their deaths were all David could think about during the date. Maybe if Rebecca had worn something a little more... revealing that would have put his mind on the right track, so to speak. Well, there wasn't much he could do about it now, so he went to Big Goose Cellars to have a look around...and at Maria.

As soon as David reached Big Goose Cellars, he went straight to the winery office to see Maria. He figured he should also talk with her; ask her some questions, even though after his date with Rebecca he didn't feel like talking to anybody with supremely shaped mammary glands.[23]

"Hey Maria. ¿Qué Pasa?" (What's up?) asked Detective Knight upon seeing Maria. "Did you find any more dead bodies in the winery?"

Maria looked at David with a horrified expression and said, "My God!" (She actually said, "¡Dios mío!") "No! I no look for dead

---

22 A man who behaves selfishly and irresponsibly in his sexual relationships with women.

23 The milk-producing gland of women or other female mammals. A.K.A. boobies, breasts, tits, knockers, jugs, fun bags, party bags, the list goes on and on. Human females have two of them.

bodies. I no like dead bodies. Are more dead bodies in winery?"

"Well, I certainly hope not. I was just messin' with ya. I do need to see Tim though."

"Messin'? What word mean?" asked Maria.

"It means...uh...'joking', 'playing around' but don't worry about it. Just forget I said anything. Is Tim around?" David asked impatiently.

"Sí, he in cellar," answered Maria. "Want me page him?"

"No, that's okay. I'll just go find him," said Detective Knight and with that, he left Maria and the winery office and walked into the cellar. Detective Knight found Tim Tauscher, along with Roberto at the site of Mark Madson's untimely demise. They had completely emptied all of the fallen barrels and were in the process of removing them from the cellar.

"Howdy," said Detective Knight. "Cleaning-up the mess, I see."

Roberto ignored Detective Knight but Tim Tauscher stopped working and greeted Detective Knight who then said, "Tim, I need to ask you a couple of questions."

"Okey dokey. I guess now is as good a time as any...shoot," said Tim as he resumed moving barrels. David reached into his back pocket, pulled out his notepad and a pen, licked his index finger, and flipped through a few pages of the notebook.

"Okay. Tim, you said earlier that Mark must have been standing on at least the first layer of barrels in this," he gestured to the fallen of barrels, "stack in order to top the barrels in the highest layer, correct?"

"Correct," answered Tim.

"How high would Mark have been if he was standing on the first layer of barrels?" asked Detective Knight.

"Well, I'm not sure exactly. Let's see, we use Bordeaux

barrels for our Cabernet, and they are...uh...oh wait a second, it's in my office. I'll be right back." With that, Tim ran through the cellar to his office and returned moments later with a brochure of Nadalie Barrels. From it, Tim read the dimensions of the Bordeaux style barrels that Big Goose Cellars was using to age their 2012 Cabernet Sauvignon.

"The barrels are 59.44 gallons. They are 37.4 inches tall, 27.56 inches around at the bilge, that's the fattest part, and 22.05 inches around at the heads, or ends. They weigh 103.62 pounds empty."

"I didn't really need for you to be so exact, but I guess it can't hurt to know," stated David Knight. He continued, "So, according to those dimensions, and assuming Mark was standing on the first layer of barrels, it would mean he was just over two feet off the ground."

"Yeah," said Tim. "But, you need to add about two or three inches to account for the rails on the floor that the first layer of barrels was resting on."

"Okay sure," said Detective Knight, "but falling from that height shouldn't cause a serious injury, let alone kill a person, should it?"

"No. I wouldn't think so."

"Okay. Now let's assume he was standing on the second layer of barrels, he would be falling just about 60 inches, or five feet. Falling from that height might bruise or scrape him but chances are it wouldn't kill him or even seriously hurt him, unless of course, Mark was a total wuss."

"Mark was no wuss...trust me. It might have *hurt* him a little, but that's it," said Tim. "Maybe if he fell just right, or wrong I should say, he could break something, but Mark was a pretty burly, buff, and a physically tough dude; lots of muscles."

"I'm having a hell of a time picturing what may have happened. I've been thinking about this *way* too much," lamented David. "I mean, it was all I could think about during my hot date last night and as a result, it became a lukewarm date at lightening speed.

"Anyway, to begin with," continued Detective Knight, "why would he just fall? As far as I know, topping barrels doesn't require much fast or sudden movement; all movements are slow, gradual and not conducive to falling. But, suppose he did just fall off for some reason. Why would the barrels then suddenly fall? Falling off the barrels wouldn't cause part of the barrel stack to fall over, would it? Especially if there is some wine in them."

"No...or yes I should say, you're right. Topping barrels does not require much movement and no, simply falling off a stack of full barrels should not cause it to fall over, but...ya never know."

David then said, "It would seem to me that the barrels falling was what caused Mark to fall off; not Mark's falling off was what caused the barrels to fall. In other words, the barrels didn't fall on Mark because Mark fell off the barrels; Mark fell off the barrels because the barrels were falling, capiche?[24] Then, of course, that begs the question, 'Why would the barrels fall?'"

Detective Knight noticed that these questions and all this talk of falling barrels had made the mood in the cellar much more somber than it was when he first arrived, and he *hated* somber moods. So, in an attempt to brighten the mood he said, "Since, everyone is falling down around here, I think you had better re-think the company drinking policy, or maybe you could re-name this place 'Falling Man Winery.'"

"No way," answered Tim, not realizing David was just joking.

---

24 Do you understand? From Italian verb "capire" which means "to understand." It makes someone sound kind of goofy when they use it.

"Our policy is that drinking is good, and the 'Falling Man Winery' sounds too much like that 'Burning Man festival.'"

"The *what* festival?" asked Detective Knight, not willing to believe his name was not totally original.

"Burning Man. You've never heard of that? It's that festival where all of the pseudo-enlightened, wannabe hippies get together, live in the desert for a few days, smoke lots of dope, and dance around to bad music. It reeks of B.O. and I think William has some sort of issue with it. He probably had a bad trip there once or something; he would never allow this place to be named anything close to that."

Detective Knight shook his head and rolled his eyes. "Well, whatever. And Tim, before I forget, your wine 'straight from a barrel' did not impress my date. At least not enough for garment removal, which was the whole point in the first place."

Tim ignored him and got the conversation back to the matter at hand. He said, "Yeah, I was up all night too thinking about this tragedy, and the only conclusion that made any sense to me is what you alluded too there at the end: The barrel stack collapsed, causing Mark to fall off, not the other way around. But I have no idea why the barrel stack would collapse. Roberto and I made that stack the same way we've been making them for years and it was stable, it certainly would not have just 'fallen over.' I mean those full barrels are heavy and they don't move easily."

"Yeah, that's what I figured also," said David. "Have you ever even *heard* of a barrel stack like yours collapsing? I sure as hell haven't."

"Yes, I have actually, but not here," answered Tim.

"Really? You have? Where? Why did it collapse, do you know?" asked Detective Knight with interest.

"Where I used to work as the Assistant Winemaker and it fell over during the Loma Prieta Earthquake, you know, the big one during the World Series between the Giants and A's," answered Tim. "But I don't think there is any doubt as to why that stack took a tumble; it seems pretty obvious to me and everyone else. Fortunately, no one was there because they were all watching the game and drinking beer. Or more likely, they were drinking beer and watching the game as a side attraction."

Roberto, who had been standing nearby during this whole conversation and apparently understood quite a bit, piped up with, "I know stack fall at Pebble Hill Vineyards. Nobody dead. Just big mess."

Detective Knight turned towards Roberto and said, "Well speak-up vato.[25] Let's hear about it."

"Oh, yes, yes. My friend José works at Pebble Hill Vineyards and a barrel stack fell over there," said Roberto—now speaking only in Spanish.

Detective Knight was able to understand the gist of what Roberto had said, and it instantly put him on a foul mood. *If he understood what Tim and I were saying so well, why the hell can't he speak a little more English a little more often? Damn Democrats!*

David Knight's mind then began to wander: He believed the current Democratic leadership had put in place policies that allowed for immigrants to get jobs, homes, financial aid, medical care, driver's licenses, and even vote without knowing a word of English. The policies weren't helping the country at all, they were just helping Democratic candidates get elected and/or re-elected.

The other day he had visited the local public library and saw

---

25   Vato is Spanish version of "dude" or "guy"; either one is acceptable.

two complete sets of voter registration forms: One set in English, and the other in Spanish. One set in two languages was wasteful enough, but a separate set for each language was preposterous! David also rightly guessed that the ballots were separated the same way. *Wouldn't you have to chop down twice as many trees to print two sets of registration forms and ballots? The tree-huggers can't like that. But since this is all helping what they must consider poor, stupid, helpless Mexicans, it's gotta be okay.*

David remembered he had been shocked and couldn't believe what the country was coming to. *Is all this for real? Are they* (meaning the government) *serious? If they* (meaning the Mexicans) *can't read or understand English, how the hell do they* (meaning the Mexicans) *know whom to vote for? They* (meaning the Mexicans) *probably just recognize the word "Democrat" and check that box. I wonder how many other languages, at taxpayer's expense of course, these voter registration forms and ballots are printed in.*

I thought we learned in junior high school that someone had to be a citizen in order to vote and they couldn't be citizen unless they could read, write, and speak at least some Basic English? Was I lied to? What other lies did they teach me? Does two plus two really equal four? Was George Washington really our first president? Was Adolf Hitler just a lonely, misunderstood gentleman?

Detective Knight was an active member of the Republican Party and was staunchly conservative. He had no problems with immigrants; he was a great believer in the U.S. being a "melting pot." The U.S. "melting pot" contained a "stew," the ingredients of which were all the people of different races, colors, nationalities, religions, etc. that were living in the U.S. Detective Knight thought the U.S. "stew" was good, it made life interesting. It was good for everyone.

51

However, any and every, stew has certain characteristics, otherwise it would not be a stew. One characteristic of the "stew," that is the United States, should be the English language, but it wasn't. David believed that because of policies put in place by Democratic Party politicians' over the years, the U.S. had gone from being a "melting pot" to an "ice-tray." In other words: All of the different nationalities that comprise the U.S. are supposedly equal but remain "separate" (like ice cubes in an ice tray) because they can't communicate with each other. New immigrants did not, *could not*, assimilate into the American culture and become part (the ingredients if you will) of the U.S. "stew" because they did not know English.

Anything, and everything, a new immigrant needed to understand was provided to them in their native language. They did not need to learn *any* English and so could keep to themselves, thus becoming a "cube" in the ice tray that the United States had become. It is virtually impossible for a bunch of people who don't know one another to mix and mingle and understand each other when they can't communicate.

David couldn't help but think of some of parties, in both college and the real world, he had been to where groups of people did not talk to one another because they were all stuck in their own group or clique and so remained separate, much like ice cubes in an ice tray.

Those parties were a nightmare...until everyone got drunk and no one cared what anyone said, or didn't say, just so long as they looked good at the time and were horny. It was as if the "ice trays" had been emptied into a large container and the ice cubes began to melt—the different groups began to mingle and get together as one. David did realize this analogy was shaky, at best, but he figured it would get his point across.

In addition to the voter registration form tragedy, all governmental forms that needed filling out for any necessary services, were printed in English, Spanish, and who knows what else. Furthermore, the recorded phone messages on answering machines in all government offices were available in both English and Spanish. To add insult to injury, the caller was often told to press "1" for Spanish and "2" for English, thereby making Spanish the first choice and English the second choice...in an English speaking country.

Just a few weeks ago, David Knight had to re-new his Drivers License at the Department of Motor Vehicles (DMV). He was required to fill out a couple of forms and take a test, all of which were printed in both English and Spanish. *If you can't read the test for a Drivers License, how can you read any sign on the road? Any warnings? Gee, how much of my paycheck goes to printing this in two languages? Probably not much but still...it adds up, and this is just the DMV!*

David believed that language barriers between the immigrants and natives (well, not the *actual* natives, the European ones) were the root of many of the social problems facing the country and its people. Detective Knight knew a number of workers in the valley, both legally and illegally, who had migrated north and had been living and working here for years but could only speak a few words of English. Not because they were stupid or lazy, but because they had no need to learn English and so chose not to. Apparently, however, some of them, namely Roberto, could understand English pretty well...when they wanted to.

Putting all these rage inducing thoughts aside, Detective Knight got back to the matter at hand and said, "Wow! So, why did the stack fall? Do you know?" David now assumed Roberto would understand the questions; he did.

"No sé," answered Roberto. "I hear boss Pebble Hill say that mi amigo stack barrels wrong. That all I know."

Detective Knight no longer knew what to think when Roberto said, "That all I know," or told him what he heard or didn't hear. *Is that really all he knows? Maybe he does not want me to know what he knows or heard, and if that's the case, why the hell not?*

Detective Knight didn't have any idea as to how much Roberto *had* understood. Not having any idea about a vital aspect of a murder investigation is not good for the health of a homicide investigator and it was certainly not helping to alleviate his headache; in fact, it was making it worse.

"Was Scott Garett your boss at Pebble Hill?" asked Detective Knight. Scott Garett and Detective Knight had been friends since Detective Knight had brought to justice the miscreant that had stood-up Scott's daughter on Senior Prom night.

"Sí. Sí. Scott Garettt," answered Roberto excitedly.

"Yeah, come to think of it, I also remember hearing about that barrel stack collapsing a couple of years ago. As I recall, it really shook Scott up. I had never seen him look that way, and I've known Scott for a long time," said Tim. "He and I went to UC Davis together. God could he put the beer away! In one class we had together, he came up with what became our class motto: 'It takes a lot of beer to make good wine'. After you have worked a harvest, you will think that motto is very...uh apropos.[26] Boy, he sure was a hell of a lot of fun to have around back then."

"Yeah, I remember when I used to work the harvest," said Detective Knight, "we spent a lot of time drinking beer. We had to, otherwise we just couldn't do it; the grapes just kept coming and coming and the needed equipment was either broken or

---

26   Very appropriate to a particular situation.

nowhere to be found. It would get later and later and we would get hungrier and hungrier, and more and more tired, but the grapes *had* to be crushed and put into a tank. *Then* we had to clean up the mess we made or else we would end up with all kinds of little bugs flying around and some really bad smells."

When Detective knight began this bit of reminiscing, he sounded rather nostalgic, but by the time he finished, he sounded pissed-off.

"Well enough of that, I should probably go speak with this Scott Garett and see what he has to say, so I'll go as soon as I am done here. Speaking of which," said Detective Knight as he looked around the winery and then at Tim, "I guess I *am* done here, at least I can't think of anything else, unless you know some good cure for a hangover."

Chuckling, Tim said, "No, I don't have any cure for one, but I do know the best way to prevent a one."

"Yeah, me too," said David. "Don't drink so much."

"No, no, no, even better," said Tim. "Drink all you want, that's the good part. But before you go to bed drink a lot of water. I mean *a lot*. You'll have to get up and pee quite a bit, that's the bad part. But trust me, it will be worth it in the morning. In fact, it's the most useful thing I learned in college. Well, it's the thing that I *use* the most."

Detective David Knight chortled and then with that nugget of knowledge, returned to his 4Runner and drove to Pebble Hill Vineyards to speak with Scott Garettt.

Chapter 5

José Is a Buffoon

Upon arriving at Pebble Hill Vineyards, David Knight immediately sought out Scott and found him in his office drinking coffee, at least he assumed it was coffee; you never knew with winemakers.

"Howdy Scott. How is Melissa doing these days?" asked Detective Knight.

"David! Come on in. Want some coffee? Melissa is doing fine. She just got a rejection letter from Stanford and that upset her, but I wasn't so upset. It made my day, actually."

"Your daughter got a rejection letter from Stanford and it made your day? Shouldn't you feel bad for her? And no...no more coffee for me or I'll be peeing all day."

"I *do* feel bad for her, but there was, and still is, no way in hell I could have afforded even one year at Stanford, let alone four. She would need at *least* one scholarship and it doesn't take a genius to know that Melissa is not exactly scholarship material, either academically or athletically. I really didn't want to have to tell her she couldn't go there if she had, by some miracle, been accepted."

"Yeah, that would suck, and Stanford definitely ain't cheap," agreed David.

"That's an understatement. So anyway, what brings you by David? Tell me you didn't come here just to ask how Melissa was doing? I know you, David, you're probably having some... uh...impure thoughts about Melissa, even though she's a little young for you."

"Aww come on Scott! Gimmee a break! She is way to young for me. Don't you know that I prefer 'mature' women? Melissa doesn't do 'it' for me, in *any* way," said David Knight in good-naturedly.

"Ahh yeah, sorry. I'm just a little sensitive to that sort of thing. Way too often on the news, I hear of some older dude in some small, country town, knockin'-up someone's daughter and messing-up her life. I live in fear of something like that happening in this 'quaint' little town. I don't really want any grand kids for a while."

"Yeah, I don't watch any news. It's to depressing. But relax, my reason for being here has nothing to do with Melissa. I am here to ask about your barrel stack that collapsed when Roberto was working here a couple of years ago. Do you remember that?"

"Ooohh yeah, I won't forget that anytime soon. It kind of freaked me out. It still gives me the willies when I think about what *could* have happened. Now, what the hell brought that up?" Asked Scott.

"Well, a stack of full barrels collapsed over at Big Goose Cellars and the new cellar hand, Mark Madson, got put on the 'Stairway to Heaven', unless of course, he was put on the 'Highway To Hell'."

"Holy Christ! A stack of *full* barrels? How did that happen?" asked Scott.

"Well, it was just a few barrels, not the entire stack and I don't *know* how it happened. That is what I am trying to ascertain; that means 'to find out' for all you winemakers."

"It does? I didn't know that. I mean it's such a big word and I'm just a dumb winemaker with a Bachelor of Science degree," said Scott.

"Okay, okay, so you're not that dumb. What can you tell me about your stack that fell over?"

"Well, it was total negligence," said Scott. "It could, and *should* have been avoided. The barrels were not stacked properly. The guys were only putting in barrel chocks when they felt like it and they didn't feel like it very often. I think the guys were thinking...well I don't know what the hell they were thinking but they weren't thinking about stacking barrels; that I *do* know. The whole stack was more than a bit crooked when finished. But despite all that, it still should not have been a problem because barrels, once full, don't just fall over...without some help."

"What do you mean? Are you saying the stack had help falling over?"

"Yeah. I think so anyway."

"Are you saying it was *pushed* over?" asked Detective Knight with a tone of disbelief in his voice.

"Well yeah, but not intentionally, at least I don't think it was intentional, but you never know. You see, at the time we had José Mendoza working here along with your Roberto and Richard and Felipe, who were a couple of foreign interns. José was, and probably still is, a real piece of work. He didn't like anybody, especially not gringos, and he was mad all the time. He was always eating beans in some form or another. I think that is why he had chronic, putrid gas...issues. I have no idea where he is now. The last I heard he was in jail in Tijuana for farting in a crowded theater and yelling, "fuego," which means "fire" in Spanish. I think some lives were lost.

"Anyway, José was tearing around on the forklift that day, acting like an ass, and trying to...well I don't know what the hell he was trying to do. He lost control of the forklift, maybe or maybe not intentionally; no one really knows, and ran into the barrel stack that was being constructed *and* filled with wine. I don't think he hit it too hard, but since it was stacked so poorly, it fell over. Thankfully, Roberto, Richard, and Felipe were taking a break at the time and were outside. If those guys had been on the stack when José had hit it, well...I don't even want to *think* about it, if I do, I'll have nightmares again. Those guys would have been crushed and I would have had to explain it too their families. That would not have been good; it would have been bad *and* ugly."

"Yeah, that *would* have been bad and ugly. I had to do the 'family explanation' routine once, and it sucked," said David somberly. "So, is that everything? Where are Richard and Felipe now?" David continued in a more upbeat tone.

"Yeah that's everything," answered Scott. "Unfortunately, Richard and Felipe are no longer with us."

"They're dead?" Detective Knight asked in a shocked voice.

"No, no, no," chuckled Scott. "They were foreign interns that were here just for the harvest. Richard is back in Australia and Felipe is back in France."

"Oh...okay I see," said Detective Knight but he was again instantly put in a foul mood. The reason being: The unemployment rate in the state was a whopping 12.1% and David knew a number of guys who were out of work, just scraping by, and barely able to feed their kids. These guys would have given one, or possibly both, of their family jewels for *any* kind of job: temporary, seasonal, part-time, full time... *any*time. Here had been a couple of good jobs that had been given to *foreign* interns.

First, why interns? Why not people who need work? Second, why *foreign* interns? Why not American interns? What is wrong

59

with them? David figured the answer had something to do with labor costs, and that just upset him more.

David thought the ideal deal would be for each winery to hire a couple of viticulture (that's grape growing) and/or enology (that's winemaking) students from either UC Davis, Sonoma State, Cal Poly, University of Oregon, or *any* American school for that matter. It would be a "win win" situation. The wineries would get needed labor and would in turn be helping young Americans pursue their degree and gain invaluable work experience..

"There was an investigation," continued Scott, "but I have no idea why...I mean it was pretty obvious what happened. I guess it was just a case of typical small town cops: A crime has been committed, at least it's *possible* one has, and they get all excited because they get to look real tough and do 'cop stuff.' They would get to play around with all their tools and equipment and pretend to be the cops they see in movies and on TV.

"Anyway, after a couple of weeks they made the brilliant conclusion that they should probably talk with José, but they couldn't find him. They looked for him until they got tired of acting like cops, then they just quit; maybe they were feeling the onset of doughnut withdrawals. In any case, they never talked with him, obviously.

"As far as José goes, no one has seen him since the incident. He's from Oaxaca, but the last I heard of his whereabouts, he was in jail in Tijuana."

"Oaxaca?" asked David Knight.

"Yeah. It's a state in Mexico...it's way down South near Guatemala, at least I'm pretty sure it is," explained Scott. "That is where a lot of the Mexican workers that come here are from."

"So, they investigated the whole barrel stack collapsing incident but didn't learn anything? Nothing came of the investigation?" asked Detective Knight incredulously. "They knew as much before the investigation as they knew after? José was never found? The interns were never questioned either?"

"No, they weren't. As far as I know anyway."

"Well why the hell not? Wouldn't it make sense to question the two guys who could quite possibly know something?" said David as he fought his rising anger.

"Yes it would, but like I said, we're talking small town cops. The 'investigation' did draw one conclusion, however," Tim said as he made finger quotes whilst he said investigation.

"Oh yeah? What was it? That the barrel stack did, in fact, fall over? Or that this town has pretty damn good doughnuts?" said Detective Knight sarcastically.

"No," chuckled Scott. "It was determined that the accelerator on the forklift is, or was, faulty and it became 'stuck' while José was driving it so, José was not at fault. No one told José because no one knew where he was. Now Toyota on the other hand –"

"Did anyone go after them, *legally* I mean?" interrupted Detective Knight. "I bet they have some pretty deep pockets."

"Uh, yeah they do, *and* they have the best lawyers money can buy," said Scott. "They convinced the court that because José was driving in 'a manner specifically warned against in the Owner's Manual,' Toyota's design and construction of the forklift were not at fault.

"I do know that when the lawsuit was first filed, Toyota had guys looking for José, but they never found him. I don't know what they were going to do if they did find him...maybe break his legs or something."

"Hmm...well I'll be damned. Thanks Scott. I better get back to Big Goose Cellars; people keep dying over there, plus I want to have another look or two at Maria."

"Yeah, you and every other guy in Fiasco[27] Valley," said Scott, "and put your pants back on. I'm pretty sure she's already married to some Mexican guy named Júan, or Tomás, or Raúl or something like that. She'll probably quit her job before long, have lots of babies, live off the American taxpayer, and send money back to her folks in Mexico. That's what they all do.

"You can't really blame 'em though," continued Scott, "it's a pretty sweet deal if you stop and think about it. The American taxpayer provides for you and your family and you don't have to do diddly-squat."

Scott was referring to the fact that *illegal* immigrants were able to receive tax-revenue funded assistance, such as: TANF benefits (Temporary Assistance for Needy Families), SNAP benefits (food stamps), WIC payments (Women Infants and Children), Medicaid, Child-Care, foster care, emergency assistance and other medical and health benefits. But the coups de grâce was: They could receive an ACTC (Additional Child Tax Credit), which is a "refundable" tax credit, even though they didn't pay any taxes.

"They, meaning the Mexicans who are being provided for," continued Scott, "say that it's payback for us, meaning the

27   A round-bottomed glass flask for wine, especially Chianti, covered with a straw basket—the valley name is very appropriate because fiasco *also* means: "A thing that is a complete failure, especially in a ludicrous or humiliating way." If you are a young, single, vibrant male working in the valley, your social life will be a total fiasco.

United States, taking a lot of their homeland...even though we didn't actually *take* it. Well, I shouldn't say that exactly."

"What *should* you say exactly?" asked Detective Knight with renewed interest.

"Well I don't know too much about it really. Just that the U.S. Army captured Mexico City in the Mexican-American War and forced Mexico to 'give' us all of their northern territory, part of which you are standing on right now. So technically, we didn't take any land; they *gave* it to us."

"Yeah, kind of like in fourth grade I used to 'give' Bully Bob my lunch money; or else I would get a purple-nurple."[28]

"Yeah, I guess so," said Scott. "Bob didn't take anything from you; you gave it to him, under duress, but nonetheless, you *gave* it to him."

David stood there and looked at Scott for a moment and then said, "Hmm. A thought just occurred to me. Maybe this is really called Fiasco Valley because of everything you just said, I mean the part about providing all the assistance for immigrant families. If we keep giving illegal immigrants all those benefits, it will be okay for a while but eventually it will turn into a total fiasco for us, meaning the U.S. It has nothing to do with a wine flask."

"Gosh." said Scott. "I never thought of it that way. You could be right. I always assumed the name *did* come from those flasks the Italian immigrants used for holding their wine, but maybe I assumed wrong. It's happened before."

---

28 Painfully twisting someone's nipples where the goal is to bruise it. A.K.A. Texas Titty Twister. I got one of those in junior high. Oh man! Not good.

Chapter 6

Marital Bliss?

Maria walked into her house and went straight to the kitchen; it was a mess. There were dirty dishes, two half-eaten burritos, and a pot full of cold beans that had been left on the stove all night. Her boyfriend, Ernesto was sitting in front of the TV drinking a Coors Light—because the bars on the can told him the beer had gone from "cold" to "super cold."

"What's for dinner?" bellowed Ernesto.

"Ohh, Tacos," sighed a wearied Maria.

"When are we eating? thundered Ernesto.

As soon as you get your fat ass off the couch and make dinner, you lazy Mexican thought Maria. But she said, or sighed rather, "In about an hour." This was all in Spanish, of course.

Maria was miserable living with Ernesto. He was great at first and Maria had looked forward to living with, and marrying him. At the time, he was an extraordinarily loving, caring, sensitive guy who was funny, devilishly handsome, and simply made her feel comfortable. They began living together about a year ago, just to save money, of course. The situation was great until Ernesto met some Spanish-speaking janitors, working for a neighboring school district, at the local SEIU (Service Employees Intenational Union) meeting.

Shortly after meeting these fellow janitors, Ernesto became much more difficult to live with. He was becoming abusive and was always fuming about something. All he did was denigrate the United States and all of its "stupid gringos."

Well where would you be and what would you have without

the United States and all of its "stupid gringos?" You'd be nowhere and have nothing thought Maria.

She loved Mexico but there were no opportunities there for...anything, unless one became involved in the illegal drug trade. Sure, the U.S. had problems but anyone and everyone had an opportunity to improve their life, maybe not an equal opportunity, but an opportunity nonetheless. Maria had definitely improved her life and Ernesto had greatly improved his. Yet, he was not at all grateful to America or Americans. He hated them all and seemed to be throwing away everything the U.S. had given him the opportunity to gain.

It had all started when Maria and Ernesto met as they were both illegally entering the U.S. via a "tunnel" that began in the bathroom of a taquería in Mexicali, Mexico and ended when it came-up through a storm drain in a Home Depot parking lot in Calexico, California. It wasn't much of a tunnel really; it was a long, narrow hole in the ground that went from one side of the border to the other. It had been dug by hand and was not up to *any* building standards or regulations and would not have passed *any* inspection by *any* agency in the U.S. or even in Mexico...well *maybe* in Mexico. That "tunnel" saw a lot of one-way traffic.

It was only one-way because no one in their right mind would begin in Calexico, California and go to Mexicali, Mexico, with the possible exception of some college kids on a drunken dare during Spring Break. The vast majority of Americans couldn't have used the tunnel even if they had wanted to because their girth would have been too large.

Ernesto had looked at Maria's cute little rear end the entire time he had been crawling through the tunnel from Mexico to the United States. Upon exiting the tunnel, and being picked-up by a relative of one the other fleeing Mexicans, Ernesto decided to learn more about whom that nice butt belonged to; a beautiful relationship would soon be born.

There is a large and complex network of Mexicans in Southern California that help illegal immigrants enter the United States and then stay in the United States. Maria, Ernesto, and the other illegal immigrants were transported to Los Angeles, via this network, and were then housed in an abandoned warehouse.

While in the warehouse, the illegal immigrants were taught some essential English phrases, such as: "What's on TV? Where's the remote? I want that...*now*! I need a latte. I love cappuccino. I ate too much. What's for dessert? This card is maxed out. Republicans are evil racists. Vote for the Democrat...that's the one with a 'D.'" They were taught these phrases in order to "fit in" better and not arouse any suspicion as to their lawful status. Maria, Ernesto, and the two other illegal immigrants were then driven up to Birchwood because there were four jobs available...for cheap labor.

Maria's job was to be the housecleaner for William Strong; the owner of Big Goose Cellars, and Ernesto's job was to be a janitor with a local janitorial service company. Upon arriving in Birchwood, Maria, Ernesto, and the two other illegal immigrants were taken to the small, over-crowded, county-run, Farmworker Housing Facility, or FawHF, where they were to live until they got permanent housing.

The county officials were not too concerned about the lawful status of the inhabitants of its FawHF. They just wanted to provide "a temporary safe place for migrants who were working simply to feed their children and better their lives." That was their official stance, but really they just wanted to make sure they appeared caring, understanding, and enlightened to the majority of the county's voters (who were Democrats) so they would win re-election.

The FawHF was important in the valley because its residents provided cheap labor for all the wineries, which increased the winery's profits and made their owners happy. That, in turn, increased campaign contributions to the incumbents, which would greatly help in their re-election bids. The elected government officials would then increase the county office's budgets and therefore the salaries of those who worked for that office. Cha-Ching! Everyone wants more money, except for the Occupy Wall Street chowderheads[29] because they know they'll never be rich so no one else should be either, or because they are content to live off the American taxpayer, or because they already have everything paid for by Mommy and Daddy, or the most likely reason: They had been so stoned for so long that they didn't care about anything, except maybe the price of marijuana. The illegal immigrants were being portrayed as a big win-win for the county.

So, Ernesto and Maria were finally in America. They were full of dreams. They would buy a big house, a nice car, a nice stereo, a DVD player, and have cable or satellite television. They would buy anything and everything they needed or wanted because this was America and that's what Americans did. It was the American Dream and they were going to live it. At least that was the plan.

Their plan began to unravel shortly after they arrived, when Maria told her intensely Catholic mother, over the phone, that she and Ernesto were sharing a room at the housing facility.

"Oh no! God will not like that. You'll go to hell! You need to

---

29   A stupid person with no common sense. It's one of my favorite words.

marry first. No sex!" wailed Maria's mother in loud and rapidly spoken Spanish.

Ernesto also told his intensely Catholic mother, also over the phone, about his current living arrangement and she basically said what Maria's mother had said. The two mothers had not been fond of each other before, but now they had abject hatred for one another.

Maria and Ernesto received calls from each of their mother's at least three times per day. The calls (in Spanish of course) were just a constant barrage of rapidly spoken insults of the other mother's child and how that child was violating religious doctrine.[30] It was also becoming a problem because there was only one phone in the housing facility and there was no time for anyone else to use it. Maria, Ernesto, and the other FawHF residents were growing tired of the whole situation so, Maria and Ernesto decided to just get married and hopefully stop the calls. Everyone at the housing facility cheered.

Maria and Ernesto hitched a ride to Las Vegas, got married, and then hitched a ride back. Their "Honeymoon" was dinner at the local Mexican restaurant followed by "dessert" in the local park. Now that they were married, Ernesto and Maria wanted their own place so they could make a lot of little Ernesto's and Maria's. That would also make their mothers happy and keep them quiet.

They quickly discovered that the housing part of the American Dream costs quite a bit of money, especially in Birchwood. They looked and looked and finally found a place they could afford. It was an enormously small apartment in the low-income housing complex near the creek at the edge of town.

---

30   A belief or set of beliefs held and taught by a church, political party, or other group—the Catholic church in this case.

They wanted that apartment. They *needed* that apartment.

When they went into the manager's office to inquire about the apartment, there was a young, tall, arrogant looking gringo wearing a suit and signing some papers at the manager's desk. When they were finally able to ask about the apartment, Ernesto and Maria were told that the apartment had just been rented; their plan continued to unravel.

Considerably dejected, they left the manager's office and began the hot, two-mile, skin-cancer-producing, trek along the road shoulder back to the temporary housing facility, which Ernesto was beginning to think would become their permanent housing facility. *I don't want to make babies there; everyone will know what we're doing and probably try to watch.* (Yes, she thought in English...amazing!)

While walking through the apartment complex parking lot, Maria and Ernesto noticed that there weren't many cars in the parking lot, and the vast majority of cars that were there were rather expensive, i.e. Porsche's, Mercedes, Audi's, BMW's, Ferrari's, and even a Lamborghini. *These people are low-income?*

Maria and Ernesto saw the guy, who had just rented the last apartment, getting into a 2014 Audi R8 sports car, which has a base price of $114,900.00. Ernesto knew about this car because one of the guys he worked with constantly talked and read magazines about sports cars, and this particular Audi model was often the topic of conversation. Anyone who owned that car, should not be living in low-income housing. The guy backed out of his parking spot, peeled-out, and drove out of the parking lot in a big hurry. The car had a personalized license plate that read: FUN4TOD.

Chapter 7

Maria

After walking from the apartment complex back to the Farmworker Housing Facility, Maria re-heated some leftover beans while Ernesto drank a Coors Light, then another, and then one more because the can told him the beer had gone from cold to super cold. Maria left Ernesto in charge of clean-up because she had to go to work, although she didn't think anything would actually get cleaned—typical male.

Maria's job as a housecleaner for the Strong's turned out to be extremely beneficial...eventually. When Maria first began working for them, Mrs. Strong only spoke two words of Spanish: "sí" and "coño,"[31] therefore she could not really talk to Maria. Initially, she would just *show* Maria what was to be done and then leave her alone to hopefully do the job correctly. This resulted in a couple of minor...uh...mishaps.

To remedy this, Mrs. Strong could have learned a few Spanish phrases but she didn't really want to and she figured it would benefit Maria more, in the long run, if she learned English. *This is the United States; we speak English here. Why should I learn Spanish? She is living and working here so she should speak at least some English.*

To this end, Mrs. Strong purchased some "Learning English Through Listening" CD's and had Maria listen to them on their home stereo whilst doing her chores. It wasn't long before Maria could understand short, rudimentary instructions in English. She could also ask simple questions, and she was getting better every day.

---

31   I'll let whoever is reading this translate that word...or not.

Now that Maria could communicate with Mrs. Strong, somewhat, they were actually becoming friends. Maria expressed, as best she could, her and Ernesto's desire to have their own place to live because they wanted to make babies (those were Maria's words) and they couldn't really do that where they lived now.

"They drink much beer, always make noisy, and probably look by crack in wall," said Maria to Mrs. Strong. She also told Mrs. Strong how she was worried about Ernesto's new proclivity (she did not use that word) for drinking and his perpetually (nor that one) pissy (or that one, either) attitude. She said he constantly whined and complained about rich people—at least those whom he considered rich—and their houses and businesses that he cleaned.

Mrs. Strong would console Maria as best she could, which wasn't very well considering the vastly different worlds the two women came from. She mainly consoled Maria via the seemingly useless (to any male) but universal female language of facial expressions, tears, and hugs.

These consolations were ultimately quite useful for Maria because Mrs. Strong, out of pity, convinced her husband, William, to give Maria the receptionist/secretary job that had recently opened-up at Big Goose Cellars. That was where Maria was going now.

Maria, to the relief of both Mrs. Strong and her husband, turned out to be very capable of doing the job she had been given. She could answer the phone and handle basic questions, as long as they weren't spoken too fast. She was extremely organized, which was good because William Strong was an extremely muddled individual. Plus, William thought she was as cute as a button, had a great figure and, and he just liked having her around; so long as Mrs. Strong didn't catch on. To top it all off, she gave off an aura of sensuality and William really dug that. After all, he was a horny old man and his wife was not nearly as...frisky as she used to be.

Chapter 8

Another Day

Ernesto got to work at 7:30 AM, a half an hour late. His two co-workers, Carl and Mike, were already there and not happy with his tardiness.

"Hey chief, where have you been?" they asked in condescending unison.

Ernesto ignored them. He was thinking ahead to the Service Employees International Union (SEIU) meeting that evening, so he just went about preparing the van for the day's work. Ernesto hated cleaning the houses of these rich Americans but it did not seem to bother Carl or Mike at all. In fact, they seemed to rather enjoy the job. If they were on a job and the man of the house was around, baseball, basketball, football, and sexy models or actresses were popular topics of conversation. If the lady of the house was around, increasing weight, diets and exercise, and kids were popular topics.

Ernesto did not understand how the people doing these menial jobs for rich schmucks could be so friendly toward them. He hated all these rich folk because they had more than he did...a lot more. Of course, Ernesto did not understand a lot of things; no one had ever accused him of being a genius.

Ernesto couldn't wait for the SEIU meeting because it would give him the chance to talk Pedro and Tomás, who were also janitors in the area. Like Ernesto, these vatos were in the U.S. illegally and had garnered a deep contempt[32] and animosity[33]

---

32   The feeling that a person or a thing is beneath consideration, worthless, or deserving scorn.

33   Strong hostility.

of wealthy Americans. At every SEIU meeting they attended, Pedro and Tomás would willingly spread their feelings to the other members.

They had come to America with dreams of riding around on speedboats with naked women, drinking beer and champagne, doing drugs, and running from the police. Apparently, the 1980's TV series *Miami Vice* was available on VHS in Mexico and these two vatos had watched a few too many episodes. Cleaning the toilets of rich, old, snooty, crackers[34] was not part of their dreams.

Once the van was ready to go, Ernesto and his two co-workers piled in and drove to the house, Ernesto considered it a mansion, that was to be cleaned that morning. On the drive, Ernesto's mood did not improve, because, as always, the van was rather odoriferous. His two co-workers were much more concerned with watching porno movies and drinking beer than with showering and washing clothes. All they talked about on the trip was the latest porno movie thay had seen and how many beers they had drank before passing out. Ernesto did not think it was very stimulating conversation.

---

34   A racist term for a white person. I've been called that more than once.

Chapter 9

Todd

"Alright dudes, the limo should be here any minute, and then...woohoo! We're off like a brides pajamas," shouted Todd with great enthusiasm. He and his drinking buddies were going to spend the entire weekend in Birchwood and stay in Todd's apartment, which he kept for just this type of getaway. They would visit wineries in Birchwood and the surrounding area, taste wine, drink wine, and hopefully meet some lonely, rich, women; even if they were "mature" widows just out looking for some "fresh meat." They would wine and dine them, then take them back to Todd's apartment and put the claims of their male enhancement pills to the test.

Todd had recently graduated—he had been on the 7½-year plan—from Chico State with a degree in Economics and was now a financial advisor for an *extremely* successful wealth management company in San Francisco.

Even though he had graduated from college, Todd had the intelligence of someone who would try to eat soup with a fork. He had gotten his job partly, or more likely wholly, due to the fact that Sam, the owner of said company, had been a fraternity brother of Todd's father at the University of Chicago. They had both been economics majors and after graduating had done extremely well in the world of high finance.

However, the two did not exhibit any brotherly love towards one another and had never even been friendly with each other. Todd did not know why he was given the job, he just figured his Dad must know many 'o skeleton in Sam's fraternity closet and

Sam wanted to keep them there. So much so, that he had given Todd a job at his company to ensure his father did not let any of those skeletons out.

Todd's drinking buddies also worked in the financial district of San Francisco, but not for the same company. They did, however, do the same kind of work. That work being: Managing wealthy, *very* wealthy people's money, many of whom lived in Birchwood. Todd did not like his job, or his boss, Sam, and Sam did not particularly like Todd. Todd's co-workers did not hold much, if any, regard for him.

First, they knew that Playboy Magazine had once rated Chico State as the Number One party school in the U.S. and that, for some baffling reason, did not garner much respect for Todd in the world of high finance.

Second, and more importantly, they had all either graduated from the University of Chicago, Yale, Princeton, or the University of California at Berkeley, all of which were held in high regard amongst those in the financial community and they did not want the company's reputation to be sullied[35] by some "partier" from Chico State. Secretly, however, they were jealous of Todd because they figured that, unlike them, he had gotten *some* poontang[36] in college or at least had a lot of fun trying. This juxtaposition of feelings in the minds of his co-workers caused jealousy, stress, discontent, and did not promote cooperation. Not surprisingly, this was not good for job performance, worker morale, or anything else for that matter.

Furthermore, Todd was sick and tired of managing *other*

---

35   Damage the purity or integrity of; defile. Then defile means: to make a holy or sacred thing or place no longer fit for ceremonial use.

36   The part of a female's body located between her legs and used for sexual activity. "Get some poontang" is another way of saying, "get laid" and is chiefly said by guys trying to make other guys *think* they get lots of action.

people's wealth. They were all a-holes and he wanted to manage his own wealth; of course, he had to get wealthy first. Todd figured that going to Birchwood and being around wealth, might inspire him to get wealthy. So, he and his buddies, all of whom were the low men on the Totem Pole at their respective companies, jumped into the rented limousine and headed for Birchwood to begin their weekend.

Death Número Tres

Chapter 10

Was Ted Tipsy?

Detective Knight returned to Big Goose Cellars. Officially, he went there to work on the investigation of the deaths of Frank Finnegan and Mark Madson. Unofficially, he went there to see that hot little tamale, Maria. When Detective Knight drove up to the winery, there was a limousine parked near the tasting room.

Upon seeing the limo, Detective David Knight was again instantly put in an exceedingly foul mood. All he heard on the news was how bad everything was economically. No one had jobs or money and poverty was rampant. David Knight did not exactly see it that way. All he saw was that a lot of people couldn't buy all of the solid material that periodically exudes from one's colon that they thought they had a right to have, and so didn't have to work for it.

He had been all over the country, in the last year or two, and had seen a lot of "poor" people with all kinds of crap they did not need, i.e. Big-Screen HDTV's, PlayStation 4 or XBOX video game systems, iMac's, iPhone's, iBook's, iAnything and iEverything that was available, beer, liquor, and cigarettes. *Well apparently, some people have money to spend. I wonder why MSNBC isn't reporting that? Probably because it's something they can't blame on President Bush and make Republicans look bad. If those "poor" people were truly in financial straits, they couldn't, or at least shouldn't, have any of that crap.*

Also, many of these same people lived in nice houses with garages that had nice cars in them. The economy was being portrayed by politicians as being worse than it really was because you can't fix something that isn't broken and politicians want to get credit for fixing something. The news media was in cahoots with them for some reason...David had not quite figured that one out yet.

It was probably because the vast majority of reporters are liberal Democrats and it makes them feel warm, fuzzy, and superior—to anyone who isn't a reporter—to report and talk about the problems of poor people who, they believe, would not be poor if the Democratic candidate was always elected, no matter what the office. The reporters felt that their reporting the problems of the poor was just as good as solving them and was far easier because they did not have to do anything except collect their paychecks and look good on TV.

Upon arriving, David went directly into the winery office to see Maria but she was not there, nor was anyone else. *Hmm. Where is everyone?* He then heard voices emanating from the tasting room, so he went in there because that seemed like the logical thing to do, and he was a logical man. Maria was there, along with Tim Tauscher, William Strong, and three young guys that David Knight did not recognize. They were all drinking...I mean tasting wine, carrying on, and getting louder by the bottle...I mean taste.

"There he is," bellowed William Strong, "the detective who will solve all of our problems!"

"Problems? What problems could you have here in paradise?" asked one of the three guys that David did not recognize.

Detective Knight took a gander[37] at the three young, overly well-dressed, gentlemen standing near William and Tim at

---

37 A look or glance. It's also a male goose. Since my last name is "Gosling" maybe there is some subconcious reason I chose that word.

the tasting-room bar and shook his head. After his quick look, David Knight approached the bar while giving a questioning glance to William and Tim.

"Detective Knight, these gentlemen here work for the wonderful company that manages my moola. They make sure I stay part of the 1%," chuckled William, "and they're helping Timmy boy here get in *to* that 1%." He gave Tim Tauscher a hard slap on the back as he said this.

Todd, one of the three gentlemen David did not recognize and who was ogling Maria, repeated his question, "Problems? What problems could you have here in paradise? If you can make wines this good, you can't *possibly* have any problems."

"Unfortunately," said Detective Knight as he turned toward the three dimwits, "the problems William is referring to have little to do with wine quality, as far as I can tell anyway."

Detective Knight then walked over to the bar and gave William and Tim the lowdown—or was it the downlow?—on the investigations into the recent events at the winery. During this rundown of events, Todd sidled up to the bar so that he could also hear Detective Knight's rundown on the lowdown, or maybe it was downlow on the runup. Whichever it was, Todd heard it and became awfully excited.

"Holy cow!" exclaimed Todd. "That's really exciting. I had no idea something like that would, or even could happen here in Birchwood. I mean, I have read the Police Log in *The Birchwood Star* a number of times and I thought all that ever happened here was that dogs barked late at night and parties were too loud at 2 A.M."

"Don't forget the lady who called the cops at 9:28 P.M. because her water softener was making a strange noise," quipped one of the other three guys.

"We like to have our Police Log like that," retorted David Knight, "it makes my job a lot easier and keeps the bakeries in business...which means jobs." David instantly did not like these three young guys in the tasting room; they gave him the impression as being haughty and just plain lame. So, he immediately turned toward Maria and asked if she had heard or learned anything that might be useful in the investigation of the death of Frank and/or Mark. She hadn't, at least that is what she said.

While this was all taking place, a cacophonous[38] racket of sirens began and could be heard in the not-to-far-away distance. No one really paid attention to them because A) hearing sirens in the distance wasn't exactly newsworthy, and B) everyone in the room was becoming so besotted[39] with the wine and themselves, that they didn't really care about anything outside of their individual realms. The sirens continued but did not seem to get any nearer or farther.

"It sounds to me like those sirens are stuck on the road that goes to our Vine Cliff vineyard," said William with a sense of perturbation. "I wonder what's going on there. It better not be costing me money...whatever it is."

"Do you mean your Vine Cliff Reserve Cabernet comes from a vineyard named Vine Cliff?" asked Todd in wonderment. "Is there a vineyard there? Is there a cliff there?"

"No. There is just one big vine over there that we named 'Cliff" after my grandfather," said William sarcastically. "Yes, there is a cliff there, and believe it or not, there is also a vineyard there with more than one vine. It has quite a few actually, because

38 A harsh, discordant mixture of sounds.
39 1. Strongly infatuated. 2. archaic: intoxicated; drunk. Bonus: both definitions apply here.

84

they're pretty small." Normally, William did not interact with tourists much because he was a bit of a smart-ass and that did not bode well for sales.

"Gee Todd, you didn't know that?" piped up one of his buddies. "I looked it up on Google Earth and Google Maps and the vineyard goes right, I mean *right* to the edge of about a 200 foot cliff, which then drops straight down to the road we used to get here.

"Man, I love Google. I've decided you can do just about anything with Google and apparently a lot other of people feel the same way. Their stock was $85 a share and now it is over $1000! Man, if I had bought a lot of stock early on when I had the chance, I could buy my own winery now."

"If you love it, why don't you marry it?" said Todd's other buddy.

"It seems as if the sirens have stopped. They're not moving anyway," said William as he ignored Todd's two dimwitted friends. William was correct. Over the last half-hour or so, the sirens had remained in the same spot; they hadn't gotten louder or quieter.

All the people in the tasting room just kept right on drinking...I mean tasting wine. However, Detective Knight was not part of the group anymore, for as soon as he had heard the sirens, he left the group and got on his car radio to see what he could find out.

What he found out was that the sirens belonged to an ambulance and two police cars en route to an accident. Apparently, a tractor had fallen off the cliff at the Vine Cliff Vineyard and landed on an SUV traveling on the road below. All indications were that the SUV did not cushion the tractor's fall very well.

Normally, a tractor falling from the sky onto an evil, deadly, air-polluting SUV would be something for the citizens of this mega-liberal state to cheer about. In this case, however, it was an unspeakable tragedy because one of the vehicles involved in the gruesome, multi-car, pile-up that immediately followed was a VW Bus carrying a group of UC Berkeley students who were on their way to live in some trees in order to prevent them from being cut down to make room for a vineyard. Suffice it to say, those students weren't going to be living in those, or any other trees, any time in the future. To make matters worse, or better depending on your upbringing, the emergency vehicles that had been summoned to help the victims were hopelessly mired in the Friday afternoon traffic and could not reach the horrific scene in a timely fashion.

By the time an ambulance *did* reach the scene and the medics were able to treat the tractor driver, Ted Templeton, it was too late. Ted was on the wrong side of the grass, he was pushing-up daisies, he was circling the drain, all of his problems were solved, he was an *ex-parrot*!

Chapter 11

Dead Ted's Tractor

Detective Knight was not able to look at Ted's tractor until after it had been taken to the police impound yard. He would have liked to see it sooner, but a plethora of personal injury lawyers had managed to reach the crash before him. Detective Knight, for the life of him, could not figure out how these personal injury lawyers had been able to reach the accident scene before he did. He thought they may have even managed to reach the crash scene before the ambulance. He also discovered that they can be a rough bunch at the scene of a personal injury. They managed to keep David so busy trying to decipher—they used a lot of Latin or Latin *sounding* words—and answer their inane questions that he did not have a chance to look at the tractor until it was too late.

David succeeded in pulling himself away from the lawyers, got back in his 4Runner (he was dreading having to face the horde of tourist traffic again) and eventually made it to the police impound yard. Once he was there, Detective Knight spoke with one of the mechanics who serviced all of the police department vehicles and who was looking at dead Ted's tractor.

"So, what can you tell me about this tractor?" asked David.

"Well, I was looking at this tractor when, wouldn't ya know it, Chief O' Wonkler showed-up," explained the mechanic.

Detective Knight knew, from all the gossip that was rampant in Birchwood, that Chief O' Wonkler was not happy with the job performance of this particular mechanic.

"As you probably know," continued the mechanic, "the Chief

and I don't...uh...'see eye to eye' on a lot of things. I need this job, so I was trying to impress him. Problem is, I don't perform well under pressure and because of that, I think I effed-up[40] the whole works."

"The whole works?" questioned David. "How do you mean?"

"Well, the whole steering mechanism was somehow jury-rigged,[41] that part was rather obvious. But in my attempt to impress the Chief and explain what must have happened, I took it all apart while just making-up how everything worked, because I really had no clue. I figured after O' Wonkler left, I would put it back together the way I found it, relax, take it apart slowly, and figure-out what *had* actually happened. I neglected to account for the fact that I suck at putting things back together," said the mechanic.

"How did you know it was jury-rigged in the first place?"

"Oh, like I said, it was obvious. There were parts from the bottom of the tractor all bent and wired to the steering column. There were ignition, and all other kinds of wires, attached to the steering wheel and gas pedal. It was quite the set-up actually."

"But you have no idea how it worked or what happened?"

"Well not really, but as near as I could tell, from before O' Wonkler showed-up, the gas pedal and the steering wheel were somehow hooked together so that the speed of the tractor was being controlled by the steering wheel. When the tractor was turned sharply, as it would be at the end of each row in order to go back from whence it came, it was rigged so *that* sharp of

---

40 An acceptable way to say "fucked-up," according to my Mom anyway.

41 Refers to makeshift repairs or temporary contrivances, made with only the tools and materials that happen to be on hand, originally a nautical term. On sailing ships, a jury rig is a replacment mast and yards (which hold the ship's rigging) improvised in case of damage or loss of the original mast.

a turn would be like stomping on the gas pedal. In other words, the tractor would be 'floored' every time it was turned sharply to go around the end of a row."

David did not hear this explanation. He was too busy wondering if, and why, the phrases "as near as I could tell" and "as far as I could tell," meant the same thing. In spite of his wandering mind, David did realize that Vine Cliff Vineyard was the worst vineyard on planet Earth (probably) to drive a tractor with a jury-rigged steering system. The reason being: Each row of vines ended no more than a few feet from the edge of a cliff (hence the name) which dropped straight down to a well-traveled road.

"Then, that begs the question," said Detective Knight, "How did the tractor get to the vineyard in the first place? What I mean is, Ted had to steer the tractor to get *to* Vine Cliff Vineyard. Why didn't it break then?"

"My job is just to fix stuff that is broken. Isn't it *your* job, detective, to solve those little mysteries?"

That last question caused David a considerable amount of vexation[42] and he gave the mechanic a look that said as much. The mechanic actually recognized the look, and said, "But I'll keep working on it and see if I can come up with anything new."

---

42 The state of being annoyed, frustrated, or worried. This particular mechanic caused a lot of people a considerable amount of vexation.

Chapter 12

Todd Tours

Todd thought Birchwood was not only the cat's pajamas but the cat's meow as well, and because of that, he thought that even *he* might be able to get some pussy there...eventually. Unfortunately, his buddies weren't as enamored with the town. They thought it was dull, snooty, and way too expensive. They hadn't met any lonely, rich, single women; of course, they hadn't met any sociable, poor, married women either. In fact, the only woman they met who was "doable" was Maria. They couldn't wait to get back home and go out eating in restaurants drinking in bars and that had wo*men* (notice it's plural) in them.

Todd, on the other hand, did not want to leave. In the limo, on the ride back to San Francisco, he was already planning his next trip to Birchwood. He would call in sick on Friday morning and go by himself. He would sleep in his apartment (unless of course he got lucky) and visit wineries and eat at nice restaurants. He would go back to Big Goose Cellars, because their wines were the best, and hopefully talk more with Tim Tauscher and William Strong. There was also an extremely good chance he would see Maria and she would see him...and his car. If that happened she would not be able to resist him because everyone knows that women are powerless when it comes to guys in expensive sports cars. If, by some chance, Maria was able to resist a wealthy guy in an expensive sports car, possibly because of her Mexican heritage, or culture, or something, there had to be at least one betty[43] in Birchwood who couldn't. And if, by some amazing fluke, he

---

43   A hot-looking female. Betty Page was the inspiration for calling a good-looking female a "betty."

didn't meet a betty, just having the chance to drive his Audi R8 and be *seen* in it was reason enough alone for Todd to make the trip, at the very least it would make him feel good. He was quite confident that his car would play a key role in him having a good, possibly even an amatory[44] weekend because on his first trip to Birchwood, Todd noticed that the people paid close attention to what other people were driving and because of that, no one was cruising around in a beat-up, old jalopie. Todd figured that his sports car would turn some heads, and quite possibly a good-looking blonde's head assuming, of course, there was one.

The first Friday after he and his two buddies returned from their Birchwood excursion, Todd got out of bed particularly early, took a shower, threw a few clothes and a toothbrush into a Nike sports bag, jumped into his Audi, and headed for Birchwood. While driving to Birchwood he, like everyone else, flouted[45] the law by using a cell phone—he didn't think anyone would mind since cell phones are ubiquitous[46] nowadays—and called in sick at work. As a bonus, making a call while driving drew attention to him and so helped him flaunt[47] his *ridiculously* expensive car that he figured chics would dig...big time. Todd was happy because he was able flout and flaunt at the same time. Not many guys can say that.

He was starving when he arrived in Birchwood at about 8:00 A.M. So, he stopped at The Birchwood Café for a bite, or two, or maybe even three to eat. The café was nearly full of people but Todd was able to get a table next to three guys

---

44   Relating to or induced by sexual love or desire.

45   Openly disregard – a rule, law, or convention.

46   Present, appearing, or found everywhere. Cell phones annoy the hell out of me.

47   Display something in order to provoke envy or admiration, or to show defiance.

wearing jeans, boots, and Ben Davis work shirts. Based solely on their appearance, Todd pegged these guys as locals, so he eavesdropped on their conversations to hopefully gain some insight as to life in Birchwood. He quickly learned that these guys often played in local Bocce Ball tournaments—one of which was this afternoon—they all had wives, and their lives in general weren't too exciting. He did however, eventually discern that these guys worked in vineyards and that at least two of the guys actually owned the vineyards where they worked.

During his eavesdropping, Todd heard them mention, in concerned voices, something called *phylloxera*. He deduced that it was some sort of small bug that ate the vine's roots and would eventually kill the vine. Dead vines meant no grapes. No grapes meant no wine. No wine meant no money. No money meant no num nums from the ol' lady, and that meant *phylloxera* was a major problem.

The other scourge he learned about was nematodes, which are round worms that feed on the roots of a grapevine but don't kill it; just greatly reduce its growth and vigor. Problem for Todd was, every time he heard the word "nematodes" he had to bite his lip to keep from laughing because all he could think about was Bikini Bottom, SpongeBob SquarePants, plankton, Patrick, and the Krusty Krab.[48]

He later heard them talking, rather excitedly, about a rootstalk which had been developed at UC Davis and that *phylloxera* did not find delicious. Todd had heard about UC Davis from a couple of co-workers who had graduated from UC Berkeley and they had given him the impression that UC Davis was a bunch of stupid hicks that drank Lucky Lager, roasted marshmallows,

---

48 Those are all elements of the children's cartoon, "Spongebob Squarepants." I like the cartoon.

and tipped cows for fun on the weekends. Apparently though, UC Davis did know a thing or two about growing grapevines and the bugs that ate them. He also heard that this new rootstock was resistant to nematodes and so could be the Holy Grail of Viticulture, which is the growing of grapevines.

He also learned, from his eavesdropping, that the natural roots of the grapevines currently grown in the Valley were being replaced with the roots of grapevines whose roots were not delicious food for the aforementioned dastardly devils. These new roots would render the vines resistant to those varmints and so were desirable to vineyard managers and owners, not only in Fiasco Valley, but throughout the world.

Todd learned there was no cure for *phylloxera* and there was no way to get rid of it once it was in a vineyard, unless all the vines comprising the infected vineyard were destroyed and replaced with vines that grew on *phylloxera*-resistant rootstalk. Not surprisingly, all grape growers feared this expensive, time-consuming "fix."

After eating his delicious, home-style breakfast in The Birchwood Café and hearing the conversation between the three locals, Todd decided that Birchwood was the place for him. He looked at his watch and saw it was only 8:45 A.M. He had made better time getting here than he had anticipated, and the Big Goose Cellars Tasting Room did not open until 10:00 A.M. so, he had some time to kill.

The Birchwood Café was right on the town's main street and it was an ideal day: Cool, bright blue sky with not a cloud in sight, and just an occasional slight breeze. So, Todd decided to walk up the street—or down the street depending on your sense of direction—and get a feel for the town.

He had only been walking for about five minutes when he

happened upon a busy coffee shop. Todd loved espresso drinks so he entered the coffee shop in order to get a Mocha and kill some time. Possibly, he thought, he could learn more by eavesdropping on some additional locals. Todd got his espresso drink (which was lukewarm) and went out on the patio to sit at one of the tables.

Sitting at the table next to him were a couple of middle-aged women. Each woman was wearing a big, wide-brimmed, ridiculous looking—in Todd's opinion—sun hat, each had a large, shiney boulder on her ring finger, and each was holding a small, shivering dog on her lap.

Todd eavesdropped on their conversations but didn't learn much. In fact, he felt dumber after having heard the conversation. He made a note to himself that he should avoid middle-aged women wearing big hats, sporting boulders on their ring fingers, and holding small dogs that shivered constantly.

Todd finished his Mocha, looked down at his watch and saw that it was 9:50. So, he got up and began to walk back to his Audi R8 that he had parked in front of The Birchwood Café. When he reached his car, he got in and drove off to Big Goose Cellars.

Upon arriving and exiting his car, Todd noticed Tim Tauscher, William Strong, and some dude with a good-sized boiler[49] standing outside the tasting room. There was a lot of motioning of arms and foot stomping, and no one appeared to be in a good mood. As Todd approached, he heard the dude with the boiler say, or rather yell, "...fucking fine! See ya a-holes later!" The dude then galumphed[50] over to his car, lumbered in, slammed his door shut, and drove off in a big hurry. Todd

---

49 A potbelly. Some people think it shows the owner of the boiler is successful, wealthy, and doesn't have to work. Some people have trouble with reality.

50 Move in a clumsy, ponderous, or noisy manner.

94

continued walking towards Tim and William and said, "Is this a bad time? I can come back later if it is."

"No. No. No. Don't worry about that. We just got rid of some dead wood that's all," said William.

"Bill, you do remember we've got that large group coming this morning, don't you? What are we going to do about them?" asked Tim.

"Is that today?" said Bill with an incredulous gasp. "I thought that was *next* weekend."

"Nope, it's today at eleven."

Todd, who had sidled up to Tim, noticed that William had suddenly turned pale and gotten a look of pure panic on his face. He asked, "What's going on? Problems?"

"Well there certainly could be. We just had to let John go. He's our tour guide and tasting room manager, and at eleven o'clock we have a large group of investment bankers and other assorted financial professionals from New York arriving for a VIP tour and tasting...with John."

William, who was known for his sangfroid[51] and had regained some color in his face, jumped in and said, "Let me make some phone calls. I'll see what I can do, but...don't hold your breath." William turned and walked briskly into the winery offices, and then into his own private office. At least that is where Todd assumed he went because he couldn't quite see through the walls.

Tim stood there for an interminable amount of time, just looking out at the vineyard, while Todd just stood there wondering what the hell he should do now. Desperate to break the silence, Todd asked Tim if Nematodes were any sort of

---

51 Composure or coolness, sometimes excessive, as shown in danger or unnder trying circumstances.

problem in their vineyards.

"Uhh...what?" asked Tim. That was the last question Tim thought anyone would ask him right about then.

"Do you have any problems with Nematodes?" Todd asked again. Fortunately, he managed not to laugh while doing so.

"No," answered Tim, "We wage chemical warfare against those little buggers."

"You use chemicals in the vineyard?" Todd asked with surprise. Todd had been living and working in San Francisco—a bastion of liberal thinking—and had seen, and read, all kinds of literature and heard all kinds of self-righteous groups talk about the dangers of chemicals, pesticides, and fertilizers that were used on farms. He had even been to a rally with a lot of women, and men, with hairy armpits and legs, protesting the use of chemicals on farms. But he had gone only to laugh at the "wannabe hippies," as he called them, not to support their cause.

"Uh, yeah. Bill is not too concerned about being 'organic' or 'all natural', which is all the rage now; he would rather have healthy vines and good wines. We use chemicals liberally in our vineyards to murder all kinds of little critters"

"So, 'better living through chemistry' is Bill's motto?" asked Todd.

"Sure is. Mine too."

"Well don't let CNN or MSNBC, or any other news organization find out, because they'll have a cow and try to shut you down. Now, what about *phylloxera*? Can it also be killed with chemicals?" asked Todd.

Tim gave Todd a look that was all at once disturbed, angry, stressed, frustrated, and defeated. He then answered, "Nothing kills those little effers. All you can do is tear out the whole damn vineyard and replant it with vines on *phylloxera* resistant rootstock. We've had to replant a couple of vineyards and we have another one that looks like it has the dastardly little pricks, but were not certain yet. Christ, Todd, you must have been doing some reading since you were last here."

"No, not really. I just overheard some old dudes during breakfast at The Birchwood Café, and then I did a Google search with my iPhone."

"Oh, okay. Well that explains it then. Everyone around here goes to The Birchwood Café for breakfast and, as far as I know, you can look-up anything with Google. It may not be true, but... What else have you learned, anything?"

"Well, I heard about Nematodes and *phylloxera* and that neither one is good for grapevines."

Tim then said, "Well Todd, you *almost* sound like you know what you're talking about. I must say I'm quite impressed."

"Oh no, don't be. I don't really know squat! I'm just repeating stuff I heard this morning, and...well...okay, guess I did learn a little using Google on my iPhone, but not much."

During this last exchange between Todd and Tim, William Strong came out of the winery offices and, as he approached them, Tim yelled, "So what did you find out, Bill? Did you find someone to cover for us?"

William said with a defeated sigh, "No. No luck at all. And it gets worse; my wife is in the hospital. It seems she fell and couldn't get up. The neighbor lady found her and dialed 9-1-1. She broke her hip. I've got to go."

"Oh hell Bill! Remember last week I said that I had to pick up my niece at the airport this morning. I have to leave like... right now."

As this was taking place, two large, black limousines approached the winery. Tim glanced at his watch and said, "Oh hell! Wouldn't you know it? They're early."

By Tim's watch, it was only 10:35 A.M., and now the panic set in. Two limousines full of wealthy financial bigwigs were coming to the winery for a pre-booked, pre-paid VIP tour and tasting, and there was no one to deal with them...well, except maybe...

"Hey Todd," said Tim. "Do have any plans for awhile?"

"No. I was playing it by ear."

"Well how about this? You take these guys around the winery, answer questions and then pour some wine for them. The tasting room is not set-up yet, but everything you'll need is in there," said Tim.

"Are you serious? I don't know anything about this winery, or making wine, or tasting wine, or pouring wine."

"Well neither do they, so just make stuff up. They won't know the difference. You know about *phylloxera* and Nematodes, talk about that. You know the difference between Cabernet and Chardonnay, so you already probably know more than they do."

The approaching limousines stopped, and a group of twelve well-dressed and distinguished looking gentlemen, gathered and walked over to Tim, Todd, and William.

"Hi. We're the group from New York here for our tour. Man, this place is incredible! All I could think as we came up the driveway is, 'Wow! We are getting a tour of this place? It's amazing!' I, well we, can't wait. We are so excited and happy to be here," said one group member.

Put on the spot, not having a clue as to how things would work out or what was going to happen, not having any sort of plan, and without even thinking William said, "Welcome. I'm William Strong, the owner of Big Goose Cellars." He extended his hand towards the guest who had just spoken. The two men shook hands and William continued as he pointed to Tim, "This here is Tim Tauscher, our winemaker and that right over there is Todd, he will be your tour guide today." As he said this, he looked at Todd and gave him a wink. *I will?* thought Todd. *I don't remember agreeing to this. I have never given a tour of anything, let alone a winery. I have no idea what the hell I'm doing.*

"Unfortunately," continued William, "my wife had a bit of accident this morning and I have to go see her and Tim has some family business that needs attending, so you will have to do with just Todd today. But he's more than capable and I am really sorry."

I am? Capable of what, exactly?

"Oh, no need to be sorry. That's too bad about your wife, is she okay?" said the man who had shaken hands with William.

"I don't really know. That's why I have to leave."

"Well don't let us slow you down."

With that, William said goodbye to Tim, gave Todd a wink and a slap on the shoulder, and left. Tim pulled Todd close to him and whispered, "No worries. You can do this. You can say anything and they'll buy it. Just look and sound confident. Bill and I will owe you big time if you pull this off. Good luck." With that, he also gave Todd a wink and a slap on the shoulder, walked to his car, and drove away.

So, Todd was left standing there with twelve well-dressed guys who just stood there looking at him expectantly or, in words less "boring-literature-class-friendly," they looked like "puppy dogs waiting to be fed." Todd saw their tongues literally hanging out and he didn't know where to begin, so he just asked, "How was the trip out?"

"Great. We didn't think there would be so many grapetrees," said one guy as he pointed to the vineyard. *Grapetrees? Boy, these guys really are clueless.*

"Those are actually called grape*vines* and yes, there are quite a few," said Todd. "Any questions before we get started?"

"So, how many grape*vines* does it take to make a bottle of wine?" asked the guy who had called the vines grapetrees.

Todd had absolutely no idea, so he said, "Well, that depends on a lot of factors, but as a general rule we say that one vine can produce about two cases of wine."

"Per year or over its lifetime?" asked a different guy from New York.

"Over it's lifetime."

"How many grapes does it take to make a bottle of wine?" asked someone else.

Again, Todd had absolutely no idea, so he said, in the most confident voice he could muster, "Well that would depend on the size of the bottle and the size of the grapes. But as a general rule we say about 200–300 grapes per 750-mL[52] bottle, which is the most common size bottle you see," answered Todd. In an attempt to end this line of questioning, Todd asked, "Shall we begin the tour?" *Hopefully they won't ask anymore grape questions.*

Before anyone moved, another member of the group said, "Before we go, I have a question. What are those giant propellers in the vineyard for? Do they keep the vines cool when it gets hot?"

---

52   mL is short for milliliter for all you people stubbornly stuck on the old and silly English measurement system.

"No," said Todd with a chuckle. "They blow the flies and other bugs off the workers when they are picking grapes, and it cools them down a bit; which does keep them happy...or at least happi*er*. But, if it does happen to get really cold at night, they start all the propellers and fly the valley down south where it's warmer, and that keeps the *vines* happy. It is a proven fact that happy vines make happy grapes, and happy grapes make good wine, and good wine makes happy people," said Todd as he winked at the group. *And happy people spend more money.* "Does anyone have another question? No? Okay. Let's go."

He led the group to the crush pad because he figured he would start the tour where the grapes start. Along the way, he told the group about the dangers of Nematodes and the bane,[53] both financially and otherwise, of *phylloxera*.

Upon reaching the crush pad, Todd had everyone gather around the press (he had no idea that it *was* the press, but it was big and looked important) and said, "Every year, we have what is simply called 'The Crush.' Surprisingly enough, that is when the grapes are physically crushed into juice. The crushing is accomplished by putting the grapes that have just been picked, or harvested, into this contraption here," Tim said as he pointed to the big, important-looking machine that was the press and had nothing to do with crushing the grapes. "This machine literally crushes the grapes into juice and that juice is then put into one of the tanks that you see behind you."

"Well, how does it crush them?" asked a member of the group.

"I'm glad you asked," said Todd. *Oh, crap! Think Todd, think.* "Inside the crusher are blades, similar to an airplane propeller. The blades rotate at an extremely high speed, again much like

---

53 A cause of great distress or annoyance. Most people are a bane to me.

an airplane propeller. The grapes hit the 'propeller' blades and as a result, break open. Hitting the fast rotating blades also throws the grapes, at an incredibly fast speed, against the edge of the crusher. This again smashes, or crushes the grapes and all the juice is released. Do this to a ton of grapes, and you end-up with a lot of juice which, with time and care, becomes wine." *Okay, that went pretty good and sounded okay. I think they bought it.*

"Well, how do you turn the juice into wine?" asked another member of the group.

"Now that is an extremely pertinent question, considering this is a winery. The actual process is rather complex and takes years to fully understand, so I'll just give you the dreadfully basic, minimal, process" (which is all Todd understood.) "The yeast eat the sugar in the grapes and then poop-out alcohol. That's all there is to it. You still want to try some wine?"

"Oh, of course. But is there special yeast for making wine? I mean, do some yeast prefer grape sugar and so have better 'poop' than others?" The questioner made quotation marks with his fingers as he said poop.

"Yes, there are a number that work well. It all comes down to the winemaker's preference as to which one to use," answered Todd.

"Which one do you guys use?" asked another member of the group.

"I'm not really sure, because I think they began using a different yeast this year...uh vintage." *No more yeast questions, please! I don't know anything about yeast...except that women can get some sort of infection.* "How about we head into the cellar now and see what goes on in there?"

"What's this doohickey over here?" said someone from the group as he pointed to the actual destemmer/crusher.

Oh, crap! I have no Idea. What did Tim say? 'You can say anything and they'll buy it. Just look and sound confident.' Well okay, we'll see about that.

"That is the grape washer. The grapes often come in from the vineyard all covered with dirt, bugs, and who-knows-what-else, so we put them through the washer to clean them off before we crush them. You don't want grape juice full of dirt, dead bugs, and who-knows-what-else because then you would have wine full of dirt, dead bugs, and who-knows-what-else. I suppose if you didn't wash the grapes, your wine would be higher in protein, but people don't drink wine for its protein content."

The members of the group just chuckled and said, "Oh wow. That's interesting." *Holy cow! They are actually buying that* thought Todd.

"Okay, if you'll follow me we will go into the cellar." Todd motioned the group to follow him and he led them into cellar.

Death Número Cuatro

Chapter 13

Stuck in a Rut...uh...I Mean Hole

As Detective Knight was at the police impound yard examining the tractor that killed Ted, his cell phone rang.

"YYeellow. Oh hi Joanie. Speak to me. Uh-huh. Uh-huh. Okay. What? Sure thing, gotcha." Detective Knight closed his cell phone and informed the police mechanic that he had to leave immediately but he wanted to know precisely what, if anything was done to Ted's tractor while he was away.

Detective Knight then got into his 4Runner and drove like a maniac—or just your typical driver these days—to Big Goose Cellars. Once there, he sought out Maria and asked her what the hell was going on.

"Someone find Jim in new vineyard by Vine Cliff Vineyard. He find Jim in hole," Maria said while trying to hold her composure, which she did not do.

In a hole? thought Detective Knight. *Geez, this ought to be good. Boy, she sure looks good when she is excited and upset.* Detective Knight managed to learn, between Maria's shrieks and prayers, that Jim Jaushki was not an employee of Big Goose Cellars. He worked for the Zeebadul Vineyard Management Company, which was the company now used by Big Goose Cellars when they had extra vineyard work to be done. They often requested to have Jim Jaushki do the work because his father was good buddies with William *and* he spoke English.

"Well uh, who found him and where are they now?" asked David. "I should probably talk with them pretty soon."

"No sé. I know nothing about it," answered Maria.

"Well crap," mumbled David as he turned and left the winery offices, but not before asking Maria where this new vineyard was. He didn't know what the hell to do except go to the scene and collect evidence so that he would at least look competent.

When David had become a detective in Elviño County, he hadn't planned on having to solve many, if any cases; especially not murder cases. Murderers scared him, the cases were too much work, he was terrible at finding clues, and he figured the killer just might kill him.

On the bright side, however, this might turn into something that would become legendary. David thought of both the Zodiac Killer and the whole Charlie Manson "Helter Skelter" rigmarole. David could picture his name up in lights when the movie came out that depicted him as the incredibly smart, tough-minded, no-nonsense detective who solved the case. He could imagine himself in Hollywood, walking down the Red Carpet arm in arm with Maria (or maybe some hot, helium-head,[54] buxom blonde) on his way to receiving his Oscar. David did not know who the hell Oscar was and he didn't really care, but he would have to win one in order to realize his Red Carpet Fantasy. This case could be worth all the work, after all.

Detective Knight got into his 4Runner with dreams of buxom blondes and Oscar dancing in his head and drove towards Vine Cliff Vineyard all the while hoping that this new vineyard with Jim in a hole would be easy to find. It was.

Officer Kendry, Officer McMillan, and another officer that Detective Knight did not recognize had already arrived at the scene. They had taken pictures of the scene and were currently talking with a fourth guy, who appeared to be a vineyard worker.

---

54   Helium is lighter than air, so an "air-head" would be relatively smart compared to a "helium head."

"Howdy boys," said Detective Knight as he walked up to the four men. "What's this about Jim in a hole?" All Detective Knight saw, other than the four guys standing there, were two police cars, dirt, a lot of grape vines, and a backhoe.

"Well," said Officer McMillan, "Jim Jaushki is in a hole and he appears to be dead."

"What hole?" asked David.

"The one under that backhoe right there," said Officer McMillan as he pointed towards it. "What we've learned from Alejandro here," said Officer McMillan as he pointed to the fourth member of the group, "is that Jim was digging a soil sample hole for the new vineyard that is going in, and somehow he got *into* that hole and the backhoe somehow ended-up *on top* of that hole. Jim was supposed to meet Alejandro at the shed when he finished, but he never showed-up. So, Alejandro went looking for him, found the backhoe, and then luckily found Jim."

"What do you mean 'luckily found' and what is a soil sample hole?" asked Detective Knight.

"Well, Alejandro was looking for Jim, but didn't see him and so decided to leave. As he was leaving, he happened to notice a pair of sunglasses lying in the bushes. He walked over, picked-up them up and recognized them as the ones Jim always wore. He was putting the sunglasses back in the backhoe when he dropped them. As he stooped to pick them up, he noticed the top of Jim's noggin under the backhoe. That seemed pretty lucky, to me anyway.

"As far as what a 'soil sample hole is,' the name pretty much says it all: You dig a hole to take samples of the soil. You dig it as deep as the roots go down, and they will go down pretty deep."

Detective Knight turned towards Alejandro and started to ask a question, but Officer McMillan stopped him because Alejandro spoke no English. *Oh yeah, sure he doesn't, and I'd turn down a night of passion with Carmen Electra* thought David.

Officer Oscar Ruiz, the third officer there and the one Detective Knight did not recognize, had been summoned to the scene to act as a translator and he asked David what question he wanted to ask Alejandro. Detective Knight told Officer Ruiz that it could wait because he first wanted to look at the backhoe and at Jim in the hole.

Before he did that, however, Detective Knight returned to his 4Runner and got his evidence-gathering equipment. He then walked up to the backhoe, took a quick look at it, and then looked underneath. He couldn't see much, just the bald spot on the top of Jim's head, which was just a couple of inches below the top of the hole. David then went back to Officer Ruiz and said, "Ask Alejandro how deep the hole is." Officer Ruiz asked Alejandro the question and then told Detective Knight that Alejandro had answered about five or six feet.

Detective Knight surmised[55] that Jim was in a standing position in the hole, not that it made one iota[56] of difference to anything right now, but he did think it was a brilliant observation. He then looked at the backhoe and saw that there was blood all over the driver's seat, steering wheel, and there were puddles of it on the floor.

So, David being David, collected blood samples. He also found a bit of torn flannel cloth. David could not tell if the cloth

---

55 Suppose that something is true without having evidence to confirm it. It's a very "detective" sounding word but detectives probably shouldn't surmise too often.

56 An extremely small amount.

matched anything Jim was wearing because Jim was still in the dark hole. David then told Alejandro, through Officer Ruiz, to move the backhoe so that Jim could be removed.

Once Jim was out of the hole, it was rather obvious how he had been killed: He had a nasty bump on his head and his throat had been slit. He also had numerous scratches, a split lip, a black eye, and a torn flannel shirt. It appeared as though he had been in a nasty fight. That was good news, because quite possibly the fight had left blood from both Jim and whomever he had fought. Therefore, Detective Knight may have a blood sample of the killer and that would help immeasurably in catching the killer. Wouldn't that be nice?

By now, Detective Knight was sick and tired of being out in the vineyard with a dead body and listening to rapidly spoken Spanish. So, he took his blood samples and every other piece of evidence he had collected and drove to the Sheriff's Office Crime Lab to have it analyzed.

Detective Knight didn't analyze any of the blood samples because he had no idea as to how. He turned that job over to a "trained" lab technician; trained in taking orders and following instructions, that is. David *did* look at all the photographs (he did know how to do that) and re-read the *translated* statement from Alejandro.

He then took the piece of torn flannel he had found over to the coroner's office to compare it with what Jim was wearing. It matched perfectly to a ragged hole in Jim's shirt. Based on that evidence, David made the bold conclusion that the piece of flannel was indeed from Jim's shirt, not the killer's. Therefore, it was of no use. Well, no use in solving the crime, but he could use that knowledge to save money by not buying that brand of flannel shirts; they were obviously of inferior quality.

Detective Knight then returned to the Sheriff's Office Crime Lab to see how the blood work was coming. It was completed. It turned out that all the blood samples were of two types: O+ or AB-. The work also showed that whomever had the O+ blood type had syphilis.

David then called the coroner to see if they had any information on the deceased, a.k.a. Jim, other than the fact that he wore cheap flannel shirts. They did. Jim had died of blood loss—surprise, surprise. The blow to his head had just knocked him out thus enabling the killer to slit his throat.

Detective Knight then asked what Jim's blood type was and was told it was O+. David now knew that Jim had at least died a satisfied, if not a happy camper. *Wow! I wonder if he's married and if his wife has syphilis. If she doesn't... Well, I won't say anything.*

Detective Knight also knew, by process of elimination, that Jim's killer had AB- blood type. David was extraordinarilly pleased with that bit of information because he happened to know AB- was a rare blood type and that should prove to be quite helpful in finding whomever had slit Jim's throat. All Detective Knight had to do was find a young male in, or near Fiasco Valley, who had AB- blood type and did not like Jim. That shouldn't be too difficult.

All this bloody information gave David an idea: Maybe, just maybe, the killer had been hurt badly enough, or more likely was dumb enough, to seek medical treatment at the local hospital's Emergency Room. To find out, Detective Knight called the the local hospital to ask some questions.

The female nurse who answered the phone was a rather large, 42 year-old single woman, named Crissy, whose biological clock was just about to stop ticking. She happened

112

to know Detective Knight, thought he was a hunk of burning love, and that he would make a great father for her child, or at least a good sperm donor—via the the age-old tried and true method, of course.

As one might imagine, she gave Detective Knight full cooperation; patient confidentiality was not a concern for her at the moment.

"So tell me, did a relatively young, possibly Hispanic, male come to the Emergency Room recently for treatment of at least one serious cut, or that looked like he had been in a fight?" asked Detective Knight in the most sensual voice he could muster.

"Well let me look." Crissy put down the phone, took a deep breath to calm herself, rummaged around for a moment, then picked-up the phone and said, "Okay yeah, here it is. A Hispanic gentleman did come in earlier today with a couple of lesions, an abrasion or two, a split lip, and a black eye. He was stitched-up and that was it."

"What was his name?" asked David.

"Ah, let's see. It was...ah...here it is, Ignacio Queso."

"Ignacio Queso?" repeated Detective Knight. "Would you spell that for me, please?"

"Sure. First name: I-g-n-a-c-i-o. Last name: Q-u-e-s-o."

"Did he leave an address or phone number?"

"No."

"Did he have an I.D.? Anything?"

"Yeah, I think he did. Just a sec, let me look. Okay, here it is. He showed a California Driver's License, one of those new ones for illegal workers."

Aside: Some arguments I've read as to why illegal immigrants should be allowed to get a driver's license: 1) A driver's license is a way integrate immigrants who must drive to work and shuttle children to school. *Why do they have jobs to earn a living and many US citizens don't? Why are we educating their kids? Why are we concerned with integrating people that are here illegally?* 2) Ensuring that immigrants in the U.S. illegally know how to drive safely does not reward them for violating the immigration laws. *They can drive to work. They can drive to school. They can drive to the doctor or hospital for free healthcare—not a reward?* 3) The roads will be safer. *Huh? They will? How do you figure? If they are here illegally and we give them an official document saying as much, why not arrest them?* One answer David had heard to all of his questions was: If the license is their "official authorization" to be here, then they aren't illegal and so are entitled. That reasoning made David want to spontaneously combust because that would have been easier to understand. Okay, enough of that.

"Oh, wait a minute," said Crissy, "here is some more. He's from Yukankysomiasso. That's spelled Y-U-K-A-N-K-Y-S-O-M-I-A-S-S-O and it's in Tamaulipas, Mexico, but there is no mailing address."

"That's all you've got? You stitched a guy up in the ER and all you've got is his name and the town he is from in Mexico?" asked Detective Knight pessimistically. "Oh yeah, I almost forgot, you also have his Drivers's License for illegals. You can't send him a bill or anything, can you?"

"No, we sure can't."

"Well who pays then? How can he can get away with that? Because I sure as hell couldn't," said David into the phone rather loudly.

"Well, you ever heard of EMTALA?" asked Crissy patiently and sweetly.

"No."

114

"It stands for the Emergency Medical Treatment and Active Labor Act. Congress passed it in...oh...I don't know, the mid-eighties I believe. It says we have to treat anyone who comes into the Emergency Room, no matter what. If they can't pay, or they are an illegal immigrant, it doesn't matter, we have to treat them."

"Ohh...yeah that's right, I think I have heard of that. It was all over the news a few years ago, wasn't it? Well, thanks anyway Crissy. This *is* Crissy right?"

"Yes" *Ooh! He remembered my name.*

Detective Knight hung-up the phone and became so effing pissed-off he almost started shaking. He was, in fact, *extremely* familiar with EMTALA because just recently a fraternity brother of his had died in Brownsville, Texas in a car crash. The crash wasn't what killed him. It was the lack of treatment in the Emergency Room that did him in. Well, that is not exactly true, because he never made it *to* the Emergency Room. He died in the overcrowded hallway that led to the also overcrowded Emergency Room. The ER was hopelessly overcrowded because there had been a soccer match in Matamoros, Mexico that had ended with a huge melee between the exceedingly crapulous[57] fans.

Most, if not all, of the people injured in the melee either snuck, if they were physically able, or were brazenly brought across the border to get free treatment at the Brownsville Surgical Hospital Emergency Room. There were a number serious injuries but the vast majority were just cuts, bruises, sprains, split lips, and black eyes.

---

57   Drunk, hammered, shit-faced, tanked, blotto, effed-up. The fans were all dipsomaniacs, or in words everyone who isn't an author can understand: They had cravings for alcohol.

115

Nonetheless, David's fraternity brother could have had his treatment started, and life saved, while stuck in the hallway but, due to the sheer volume of patients, the hospital was out of many needed supplies.

He also knew, from personal experience, that insured and paying patients were getting totally screwed because their medical bills and insurance rates were significantly higher due to the fact that they were ultimately paying for this "free" healthcare that covered...*everyone*. There was plenty of "cost shifting"[58] going around and David did not like it.

That however, was not what was making David so upset. What was making him almost shake with fury was the fact that it was later determined the other car involved in the crash was being driven at the time by an *illegal* alien from Mexico who had a *legal* California driver's license. Of course, he had no registration or insurance for his car, like all *legal* Americans who drive must have, and he apparently could not read any of the road signs that said "Lane Closed Ahead," "Reduce Speed Ahead," "Use Right Lane Only," "No Passing Zone," and "Merging Traffic."

The driver had been able to exit his vehicle and leave the scene but was nabbed a couple of hours later at a rathskeller[59] in Brownsville. He was taken to the Brownsville jail and thrown in with all the other remarkably well-oiled soccer fans who had been arrested in the melee. Unfortunately, he managed to escape the next day in all of the Spanish/English speaking confusion as the sobered-up soccer fans were being dealt with.

---

58   "Cost shifting" occurs when an insured patient is charged more than an uninsured patient for the same procedure or service. So, in effect, those with insurance pay for those without insurance. Of course, now everyone has health insurance thanks to Obama, so this little issue has been solved. I also have a bridge in Death Valley that is for sale, if anyone wants to buy it...cheap.

59   A beer hall or restaurant in a basement.

After Detective Knight hung up the phone, he left the crime lab, and was still so spitting mad that he made the not-so-rational decision (So that would mean he made an *irrational* decision—David Knight was good at making those.) to go see Maria and ask her if she knew Igancio Queso because he figured that all Mexicans in Birchwood knew each other. It was also a cold day and he wanted to get a look at Maria's mammary glands in what he hoped was a tight sweater; he didn't bother with the fact that she would be in the nice warm office and he was going too see her about a murder investigation. David was "one chopstick short," "smart as bait," and had redefined the term "third grader," when it came to anything having to do with beautiful women.

When Detective Knight reached Big Goose Cellars, he went straight for the winery offices and Maria.

"Howdy Maria. How's it going?" said Detective Knight as he entered the office.

"Oh...bueno," sighed Maria.

Damn! No sweater. "Hey Maria, I've got to ask if you know someone and know anything about them," said Detective Knight, in the most authoritative voice he could muster while looking at Maria's front side.

"Sí. Sí. Who?"

"Do you know someone named Ignacio Queso?"

"Ignacio Queso...Ignacio Queso...hmm," said Maria as she looked down at her desk. "No. No. That no sound..." her voice trailed off and she started to giggle. "Is joke?"

"No. What? Joke? Why? What's so funny?" asked David.

"Well," said Maria trying not to smile, "in Spanish 'queso' mean cheese and we sometime say 'Nacho' for Ignacio. Ignacio

117

Queso is Nacho Cheese. It silly name."

David, who was trying to remain composed now that he realized he had been fooled, sheepishly showed Maria the name of the town he had written down and asked, "Well is this a joke town then? I was told it is in Tamaulpias."

Detective Knight showed her what he had witten down: Y-U-K-A-N-K-Y-S-O-M-I-A-S-S-O. Maria looked at the name and said, "I no hear of it." She kept looking at it while rubbing her chin and thinking, then she began giggling again.

"You're laughing again. That's not good. I've been made a fool again, haven't I?" asked Detective Knight sourly.

"I think so."

"So what is it? There is no town in Tamaulpias named Yukankysomiasso?"

"No. It joke name too."

"Oh hell!" groaned Detective Knight, "You sure?"

"Sí. Sí. I try explain. Yukan is 'you can.' Kys is 'kiss.' Miasso is 'my ass.' He say town name is 'Youcankissmyass' but added "o" to make sound Spanish. That what I think," said Maria.

Upon hearing this, David not only became spitting mad again, but he started turning red and his neck veins were rapidly enlarging. He was being made a fool *again* and he did not like that. There aren't many detectives that like to have the word "fool" associated with their name, especially not twice in one day.

Chapter 14

Cellar Tour by Todd

"We are going into the cellar now," Todd said to the group of financial bigwigs, "it is where the new liquid, full of yeast ordure,[60] comes to be transformed into fine wine." Todd led the group into the cellar where there a was barrel stack and all kinds of hoses, clamps, pumps, and equipment laying around. He had them gather around the barrel stack. *Oh man, I don't know what any of this excreta is. I don't know what the hell goes on in here.* Todd took a deep breath, *remember: Just think and sound confident, they don't know what the hell is going on, either.*

"These are the barrels that the newly made 'wine' is aged in." *I hope anyway.* Todd made quotation marks with his fingers again as he said the word wine. Todd didn't think the liquid that was just pumped from the tank was considered wine yet, but he wasn't sure. He then continued, "The 'wine' is moved from the tank out there," he pointed to the door through which everyone had just come, "into these barrels here, where it sits until it tastes good...as determined by the winemaker."

"How long does that take?" asked a member of the group.

"Well, that depends," answered Todd, "on a number of factors." He held up one finger and said, "One: The actual grapes." He held up another finger, "Two: The temperature of the cellar." Todd had absolutely no idea about this but it sounded good. He then held up a third finger and said, "Three: The weather

---

60   Manure, dung, muck, droppins, feces, stool...you get the picture. Only people who are cultured, intelligent, wealthy, and have been educated at an Ivy League university use this word.

119

during the entire year. Four:" Todd held up a fourth finger, "The number of nematodes that were in the vineyard. And finally five:" He put up the thumb on the hand he was counting with, "Was there any *phylloxera* in the vineyard where the grapes came from?" *Ooh, that sounded impressive. I can fake it. Hmm, that's probably what most women tell themselves at night before the old man gets in bed.*

"What are nematodes and ph...phyl...whatever you said?" came the question from someone in the group.

Oh man, I knew this coming thought Todd, but he said, "They are both tiny little bugs that do dastardly deeds to the vines so they produce bad grapes, and bad grapes make bad wine, or in other words: Wine that tastes like it came from some other winery." Todd waited for the chuckling to die down and said, "Nah, I'm just kidding and, of course, plugging this winery. Seriously though, all wine made in In Elviño County is good, because all the grapes grown in Elviño County are good. The wines made from lower quality grapes, or ones from any other county, will be of much lower quality and therefore will be in much less demand. As a result, the price will not only go through the floor, but the basement as well." Todd was now beginning to talk in a language that this group would understand: Money and how not to lose it.

He continued, "A prophet once said, 'You can make bad wine from good grapes, but you can't make good wine from bad grapes.'" Todd figured that sounded like a good ending to the tour so he said, "Now let's go to the tasting room, start drinking, and you can decide for yourselves how good the wine is."

An enthusiastic cheer came from the group and someone piped up with a good natured, "It's about effing time!

Chapter 15

Back at the Yard

David left Big Goose Cellars in a pissy mood. He had been made a fool and in front of Maria, no less. He hated that. He stewed over the whole episode the entire way back to the Police Impound Yard. By the time he reached the yard, he was so embarrassed and worked-up over the whole "Yukankysomiasso" joke that he was not thinking to clearly. He alighted and saw the same mechanic he had talked with earlier about Ted's tractor.

"Hey dude, what's up?" asked David even though he didn't really care what was "up" with this guy and he didn't want, or expect an answer. "Were you able to learn anything else about that tractor that was driven off the cliff the other day?" David *did* want an answer to that question.

"Yeah, I did and it's rather interesting. Come in the office and I'll fill you in." The two men walked into the small office in the police garage at the impound yard. "Can I offer you some coffee?" asked the mechanic.

"You can offer me some, but I won't take any." David felt like he owed an explanation for not wanting coffee in order to retain his manliness card. So, he said, "I'll just end up having to go pee all day and that will just piss-me-off...pun intended. Now, if you have decaf... " As soon as he said that, Detective Knight chided himself because knew he *had* just lost his manliness card.

"Decaf? What the hell is decaf?" said the mechanic with a hint of disgust as he sat down behind his desk and pointed to the beat-up, metal folding chair in front of his desk, "Have a seat and get comfortable, if you can on that damn thing."

Detective Knight sat down, tried to get comfortable in the chair; didn't, but tried to look as though he had, and asked, "So what did you find out?"

"It seems I have done part of your job for you," answered the mechanic.

"Really? Which part?" asked david in a sarcastic voice.

"Really," answered the mechanic. "I solved a couple of your mysteries."

"You did? Which ones?" David asked skeptically. This guy was starting to get on his nerves.

"You asked me why the tractor steering didn't break sooner than it did, i.e. when it was being driven from the vineyard shop to the vineyard. Well, I can tell you. Like I said, it was rigged so that certain parts of the steering assembly would break, but *only* when a significant amount of force was being applied them. I checked the route from the vineyard shop to the vineyard and there are no turns that would have required that much force.

"However, when the tractor was going through the vineyard it had to be turned around the end of each row. In other words, it had to be turned one hundred and eighty degrees, or sharp enough to go in the opposite direction," said the mechanic in a condescending tone of voice. He believed he was one sharp cookie and therefore, sharper than any cop or detective. "Then, and only then," he continued, "would enough force have been applied to the steering mechanism to break those certain parts." He made quotation marks with his fingers as he said "certain parts." He perservered, "So, when Teddy Boy was driving *to* the vineyard the gentle curves did *not* have the Long Cord Length, the Curve Length, the Middle Ordinate, or the External Distance to produce enough force to overcome the Coefficient of Side Friction. Therefore, he didn't slide, swerve, or lose control." When the mechanic was done speaking, he folded his arms on his chest, shut his eyes, gave an emphatic nod and a satisfied grunt. He was making stuff up. He had no idea what either the "Long Cord Length" or the "External Distance" was, and he certainly had no idea what the "Coefficient of Side Friction" was. He had heard the terms while eavesdropping on some officers talking around the garage one day.

"Well I'll be damned. What happened then? Why did the tractor speed up?" asked David as he ignored the mechanics condescending tone for he knew the mechanic was just trying show he was as smart, if not smarter, than a detective, *and* that he was more learned[61]—even though he wasn't.

"Well", answered the mechanic, "when the original steering assembly broke, a secondary system that had been hastily installed took over. With that secondary system, every time the steering wheel was turned, it caused gas to be fed into the carburetor and therefore the tractor went faster, capiche?"

"Yeah, capiche. Now this 'secondary system', is it some complex thing? Would it be easy to install? I mean, could anyone do it?"

"Yeah. I think even *you* could do it. It wouldn't take long either. What I don't get, however, is why the driver didn't notice anything when he first got on the tractor. I mean, there are a couple of extra levers sticking out and there is even an extra bar going from the steering column to the gas pedal. I mean golly, it's pretty obvious something had been done. I don't see

---

61 That's learn-*ed* (emphasis on the ed) – meaning: having much knowledge acquired by study.

how someone could miss it."

"Well, I didn't notice anything, either. Of course I wasn't looking..." Detective Knights voice trailed off as he realized that any detective worth his weight in plumbum[62] should have noticed a tractor that had extra levers and a bar running from the steering wheel to the gas pedal, even if it *had* just fallen off a cliff. *How could I miss that? I gotta pay better attenion. What was I thinking? I must be thinking with the wrong head.*

"Well the driver didn't notice it either," replied the mechanic. *And he sure as hell should have.*

"Oh gee, that makes me feel better. It's well known that Ted, who was the driver, was prone to 'tipping the bottle' on occassion. That occassion being whenever the sun came up. So, he either didn't notice the extra parts, thought they were supposed to be there, or thought he was just seeing things again."

"Yeah, that could explain it...I suppose" agreed the mechanic.

---

62 Lead – its atomic symbol is Pb. It's very heavy.

Chapter 16

Maria Overborne[63] by Ernesto

David Knight was not exactly a "people person." In fact, he did not like people at all and avoided them whenever possible. But, he disliked even more knowing that a person, or persons, was killing other people, or people's;[64] especially when the those being killed were honest, hard-working folks just trying to to make ends meet. He didn't mind seeing lazy people who didn't work and were just scamming the system get killed. That sounds brutal but that is how he felt and he was always taught, by his multitude of female teachers throughout his young life, that feelings were never wrong. Since it was the hard-working people being killed, David Knight decided he had better get serious about being a detective and catch whoever was doing these murders. *Too bad he's not killing politicians, especially Democrats; I might enjoy that. Hmm, I wonder why I thought it was a "he." Maybe it's the male chauvinist pig in me. I suppose it could be some dyke[65] doing all this, but I doubt it.* David's mind was wandering again, as it was prone to do in stressful situations.

To that end, i.e. catching the murderer, Detective Knight decided, for some inexplicable reason, that he needed to go to Big Goose Cellars and see Maria. Upon reaching Big Goose Cellars, he went straight for the offices and Maria.

"Hey Maria, anything new?" asked David, as a certain

---

63   Overcome by emotional pressure or physical force. Ernesto liked bullying people, especially women.

64   That is not proper English—I don't think—but it sounded cool to me.

65   A masculine lesbian.

appendage of his grew significantly larger, although that is not saying much in his case.

"No. Nada," sighed Maria. Then she looked right at Detective David Knight and began to cry.

Oh man, it can't be anything I said, I just got here. I couldn't have done anything either. Should I give her a shoulder to cry on? Maybe that would lead to getting something off of her later, wouldn't that be nice? I should probably say something...but what?

"What's wrong Maria? Was it something I said?" asked David. That's the best he could come up with.

"No. No. No. It nothing do with you. It Ernesto."

"Ernesto? Who is Ernesto?" asked Detective Knight.

"He my husband, but I find out he been no telling me truth."

"He's been lying to you? About what?"

"He was janitor at school. He go to SEIU meetings and meet Pedro and Tomás. They say government pay you even if you have no job. They say you can drink cerveza and do nothing, even if no have green card or papers. So, Ernesto quit job because they tell him to. They not very nice guys. Ernesto no tell me this. I ask him about job, he say everything fine. He been collecting unemployment checks for months but I not know that. No checks now. I no make enough money for both of us. I not know what to do."

"You and Ernesto are here illegally?" asked a surprised and dismayed David. He thought that William Strong, and his wife, would have much more sense than to hire someone that was here illegally. "Your husband was able to get unemployment checks?" David wasn't sure how that had been accomplished but it didn't surprise him.

David was becoming rather upset. He could not fathom[66] the thinking that allowed immigrants to get assistance from the government of the country they were in *illegally*. The government was spending money it got from its citizens, via taxes, to benefit people who were not citizens and were breaking the law.

David felt like the U.S. taxpayer was being robbed because their tax money was not being used to benefit them or their country, as it should be, but to benefit foreigners who broke our immigration laws. At least that is what it boiled down to in David's mind. Although to be totally honest, the number of U.S. citizens who were actually paying taxes and being "robbed," was getting smaller and smaller.

David Knight's mood was buoyed[67] however, by the memory of a day in some class he took at UC Davis where he had gotten into an intensely tempestuous discussion with a few of the many sorority girls that were enrolled in the class. That fact that there *were* sorority girls enrolled in the class had absolutely nothing to do with why David took the class; he was just trying to gain knowledge and expand his mind, at least that is what he had told his parents.

Anyway, the sorority girls asserted that we (the U.S. citizens) were all illegal immigrants because our ancestors had just come over and settled on land that was not theirs and already occupied. The original occupants (the Native Americans) didn't want us (the newly arrived Europeans) to be here, but we didn't care; we just kept moving onto their lands without permission, or even without so much as bothering to ask nicely. We did it

66 Understand after much thought – there were many things David couldn't fathom, women being the most troublesome.

67 Cause to become cheerful or confident.

just because we wanted to. Therefore, *we* were and still *are*, the illegal immigrants.

David did not agree with them and asked if they knew the definition of illegal. They said, "Sure, it means 'it's against the law.'" David then argued that their line of reasoning was bogus because the Native American tribes didn't have any immigration laws, so there were no laws to break. Therefore, by definition, we couldn't be illegal.

The girls didn't buy his argument, so David then asked them if they could break a law that wasn't a law. They said, "Uhh...well...ahh...no, I guess not. You can't break something that isn't there."

"Exactly. If there is no law to break, how can you break it and do something illegally?"

The classroom became deathly quiet before one of the girls piped up with, "That doesn't matter; it's just words. They were here first! We were unwanted. It was their land. They loved it! We took it. It doesn't matter what some piece of paper said."

"Well actually, it *does* matter," said David, "a great deal in fact. Any civilization that is going to survive must have rules or laws. Just look at the history of any, and all civilizations. The Native Americans had no rules or laws about immigration so they didn't survive."

David remembered that this argument...uh...I mean *discussion*, went on until everyone got sick of yelling at each other and just wanted to go to The Graduate and drink beer; it was Friday afternoon after all. From that day forward, David was called "D&D." It had nothing to do with Dungeons & Dragons, the game popular with high school dorky geeks...or geeky dorks; it stood for "David Diatribe."[68] He was proud of that nickname.

David shook his head to get the thoughts of the past out of his head, so that he could fill it with thoughts of the present, namely Maria crying because her husband Ernesto, the illegal immigrant, was unable to collect any *more* unemployment checks from the government.

"That not worst part," said Maria.

Oh no! Here we go. "What's the worst part?" David asked as he stood on tenterhooks.[69]

"I...I...kill...Frank," said Maria between sniffles, sobs, and nose drippings.

"Excuse me?" said David in a shocked voice. He couldn't believe he had heard correctly.

Maria let out another huge sob and said, "I kill Frank. Ernesto told me do it."

Okay. Okay. Frank...Frank...now is he the dude who fell in the tank and died from CO_2 poisoning? What did they call it? Oh yeah: Hypercapnia. Yeah, that was Frank. I guess he didn't just fall in. Well, that sure makes my job a hell of a lot easier. Case closed. Mystery solved. Job well done. But how the hell could this sweet little empanada[70] kill Frank?

David wasn't sure what to say or do now because nothing like this had ever happened to him before. He knew he should probably arrest her but he didn't know if he could actually do it, although the thought of putting her in handcuffs wasn't

---

68   Diatribe – a forceful and bitter verbal attack against someone or something.

69   In a state of suspense or agitation because of uncertainty about a future event.

70   A Mexican dessert; a spicy or sweet turnover—Detective Knight certainly wanted to turn Maria over and over and over and...

without some appeal and was certainly erotic. David just stood there with his mouth open, gaping at Maria because he was completely flabbergasted and more than a wee bit aroused.

"Why?" was all David could think to say, and before he got an answer, he blurted out, "How?" David did not see how a cute, petite, sweet Mexican girl could possibly kill Frank, or anyone else for that matter. David's mind was trying, and failing miserably to get some sort of grip on the situation.

"Ernesto say to me, 'If love me, kill Frank. If you no love me, I leave.' I want be married and have babies so I kill Frank. He told me how. It easy."

Holy cow! What a dick! What kind of a guy asks his wife to kill someone for him? A total wuss, that's who. Maybe Frank aroused him and he didn't want to realize he was gay, so he offed him... well, he got Maria to off him.

"So how did you kill him and get him in the tank?" asked David.

Maria, who had had regained some composure and stopped most of her crying and sniffling said very matter-of-factly, "It no hard. I just push head down and hold in tank for minute when he get sample before pump-over. Then I pick-up feet and push down. He go in. I come back to office, clean-up, and then I see you."

David was thinking as best he could, which wasn't very good at the moment, of the day Frank Finnegan had wound up dead in a tank full of wine. Then he thought of Mark Madson, Ted Templeton, and Jim Jaushki.

"Did Ernesto also ask you to kill Mark, Ted, or Jim?" David asked this question rather eagerly because if Ernesto, for whatever reason, wanted these guys dead and he had gotten his wife to do the dirty work, David's job was essentially over and he could go grab a beer and maybe talk to that new, blonde waitress.

"No. No. Frank only one. Ernesto not know Mark or Ted or Jim," said Maria as she wiped her nose with her sleeve.

Well crap! No beer for me now, still more work to do. This was all fine and dandy, but Detective Knight wanted to know why Ernesto wanted Frank dead, because maybe it would lead him to whomever had offed Mark and/or Ted and/or Jim.

David proceeded to ask Maria why Ernesto wanted Frank killed. She had no clue...at least that is what she said.

"Well Maria. I hate to do this, but I've got to arrest you and unfortunately, you're going to the pokey."

"Pokey? What is pokey?" asked Maria.

"Jail."

Maria then lost all the composure she had regained, let out a terrible shriek, and fell to her knees wailing in Spanish, "Oh my God, what have I done? Have mercy on me." Apparently, Maria hadn't thought her crime all the way through.

Detective Knight let out a big sigh, rolled his eyes, walked behind Maria, grabbed her by the armpits, and proceeded to stand her up and handcuff her. He noticed this caused a bit of arousal in him and wondered if, by some chance, Maria felt the same thing. *Too bad we're not doing this in my free time at my place. She looks hot in handcuffs and I think I might even have a pair of manacles[71] at home.*

As Detective Knight was escorting Maria to his 4Runner in order to take her to the local police station, Tim Tauscher and William Strong came out of the wine cellar, saw them, and hurried over. Their eyes got awfully big and round when they

---

71 A metal band, chain, or shackle for fastening someone's hands or ankles.

noticed Maria was in handcuffs and that she had been crying.

"What the hell is going on here?" demanded William.

"I'm arresting Maria for murder," said David matter-of-factly as he stopped walking and halted Maria.

"Maria? Murder? What the hell have you been sniffin' David?" asked William. "You're must be confused or there must be some mistake."

"No mistake and she just confessed."

"Well I don't buy it."

"Neither do I," said Tim.

"It true," Maria managed to say between sniffles. "I kill Frank."

With that, William and Tim looked at each other with their mouths agape. They were completely flummoxed and so just stood there with baffled expressions on their faces.

Detective Knight hesitated a moment and then continued to lead Maria into his 4Runner so that he could take her to the Sheriff's Department jail cell. As they drove away, William and Tim just remained frozen where they stood and watched them leave. They could not speak; they could not move.

Eventually, William said, "Well that's a fine kettle of fish. Now I have to find another receptionist slash secretary. That'll be a pain in the ass and take forever."

"Christ Bill, that's all you have to say?" said Tim. "I mean we just found out Frank was murdered...by Maria no less," he paused for long moment and waited for Bill to say something else, but Bill kept his mouth shut. Tim then said, "Shouldn't we notify...uh...well...someone...anyone?"

"Who? Why? He'll still be dead. Notifying someone won't change that. Besides, that's the cop's job, isn't it? Let them do it," said Bill. It was clear he was rather annoyed.

"Yeah, I know. But...I just feel like we should tell *someone*. Isn't she married? What about her husband?"

"Yeah okay, you're right," conceded Bill after a long pause. "She was married. I think her husband's name is Ernesto or something like that, and I suppose *he* would want to know. He will probably wonder where she is when his dinner is not ready and he will definitely wonder where she is at bedtime," answered Bill with a slight titter.[72] "But I have no idea how to reach him or where he would be. I do know he is a janitor with that service...uh...what's the name? Oh, hell...it's...um...oh yeah: Jumpin' Janitors, yeah that's it. My wife likes them. Call them and see if they know where he is."

Tim quickly returned to his office to make that call, but first he called Maria's house on the off chance he was there; no answer. So, he called Jumpin' Janitors, and yes, Ernesto *did* work for them, until he quit a few weeks ago.

"He quit? Did he say *why* he was quitting?" asked Tim.

"No, but he had been mumbling for days something about how all Americans were rich, fat, lazy, stupid, greedy, and total racists. He also mumbled something about how the stupid gringo government will pay you for not working. Um...can I ask why you need this information? Is there some sort of problem?"

"Yeah, you could say there's a problem, a pretty serious one, actually. Our secretary, Maria just confessed to killing one of our cellar worker's at Ernesto's bidding. This is Tim Tauscher, by the way, over at Big Goose Cellars."

After an awkwardly long silence, the person at Jumpin' Janitors said, "You mean Ernesto's wife, Maria?"

"That's the one."

---

72   A short, half-suppressed laugh.

"Aww come on, is this a joke? Maria didn't kill anyone. I've met her. She's the sweetest thing. She wouldn't kill a cockroach, let alone a person."

"Well, she will and she did," answered Tim. "You must have her and Ernesto's home address and phone number. I need to get those from you."

"Well, yes I do have them, but I can't give them to you, unless of course, you are a cop or something."

"Well, I am certainly something, but it's not a cop. Why can't you tell *me*?"

"Because it's illegal. I can't go around divulging employee's personal information to just anyone. I'll need some sort of proof that you are who you say you are."

"But he is not your employee, you canned him. Now, he is just your average Joe...or medio José in this case. There isn't any law against you divulging information for the 'average Joe' is there?"

"No, but you are *also* just an 'average Joe' and I'm not about to give out personal information to anyone just willy-nilly."

Tim knew he was barking up the wrong tree, plus he just thought of someone who would probably know all the needed information, so he said, "Okay, I suppose you're right. Thanks anyway." He hung-up the phone and poured himself a glass of wine so that he could drink and think better.

Chapter 17

Prom Dress (Don't worry, there weren't any stains.)

The trip to the Sheriff's Office was deathly quiet and Detective David Knight absolutely abhorred deathly quiet trips because they made him nervous and uncomfortable, especially when the other person in the car was a supremely sexy, female murderer. So, to remedy the situation, David said, "I spy with my little eye something that starts with the letter 'C.'"

Maria, who was dumbstruck by what Detective Knight just said, stared straight ahead with her mouth agape and didn't move. Finally, she asked in Spanish, "What did you say? I don't understand." Her tone of voice was surprised and confused. David repeated himself and so did Maria. *Gee Maria, that's convenient. You no longer speaka da Ingles? Amazing!*

"Oh, sorry," David said. "You probably aren't familiar with that game. It's a game kids play in the car to pass the time."

Maria was, in fact, extremely familiar with the game. She and the other illegal immigrants had played it (in Spanish, of course) on the trip from the abandoned warehouse in Los Angeles to Fiasco Valley. However, now she could speak English pretty well and had understood everything Detective Knight had said. She also knew from American TV and movies that no one in trouble ever spoke to the fuzz without their lawyer being present. Sprinting continuously through her mind were the phrases "Talk to my lawyer" and "Let me see what my lawyer says," or something to that effect. Maria figured that all Americans must have a lawyer. She didn't know why, but apparently, they did;

it must be in the Constitution or something she guessed. She decided not to say *anything* until she had a lawyer.

David didn't say a word for the remainder of the trip. He was absorbed in thoughts about his lack of instincts regarding *anything* involving hot women. He thought about the time in college when he was taking a required general psychology class and during a lengthy class discussion, David was found to be afflicted with Caligynephobia, or fear of *beautiful* women. So, he supposed he did have at least one instinct about women (the hot ones at least) and that was to be afraid.

Fortunately, well David thought it was unfortunately, it turned out that he didn't have Gynophobia, or fear of women in general. David felt comfortable with, and could easily talk to, ugly chics all day long. That is why David always ended-up talking, and just *talking*, with the bus driver[73] at parties.

He was not just surprised; he was shocked when Maria confessed to the murder. He hadn't even considered the possibility that Maria could have done such a thing. All David thought about when it came to Maria was her perfectly sized and shaped mammary glands and her nice derrière.

Her confession also blindsided him because he hadn't even thought a woman would commit a crime that was so male-dominated. Although, he shouldn't have been too surprised because the equal rights movement was changing gender roles and women were acting more and more like men every day.

David's thoughts of his having no instincts about females led to thoughts of what other instincts he was missing. *Do I actually have any investigative instincts? How would I, or anyone, or*

---

73 "bus driver" – the least attractive of a group of girls. The "bus driver" stays sober because she has no chance of "hooking-up" with a guy and "disappearing." Therefore, she can drive all the other girls wherever they need to go.

*anything, know if they were missing an instinct? An instinct is
an instinct. You know it or you don't. You can't learn an instinct.
Otherwise, it wouldn't be an instinct...would it?*

He had always heard detectives say things like, "There was
something about him," or "It just didn't feel right," or "I knew I
was missing something." He never had those thoughts and so
didn't think he had any instincts.

Fortunately, for Detective Knight, Elviño County did not
require him to have *any* investigative instincts, talents, or
anything like that, because there was almost no crime in the
county. It was unheard of, until now, to have a crime that
actually needed to be solved. The only crime, if you could call it
that, which had required any sort of detective work on David's
part, was the one in which Melissa Garett, Scott's daughter, had
been stood-up by her Senior Prom date. It wouldn't have been
considered a crime except for the fact that Mr. & Mrs. Garett
had spent a small fortune on Melissa's Prom dress and their
daughter had been left high n' dry.

David had been hired by Scott to find out why the guy, who
was the back-up quarterback on the varsity football team,
hadn't shown up. Scott Garett was out $950 and his daughter
was extremely upset. Someone was going to pay...for the dress
at least.

David only "solved" the case because he happened to be
down by the swimming hole in the local creek one day and
he overheard some kid bragging about how he had "ditched
the Garett bitch because she wasn't gonna put out." All
Detective Knight had to do was snap a photo of the kid with
his iPhone and then show it to the school principal, who then
told Detective Knight the kids name and confirmed that he
was the back-up quarterback on the varsity football team. It

wasn't much of a crime and it hadn't required much work, or even thought to solve.

To make the arrest, all David had to do was find out where the kid would be at a certain time and arrest him. That turned-out to be an even easier task because all he did to find out the needed information was walk behind a group of high school kids, which included the suspect, and listen to where they were all going to be after school.

Detective Knight then showed up where the evil "prom-date-ditcher" was and arrested him on fraud[74] and larceny[75] charges. The entire process took about four hours. It would have taken less time except Detective Knight ran out of gas on his way to make the arrest and as a result had to go to plan B, which was just to walk the three blocks to where the kids were.

---

74 Wrongful deception (he said he would take Melissa to the prom) intended to result in financial or personal gain (he thought he was going to get laid.)

75 Theft of personal property – Melissa's Dad was out $950 for the unused Prom dress, so David charged the kid for stealing money.

Chapter 18

Observing Maria

Once they arrived at the Sheriff's Office, Detective Knight led Maria, still in handcuffs, to the interrogation room. It was just a small room with a neon overhead light, a table with two nice comfy chairs and one metal un-comfy chair around it, and a one-way mirror on the wall opposite the un-comfy chair. Detective Knight sat Maria down in the chair facing the one-way mirror (that would be the un-comfy chair) and took off her handcuffs. He then left and went into the observation room located behind the one-way mirror.

Detective Knight and Officer Oscar Ruiz sat down in the observation room and just observed Maria for about ten minutes. David let his mind wander and so he rather enjoyed himself. He had a big smile on his face the entire time and thought, "I'm going to re-name this the 'fantasy room.'"

David did not think Officer Ruiz was enjoying himself nearly as much as he was because when Officer Ruiz was *not* observing Maria, which was most of the time, he had his nose in his notebook and was furiously writing with his pen. David tried to sneak a peak at what Ruiz was writing because he couldn't imagine what the officer was spending so much time writing about instead of observing Maria. *I wonder if he is gay.* He was never able to get a look, though, because Officer Ruiz was leaning over his notebook and kept a wary eye for Detective Knight looking his way.

Maria, who had her head on the table in the interrogation room, also knew, from all the TV she had watched and all the movies she had seen that Detective Knight, and at least one other guy, was behind that "big mirror thing" and they could see her but she couldn't see them. She figured they were letting her get nervous and scared so she would talk, or maybe they were just watching her and pleasuring themselves. Whatever they were doing, she wasn't scared; nothing scared Maria... except mice.

I bet they're just watching me. Maybe I'll have some fun and give them something good to look at. Things can't get any worse and maybe they'll like it and go easy on me. So, Maria stood up, approached the one-way mirror, adjusted her hair, and then took off her shirt (she was not wearing a brassiere[76]) and wiggled around for a few minutes. She then put her shirt back on, returned to her chair, and sat down with her arms folded on the table and her head resting on top of them. She stayed like that until Detective Knight entered the room clapping with Officer Ruiz right on his heels.

"That was quite a show," said Detective Knight with a libidinous[77] grin. "I might even pay to see that sometime."

"Pay to see what, David?" asked Officer Ruiz innocently.

David looked at Officer Ruiz and said, "Aww, don't worry about it. It was nothing."

Maria understood this exchange between Detective Knight and the police officer, was insulted, and started to cry...again, which was what Detective Knight wanted to happen.

David sat down in one of the nice comfy chairs and put his

76　That's a bra – but I am too much of a cultured, sophisticated, educated, and refined author to simply use a three-letter word, when a much longer word will do the job.

77　Showing excessive sexual drive; lustful, horny. Detective David Knight was an extremely libidinous creature.

folder in front of him on the table while Officer Ruiz excused himself because he was receiving a call on his walkie-talkie.

"Now Maria," said Detective Knight sternly, "that crying won't do you any good here. So knock it off."

David adjusted his position in his chair in order to get more comfortable and then said, "Now tell me, why did you do that? That thing with no shirt, I mean."

"I think you like it," said Maria. "You go nice on me."

"Well, you thought right...and wrong. I sure *did* like it, but I won't 'go nice on you.'" David made quotation marks in the air with his fingers as he said "go nice on you." *It sure would be nice to get on you, though.*

David then continued, "It may have made things worse for you actually, because that could be considered bribery, and bribery is illegal. However, that's only if someone knows about it, and I will make sure no one knows about it if you cooperate with me. Do you understand?" Maria nodded.

"Okay. Good. Now...why did you do it? Kill Frank I mean."

"Ernesto told me to."

"Ernesto *told* you to?"

"Sí."

"That's why you murdered another human being? Because Ernesto *told* you to?"

"Sí," answered Maria dejectedly.

"So, if Ernesto told you to jump off a bridge, you would do it?"

Maria just looked at a David with a befuddled expression and said, "¿Qué? What bridge? I no jump off bridge. Ernesto no ask me jump off bridge."

"I know. I'm just saying...oh never mind. So why *did* Ernesto tell you to kill Frank?"

"I no sure. He just tell me to."

"Well, did he at least threaten you?" asked Detective Knight. He knew he had no female instincts and not a lot of investigative instincts, but he figured there must be more to this story than met the eye. Of course, he could be totally wrong, and Maria could just be a psychotic virago.[78]

"Threaten? What word mean?" asked Maria.

"It means he would do something bad to you if you didn't do what he asked."

"Sí. Sí. He say he leave me if I don't kill Frank, and if he leave me I bring shame to family. If he leave me, I no have husband. If he leave me, I no have babies and I need go back to Mexico. I no want go back to Mexico. I die instead," said Maria between sobs and sniffles.

Besides all these reasons for not wanting Ernesto to leave, Maria suffered from *Isolophobia*, which is fear of solitude or being alone. Maria had a severe case and had been prescribed Zoloft, Klonopin, Paxil, and aspirin, which she took daily. If Ernesto was late coming home on a particular day, she would take a couple of extra pills.

Detective Knight took a deep sigh and said, "Okay, okay. Now calm down and let me see if I got this straight: You killed Frank because your loving husband *told* you to. He said if you didn't kill Frank, he would leave you. You felt if he left you, that would bring shame to your family *and* you wouldn't have any babies." *Hmm. I would have gladly made babies with you...and you wouldn't have had to kill anyone.*

David continued, "You also thought you would have to go

---

78 A domineering, violent, or bad-tempered woman. I am willing to bet that Hillary Clinton is a virago.

back to Mexico if Ernesto left you, but you would rather die than go back to Mexico. Does that about cover it?"

Maria just stared straight ahead and immediately clammed up. She had also learned from watching television that someone talking to the police better not say too much or else they would end up in the hoosegow (she didn't use that word) for a long time. She had learned from watching the news that Hispanic Immigrants were looked upon by the news media (she called them "news people") as being stupid, helpless and not being able to function in American Society without *their* help. So, she figured if she only spoke Spanish, the "news people," who always followed stories of helpless immigrants being abused by the police, would portray her as the victim and somehow come to her aid, because the police were all bigoted, ignorant, white males, and "news people" hate bigoted, ignorant, white males.

"What? I don't understand what you are saying," Maria said in Spanish.

David just stood there staring at Maria and contemplating. It was truly amazing: Maria had instantly and miraculously lost her ability to speak and understand English. David Knight knew a little Spanish, but not enough to get any more answers or information from her. Officer Ruiz was not available to act as a translator, as he had been called away to a traffic accident involving people who spoke nothing *but* Spanish.

The only thing David got from his time with Maria was a headache and the knowledge that he didn't need Viagra, Zenerex, Cialis, Staxyn, or Levitra,[79] as of yet. As Detective Knight was leaving the interrogation room in order to relax

---

79   These are all Erectile Dysfunction medications, a.k.a. "woody pills." There are a lot more, but these are the only ones David knew about and he could "get it up" without any of these so...

and take a leak, he thought maybe he should call Stanford University or UC Berkeley and let someone know about Maria's amazing and miraculous language...uh...development. But he decided against it because he knew Maria, like many of the immigrants in Elviño County, was probably just faking her language "development," and he didn't want to make himself look silly and/or stupid in front of some pompous college professor.

Chapter 19

Maria and Officer Oscar Ruiz

When Officer Ruiz returned from the car crash that had involved only Spanish-speaking drivers, Detective Knight filled him in on Maria's newly acquired language deficits and asked Officer Ruiz to be so kind as to conduct the interrogation in Spanish. Officer Ruiz was more than happy to do so, as he, like David Knight, was a young, single, virile male Homo sapiens, who also had no need for "woody pills" and Maria was just what his libido ordered.

He began to question Maria and ogle her chest as soon as Detective Knight left the room. In spite of this, Maria felt more comfortable with Officer Ruiz for the obvious reasons: He was a Mexican, he spoke Spanish fluently, and he was tall, dark, and handsome; just what Maria liked. After the two exchanged pleasantries, Officer Ruiz got down to business.

He sat down at the table and looked through David Knight's notes. He saw that Maria had killed Frank. He also saw that David, probably on a whim, had asked Maria what she knew about the murder of Mark Madson. Maria denied having anything to do with his murder or even having any knowledge of it.

Officer Ruiz kept going through the motions of looking through Detective Knight's notes, but he was actually studying Maria. She looked fidgety and glanced around furtively[80] the entire time.

---

80 Attempting to avoid notice or attention, typically because of guilt or a belief that discovery would lead to trouble; secretive. Only authors are allowed to use this word.

Unlike Detective Knight, Officer Ruiz *could* tell when someone was not being forthright with him. Since she had just admitted to Killing Frank, Officer Ruiz figured maybe Maria was not being candid about her role in Mark Madson's death. He also got the sense that she wanted to get something off of her very perky and lovely chest.

Whilst he pretended to look through Detective Knights notes, Officer Ruiz watched her squirm, which for some inexplicable reason, prompted Officer Ruiz to fantasize about what he could do with, and to her.

After an interminable couple of minutes, in Maria's mind anyway, Officer Ruiz looked up from the notes, shook his head to clear it, and told Maria that he was going to ask her some questions and that it would be mucho better if she told the truth.

After an hour or so of questioning, Officer Ruiz decided he had gotten all he was going to get from Maria and left. Besides, he knew that interrogations in the interrogation room were always video taped and he could always watch the tape of her perky chest heaving up and down later in the evening.

Upon leaving, Officer Ruiz immediately sought out Detective Knight in order to fill him in on what he had gleaned from Maria and that a few of the nagging questions had been answered. The big piece of information learned was that Maria didn't actually kill Mark Madson, but was certainly a confederate[81] because she had set-up the ropes that were used to collapse the barrel stack.

One evening after everyone had left, Maria had gone into the cellar with a sledgehammer and some coils of rope. She used the sledgehammer to knock some key chocks out of

---

81 A person one works with, especially in something secret or illegal; an accomplice.

the middle of the barrel stack, not enough for the stack to fall over, just enough to de-stabilize it. She had then looped a rope around the two front chocks underneath the first barrel on the bottom layer of the stack and another rope around the bilge of that same barrel. She had also fastened a carabiner to the end of each rope and fed them out to the large doors of the barrel room.

Maria, each day for weeks prior to this set-up, had saved the grease that came from her daily lunchtime burrito that she purchased at El Vato Guapo Market. She rubbed this grease, or oil, on the barrel chocks and some of the barrels themselves with the hope that it would cause them to slide and fall easier. After that task had been completed, she unlocked the large doors and left.

The next day Pedro and Tomás, who were the SEIU members that hated all Americans and had befriended Ernesto, opened the doors and used the carabiners to attach the ropes to Pedro's truck which, by the way, Maria had described to Detective Knight as a "Silver, Chevy, big number, and a some letters thing." (It was a Chevy Silverado 3500HD.) They then drove away pulling the ropes, thus removing the chocks and the bottom barrel at the end of the first row causing the whole stack of barrels to come crashing down and their contents to be spilled.

After Officer Ruiz had finished filling him in on all he had gleaned from Maria, Detective Knight wondered why Mark, who had been on the stack topping the barrels, did not notice two guys opening large doors, grabbing ropes, and attaching them to a truck. He asked Officer Ruiz about that and was told what Maria had said when he had asked her a similar question.

"Maria said Mark wasn't exactly genius material and he was not very observant either. She told me a story that proved as much, in her mind anyway. He was recently divorced and what led to the divorce was that his wife, ex-wife now, was sleeping with another guy who, unbeknownst to Mark, had been living in their garage for eight months. Maria said he probably never would have noticed him, or figured out what was going on, except one day he came home early from work and walked in on his wife and this guy 'follando en el piso de la cocina,' which translates to 'fucking on the kitchen floor.'

"As to why Mark didn't hear any of the commotion going on around him, it could be because he was *always* listening to his iPod...*really* loud. Maria doesn't think he even took it off when he went home. I think between the loud music, being recently divorced, and not having too much upstairs, it's not to surprising Mark was unaware of what was going on around him."

"How the hell does Maria know all this?" asked David skeptically.

"I don't know. Except that this *is* a small town and well...you know how small towns are."

"Okay, well yeah, I suppose," said David resignedly.

"So anyway, I guess we need to locate these Pedro and Tomás characters. You say they go to all the SEIU meetings?"

"Well yeah, according to Maria anyway."

"Okay, it should be easy enough to find out when the next meeting is and we can check it out...or we *could* just check the list of members in local SEIU chapter and find a Pedro and Tomás that live around here."

Officer Ruiz said, in a voice dripping with sarcasm, "Oh sure, that'll narrow it down to a hundred or so."

"Maria didn't give you any last names?"

"No."

"Did you ask?"

"No."

"Well, of course not. That would make too much sense."

Detective Knight went to speak with Joanie and asked her if she would be so lovely as to find out when and where the next SEIU meeting was for Elviño County, or the for local chapter, or for this part of the state, or however they broke it down. David never bothered himself with those kind tedious details, especially when it came to unions. Joanie said she would let him know as soon as she knew something.

This whole traumatic ordeal of learning that sweet, innocent Maria was actually a cold-blooded killer, her subsequent arrest and questioning, and her conveniently forgetting how to understand and speak English had tuckered Detective Knight out. He needed a good meal and some sleep. Unfortunately, these two needs caused David some unneeded apprehension. The reason being: David lived just outside of Birchwood in a small one-bedroom apartment just off of a main, larger house. Living in the main house were five (sometimes 6) foreign interns that worked the harvest for the winery that owned the house and apartment in which David lived.

The interns were all young males, full of vim and vigor, living in a foreign country, and making money. They drank enough beer and liquor and smoked enough pot to put Detective David Knight's college fraternity brothers to shame. As a result, they revealed where many stereotypes involving young, energetic males, alcohol, and pot originate. Suffice it to say, David did not get much sleep when the main house was full of interns, which it was at the moment. Just when David had given-up on catching a nap, his phone rang and Joanie informed him of when and where the next SEIU meeting was to be held.

Chapter 20

SEIU Meeting

It was a miracle. The next SEIU meeting was to be held that very night in Calinaspa, which was a larger town about 20–30 minutes from Birchwood. David contacted Officer Ruiz and asked if he could accompany him to the meeting to act as a translator because David rightly guessed there would be an inordinate number of members that only spoke Spanish. Officer Ruiz readily agreed because it was possible that he would see someone from his hometown in Mexico and they *might* know how his mother was doing. Officer Ruiz hadn't spoken to his mother since the great Burrito Boondoggle of '99 and was growing a wee bit concerned, as he had heard rumors that she was not doing well health wise.

Detective Knight and Officer Ruiz arrived at the meeting one hour after it had started and walked to the front of the hall in an overly confident and forceful manner; flashing their ID's the whole way. Once they reached the front of the meeting hall, they commandeered the microphone and asked for Pedro and Tomás to come forward.

They quickly realized, well as quickly as David Knight and Officer Ruiz could realize anything, that they should have had some sort of plan prior to coming here, as about 15 or 20 hombres stood up and started to come forward. Detective Knight and Officer Ruiz exchanged glances with sheepish grins and shook their heads because they realized that this had been an asinine[82] attempt, at best, to apprehend the Pedro and Tomás who were responsible for getting poor ol' Mark mashed.

They held-up their hands to stop all of the vatos who were coming towards them and told them to retake their seats, with the hope that they would figure out a way to get the right Pedro and Tomás to come forward. However, concocting a plan was beyond their capability, so Detective Knight just turned to the microphone and said, "I need the Pedro and Tomás who know Ernesto Martinez and have done stuff for Maria, his hot little woman."

Instantly, two Mexican guys from the back row practically sprinted up to Detective Knight and Officer Ruiz. Apparently, they understood English pretty well...for now, and the thought of letting everyone know that they knew Maria was worth whatever the consequences may be.

David was shocked that his spur of the moment "plan" actually worked and so he hadn't thought of what to do next. Fortunately, Officer Ruiz figured something like this may happen, so he formulated a plan and quickly whispered it to David.

When Pedro and Tomás reached the microphone Officer Ruiz told them, in Spanish, that they needed to go outside with Detective Knight because Maria had a surprise for them. They bought it hook, line, and sinker—remember, they aren't too bright.

Once outside, Pedro and Tomás asked incessantly, "¿Dónde está Maria?" (Where is Maria?) They had one thing on their mind, and it wasn't union dues. Detective Knight didn't answer. Instead he removed, from a bag he was carrying, two of the chocks that had been pulled from the barrel stack that had fallen on and killed Mark Madson.

---

82 Extremely stupid or foolish. I've seen and read that word a lot but I never knew what it meant.

"Either of you boys recognize these?" asked Detective Knight as he shoved the chocks right in the faces of Pedro and Tomás. He was rewarded with two big, wide grins, two looks of disdain, and two innocent voices saying in Spanish and in unison, "What? We don't understand. We are just here for the meeting."

David berated himself for giving these two wankers[83] the satisfaction of him making *them* look like some sort of innocent "victims" because *he* didn't speak *their* language. Fortunately, Officer Ruiz wandered out of the meeting hall and joined Detective Knight in his confrontation of Pedro and Tomás. When Detective Knight saw Officer Ruiz, he gave an exasperated sigh, surrendered the barrel chocks to him, and loudly said, "You handle these two wankers, I'm sick of their crap."

Officer Ruiz took the chocks from Detective Knight, walked-up to Pedro and Tomás, and began to question them in rapidly spoken Spanish. Within minutes the two vatos were on the ground sobbing and in handcuffs.

"Well I'll be damned," said Detective Knight in wonderment as he rejoined Officer Ruiz. "What in the hell did you say to them?"

"I just told them what a 'wanker' was and that I would tell everyone I knew in Mexico that they were wankers. I also explained that this information would undoubtedly reach their devilishly[84] Catholic mothers and they would know that their boys had committed a mortal sin.

---

83   1. An offensive term for someone who masturbates (jacks-off) a lot—they both did quite a bit of that as they were overweight, had bad teeth, bad complexions, didn't smell too good, and often watched porno movies.
2. An offensive term for somebody considered unpleasant, self-indulgent, pretentious, or arrogant – you wouldn't think they'd be arrogant if they were jacking-off all the time, now would you?

84   A submodifier meaning "very" or "extremely" – a submodifier is an adverb used in front of an adjective or another adverb to modify its meaning. It's like using "really" or "very." They are one of the many reasons I hated English classes.

"Then I told them, in case they didn't already know, that committing a mortal sin makes it impossible for them to follow Christ and therefore they would go to hell, and *that* would make their mothers very, *very* sad. No Mexican child, especially a male one, wants to make his mother sad, so they just fell to their knees blubbering and repeating over and over again, 'Estoy tan triste Mamá,' which translates to, 'I am so sorry Mom.'"

Detective Knight grinned widely, slapped Officer Ruiz on the back and said, "Oscar, you bust me up. I'll buy you a beer, that's means cerveza in Spanish, after we're done with these two hombres."

"Oh sì, sì señor. I didn't know that word was. Muchas gracias," said Oscar Ruiz sarcastically.

Detective Knight and Officer Ruiz then proceeded to collect the still blubbering Pedro and Tomás, put them in Officer Ruiz's squad car, and take them to the Sheriff's Office. Once there, they were shown into the same observation room Maria had been in and Detective Knight and Officer Ruiz again went behind the one-way mirror. They just observed the two vatos for about ten minutes. During this observation, Officer Ruiz did not bury his nose or furiously write in his notebook. Detective Knight noticed this and wondered what, if anything, it meant.

The two vatos just sat there and looked extremely bored. After a few minutes, they both stood-up and began to inspect every 2.54 cm's (that's an inch) of the room. Detective Knight and Officer Ruiz couldn't figure what they were doing, so they entered the interrogation room and asked, "What the hell are you guys doing?"

"Nothing. We are just bored," replied both vatos in Spanish and unison. They obviously had understood the question and could, in all probability, answer in English, but chose not to.

154

"Well damnit, sit your asses down!" ordered Detective Knight in his loudest, most authoritative voice he could muster. His outburst in English did not have its hoped for affect, because Pedro and Tomás just stared at Detective Knight with smirks on their faces and said in unison, "¿Qué?"

This ability to speak and understand English only when it was convenient for them, really pissed Detective Knight off, so he screamed, "I know you can understand me, so just sit down and shut the hell up!"

David then took a deep breath, tried to relax, failed, and so went to Officer Ruiz and told him he had better do the interrogation in Spanish because these two wankers were playing the "we only speak English when we want to" card and he couldn't deal with that right now. Detective Knight could not deal with a lot of things, so here he would have someone else deal with the problem.

Officer Ruiz agreed with Detective Knight's assessment of the situation and so agreed to handle the interrogation, even though he'd never done one before. Unless, of course, you count the time he tried to figure out which hooker took his wallet during his last short sojourn[85] to Tijuana.

Officer Ruiz sidled up to the table in the interrogation room at which Pedro and Tomás were now seated and threw down a brown folder...hard. The folder was empty; it was just a prop. But Officer Ruiz thought throwing it down hard on the table would make him look like an experienced, no-nonsense, tough, and formidable interrogator, none of which he was.

He hoped to rattle these two vacuous[86] vatos into telling the

---

85 A period of time when you stay in a place as a traveler or guest. I always thought it meant a leisurely trip, but noooo...I was wrong.

86 Having or showing a lack of thought or intelligence; mindless.

truth. So, he stared hard at the two wankers for a full minute and then started speaking to them exclusively in Spanish. After a few minutes of fruitless questioning and intimidation, Officer Ruiz decided to try a different tactic. He planned to get them comfortable and talking by asking them questions that had nothing to do with the case. Once they were talking, he would hit them hard.

Officer Ruiz knew how Mexican males revered their mothers, so he asked, exclusively in English mind you, how their mothers were doing. They both answered, "Fine." That made Officer Ruiz teary-eyed and he told them how he had not spoken with his Mother for a year or two and he didn't even know where she was. He took a shot in the dark and asked if either of them knew a Juanita Garcia-Sanchez-Feliz-Gonzalez-Smith-Thompson-McFarly-Romero-Ruiz, who was his mother and still living somewhere in Mexico.

Tomás answered, "No." His intermittent understanding of English was in the "On" mode.

Pedro, whose understanding of English was also in the "On" mode said, "Yeah, I know her, she's a good, dumb, lay."

Officer Oscar Ruiz reared back and clocked him. Pedro hit the floor and did not move. After a few minutes, he began to stir and eventually got up moaning and rubbing his head. He stared at Officer Ruiz, who was sitting in a chair at the table, and managed to say, in English, "What did you do that for? I was just kidding. You gotta relax."

"Well don't kid about that. I won't stand for it. That's mi madre you're talking about. If there *is* a next time, you won't get up." Officer Ruiz didn't think this interrogation could have started out better even if it had been planned. His intimidation factor went up tenfold.

"Okay boys," said Officer Ruiz as he continued with his interrogation speaking exclusively in English, "let's get one thing straight. I won't stand for any smart-ass answers and if either of you boys ever say anything like that again about mi madre well..." Officer Ruiz would just let their imaginations finish his last sentence. Even though these two guys had imaginations that were, shall we say...limited they were still cowed[87] into cooperating with Officer Ruiz. Pedro, while rubbing his jaw ruefully[88] said, "Okay buddy, no problem. Whatever you say."

"Good. Now let's get down to business."

Officer Ruiz began to question the two guys who had killed Mark Madson. First, he asked them if they knew Maria. They each grinned widely and said they did. Then, Officer Ruiz asked them if they knew how prisoners were executed. After they exchanged galances with growing trepidation,[89] Tomás and Pedro turned to Officer Ruiz and said they had heard some stories. They *were* smart enough to realize that the question was hinting at some rather unpleasant business, and they instantly became conspicuously nervous. Officer Ruiz recognized this and decided to go for the kill...pun (I guess it is anyway) intended, as you will see.

He immediately went on to describe, in great detail what happens to someone when they are executed by electric chair. He continued with detailed descriptions of what happens to someone when they are executed via lethal injection or the gas chamber. As Officer Ruiz was describing these various modes of execution, Pedro and Tomás broke down in tears, again.

---

87 Cause someone to submit to one's wishes by intimidation.

88 Expressing sorrow or regret, especially when in a slightly humorous way.

89 A feeling of fear or agitation about something that may happen. They had heard about "The Chair" and certainly did not want that.

"Quit your crying!" yelled Officer Ruiz. "You're embarrassing me as a Latino. Only wimpy, fairy, crackers cry. Be a real man!"

Pedro and Tomás did not want to look any more wimpy than they already did and they certainly did not want to have anything in common with a cracker, so they quit crying and pulled themselves together. Once they had gathered themselves, which took a while, Officer Ruiz continued with the interrogation.

During the subsequent interrogation, Pedro and Tomás admitted to driving the truck that pulled the barrel chocks out of the stack. They said that Ernesto had persuaded them, during their SEIU meetings, to do the "job" by offering them some num-nums[90] from Maria. All they had to do was drive their truck away after attaching the ropes to it that Maria would have already set-up for them.

Thinking of getting num-nums from Maria was more than enough to convince both of these not-to-bright vatos to go along with anything Ernesto said. It's a good thing for Ernesto that Maria was unaware of what he had offered them, or he would have become the first Latin Eunuch.[91]

When Pedro and Tomás were done with their confessions, Officer Ruiz left the interrogation room, tracked down Detective Knight, and informed him of what he had learned.

"Well that's just great," said Detective Knight. "But it's only *one* mystery solved. We still don't know *why* Ernesto wanted Mark dead and we certainly don't know *why* Maria helped kill him." Detective Knight always wanted to know why things happened. That's one reason he was so unpopular with his fellow students in his high school classes. He asked a lot of questions.

---

90 Can mean anthing sexual.
91 A man who has had his sexual organs removed.

"Yeah that will take some more work," agreed Officer Ruiz, "but–"

"But what?" interrupted Detective Knight in a confrontational tone, "I hate 'buts.' Nothing good ever comes of 'buts'...unless it's Jennifer Lopez's nice butt. Now, explain to me Oscar, if you would be so kind, how you got these two jack-off's to start crying?"

"Oh, it was easy. I just described to them what it was like to be executed and they started balling like little bambinos."

Detective Knight got a wide grin on his face, slapped Officer Ruiz on the back and said, "Well Oscar, for that, I'll buy you a cerveza. How 'bout we get it now?"

"Sounds good to me. I'd love to," answered Officer Ruiz sarcastically in Spanish.

Chapter 21

Maria's Motive

Officer Ruiz and Detective Knight went to the local cantina, got beers, sat at a table, and started talking about their harrowing day, in their minds anyway, at the "office."

"I'm still having a hard time believing Maria had much to do with this. I mean holy cow...have you seen the chest on that babe?" asked David as he took a swig of his beer.

"Oh sí señor. Her chest is very beautiful. But I don't see how that has anything–"

"Yeah I know," David cut him off. "I'm just saying." *What the hell am I saying? That she is very proud of her "twins" and kills anybody who isn't?* "Well actually, I don't really know what I'm saying. I was just thinking that maybe Maria..." Detective Knights voice trailed off and then he said, "When I was sick and stuck in bed for a week last year, I saw this episode of Maury Povich, about women who were so distraught over the fact that nobody stared at or complimented them on the size and shape of their breasts that they felt worthless, ugly, and un-loveable and they believed their husbands were going to leave them. They were so emotionally distraught over it that they nearly became homicidal. I couldn't believe it. I was like, 'Yeah whatever. Gimmee a break.' I mean I could *maybe* understand if they became *suicidal*, but *homicidal*? No, it made no sense to me. But then what the hell do I know about women?"

"About as much as me. Well, American women anyway," lamented Officer Ruiz.

"So anyway, I was thinking maybe Maria should have been

on with Maury that day."

Officer Ruiz shot beer across the table, though his nose, and guffawed at the thought of Maria on "The Maury Povich Show." He then managed to say, "Well, you know she didn't actually *kill* the dude. She just set it up. What's the word you gringo's use? *Accomplice?* Yeah that's it. She was just an accomplice. But then again, she *did* kill poor 'ol Frank Finnegan. Maybe he didn't like her boobs either."

Detective Knight, who had graduated to Tequila shots said, "Yeah, I still can't quite understand that one." He took another shot of tequila and as he slammed the empty glass down on the table said, "She certainly was no accomplice that time. She did the deed...the psycho wench."

Officer Ruiz took another swig of beer and ruminated about Maria as he stared at the ceiling with a smile on his face. He then looked thoughtfully at Detective Knight, and said, "Hold on, back-up. Let me see if I can follow your tiny little gringo mind on this one. You think Maria was so distraught over the fact that no one stared at, or complimented her on the shape and size of her boobies, that she became homicidal and had Mark killed? I don't know about that one Dave. Have you been smokin' something you shouldn't be? I mean come on, you're stretching...big time. Besides, Mexican women aren't that stuck on their appearance, nothing like American women anyway; they aren't that shallow.

"Here's what I think the problem is, or was," continued Officer Ruiz. "Ernesto wasn't getting any action from his lovely wife because she was so upset about Mark not noticing or staring at her...uh chest. She felt that she must be ugly, or gross, or undesirable, or...something. She was that regardful of her appearance.

"Since she was so upset, she was never 'in the mood,' and as a result, certain parts of Ernesto were turning blue.[92] Anyway, Ernesto figured Mark was the reason he wasn't getting any lovin' so, get rid of Mark and...problem solved." Before continuing, he took another swig of beer, contemplated the bar ceiling again for a long moment, and then said, "But then again I could be wrong. I mean she *has* been living in California for a while so... who knows? You may be right."

"Oh hell!" Detective Knight suddenly shouted. "We left good ol' Tommy and Petey Boy in the interrogation room. We gotta get back there and deal with them. Come on! Let's go!"

Detective Knight and Officer Ruiz jumped, well stumbled, up from their table and managed to get into Officer Ruiz's squad car. As soon as Officer Ruiz got the key into the ignition, which took a couple of tries, he started the engine along with the sirens and lights. He was hoping to clear a wide path for himself and Detective Knight all the way to the police station, since he was in no shape to drive on a narrow path. In fact, he was in no shape to drive on any path because he was totally hammered.

Once they were on the road with sirens blaring, Officer Ruiz instructed Detective Knight to reach into the glove box and grab the bottle of Binaca[93] he kept in there. Detective Knight began to laugh as he did so.

"Why the hell do you have Binaca in your car? You don't

---

92 He was getting "blue balls," which is the slang term for the condition of temporary fluid congestion in the testicles accompanied by intense testicular pain caused by prolonged and unsatisfied sexual arousal in the human male.

93 It's a mouth spray specially formulated to freshen your breath instantly. It is widely used by high school kids to mask the smell of alcohol on their breath. I was never part of the "in" crowd so I didn't go to where Binaca would be needed at some point later in the evening.

want Mommy to know you've been drinking?" said Detective Knight while laughing nearly hysterically.

"Um...Halitosis.[94] I have Halitosis," answered Officer Ruiz matter-of-factly while socking Detective Knight hard on the shoulder. Officer Ruiz and Detective Knight then each shot three squirts of Binaca into their mouth hoping to negate any smell of alcohol on their breath.

They managed to return to the police station (without wiping out a family of six) and ran straight, well as straight as their condition allowed, for the interrogation room. Fortunately, for them, there were no lieutenants, commissioners, detectives, other police personnel, or anyone else for that matter, anywhere near the police station that would care about their lack of sobriety.

There was, however, a large M.A.D.D. (Mothers Against Drunk Drivers) poster on the wall inside the station and Detective Knight stopped right below the poster, pointed to it, managed to stop laughing, and said, "Hey Oscar, we should make a D.A.M.M. poster."

Officer Ruiz stopped next to David and said, "Oh yeah? What does D.A.M.M. stand for?"

"Drunks Against Mad Mothers," answered David. Both men started laughing uncontrollably and each blew snot out of his nose.

While still laughing, they made their way to the interrogation room. Once there, they found something both impressive and disgusting.

The two vatos, Tomás and Pedro, who had been stuck in there for hours, had drawn all over the walls. They had used

94 Disgusting breath that people always seem to have when they lean in really close and tell a secret.

the black and red Sharpie pens that Detective Knight used for labeling evidence bags and had accidentally left on the interrogation room table. Their drawings were extremely pornographic, vulgar, and offensive, but incredibly good.

Detective Knight stood in awe for a moment when he first entered the room. He had taken art classes in high school and college, but never got past drawing much more than stick figures. Here, these two hoodlums, with just two pens, had transformed the walls of the Sheriff's Office Interrogation Room into the vato version if the Sistine Chapel. That was the impressive part. The disgusting part was the drawings themselves. They were not only of the lewd, crude, pornograhic variety, but also the grahic, gang-violence variety.

"Ahh. Goddamn!" yelled Officer Oscar Ruiz exasperatedly as the room's fetor[95] hit him with full force after he and Detective Knight barged through the door. "What the hell you boys been doing in here?" It was a rhetorical question.

Tomás and Pedro didn't say anything because they were ignoring Officer Ruiz. They were too busy watching Detective Knight, who was standing in awe of the wall art and paying absolutely no attention to them, and they craved attention.

As Officer Ruiz continued walking towards the two vatos, he stepped right in the middle of a pee puddle on the floor that had been left by one, or both, of these vatos. Now, he was really pissed-off. The worst part of stepping in the puddle, however was that it reminded Officer Ruiz that he had to pee rather urgently, as his recently consumed tequila shots and beers were begging to get out.

---

95 A strong, foul smell. Remember, these two guys didn't shower much...if at all and they had "relieved" themselves on the floor. In their defense, they had no choice.

Detective Knight, who had finished gawking at the "artwork," was now trying to cuff the dastardly duo of not too bright vatos. They resisted of course, and Detective Knight needed Officer Ruiz to assist him. Since Officer Ruiz and Detective Knight weren't exactly sober, and drunken guys often can't control their testosterone tendencies; a fight ensued. During the fight, Officer Ruiz and Detective Knight managed to wet their pants, thus adding more pee to the interrogation room floor and worsening the room's miasma.[96] However, they were professionals and did manage to eventually get Tomás and Pedro cuffed and into the only jail cell at the Sheriff's Office. As soon as they were put in the cell, Tomás and Pedro said a heartfelt "Thank you" to their God for already in the cell was... wait for it...wait for it...Maria...and she was looking *really* good to them; of course, a 299 lb. German female wrestler who hadn't shaved or showered for a few days would have looked good to these two wankers right about then.

To their chagrin however, Officer Ruiz led Maria out of the cell because he and Detective Knight wanted to look at...I mean interrogate her some more. They led her to the Interrogation Room to begin their questioning.

"Okay Maria," began Detective Knight, "we know you pushed Frank into the tank and killed him because your loving husband told you to. The question now is—"

"Will you go on a date with me?" interrupted Officer Ruiz in Spanish and the most sensuous voice he could muster.

"Oscar, what the hell are you doing?" yelled Detective Knight. He did understand a little Spanish and he had heard Oscar ask this question time and time again, but never with anyone in

---

96   A highly unpleasant or unhealthy smell or vapor.

police custody.

"Uh, is this a trick question?" replied Officer Ruiz.

"No. But we're *supposed* to be getting information on a murder, for Christ's sake. Not trying to scare-up some action for later on."

"Well, *exxcuuuuse* me. Unlike you apparently, some of us have normal needs and desires. Plus, she is a captive audience and can't really ignore me."

Detective Knight had to give Oscar kudos for that line of thinking, even though it was totally inappropriate and reeked of desperation.

Officer Ruiz looked at Maria and said in his sexiest voice, "Maria, I'll make it worth your while if you say 'yes.'"

Fortunately, for everyone involved, Maria ignored him, although she was curious about what he meant by "worth your while." Maybe she could get off scot-free if she worked it right.

"That's right, just ignore him," Detective Knight said to Maria. "As I was saying, the question now is, why did Ernesto want Frank dead?"

Maria just sat there for a long moment, looked at Detective Knight and Officer Ruiz, let out a deep sigh, and seemed to come to a decision. She said, in English mind you, "Well, Ernesto hate all Americans. He think they all fat, stupid, lazy, and rich. Frank no go to SEIU meetings, because he no member. Ernesto love SEIU. They help him get much money from job. Ernesto know Frank was a Republican so he hate Mexicans. Ernesto say his cousin from Oaxaca need job badly. Ernesto think he can get Frank's job if Frank no there and I tell William to hire him. Then Ernesto give old job to cousin. Then we all be in America, rich, happy, and I could have many baby."

So there it was. Ernesto wanted Frank dead, so that his job would be available and he would get it. He would then give his old job to his cousin from Mexico. Then, they would all be together in America, they would all get rich, be happy, and Maria could have a lot babies. *Un-effing believable* thought David.

Chapter 22

Alice in Wonderland

Todd was fed-up with working in the Tasting Room of Big Goose Cellars. He could no longer deal with the tourists; their ignorance was staggering and the vast majority were rich, snooty, arrogant, stupid, and just plain lame. All the women were middle-aged, wore big silly hats, high heels, loads too much make-up, and no one could smell the wine because they were wearing so much Chanel No. 5 that the olfactory[97] senses were overwhelmed.

All the men had blinding white skin, big boilers,[98] and wore collared shirts tucked into their shorts that needed to be held-up with belts or suspenders; both in some cases. They wore nice, clean Teva sandals with knee-high socks. Todd thought they must be either utterly injudicious[99] or just plain dumb. More often than not, the men were partially sunburnt and reminded him of marshmallows on sticks that needed to be roasted just a tad more.

One day, soon after a lady tourist asked him if Mexicans were the only workers short enough to climb the grape trees and pick the grapes, Todd went in to William Strong's office and asked if he could work in the cellar instead of the tasting room.

"Why?" asked William.

"Because...uh..." Todd couldn't tell William that the tourists

---

97   Of or relating to the sense of smell.

98   A large protruding gut on a man.

99   Not having or showing good judgment: not sensible. I'm very injudicious nowadays.

were incredibly annoying and he wanted to kill at least half of them, "...I want to see how the wine is actually made because I get asked a lot of questions about it and I have no idea, so I just make stuff up."

William was glad to hear Todd was so solicitous[100] about giving the tourists accurate answers and said, "Well let me talk with Tim and see what he says. I am sure we can work something out."

"That'd be Great," answered Todd.

But that would potentially solve only one of Todd's problems. One of his other problems that wouldn't be solved by this was that Birchwood was extremely dull and boring, especially at night. The town was dead by 8:00 P.M. on weekdays and 9:30 P.M. on weekends, *if* you were lucky. There was one bar, or cantina, in town but it catered to the young Spanish-speaking migrant workers and they did not look kindly upon gringos on their "turf." Plus, they only played rap music in the cantina, which Todd absolutely abhorred, and it was played so effing loud that he figured he would go deaf in the time it took him to have one beer. *I suppose that could be one reason why so many of the young Hispanic migrant workers don't speak English: They can't hear it to learn it.* Since he was used to living in San Francisco, which has a good and varied nightlife, Todd was going stir crazy.

But that wasn't the worst problem. The worst problem was that Todd's father refused to send him any more money; and he needed money because tasting room workers make diddleysquat. His father thought he was an idiot for leaving his job, and throwing away his future as a financial advisor, in

---

100 Characterized by or showing interest or concern – archaic: eager or anxious to do something. Both definitions work here.

order to work in the tasting room of a winery. To make matters worse, his father had recently been diagnosed with Alice in Wonderland Syndrome[101] (AIWS), which is a disorienting neurological condition that affects human perception. People with AIWS may experience micropsia, where things look smaller than they really are, or macropsia, where things look larger. It is a temporary condition often associated with migraines, brain tumors, or the use of psychoactive drugs.

Todd knew that his father did not, had not, or ever would take psychoactive drugs. Therefore, the cause must be migraines or a brain tumor. Todd thought it was most likely migraines because all during his childhood when he had upset his father or done something to disappoint him, he would complain of a terrible headache.

Now that Todd was a "man," and not only upsetting his father but disappointing him as well, the migraines became so bad that they were causing his AIWS; at least Todd hoped that was the reason and not a brain tumor. His father needed every cent of his retirement money for treatment, and to be sending money to what he considered his dim-witted son was just too much for him to bear.

---

101   There really is such a thing; I'm not making this up.

Chapter 23

Todd Is bottled up

Capsule

Label

Bottle of Big Goose Cellars Cab

The next day William gave Todd the good news that Tim said he would love to have him work in the cellar. Todd was so excited that he ran into the cellar to find Tim so he could get started right away. He found Tim among a bunch of equipment he had never seen before and so became even more excited.

"Tim. Tim. What should I do? Huh? Where should I go? Where should I start? Where? Where? Huh? Huh? Tell me. Tell me."

Tim half expected to see Todd stick his tongue out and start panting, and then start barking and running around in circles trying catch his own tail. Tim hadn't seen a person this excited since he had given his nephew a remote control Tyrannosaurus Rex for Christmas a couple of years ago.

"Don't do anything and don't go anywhere. I need you right

here, right now, to help because we're bottling today," answered Tim as he waved to all the equipment Todd had never seen before. Todd almost passed-out he was so excited. *Would he be putting the wonderous essence into the bottles for sale?* This thought was almost orgasmic for him.

Right at that moment, a beat-up old car drove up, parked, and out piled four people that did not look like they belonged anywhere near a winery—you, beloved reader, can use your own imagination to conjure up what these four knuckleheads looked like.

Todd saw them and immediately thought they must be lost and were asking for directions...or something else. To his shock, Tim said as he walked towards them, "There are your fellow bottlers now. Come and say 'Hello.'"

My fellow bottler's? thought Todd. *You gotta be kiddin' me. That's with whom I am working? Oh Christ almighty!* Todd was not used to working with, or even associating with people whom he considered lower class; people who most likely had not even graduated from high school, people that were wearing clothes that probably hadn't been washed recently, people that smoked and managed to insert the "F" word at least once into every sentence, no matter what the subject.

"Okay you guys," said Tim to the bottling crew, "this here is Todd, he'll be working with you for awhile. Be nice to him," Tim added as he winked and smiled at Todd. All that Todd heard from the group in the way of a greeting were some grunts, groans, and moans.

"Now Todd," continued Tim as he pointed to an overweight woman missing a couple teeth and smoking a cigarette, "this here is Sandra. She is the foreman of this crew and she'll be telling you what to do, and more importantly what *not* to do."

Todd immediately knew he was not in San Francisco anymore with pseudo-intellectual feminists, because Sandra did not point out she could not possibly be the fore*man*; she was the fore*woman*. Todd's opinion of her changed instantly and drastically and he found it very refreshing. He figured he would get along with her nicely, as long as he didn't look at her too closely.

Sandra, however, wasn't to impressed with Todd and gave him one of the tougher jobs on the bottling line. Not that any of them were tough, but this was one of the "less easy" jobs. All he had to do was stand next to the conveyor belt, just past the machine that put corks in the newly-filled bottles, and place a capsule on top of each bottle before it went through the "spinner," or the machine that tightened the capsule on the bottle so that the finished bottle would look like it should at the time of purchase. Todd was shown how to do this—which took about three point five seconds—and was then given a pair of earplugs to put in his ears (That's a great place for *ear*plugs.) The bottling line was exceptionally noisy, what with the all the machines on the bottling line, the empty bottles being moved along the line, and the full bottles being inserted by hand into empty cases. That's not to mention the radio being played loud enough to be heard over the whole operation.

Todd hadn't even gotten both earplugs in when the bottles started coming by, with corks but no capsules. Todd began placing the capsules on the tops of the bottles as they came through the corker on their way to spinner. At first, Todd did not place the capsules down completely on the bottles. Therefore, when they went through the spinner, the tops of the capsules were smashed down on the tops of the freshly filled and corked bottles. This looked extremely bad. Those bottles then had to be removed from the line, their smashed capsules removed, new capsules put on, and then run through the spinner again.

After about four bottles and five seconds, Todd figured out to *gently* push the capsules down completely on the tops of the bottles before they got to the spinner. Todd thought his job on the bottling was fun and interesting for about thirty-one seconds and then it became mind-numbingly dull. The bottles just kept coming...and coming...and coming.

The line was terribly noisy so there was no conversation among the workers, not that it mattered much because Todd had nothing to say to any of them and they had nothing to say to him.

After about an hour, which seemed like about two days, Sandra stopped the line and said it was time to rotate. So, Todd who had never worked on a bottling line before, started to rotate in circles because he thought it must be some new-fangled technique the Japanese used to help keep the workers healthy, or happy, or more engaged with their task...or something along those lines. The other workers had no idea what the hell this new guy was doing and so just stood there sniggering at him. Finally, Sandra said after she took a long drag on her fifth cigarette, "No, no, you fucking idiot. Not in fucking circles, rotate *jobs*. So, now you will be checking the fucking labels."

"Oh, okay," said Todd with a sheepish grin.

He moved a few feet to his right, replaced his earplugs, and the bottling started-up again. Now all Todd did was stand in one spot and make sure the freshly-applied labels on the newly-filled bottles were straight, right-side-up, and not torn or damaged in any way. After about two minutes and twenty-nine seconds of this, Todd was praying for upside-down labels,

174

or torn labels, or something, *anything* to break the monotony. After another hour, which seemed like a month, Sandra said it was time for a fifteen-minute break. Todd had never taken a "bottling break" before, so he didn't know what to do for fifteen minutes. He just followed the other bottlers out of the cellar because he figured he would just "hang with them."

However, to Todd's dismay, all the other bottlers went straight to their cars, lit-up cigarettes, and started puffing away. A couple of the workers also started to get themselves "lit-up."[102] Todd couldn't believe what he was seeing; he was shocked actually. Yes, the bottling line was dull and boring, but getting drunk while on the job? *No wonder they were bottlers. At least they will die young...hopefully.* They must already be mentally dead because they are total numbskulls. After what seemed like about twenty-four seconds, Sandra yelled for them to come back because the fifteen minutes were up.

The bottling torture went on for the entire week. By the time the final drop of wine was safely in a 750 mL bottle, Todd was so effing sick of bottles, corks, capsules, labels, and anything else that had to do with wine, he swore he'd only drink beer from then on.

Despite all this, when Tim came by to check on the bottling line clean-up and ask Todd if he wanted to continue working in the cellar for the harvest, Todd gave a wholehearted "Yes." *Harvest? Really? Me? Finally, I can learn to make wine and see the magic happen.* Instantly, his newly formed aversion to wine and affinity for beer was gone.

Tim was utterly relieved because it was hard to find harvest workers nowadays, even though the unemployment rate in the

---

102   Drunk in this case, but it could be stoned, or anything really, as long as it has been caused by some substance.

state was a whopping 9.3%. One reason the rate was so high, according to William Strong anyway, was that a lot of wineries in the valley, and elsewhere, were hiring foreign interns rather than U.S. citizens to work the harvest. These seasonal jobs, which are still *jobs*, occasionally led to permanent ones. Case in point: The Winemaker for Donaldson Winery had simply started out as a harvest intern from South Africa but now held the permanent winemaker position, which was a position highly sought after by qualified Americans. Tim knew that William simply did not like this new trend. "Why give foreigners preference over Americans?" he would ask. "Do they know something we don't?"

It turns out the trend was partly due to the fact that American harvest employees were just too greedy. They wouldn't do *anything* extra without demanding extra pay and they were continually badgering the winemaker and owner for free wine. It was an aggravating, not to mention an expensive, nuisance the winemaker and the winery owner did not need during the hugely hectic harvest. It was also partly due to the fact that the American workers were just to damn lazy which, of course, is like saying all Mexicans are stupid and lazy. Nothing could be further from the truth, at least when it comes to the Mexicans. Tim told Todd that harvest would begin in a week or so, but that he should show up Monday morning, as there was a lot of prep work to be done.

"Okay, I'll be in Monday at ten," said Todd as he wearily turned to go to his car.

"Ten?" chuckled Tim. "No, you better make it eight."

Eight? Aww Crap! Thought Todd. *That's too friggin' early.* "Okay. Eight it is."

Chapter 24

Ted Was Never "On the Wagon"[103]

Detective Knight was feeling quite good about his professional life. The murder cases, which he never wanted anything to do with, were practically solving themselves. No, they *were* solving themselves. The killers were all confessing and it was making him look good in the eyes of the higher-ups, whoever the hell they were.

Now, however, he still had to deal with dead Ted's tractor because no one had confessed to killing him. David went back to the impound yard to talk with the mechanic and find out if he had discovered anything new about the tractor or possibly had forgotten to mention something that could shed even a small amount of light on Ted's death. He didn't have any new information, but he did admit to forgetting to mention an interesting fact: The tractor, in addition to being jury-rigged, had been littered with alcohol containers (everything from smashed light beer cans to broken Jägermeister bottles) many of which had been used in the jury-rigging of the tractor.

"Apparently," said the mechanic, "your tractor driver, Ted was it?"

"Yeah, Ted."

"Well, he apparently had a drinking problem. He was probably driving this tractor drunk and was definitely *a drunk*, assuming all these bottles were his, that is."

Detective Knight's mind started wandering again. *A drunk?*

---

103 "On the wagon" refers to an alcoholic *not* drinking. I can never remember if it's good for an alcoholic to be "on the wagon" or "off the wagon."

177

I wonder what his definition of a drunk is? Detective Knight's definition of drunk was: "A glorious way of existing in a world full of idiots." Detective Knight hoped that had also been Ted's definition and he had just been trying to gloriously exist. Detective Knight didn't think the police mechanic would have such an enlightened definition of the word. He figured the mechanics definition was the plain-old, unimaginative, dictionary definition: "Person who habitually drinks to excess." It was. How boring, unoriginal, and unimaginative.

"I still haven't quite figured out exactly how the jury-rigging worked," continued the mechanic, "but again, I do know it would have taken a lot of force to make it do what it did."

This sounded vaguely familiar to David and he figured he should check his notes, but that would require too much work, so he figured he would just play dumb and let the mechanic repeat himself. The mechanic noticed David standing there with a baffled expression on his face and said, "You would have to make a really sharp turn in order for the steering to break down and fail like it did." *I thought I already told you this. Shouldn't you have written this down in a notebook or something? Aren't you the fancy-shmancy detective?*

Finally, David asked, "So, you're saying the steering would not have broken down driving on the nearly straight, dirt roads used to get to the vineyard?"

"Yep, that's what I'm saying...*again*," answered the mechanic.

"But the one-hundred-and-eighty-degree turns required to get around the end of each row in the vineyard would have done the trick?"

"Yep, I'm saying that again too," agreed the mechanic. *There, I solved this mystery for you...again. That means I'm doing your job...again, detective.*

178

A number of questions had been answered, except for the two that Detective Knight was being paid to answer: Who the hell killed poor ol' Ted, and why?

Instantly, Detective Knight thought of Maria. *That damn señorita. I bet she probably either killed him, knows who did, or arranged for him to be killed. Maybe poor ol' Ted made a pass at her, which is understandable because, man her chest is so...*and there was the problem: David couldn't think about her without thinking of her party bags. *Is that really a problem? It must be, because I can't seem to focus on the case, all I see are her glorious glands.*

Maria's show in the interrogation room was now paying her nice, big, firm...uh...dividends because it had become so firmly ensconced in the mind of Detective Knight that it was blocking all of his crime solving thoughts and abilities; not that there were too many to begin with. There was however, one thought that wasn't blocked: *If she had also taken her pants off, would I have even arrested her? Hell no! I probably would have helped her escape and then not let her out of my sight.*

Upon thinking this, David berated himself for having such a ridiculous, inappropriate, and unprofessional thought. It was not surprising however, because he was single and living in Birchwood and therefore, had a myriad of pent-up, testosterone-induced feelings and found himself thinking with the wrong head occasionally...well more than occasionally, actually.

David tried and tried to shake the thought of Maria with no pants on out of his head. It took awhile, but he finally succeeded. Unfortunately, he had no thoughts to replace it with and so had no idea what his next step should be in figuring out who killed Ted, and why.

He was a detective in a county full of hoity-toity towns in which not much needed detecting. He had done some research prior to his accepting the job and he couldn't believe the job even existed, much less was being offered to him. His "research" had consisted of going on-line and browsing through past and present newspapers from each town in the county. Each town's paper featured a "Police Log" of the local Police Department's activies and Detective Knight read all of them. They were more amusing than anything else. Especially the entries he read in *The Birchwood Gazette*. One entry in particular convinced David to take the job. That entry was:

"Monday, May 17

0016   A resident on McCinkle Avenue reports a rooster crowing loudly and frequently. Fifteen minutes later, the resident reported the rooster had stopped."

Is 0016 hours 12:16 at night? Don't roosters crow at dawn? Maybe it was a retarded rooster. Did the resident kill the rooster? Maybe the rooster agreed to be quiet...but at what cost?

After reading the police logs, David figured all this job would entail would be to figure out where some raucous party was, whose dog had been barking all night, or whose uncommonly rude rooster couldn't tell time. None of the entries reported anything that could prove detrimental to his health, so he had become the detective for Elviño County.

Now however, instead of dealing with a rude rooster, a barking dog, or a raucous party, he was going back to the Sheriff's Office jail cell to talk with two murderers in the hope of getting some sort of clue as to what he should do now. Once he got to the Sheriff's Office, he discovered that Pedro and Tomás had been moved to the Elviño County Jail, so now he *did* know what he was going to do: He was going to hit on Maria, as she was all alone in the cell.

He started out by asking Maria what it had been like sharing a cell with Pedro and Tomás. In hindsight, Detective Knight decided that had been a bad way to start hitting on Maria.

"It fun and they cute and...muy grande," said Maria with a wink and a coquettish[104] smile as she held her hands about a foot apart in front of her.

"Ahh...*what?*" asked Detective Knight incredulously and with shock. *Muy grande? She can't mean what I think she means...can she? I sure hope not. Well no, wait a second; I hope she does.*

Maria didn't answer any questions or say anything else after that. She just stood there with a seductive smile on her face while sticking her chest out as far as she could. She winked at him repeatedly while having a loving smile on her face and sensually licking her lips. *Damn, she is a sybarite.*[105]

Detective Knight could not believe what he was seeing. What was she doing? Was she attempting to seduce him? He wasn't sure, but if she was...it gave David pause while he considered the ramifications of allowing himself to be seduced by her. He did not know what to do, which was typical for David when it came to women. He knew what he *shouldn't* do; but hey, he was in the midst of an inhumanly long dry spell and here was an opportunity to end it. Plus, he had handcuffs and the interrogation room was soundproof so...it could be quite interesting.

Fortunately, for David (and Maria) his head with ears won the day and his mind got back on the right track, albeit that track was a bit bizarre: A hot Mexican chic was in jail for killing Frank Finnegan and being an accomplice to Mark Madson's

---

104   Behaving in such a way as to suggest a playful sexual attraction; flirtatious.
105   A person who is self-indulgent in their fondness for sensuous luxury.

murder, and now she had the audacity[106] to hit on the detective who had arrested her and would undoubtedly testify against her in court. David figured that she probably did not think she was taking any kind of risk because men had always been putty in her hands and would do whatever she wanted. Because of this, David made the bold conclusion that she was a complete vamp,[107] and a sybaritic vamp at that.

In spite of all this, David still couldn't take his eyes off her chest, especially because it was rather nippy in the jail cell and the low temperature put her magnificent chest in a state that put a smile on his face. A good view of a nice chest in that low-temperature-induced state was a rare and welcome sight to any heterosexual male living Fiasco Valley.

Young males in Fiasco Valley, who were single and not wealthy, had to jump at any and every chance afforded (would that be considered a pun?) them to get *any* sort of sexual satisfaction; even if it was just looking and dreaming. This was simply because there weren't many females in Fiasco Valley and most women that were there, were just "digging for gold,"[108] although that wasn't necessarily a bad thing, thought David with lusty smirk on his face.

He was smirking because he knew what women coming to Fiasco Valley and "digging for gold" would do just about anything to land a wealthy husband. On any given Friday or Saturday night in Fiasco Valley, David had discovered, through trial and error, that he was highly sought after if he pretended

---

106   Bold or arrogant disregard of normal restraints.

107   A woman who uses sexual attraction to exploit men.

108   A "gold digger" is woman who is with a man solely for his money. The older the guy is the better because he'll die sooner and leave her the cash.

to be part of the jet set.[109] He had been a "movie producer," an "heir to a large fortune," a "lottery winner," a "CEO at a Fortune 500 company," and an "extremely successful, but retired, pro-athlete." David was at the age where he couldn't let any opportunity to be with a member, or better yet members, of the opposite sex go by, even if it was just with "gold diggers." He knew they could "dig" all they wanted, but wouldn't get much "gold" from him...so he let them "dig."

---

109 A fashionable social set composed of wealthy people who travel frequently by jetliner to parties and resorts.

Chapter 25

Todd the Cellar Rat

Todd showed up at Big Goose Cellars at 7:50 A.M. on Monday morning. He was so excited that he didn't realize how tired he was. He had gone to bed at around 9:00 P.M. the night before in order to be well rested and sharp, but he had been so excited that he couldn't sleep and as a result, he was neither rested nor sharp.

Tim Tauscher showed-up five minutes later and he was not surprised to find Todd waiting for him. Tim figured that the first day of the first opportunity to work in a wine cellar must be exciting for a wine enthusiast and greenhorn[110] cellar hand like Todd.

Tim took one look at Todd, saw what he was wearing, and shook his head. What he was wearing was a nice pair of pants, a nice belt, a nice collared shirt, a tie, and a nice pair of wing-tips.

"Ah Todd, we need to have a little talk," said Tim in the most dire voice he could muster.

"Okay. Sure," he replied he zealously.

Tim proceded to tell Todd that he should wear old pants, jeans preferably, an old t-shirt, and rubber boots. He told him to go home and change because they would be cleaning tanks that day and he would most likely get wet. So, Todd jumped into his Audi R8, which was parked next to Tim's old, rusty Ford

---

110   A person who lacks experience and knowledge – From the reference to an animal with *green* (that is, young) horns OR From 17th century jewelry manufacturing which used decorated horn which was impressed at a specific temperature. If heated too high (a common mistake by apprentices), the horn turned green.

pick-up truck, and drove back to his apartment. Once there, he found some old jeans, he managed to get them on, and then found an old t-shirt. He didn't have any rubber boots, so he put on some old running shoes he had lying around, jumped back into his car, and raced back to the winery. Once there, he found Tim and got approval of his habiliments,[111] except for the shoes.

"You're fine for now, but I must say your life will be much less miserable if you wear rubber boots," said Tim. *Yeah whatever* thought Todd. *I'm working in a winery, how miserable could I possibly be? Besides, I'll look like a dork.*

Tim then led Todd out to the tank pad and proceeded to show him that all of the stainless steel wine tanks were extremely dirty, due to the fact they hadn't been cleaned in months. The reason being: Tim couldn't find anyone to work at Big Goose Cellars because no one wanted to end up being worm aliment.[112]

The wine tanks had tartrates stuck to their insides, there were dried-up lees, which reeked and were stuck on the bottoms of the tanks, and there were still some seeds, pulp, and dried-up grape skins in a few of them.

Tim pointed to the row of tanks on the tank pad and said, "We have to start by cleaning all these tanks because we are going to be crushing grapes into them real soon."

"Okay great," said Todd. "Show me how and consider it done."

Tim told Todd that to clean a tank all he had to do was "remove all visible dirt and foreign matter, or in other words: Get rid of all the crap stuck in the tank." Then with a wink of

---

111   Clothing. I can't imagine why that word is not used much nowadays.
112   Food; nourishment.

his eye, he said, "And hopefully there won't be any dead people in there."

Todd ignored that last comment because he thought it must be some sort of inside winemaker joke and besides, he had no idea how to get rid of all the "crap stuck in the tank." Tim realized this from seeing the blank look on Todd's face and therefore, gave Todd his first lesson in winemaking.

He began by saying that cleaning and sanitation were, "the most boring, tedious, and unglamorous aspects of winemaking, but they were also two of the most important." He then told Todd he was to start by giving all the tanks a "Three Cycle Wash" and went on explained what that was.

When Tim was done with the explanation, Todd went to clean the first tank, which happened to be Tank 12. He found the nearest high pressure water hose but there was no spray nozzle, so he asked Tim if he had to have a spray nozzle.

"Well yeah, it's a lot easier to spray tanks when you have a spray nozzle. There should be one right over there," said Tim as he pointed to a small shelf on the wall behind the tank. There wasn't. So, Todd and Tim looked for, and found, two nozzles right away. Unfortunately, neither nozzle worked and it took them another half an hour to find a spray nozzle that did, in fact, spray.

Todd put the nozzle on the high-pressure water hose and began to spray the inside of the tank (via the upper and lower manway) to remove any dried skins, seeds, tartrates, molds, and hopefully no dead people. He sprayed and sprayed for over an hour but the tank didn't look any cleaner. Todd figured he had better find Tim and make sure he was doing everything correctly because he did not want to make any sort of mistake in this tank where the heavenly elixir would be made. He called out Tim's name, but got no response. He wandered around the cellar while repeatedly calling Tim's name. No Tim. He did this for a good twenty-five minutes, to no avail. He then walked out of the cellar, was temporarily blinded by the sun, and resumed his calls. No Tim. Finally, Todd went into the winery offices to see if he was in there; he was, just sitting at a desk (formerly Maria's desk) looking through some papers. Todd told Tim that he had been spraying the tank with hot water for nearly an hour and it was still dirty.

Tim got kind of a goofy grin on his face and said, "Well, you have to get in and scrub and use some elbow grease on those babies."

"Use what? Elbow Grease? In the tank?" asked Todd incredulously. *I have to get in the tank? I use grease to clean wine tanks?*

"Yep, that's right. Get right in and scrub, scrub, scrub. Come on, I'll show ya," answered Tim. He straightened the papers he was looking through, stood-up, and led Todd outside.

Todd followed Tim (he didn't have the nerve to walk alongside him as an equal) back into the cellar and to the tank he had been working on.

When they reached the tank 12, Tim looked into it and said that Todd would definitely have to get inside and use some elbow grease. He explained to Todd that he could enter the tank through the lower manway and then scrub the inside of the tank until it was clean.

So Todd, who nearly had an orgasm with the thought of getting into a tank that had actually held wine and would soon be holding more wine, walked up to the tank, pointed at the lower manway and asked with amazement, "Go through there? Seriously? How?" He did not think the manway was large

187

enough for him, or anyone, to fit through.

"Really serious," answered Tim. "If I can squeeze in there," he said as he pointed to the lower manway, "you can squeeze in there. I've done it dozens, if not hundreds of times."

After about twenty minutes of trying different body contortions, Todd managed to get himself into the tank. Problem was he forgot to bring any of the cleaning equipment that Tim had told him he would need. So, he contorted himself back out of the tank, grabbed the hose with the working spray nozzle, some Scotch-Brite pads, and then contorted himself back into the tank. Once inside the tank, he realized he had forgotten to turn on the water to the hose. He didn't want to go thru the manway again, so he just stuck his head out of the tank and yelled for Tim. He got no response and after a few minutes, gave up. *Oh man, where could he be? He's probably talking with Maria...oh no wait; she's in the hoosegow.*

Todd sorely wanted to impress, so he struggled out of the tank...again, turned on the hot water, then struggled back into the tank...again, and started cleaning. He started spraying the inside of the tank with hot water to loosen all of the crud. It wasn't fun and the infuriating part was that the hose got a kink in it every time he gave it a yank in order to spray a different area of the tank. Every time the hose "kinked-up" he had to struggle out of the tank and straighten it out. After he sprayed the inside of tank for a while, Todd used the Scotch-Bright pads to scrub off the crud that would not come off with just spraying; well he *tried* to scrub the crud off.

After a couple of hours of this routine, there was so much steam in the tank that Todd couldn't see what he was doing and he was sweating profusely. The tank had become like a sauna, it was starting to smell like a locker room, and it was getting hard to breathe inside. He figured with all that hot water and scrubbing, the tank *had* to be clean. So, once again, he contorted himself through the lower manway in order to take a break from the heat while allowing the steam to dissipate.

When Todd exited the tank, he was wet and so was the cement floor of the cellar. The wetness made it slippery and his old running shoes with worn out soles didn't provide enough traction. He slipped and fell, whacking his elbow and head. He stood-up, cussed at the whole world, and stumbled outside to get some fresh, cool, dry air.

When he came back into the cellar a few minutes later and looked in the tank (the steam had all dissipated) it wasn't clean, not even close. *Oh man! It doesn't look like I've done a damn thing.*

Todd gave a tired sigh, and then went through the whole tank entering rigmarole. Once inside, he scrubbed, sprayed, cussed, and smashed knuckles (inadvertently, mind you) until he finally had the inside of the tank spotless. He contorted himself through the lower manway one final time and, lo and behold, Tim was standing right there looking at the tank.

"Well, she looks pretty good," said Tim. "You only have four more to do. But it's five o' clock, so they can wait until tomorrow."

Only four more? Holy cow! That's ridiculous. Todd's shoes and socks were soaking wet, his pants and shirt weren't exactly dry, and he was in considerable pain. On his many treks in and out of the tank, Todd had managed to scrape both elbows, four knuckles (only two of which were bleeding,) smashed a few fingers, whacked both knees at least once, fallen on his butt twice, and most recently, whacked his head. He didn't mind though, because he was working in a *winery*, although he was getting rather sick of Tank 12.

Tim noticed that Todd looked tired and defeated, so he quickly went to his office and returned with a bottle of wine and two glasses. He offered a glass to Todd and said with a grin, "Looks like you could use a drink. This is our 2012 Barrel Fermented Chardonnay. Tell me what you think."

Your asking me what I think? Holy cow! All of his tiredness and pissed-offedness (I thought I had made-up that term, but *nooo*, someone beat me to it) went away instantly. There he was, standing in the cellar of a winery, being poured a glass of wine by, and then sharing it with, Tim Tauscher, a winemaker in Fiasco Valley. Todd had to pinch himself to make sure he wasn't dreaming.

Todd swirled the wine in his glass, then stuck his nose into the glass and made a point of taking a long, deep, noisy breath in through his nose. He then took a sip and made a big show of swirling the wine around in his mouth before swallowing it. He didn't know what the point of all this was, but it was what he always saw people do at wine tastings so he was playing it safe.

Todd did think the wine smelled and tasted pretty good, but that was about all he could say because he couldn't pick out any specific characteristics or give a detailed description of how the wine smelled, tasted, or felt in his mouth. He didn't want to look like a wine ignoramus (even though he was one) in front of Tim, so he just repeated (as best he could) a description of some wine he had recently seen online at a wine review website.

He droned: "It has a citrus driven nose. I get pineapple in plentiful amounts along with ample amounts of coconut, and hints of banana. It has a gentle and round entry. The oak is subtle but definitely there. The mid-palate broadcasts other flavors,

190

such as vanilla and lemon meringue pie. It is flawlessly ripened and decked out with plenty of sweet oak, yet it is measured and mannerly all the same. The finish is luxuriously rich with a viscosity that coated my mouth for a long while after my last sip."

Tim gave Todd a knowing smile and tried not to laugh, because that description, beside being snotty, snobby, and uppity, sounded eerily familiar to the review of the Pebble Hill Vineyards 2011 Barrel Fermented Chardonnay he read a couple of days ago on *The Wine Watcher* website. He nodded his head towards Todd with a knowing smile and finished his glass of wine in silence. When Todd had also finished his glass of wine, Tim said, "Well good work today. How about we do it again tomorrow? Say eight o'clock?"

"Sounds good to me," said Todd. *Aww crap! Eight o'clock tomorrow? I don't know if I can make it tomorrow. My whole body aches and I need my sleep.* He then walked out to his Audi R8 sports car, got in, peeled-out from his parking spot, and drove to his apartment in the low-income housing complex. Todd just hit the sack and conked out as soon as he got into his apartment. He had planned on going out after work to a nice restaurant with a bar and picking-up a lonely or unhappy wife, a divorcée, or maybe even a rich widow, but those plans were all shot to hell now.

Chapter 26

José Returned

Tim and William's breakfast Friday morning had gone longer than anticipated because they had run into Scott Garett at The Birchwood Café. The three men shared a table, talked Giants baseball, Golden State Warriors Basketball, 49er cheerleaders, and the possibility of Giant cheerleaders. Well, not extremely large cheerleaders, but cheerleaders for the San Francisco Giants. They did not talk about *phylloxera*, bottling nincompoops, wine ratings, or even annoying tourists.

Towards the end of their breakfast, Scott looked out the window and saw José Mendoza walking by. Unfortunately, for Scott, José saw him too and came into the café, sat right down at the table, and started talking (he spoke better English than most Americans under the age of 35.) He didn't bother to mention the "legal" problem he had in Tijuana and he didn't seem at all concerned with the "barrel stack" incident that had caused him to leave Fiasco Valley in the first place.

José told the three men at the table that there were no opportunities for jobs in Tijuana, but he had heard there were some jobs in California for guys who could drive and repair tractors.

"Well, if Melvin would ever kick the bucket, (literary note: I'm foreshadowing—give me an A+ Ms. English Lit. Teacher. All English Literature teachers are a "Ms.") Timmy here would have a job for ya," said Bill.

"Who is Melvin?" asked José.

"He is in charge of the vineyards and does anything and

everything that involves a tractor; he won't let anyone near the tractor he uses and he *always* uses the same tractor. I think he has some weird childhood issue...or something. Plus, he's getting really cranky in his old age," answered Bill.

Scott Garett then said, "I didn't think you knew anything about tractors José, at least that's what I thought when you worked for me. You could drive a forklift like a maniac, but that's about it. The last I heard about you was, you were in prison in Tijuana. Is that true?"

"Yeah, it is. It was just a big misunderstanding though," said José. He did not explain any further and he hoped no one could tell he was lying through his teeth. He continued by telling everyone at the table that it was while in Tijuana he learned all about tractor repair and maintenance.

The prison José was in employed a "trabajar en la sociedad" (work back into society) program as part of its rehabilitation strategy; or punishment strategy, depending on your point of view. In the program, inmates were taught how to fix and maintain tractors along with other pieces of farm equipment, and were then tasked with repairing and maintaining the tractors and other pieces of farm equipment for the local farmers.

Besides learning about tractors in prison, José was informed about all of the benefits he could receive if he went to the U.S.—California ideally. The prison actually held a mandatory class for the inmates that taught them how to take advantage of the American "system." A main point made in the class was that speaking English was not a requirement; so don't waste time learning it.

Having criminals "sneak" out of Mexico and into the U.S. was a win-win situation for the Mexican Government. I put sneak in quotes because there was not much sneaking involved, a little running possibly, but sneaking? No. *I can go across the border and the U.S. government will provide for me?* thought José. *I don't even need to speak English? Wow! What fools! I'm there.* Use your own imagination to come up with reasons for Mexican Government wanting its criminals to leave Mexico and go to the U.S. Whatever you think the reason is, you are probably right.

This prison in Tijuana that José had been in was nothing like a prison in the U.S. It was simply a cinder-block building with a small yard surrounded by an eight-foot tall, chain-link fence with some barbed wire on the top. The fence had one gate, which was guarded by three guards on a day shift followed by three guards on a night shift. That was it.

By sheer coincidence, the prison was within easy walking distance of a nightclub or two...or possibly three. The three prison guards working the night shift were José's cousins and they would simply allow José to walk out at night and go to the nightclubs, as long as he was back before their shift ended at 5:00 A.M.

José always came back, except for one time...the last time. On one of his earlier junkets[113] to the nightclubs, he heard that people who could maintain, repair, and drive tractors could find jobs in the valley. José couldn't believe his luck. The Mexican prison system had unwittingly trained him for a job in California where the wages, lifestyle, women, beer, drugs, and weather were much better than in Mexico...well maybe not the women. *Although my life in this prison is pretty damn good. Maybe I shouldn't leave. Nah, I gotta get outta here.*

To that end, José did not come back from his nightclub sojourn

---

113 An extravagant trip or celebration, in particular one enjoyed by a government official at public expense.

one night. He simply walked through the gate, hitched a ride to Mexicali, found the correct taquería (which turned out to be the hardest part of his escape) and then crawled through the same tunnel that Maria and Ernesto had used to enter the U.S.

Apparently no federal, state, or local agency, of any kind, had a clue the tunnel was there...so much for homeland security. He had then used the Mexican network of immigrants, both legal and illegal, to get back to Fiasco Valley and the FawHF. (That's the Farmworker Housing Facility...in case you forgot.)

Chapter 27

Wrong Valley

As soon as José had reached Fiasco Valley after his daring escape and had moved into the Birchwood FawHF, he began asking his fellow immigrants where the tractor jobs were. No one knew, or had even heard of any of those types of jobs available. José was thunderstruck by this. He couldn't fathom why there weren't any jobs for someone with his tractor knowledge and driving abilities. He never even considered the possibility that he had gotten some bogus information at the nightclub in Tijuana because it's a well-known fact that Tijuana nightclubs are a wealth of reliable information. *How could information one hears in a Tijuana nightclub be false? It's not possible, is it?*

No, it's not possible. The information José had gotten in the nightclub *was* true, but for a different valley. He had overheard a conversation concerning the Central Valley of California, which is infinitely larger (well not really; that's impossible) and has a greater variety of crops than Fiasco Valley.

Good ol' José wasn't deterred by the fact that no one knew of any tractor related jobs. He figured his fellow immigrants were just to dumb and/or lazy to have heard about any job that might require some training. He, José Mendoza, would be able to easily find a job and gain employment because jobs were plentiful for people with his skills.

He left the FawHF early the next morning on foot brimming with confidence about his abilities, his chance to get a job, and his chance to live the American Dream. He walked down a dirt road next to a nearby vineyard that he had seen a couple of pick-up trucks drive up and down numerous times the previous day. As he walked down the road a tractor being driven by an old honky drove out of the vineyard and came up beside him.

"What can I do you for?" asked the old man.

"I'm looking for a job doing pretty much what you're doing," answered José as he stopped walking. "I can drive just about any tractor and I can do all kinds of maintenance and repair on those same tractors."

The old guy chuckled and told José that he, himself, could do anything and everything that had to do with tractors and had been for forty-five years.

"Why don't you go try the ol' Spencer place? He might need someone like you," the old guy said to José. He then proceeded to tell José where the old Spencer place was. José thanked the guy and started walking towards the old Spencer place and what he hoped was a job and a better life. He had walked for over an hour, and was starting to think that a job and a better life weren't all they were cracked up to be, when he finally reached his terminus.[114] The first thing José saw was a tractor that looked to be in need of repair. *Oh yeah, that's what I'm talkin' about.*

As José was walking across the dirt and gravel yard towards the tractor an old, rusty, dusty, beat-up, pick-up truck pulled into the yard and drove right up to the tractor. An old man—according to José anyway—got out and immediately started tinkering with the tractor. José moseyed on over to the man,

---

114   A final point in space or time; an end or extremity. I sound like a British guy wearing a tweed jacket and smoking a pipe when I use that word. Either that, or an education snob who thinks they are smarter and more cultured than everyone else.

introduced himself, and asked if this was the Spencer place, and if it was, did they have any need for someone who was good with tractors.

"Well, I'm Shane Spencer so you are in the right place, but I don't really need help with anything. I've been doing this for thirty years and I think I got it pretty well figured out."

José, with a look of profound disappointment and in a voice of the same asked, "Well, do you know anyone who does?"

Shane Spencer did, and gave him the names of two fellows who owned vineyards and were getting to the age where all the candles on their birthday cake would set off fire alarms. José thanked him and said he would go see the two fellows. José, who was sick and tired of walking, went out to the highway and managed to hitch a ride with a passing truck that was being driven by another vato. I won't mention the fact that the driver was an illegal immigrant who had a *valid* California Drivers License, but who couldn't speak or read a word of English. I also won't mention the fact that he was receiving unemployment benefits and free healthcare.

José was dropped off at the vineyard of the first fellow Shane had mentioned and found the guy sitting in his tractor at the edge of a vineyard drinking beer, even though it was only 10:00 A.M. Again, José moseyed on over to the tractor, introduced himself, and said that Shane Spencer had told him that he could probably use some help.

The old codger said in an irritated voice, "He did, did he? Well, I don't need no help from no one like you sonny boy, so you can just leave the way you came...and do it fast. That's muy rápido to you. Comprende muchacho?"

José bored two holes into the ol' codger's head with his stare but didn't want to do anything he'd regret and so made a quick

198

exit, well as quick as he could on his tired legs. He walked back to the highway and begrudgingly stuck his thumb out to hitch a ride to, and see, the second fellow Shane had mentioned. José wasn't too keen on meeting anymore old, racist, country bumpkins, but he needed a job so, he had to swallow his pride and suffer through it.

Eventually, someone stopped and gave José a ride to the next vineyard. The "next" vineyard was about two miles away and when José was dropped off, he immediately walked towards the large barn that had all kinds of farm equipment around it, including a tractor. José moseyed (he liked to mosey) up to a guy who was tinkering with the tractor and introduced himself. He then asked if he had, or knew anyone who had, any kind of a job involving tractors available. He didn't.

By now, it was late afternoon and José was tired and demoralized. He tried to hitch a ride back to the FawHF but no one stopped and he ended-up walking the entire way. Once he arrived at the FawHF, he started drinking the case of Budweiser he had picked up on his way home. He had drunk enough beer to be in the marvelous condition in which he didn't care what he said or what people thought of him, when he forced himself to go to bed because he was going to continue his job search in the morning and he wanted to be well rested.

The next day was a repeat of the day before, with regards to the job hunt. He walked quite a few miles and was told by gringo after gringo sitting on a tractor that they had no use for him. Contrary to outward appearances, the valley was affected by the struggling economy and the vineyard growers were having a bit of a financial fiasco.

Tired and frustrated, José decided to call it quits for the day and find a way home any way he could. It had been another day of his dreams not coming true, with the only difference from the day before being that he got a case of Coors Light instead of Budweiser on his way home. Again, José drank until he was in the marvelous condition he had been in the previous night and then went to bed. José repeated this process (including the beer drinking) for a few more days until he became extremely discouraged, tired, and pissed-off that he couldn't find a job that he had been trained for.

Lying in bed that night, José kept thinking of his chance meeting with those vatos in The Birchwood Café the other day. Continually repeating in José's mind were the words William had said: "If Melvin would ever kick the bucket..." *Why don't I help Melvin kick the bucket? That shouldn't be too hard.*

Chapter 28

Jury-Rigging Duty

José made the brilliant conclusion that if Melvin was dead, he would get his job and all of his problems would be solved. However, José wasn't about to wait around for Melvin to more than mostly malfunction because who knows how long that would be, and he figured it would be best, for him anyway, to speed things up a bit.

José decided the best and quickest way to speed things up a bit would be to pay Melvin a visit. José managed to reach the Big Goose Cellars without walking too much, but it did take him quite a while as he had to hitchhike and no one in Fiasco Valley would stop to pick-up an unkempt and slovenly Mexican. The reason being: Everyone in Fiasco Valley was a rich, white, Republican, racist that considered themselves too good to pick-up a hitchhiker, especially a Mexican one. This did not improve José's state of mind.

At Big Goose Cellars, he looked for someone who seemed to be in charge, but there was no one around. He tried every door he saw but they were all locked. He called Maria's name but got no answer. He did hear some bad disco music coming from a nearby dirt road so he walked down that road until he came to a shed from which the music was emanating.

The shed also had various pieces of vineyard equipment around it, including two tractors. Leaning on one of the tractors, which was running rather poorly, wearing old worn-out jeans, old worn-out suspenders, a rumpled collared shirt, and drinking a Budweiser, was a big man with a large purplish-red nose.

José walked up to him, careful to make some noise so as not to startle the guy and cause him to spill his beer, and said, "Excuse me, do you happen to need anyone who can drive and service tractors and other pieces of equipment?"

Melvin turned, looked at José and said, "And you are...?

"My name is José and I was wondering if you could use any help in the vineyard."

Melvin took a long, slow, swig of the beer he was holding, and stared at José for an uncomfortably long time, seeming to contemplate something all the while. During this time, José began looking at the tractor to hopefully determine what was wrong with it. He would impress the old geezer by telling him what the problem was and how to fix it. The old geezer would be so grateful and impressed, he would hire him on the spot. José had trouble with reality.

"Your engine doesn't seem to be running too smoothly," said José.

"Yeah, I don't what the hell is wrong with it," said a perplexed Melvin after he had finished gulping down the rest of his beer. "I've checked the fuel lines, spark plugs, distributor, and air cleaner. I just checked the float valves and they are floating," said Melvin with a slight chuckle. "But so far everything is fine. I'm at a loss as to what is wrong, and to make matters worse, I need this tractor today because I have a lot of work to do in the Vine Cliff Vineyard."

José smiled inwardly and began closely examining the engine. He started by feeling around the engine and the engine compartment with his hands. He looked at hoses; he yanked on and turned a few parts; he then got down on his hands and knees and looked at the engine from below. While he was doing all this, he kept mumbling to himself, "Hmm. Hmm. No not that.

I wonder... Sí. Sí. Okay. Yeah that should work."

Finally, he said to Melvin, "The problem is you have a loose manifold."

"I do? I didn't know I had a manifold," said Melvin sarcastically with a chuckle and a big grin. His sarcasm continued, "Oh, or do you mean the *tractor* has a loose manifold? That would make a lot more sense." As Melvin said this, he reached for another beer from the cooler at his feet.

José did not recognize the sarcasm in Melvin's voice. He felt that Melvin was mocking him and he became furious. Melvin was not mocking him, he was just trying to hide his embarrassment for not diagnosing the problem earlier, which he probably would have had he only been half-soused. He'd had a lot of practice doing his job half-soused, but today he was fully-soused and had been since 8:00 A.M.

José's entire body had gone rigid during this last exchange with Melvin, but he did see an opportunity. He figured he would fix this dumb cracker's tractor, get rid of him, and then take his job.

José balled up his fists and said, or rather snarled, that he would fix the manifold if Melvin would get him the proper tools. Melvin thought that was a good idea and so stumbled into the shed to get the proper tools, but he never came back. After about fifteen minutes of standing by the tractor and doing nothing, except possibly becoming more furious, José went into the shed to see what the hell was taking so long. He found Melvin passed-out on a hay bale with an empty bottle of whiskey next to him. *Aww, the dumb gringo, just pathetic. I'll fix his tractor...I mean really fix it."*

José then went through the entire shed and gathered all the tools and the materials he would need. He went back outside and began making alterations on the tractor. What he did was a little trick he had learned from a fellow prisoner in the Tijuana prison. A full three hours later, the alterations were complete and José returned all the tools to where he had found them. He saw that Melvin was still passed-out on the hay bale but was beginning to stir, and *that* was the sign for him to leave.

Twenty minutes later Melvin rose from the hay bale, tried to remember what he was doing on there, couldn't, and so went back outside and got on his tractor because he still had some work to do that day. The tractor started right up (José had fixed the manifold while making the alterations) and he drove out to Vine Cliff Vineyard...he never came back.

Chapter 29

Job Opening?

After "fixing" Melvin's tractor, José went back to the FawHF with a case of Budweiser and a case of Coors Light. He had a lot of adrenaline pumping through his veins because he knew what *should* go wrong with Melvin's tractor and what it *should* result in. José was thoroughly familiar with Vine Cliff Vineyard because he and his buddies used to go drinking near it after work on Fridays...and then on Thursdays...and eventually on Wednesdays also. José knew that if his "trick" did its thing where it was supposed to, terrible things would happen to the stupid cracker and that excited him. *That pinche vato deserves whatever happens to him. I hope he fuckin' dies.*

Assuming his tractor "trick" worked (and José did) he would be striking a blow for all immigrant workers everywhere, at least that's what he told himself. He could even imagine a Mexican holiday being named after him. He pictured big signs in towns all across the country that read, "Come celebrate José Mendoza day!" Of course, they would be written in Spanish and would read: "¡Venga a celebrar José Mendoza día!" He imagined floats with his likeness going down the street with beautiful señorita's dancing all about. He imagined barbecues with everyone drinking cerveza, eating carne asada, and singing songs that would pass the story of his greatness on to future generations. He figured if there was a "José Mendoza Día," he could, and would, have any woman he wanted, any time he wanted, and *that* excited him in more ways than one. Again, José had trouble with reality.

Believe it or not, José was not an idiot and he did have a bit of a grasp on reality. He knew his "trick" might not work, and then all of his tractor alterations would be for naught. If that was the case, he might get caught and *that* made him nervous.

In the following days, he was desperate to hear any news about a tractor falling off a cliff in the valley. So, he furtively asked anyone he saw if they knew of, or had heard of, any type of tractor incident in the valley. He didn't specifically ask about a tractor falling off a cliff because he thought someone might get suspicious.

He continued discreetly asking about a tractor incident for a few days while just hanging-out at the FawHF and not doing much except alternately feeling ecstatic because he had struck a blow, or so he hoped, against all stupid American crackers, and feeling extremely anxious about what actually *did* happen. No one had heard anything and it was driving him nuts because he wanted to be able to brag and "puff out his chest" about what he had done to the stupid gringo and his tractor. José either didn't care, or more likely didn't realize, that bragging about sabotaging a piece of heavy equipment that resulted in someone's untimely demise was not such a good idea.

Finally, when José couldn't stand it any longer, he decided to go for a nice, long walk. He walked into downtown Birchwood and therefore, had to walk right past The Birchwood Café—it *is* a small town.

As he walked by, he saw Scott Garett having breakfast with Tim Tauscher and William Strong so he went in to ask them about a job. José reasoned that if there was a job opening at Big Goose Cellars that would mean, in all likelihood, that Melvin was now on the wrong side of the grass. That, in turn, would mean that his tractor "trick" *had* worked.

José began speaking with the three gringos and it wasn't long before he knew that a job doing vineyard work that required tractor skills had recently become available. He was relieved and exhilarated, not only because there was a job available and there was one less honky on the planet, but because his "trick" had worked.

Chapter 30

José Deere?

As Tim, Scott, and Bill, sat and talked with José in The Birchwood Café, Tim began to think that his preconceived notions about José might actually be wrong. *Well, there is a first time for everything.*

José seemed like a good guy. He spoke English well—which was a huge plus in Fiasco Valley—he was respectful, soft-spoken, polite, relaxed, friendly, and he smelled good. Tim desperately needed someone who could drive and maintain the winery's tractors because it was nearly harvest time and tractors would be needed to pull the gondolas full of grapes out of the vineyard. Then, after harvest, the vineyards would need attention, some of which would require the use of a tractor. Here sat someone who had been trained by the government, albeit the Mexican government, to drive, maintain, and repair tractors. He was experienced and eager to work. With considerable effort, Tim put aside his preconceived notions and asked José if he would be interested in helping out with the vineyard work. José jumped at the chance.

"Great," said Tim unenthusiastically. "We can start right now, if that's okay with you. Bill and I have to go to the winery but we can give you a lift to the vineyard shed. We recently lost a tractor, but we've got a couple of old ones that should do the trick and you can just familiarize yourself with them for now."

José had to try hard to keep his eyes from getting real big when Tim used the phrase "do the trick" when referring to the tractors in the vineyard shop. *He couldn't know, could he? No, impossible. Besides, he's offering me a job.*

"You can also meet the guys there," continued Tim still unenthusiastically because he did not trust José. Tim knew he was thinking rather prejudicially, based solely on José's appearance, but he couldn't help it. José had slicked back hair, was covered with tattoos, wore a lot of bling,[115] always wore a wife-beater,[116] and called everyone a "cholo." Tim would not feel comfortable having him in the vineyard shop with a lot of equipment and plenty of tools, some of which were rather sharp, but he desperately needed someone to do the work.

As they sat there, the check came and William whipped out his money clip, peeled off a few bills, put them on the table, and shoved the still full money clip back in his pocket. José saw this and his feelings towards Americans did not change, in fact, they were reinforced.

Tim, William, and José then parted ways with Scott Garett and piled into Tim's rusty, old pick-up truck. They drove to the vineyard shed, where José was dropped off, and then continued on to the winery. José went into the shed and saw a couple of his countrymen working on two tractors. Both workers saw José and greeted him warmly. José asked what they were doing and they both gave him a frustrated explanation. All of this dialogue was in rapidly spoken Spanish.

Both workers were flummoxed by their respective tractors and let José take a look and see if he could spot the problem. He could, and offered to fix both tractors. After about an hour both tractors were running like champs. The two workers were extremely impressed with José. In fact, they were nearly

---

115   Gaudy (bright, shiney, showy) jewelry worn to be noticed and impress people. Rap stars and pro athletes wear a lot of bling.

116   A tank-top.

in awe. José looked like he was at home in this shed and indeed, José did feel at home. He did not have any trouble locating tools and he seemed to know where everything went, it was almost like he had been there before.

As the three vatos were standing around looking at the tractors and discussing fútbol, cerveza, and mujeres,[117] a truck pulling a large, flatbed trailer carrying a brand new John Deere 5GV Specialty Tractor, pulled up to the vineyard shop.

Wow! thought José as he exited the shop, *that's brand spankin' new. It's friggin' awesome!* The tractor was the replacement for the one Ted had driven off the cliff. *That's a hell of a lot nicer than the tractor Ted drove. I wonder if the trick would work on it.*

The two workers also came out of the shop and joined José as the truck driver alighted and approached the three guys.

"I need someone to sign for this. Is Ted or Melvin around?" asked the truck driver as he walked towards the three vatos.

"No. Ted and Melvin are a bit under the weather," said José. *Actually, they are bit under the ground.* "What do you need them for?"

"I need someone to sign for this tractor," repeated the truck driver. The two workers, who had joined José, just stood there with blank looks on their faces and seemed to be trying to disappear. They did not understand what José and the truck driver had said; they just recognized the words "Ted" and "Melvin" and that made them nervous. José noticed this and decided to take charge. He stepped forward, signed for the new tractor, and then went about helping unload it from the flatbed, making small talk the entire time.

---

117 "...fútbol, cerveza, and mujeres..." is "soccer, beer, and women" – I'm adding a little Spanish flavor because I love Mexican food.

Once the tractor was unloaded, José drove it to the winery to show Tim...and to make himself look good. Plus, he wanted to get a sense of how the tractor operated so he could get a sense if his "trick" would work on it. José was always thinking ahead about possible opportunities to...you, dear reader, can fill in what sort of "possible opportunities" José had in mind.

When he arrived at the winery, Tim and William were standing on the crush pad discussing who-knows-what, so José drove right up to them and put the new tractor on display. He alighted and started explaining all of the tractors virtues. The problem was, he didn't know any of the virtues so he was just making them up—but he did *sound* like he knew of what he spoke.[118] William became so caught-up in José's explanation and presentation of the new tractor that he just climbed aboard and started driving it. Unfortunately, he doesn't know how to drive a tractor and Tim and José had to listen to gears grind and the engine scream. They saw the tractor bouncing and swerving all over the road, saw a few vines get taken out, and then heard a couple of god-awful noises. After an excruciatingly long twenty minutes, William managed to return the tractor to Tim and José.

The tractor was trailing a few vines, there were fence posts and wires stuck all over it, and the engine was beginning to smoke. Tim looked at José, shook his head, and quietly said, "Well, it looks like you'll be busy the for rest of the day...and probably all next week."

Great thought José *I guess I do have a job.*

William got out of the tractor with a huge grin and look of sheer joy on his face and re-joined Tim and José.

---

118   "...he knew of what he spoke." The fancy, educated way to say, "...he knew what he was talkin' 'bout."

211

"Oh that tractor is a blast! I may have gone off the road a little once or twice but everything seems okay," said William in a giddy voice.

May have gone off the road? Everything seems okay? What the hell are you looking at Bill? thought Tim. However, all he said was: "Well great, Bill. I'll have José take the tractor back to the vineyard shop to let the boys see it and learn how it works. You know, just let them get familiar with it."

Tim then sidled up to José and whispered to him that when he got back to the shop, he should remove the fence posts, wires, grapevines, and anything else that shouldn't be stuck to the tractor. Then give the engine a complete and total check-up, and be sure to check the brakes, clutch, and hydraulics... anything and everything. "And have the other guys give you a hand," whispered Tim. "They're good with engines and stuff. We want to make sure everything still works."

So, José coaxed the tractor back into the vineyard shop (William had really done a number on it) and he and the two other workers immediately went about doing what Tim had said; well not *immediately*, they got some beer first. While working on the tractor, the three vatos drank beer, made jokes about, and laughed at William.

José was doing more than going-over the tractor. He was also trying to figure out if the "trick" would work on it, and if not, what would make it work. José wanted to be ready for anything because he never knew whom he would meet next.

On the afternoon of his third day at work, when the new tractor was nearly fixed, José—who was a bit tipsy and rapidly getting tipsier—started to "puff out his chest" about what he had done to that "stupid gringo." He told, in detail, of all the alterations he had made to Melvin's tractor and what they

212

resulted in. The other two workers were aghast. They had been fond of Melvin mainly because he just let them be, and if it had been a particularly rough day, he would buy them beer. Plus, they were Catholic and they believed that murder was a mortal sin, which meant eternal damnation for the murderer. They weren't sure what it meant for people who drank beer and worked with the murderer, but they weren't about to take any chances with eternal damnation, or ED as they called it.

To avoid ED, they figured they needed to tell on José, so they immediately, and without saying a word, made a beeline for the winery. Once they got to the winery a major problem became evident: They spoke very little English (They only knew five English words: paycheck, pussy, stupid, American, and beer.) After about ten minutes of charades and one-word questions and answers, Tim and William thought it best to call Detective Knight and a translator.

When Detective Knight and the translator arrived, the two workers spit out everything that José had been bragging about so, a clear picture emerged.

Detective Knight then went to the vineyard shop to see if José was, by some chance, still there. He was. In fact, he couldn't go anywhere because he was passed-out on the floor. Detective Knight just moved all the empty alcohol containers out of the way, rolled him over, cuffed his hands behind his back while reading him his rights, dragged him over to his car, and managed to get him on the back seat.

As he drove José to the Sheriff's Office to put him in jail, David Knight just marveled at how easy his job had become, and it was getting even easier. David did not have to solve anything concerning this murder. He just answered the phone, drove to a winery, and was told "who done it." Even the arrest had been easy. There was no chase, no resistance, nothing. Just a passed-out vato lying on the floor. He supposed at this rate, the killer of Jim Jaushki would simply walk in to the Sheriff's Office and put himself in jail. *Wouldn't that be convenient.*

Chapter 31

Todd Is Tired of Toiling[119] at These Tasks

Todd was tired and hungry. It was 9:00 P.M. and a truck pulling a gondola filled with two tons of Cabernet Sauvignon grapes had just arrived. Todd, Roberto, and Brent (the American harvest intern) had been at the winery since eight o'clock that morning and the arrival of the gondola meant they had three to four more hours of work. The three of them climbed onto the grapes in the gondola and began feverishly pitching the grapes into the crusher with pitchforks.

The hydraulics on the system that the winery used to automtically transfer the grapes from the gondola to the crusher had broken down earlier that day and so the gondolas had to be emptied by hand, which was slow and a pain in the "you know where." After about an hour and a half, the gondola had been emptied and the grapes were in the process of being crushed and pumped into a stainless steel fermentation tank. After another hour, all the grapes *were* crushed, the tank *was* full, and all that remained was the clean-up.

Todd didn't mind doing the clean-up because all he did was walk around with a hose and spray everything in sight with water until it looked clean. He may have even enjoyed it had he not been at work for thirteen-plus hours.

While he was spraying the crush pad a long, black, Mercedes pulled up and two young guys wearing slick, fancy, dark suits

---

119   Work extremely hard or incessantly – then incessantly means: continuing without pause or interruption. It's also nice alliteration, eh?

got out. They approached Todd, because he was the nearest person, and asked him what was going on. Todd told them that they had just finished crushing for the day and were getting ready to go home.

"Well, we just spent the entire day driving up from LA and we saw all the lights from the highway, so we came in for a tour," said one of guys.

"Seriously? You thought we'd give you a tour now? It's after midnight for Christ's sake," said Todd in a highly exasperated tone of voice. These two numbskulls acted like the world revolved around them.

"Well, we *are* from and LA, and my buddy here," the guy said as he pointed to the other dude, "works in Hollywood and knows lots of people." He made quotation marks with his fingers as he said the word "people." He had an air of haughtiness about him and Todd was beguiled[120] by the dude's confidence, slick suit, and big, long, black Mercedes. He could picture these guys hobnobbing with celebrities, and famous movie directors. Todd's attitude towards the guy did a one-eighty.[121]

Todd had dreams of becoming a movie star, so he offered to give the two guys a tour. *Maybe they'll say something to someone in Hollywood and I'll become a movie star and get rich and famous. I'll meet and screw all kinds of famous, beautiful babes.* Todd, like José, had trouble with reality.

The tour lasted over an hour, partly because Todd was asked a lot of inane question, to which he gave long, vacuous answers, and partly because the two guys did not seem to be in

---

120   Charm or enchant someone, sometimes in a deceptive way.

121   That means his attitude was the exact opposite of what it had been: It turned one-hundred-and-eighty degrees, which is half-way around a circle or half of a complete rotation. This explanation is for all you graduates of the California Public School System.

any hurry for the tour to end and Todd wanted to please them. When the tour was finally over, the two guys said they would put in a good word for Todd around Hollywood by mentioning the winery and his excellent tour. They would recommend him and the winery at the next party they attended, which would undoubtedly include movie producers, directors, stars, and plenty of hot babes. They said if they heard of any oppurtunities for someone like him, they would certainly let him know. They were never heard from again.

The guys were not lying. They would indeed be attending a party in the near future that would have movie producers, directors, actors, etc. in attendance, but they would not be going as guests. These two guys were dishwashers for a catering company that catered a lot of parties for the Hollywood crowd. They were in their late twenties and still living at home, to boot. They had "borrowed" the car from the father of the guy who was doing the driving as he was out of the country on business.

After the tour, and quite a bit of wine drinking...er tasting, Todd managed to get home and be in bed by about 3:30 A.M. Four hours later Todd's alarm went off and he got up but could hardly keep his eyes open. His head throbbed and he was not happy; he certainly wasn't refreshed and ready for another day of crushing grapes. Fortunately, for a tired Todd, crushing grapes is extremely monotonous and does not require much in the way of complex, or even elementary thought. So, Todd figured he would be fine.

As soon as Todd got out of bed, he was dressed for work because he hadn't gotten undressed. He had been wearing the same clothes, including his underwear, for the last four days. They were grimy, getting a bit stiff, and did not smell too fresh. His shoes were wet, smelly, and sticky from all the grape juice, wine, and water he had managed to get on them. He had not showered either, because he was too tired when he got home to partake in that luxury.

Not surprisingly, he hadn't been eating too well. He had eaten nothing but donuts, burritos, pizza, and Hot Pockets for about a week. He had drank nothing but coffee, cola, beer, wine, and fermenting grape juice (which contains a lot of active yeast.) His digestive system was beginning to revolt as indicated by all of the liquid material Todd was expelling from his rectal region multiple times per day.

When Todd arrived for work on this particular day, he was told there had been a slight change in plans for the morning. A group of restaurateurs who featured Big Goose Cellars Wine on their wine lists was coming for a visit that afternoon because they wanted to see "the crush" and "the magic happen." William was determined to give these important customers the VIP treatment and so wanted the winery to look splendid. He wanted nothing out of place and everything spotless. So Todd, along with Roberto and Brent, spent the entire morning cleaning the cellar, the bottling room, the crush pad, and the tasting room. They even used the leaf blower to clear off the driveway, parking area, footpaths, and anywhere else that could be seen.

Then the grapes arrived. This made William extremely happy because the restaurateurs would get to see grapes actually being crushed and that was the Holy Grail of winery tours. It also induced VIP's to spend a lot money on wine and that thought gave good ol' William a wonderful woody...or a wicked woody depending on your point of view.

As soon as Todd, Roberto, and Brent started to empty the newly arrived grapes into the crusher with shovels and pitch forks (the hydraulics were still broken) the VIP restaurateurs arrived. William couldn't have been more pleased with their timing. He took them over to the crush pad and explained (sort of) what was going on. Todd also couldn't have been more pleased because he was getting a lot of attention, as he was the nearest worker to all the VIP's.

However, Todd's pleasure did not last long as he was peppered with fatuous[122] questions and a lot of the comments he overheard made him feel like a lower-class citizen. *Now I know how Roberto must feel a lot of the time.* Their comments made Todd feel bad, but their ignorance of wine and winemaking was astounding and that made him feel good because everyone likes to be around people that make them feel smart.

The restaurateurs continued watching the three workers process the grapes that were in the gondola, but they soon left with William so that he could show them all around his spotless winery. As they were leaving, Todd gave them the finger and then thrust his pelvis forward while grabbing his crotch, for that was the only way he knew to show his loathing for those overweight, rude, rich, sphincters as he was sorely lacking in imagination. Roberto and Brent saw his gestures and nearly fell over laughing.

This scene was repeated frequently in the following days and weeks, but with tourists, not restaurateurs. Todd was becoming extremely annoyed with the tourists, but unfortunately, it was tourist season and since Fiasco Valley's existence largely depends on tourists, they are encouraged to visit. When they visit, they are catered to by the local businesses almost to the point of ridiculousness.

---

122   silly and pointless

Chapter 32

A Permanent Cure
for Athlete's Foot

Detective Knight was sitting in front of his home computer surfing the web. He was supposed to be looking at a website, or websites, that gave information on any new technology available to detectives but he was just looking at free porn websites. He was shocked at how many there were and how easy it was to look at them. All he had to do was click a button that said "I am 18" and he was in like Flynn.[123]

After an hour or so, David got tired of looking at those type of websites and decided he should do some actual work. He had "solved" the murders of Frank Finnegan, Mark Madson, and Melvin but there was still Jim Jaushki. David didn't know where to start, so he consulted his notes, which were on his computer, and was reminded that it was possible that the killer had a blood type of AB-. *That's a rare blood type. Hmm, I wonder...*

Detective Knight picked-up his phone and called the local hospital. While waiting for the phone to be answered, David Knight remembered how he had been made a fool of because he had believed the probable killer's name was Iganacio Queso and that he was from Yukankysomiasso in Tamaulpias, Mexico. He was clenching his teeth and had the phone in a death grip by the time it was answered.

---

123   To be quickly and easily successful at some pursuit. Traditionally said to refer to classic film star, Errol Flynn, because he easily and regularly seduced women. It was pretty darn easy for him to have sex with (to get "in") any woman he chose.

"Uh yeah, this is Detective David Knight," he said as he tried to relax his jaw muscles, "and I was wondering if it would be possible for me to get the names of everyone you've treated in the last few days with AB- blood type."

"David? Is that you? It's me, Crissy." *Maybe he's calling to ask me out for dinner like he said he would. God, I hope so.*

"Oh hi Crissy. You're not in the Emergency Room anymore?"

"Well, not this week. We rotate once a week which keeps us from getting bored and keeps us sharp. Plus we, or at least I, get tired of looking at the same ol' people every day."

"Okay, well that's great, um, so is it possible for me to get a list of people who have been to the Emergency Room with AB- blood type?" inquired David.

"Anything is possible for you David," said Crissy as she batted her eyelashes, got a big smile on her face, and twirled her hair with a finger while she lovingly held the handset with her other hand. "I can get you a list of everyone we have on record with that blood type, there can't be too many." *Should I ask if he's investigating a crime?*

"Oh, just from the ER is fine. How long will that take?"

"Oh, I dunno. It may take a while to get in there," she answered. Crissy was referring to the fact that she would have to hack (she was a good hacker) into the hospital computer system to access those personal records. "Give me the rest of the day."

Three hours later, Detective Knight got a call on his cell phone, it was Crissy.

"Hi David. It was easier than I thought. Security here is not quite what I thought it would be and I've got your results. There are only two so that should make whatever you're doing easier...are you investigating a crime?"

"Great," said David as he ignored her question. "Give 'em to me."

"Well, the first person is Ignacio Queso. He just came in recently."

Detective Knight didn't bother telling Crissy that Ignacio Queso was not an actual person and that she had also been made a fool of.

Oh please, please ask me out...please she thought. But David of course, did not. Still, she persevered. "The second is a Mexican, at least I assume he's a Mexican, by the name of Vicente Gonzalez Vega."

Vega...Vega...Vega...Where have I heard that name? thought David. *Oh yeah, Vega Vineyard Management Company right near here. I wonder if this has anything to do with them. I doubt it.*

"...I really like their risotto," finished Crissy.

"Okay yeah, sure. That's great. Thanks a lot Crissy. I'll keep that in mind," responded David in a distracted, faraway voice as he hung-up the phone. Detective Knight hadn't heard a word that Crissy said after he had heard the name "Vega." The reason being: His thoughts were consumed with the Vega Vineyard Management Company and he remembered they were located just outside of Birchwood. David decided he would go over there and see what he could find out.

At Vega Vineyard Management, Detective Knight talked with Vicente Vega himself. That was good luck on David's part because Vicente Vega works long, hard hours and is normally out in a vineyard somewhere. As soon as David had introduced himself, Vicente Vega became noticeably edgy. He became even more so when Detective Knight said he had a few questions for him. *Hmm, why do you suppose Vinny here is so nervous? Maybe he does have something to do with this.* David began by asking Vicente why he had a number of bandages on his neck and face.

"Because I no good at shaving with razor blade," Vicente explained. "We no electricity in house the other morning so I shave with razor blade in dark. Cut myself much," Vicente said as he pointed to all the bandages on his face. Vicente, like all vineyard workers, arose before sunrise.

Vicente often wore a long sleeve shirt and pants to work, just as he was now, so David couldn't see if he had any cuts on his arms or legs. Cuts there could indicate a fight, or a struggle, because there was no likely reason for Vicente to be shaving his legs in the dark, or the light for that matter. Unless, of course, Vicente was just masquerading as a vineyard worker but was actually a pro-bicyclist preparing for the Tour de France. That might explain any cuts on his legs, but the arms? No. Looking at Vicente, David figured it was a pretty good bet that he was not riding in the Tour de France, because he didn't look like he could even do the Tour de Downtown Birchwood. Therefore, cuts on his legs or upper body may indicate some sort of brawl or struggle.

"Take off your shirt," demanded Detective Knight.

"What?" asked Vicente bewilderedly. "Why?"

"Because I want to see your arms and chest," stated Detective Knight firmly.

Is this guy gay? wondered Vicente as he yelled, "Hell no, muchacho!"

"Fine. Be that way. But...we know you have AB negative blood type, which is extremely rare, and a lot AB negative blood was found all over the tractor on which someone was murdered. Do you happen to know anything about that?" queried David.

"¿Qué? No entiendo?" ("What? I don't understand.") answered Vicente. David sighed and shook his head in frustration. *Okay yeah, sure. Now you don't understand English. Amazing how that happens at just the right time.* However, there wasn't much David could do about it, except either learn Spanish or get Officer Ruiz to translate. Detective Knight opted for the latter because the former would take too long, be way too much work, and besides, he didn't want to learn Spanish, or any foreign language for that matter.

Detective Knight got on his radio and said that Officer Ruiz was needed ASAP at Vega Vineyard Management Company to act as a translator. Officer Ruiz arrived within 15 minutes. He was familiar with the case and arrived eating a bag of nacho cheese flavored potato chips. He held his chips to Vincente and said, "Do you want some?" Detective Knight didn't know if Officer Ruiz was being an a-hole or just trying to be funny. Whichever it was, David thought it was pretty effective.

Vicente Vega got a terrified look on his face and replied, "I don't want," but he was thinking *Do they know? How could they know? There's no way in Hell they could know. They're just stupid crackers trying to scare me.* But, just in case they did know, he decided to play dumb because he believed that all Americans thought all Mexicans were stupid...so why disappoint?

"¿Qué pasa?" asked Vicente with a blank look on his face. "Who Jim Jaushki?"

Detective Knight turned toward Officer Ruiz and told him to tell Mr. Vega about the blood they found on the tractor that was parked over the hole that Jim Jaushki was found in. Then tell him that we need to see his arms and legs. Officer Ruiz did as he was told, and that's when Vicente figured the game was up and took off running out the back of the building and into the vineyard. Detective Knight and Officer Ruiz looked at each other with stunned expressions, and then ran out the back of the building after him, but he had disappeared.

Vicente was intimately familiar with the vineyards near his business and so quickly and easily ran between the vines and rows of vines because he knew not only where all the hoses for the irrigation system were located, but also where all the wires and posts for the trellis system were. Detective Knight and Oscar Ruiz on the other hand... They just started blindly running through the vineyard. They tripped over and got tangled up in irrigation hoses; they were almost beheaded by trellising wires on more than one occasion, and they even managed to knock over a couple of smudge pots.[124] At this point, the two were a couple of Merry-Andrew's[125] that would have made Laurel and Hardy proud...or jealous.

At he edge of the Vineyard are the train tracks for The Meritage Express, which is the sightseeing train that travels up and down Fiasco Valley. Vicente saw the train coming and scurried over to the tracks. His plan was to hop on the observation platform of the last car, ride the train for a few miles, and then jump off and disappear. Vicente had watched one to many Westerns with John Wayne, who was his male role model and hero.

124   A smudge pot – They are placed around the edges of a vineyard. The base is full of oil and when lit they give off heat to prevent frost, AKA "choofa" or "orchard heater" but...you can't beat "smudge pot."

125   A person who entertains others by means of comic antics; a clown.

However, when Vicente got a view of the observation platform, he saw that it was packed full of tourist holding iPhones so, he made a quick change of plans. He figured his best chance of escape now was to squeeze into the space between two train cars and just hang on. Vicente then found out, the hard way, that getting into the space between two cars while the train is moving is not exactly easy. He didn't quite get all the way into the space and he didn't quite hang on. What he did get was his feet chopped off by the train after he fell onto the tracks.

Detective Knight and Officer Ruiz also saw the train but didn't think much of it. The thought of hopping on a train to escape did not enter their consciousness, as they were more fans of the XXX movie variety. They had no idea where Vicente had gone, but just then, they heard a blood-curdling scream coming from the direction of the train.

They thought, and hoped, it was a damsel in some sort of distress, so they forgot all about Vicente and went towards the screaming. They were soon reminded of Vicente because he was the one screaming: "My feet! My feet are gone!" He sounded just like a woman (no offense to anyone) and Detective Knight and Officer Ruiz were profoundly disappointed that it was not a damsel in distress but a dude in despair.

They ran up to next Vicente, saw a lot of blood, heard a lot more screaming, and didn't see any shoes. Detective Knight and Officer Ruiz stepped aside, got together (they weren't to worried about Vicente going anywhere at the moment,) and tried to figure out what to do next. They decided they had to arrest him, but that it probably wasn't necessary to cuff him as he couldn't resist too fiercely and wasn't much of a flight risk.

Chapter 33

Truth Serum

Vicente Vega was taken to the Emergency Room of the local hospital, followed by Detective Knight and Officer Ruiz. They had plenty of questions for Vicente and weren't too concerned with the fact that he would never again need fast actin' Tinactin[126] as he had been thoroughly de-feet-ed by the train. However, Officer Ruiz and Detective Knight hadn't really thought their trip to the hospital through and once they arrived at the Emergency Room, there was nothing for them to do because Vicente Vega had been rushed into surgery to have as much repair as possible done to his de-feet-ed legs, and he would be in there for a while. They waited in the Emergency Room Waiting Room (What else would one do in a *waiting* room?) until they became so annoyed with Crissy fawning all over Detective Knight that they willingly went to the hospital cafeteria to raise their cholesterol level's.

After they had been in the cafeteria for what seemed like a millennium and eaten enough hospital food to raise each of their cholesterol level's at least 200 points, they returned to the ER waiting room only to hear someone screaming, "¡Necesito más morfina! ¡Ahora mismo! ¡Necesito más morfina! ¡Ahora mismo!"

"Who the hell is that and what are they saying?" asked Detective Knight.

"It sure sounds like Vicente," said Officer Ruiz, "and he is saying that he needs more morphine right now."

"Well, then he must be out of surgery. Let's go see him."

---

126   Over the counter athlete's foot medication.

227

Detective Knight and Officer Ruiz walked down the hallway and barged into Vicente Vega's room with guns drawn and dire looks on their faces as they displayed their badges. They then proceeded to herd the doctors out of the room and, once they were alone, took up positions on either side of Vicente as he lay in the hospital bed. Officer Ruiz made small talk with Vicente to distract him from what Detective Knight was doing.

Detective Knight was administering the contents of a small vial he had extracted from his pants pocket into the IV attached to Vicente's arm. He then motioned Officer Ruiz to join him out in the hallway.

"Now Oscar, you didn't see me do that, right?"

"Do what?" answered Officer Oscar Ruiz with a knowing smile on his face.

"Right. Exactly," responded Detective Knight.

"Now David, what exactly didn't I see you do? Poison the little beaner?" asked Officer Ruiz just to make sure he and David were on the same page.

"Aww nah, come on, gimmee a break. I didn't poison him. Who do you think I am?" asked Detective Knight. He then looked up and down the hallway, leaned in close to Officer Ruiz and whispered, "I gave him some sodium pentothal."

"Truth serum?" asked Officer Ruiz in a surprised voice. "Come on, that stuff doesn't work. It's a bunch of hokum or hogwash as you Yanks like to say."

"Wanna bet?" answered David forcefully. "Good ol' Vicente will be singing like a canary when we go back in there."

"Really? Sing like a canary?" asked Officer Ruiz while trying not to laugh. "How is a beaner with no feet going to sing like a canary?"

"Well, he won't actually *sing* like a canary, but he *will* talk a lot. It's just a figure of speech that you beaners have obviously never heard," answered David.

"Nope, never have," agreed Officer Ruiz sarcastically. "Of course, we 'Beaners' aren't as cultured, well read, or intelligent as you gringos are. We're just simple folk."

Detective Knight chuckled and then the pair went back into Vicente's room and began asking him questions. Vicente did sing like a canary, but it wasn't the right song. He "sang" (in Spanish) all about his boyhood, how wonderful his mother was, how she made great Gorditas,[127] and how his father had left them when he was a young boy. He then said that he had come to The United States because there was work and opportunity. He had gotten a job and eventually started his own company.

Unfortunately, none of this answered any question that could be of any help to Detective Knight. He thought the information was all very interesting, but useless, and didn't care if it was true. He was beginning to think that "Truth Serum" was a misnomer for Sodium Pentothal and it should be called "Awful Singing Serum."

To try and avoid the embarrassment of the "Truth Serum" not working, Detective Knight increased the dosage. It wasn't long before Vicente was singing like a Red-eyed Vireo.[128] The "song" he sang told how his company had not been doing so well lately because Zeebadul Vineyard Management Co. was taking away a lot of his business. It told how Jim Jaushki used to work for him, but quit to go to work for Zeebadul (they offered

127   A gordita is a small cake stuffed with cheese, meat, or other fillings.
128   A Red-eyed Vireo sings more than 20,000 songs a day. There are 86,400 seconds in a day, so that is 4.32 seconds per song. I have no idea what constitutes a "song," but if you don't like a song, it will be over soon. I wish most songs on the radio were that short.

him benefits) and that was a big blow to Vicente's business because Jim was his only worker that spoke English. He was therefore, requested by a lot of vineyard owners; all of whom were of course, rich, evil, racist Republicans.

The vineyards owned by these rich, evil, racist Republicans were, for the most part, exceedingly large and required a lot of work, so Jim was always busy. This kept Vicente happy because it meant a lot of steady contracts for him and *that* meant more money for Budweiser and to be sent home to his family in Mexico.

Now that there was no Jim, there were significantly fewer contracts, and *that* meant there was little money to buy Budweiser, or even Lucky Lager, and absolutely no money to be sent to his family in Mexico. Because of that, Vicente was no longer happy and it was all Jim's fault. Therefore, Vicente thought, Jim must die. Vicente's thought processes also left a lot to be desired.

Now that Vicente was singing so freely, he sang another song. This song told the story of how he had "Put the dumb gringo in a hole and drove a tractor on his head," or as Vicente actually sang, "Poner al gringo tonto en un agujero y condujo un tractor en la cabeza."

At first Detective Knight was relieved that Vicente had confessed to killing Jim; his job continued to be easy. However, the longer Detective Knight thought about his confession, the less relieved and more upset he became. All these criminals were just confessing to their murders and that was not liable to be the subject of a hit movie. David's "Red Carpet Fantasy" was disappearing before his very eyes or, more accurately, disappearing around his very ears and he was not happy.

Officer Ruiz left the room, went and found a hospital

administrator and informed him (or her—in case you are one of those militant people regarding gender equality) that the patient, Vicente Vega, was under arrest for murder and that there would be a police officer posted outside his door; not because he was a flight risk, but because it was standard procedure. The police were not at all concerned about Vicente Vega being a danger to the other patients as he had no feet and so wasn't likely to be prancing around the hospital killing people.

Deaths Cinco, Seis, Siete, and Ocho

Chapter 34

Tourist Tag

The harvest was winding down, so Laurent LaFlamer was splitting time between working in the cellar and the tasting room of Supercilious[129] Cellars, which is located just outside of Birchwood. He worked Tuesday, Wednesday, and Thursday in the cellar doing harvest jobs, and then Friday, Saturday, and Sunday in the tasting room pouring wine. He did take Monday off which was one day off more per week than he had been taking. *Is it even legal to work seven days per week?* He had to work six days per week because Birchwood requires more than a "harvest income" to live in, as the towns main goal is to allow people to flaunt their wealth.

His father had sent Laurent to Fiasco Valley to work the harvest in an American winery as part of a punishment/ motivational program he had concocted. His father, who was the owner/winemaker of Château Bonheur[130] in Southern France, had recently "come out of the closet" and ever since that day, Laurent had been a troublemaker and scandalmonger.[131] Out of desperation, his father had shipped him off to California to work...and get rid of him for a while.

His father chose California because A) It has many wineries and B) It is a very progressive, tolerant (as long as you don't have conservative views and just simply agree with everyone else,)

---

129   Behaving or looking as though one thinks one is superior to others. The town has a supercilious citizenry.

130   Pronounced BONE-uhr—the French word for happiness.

131   A person who stirs up public outrage toward someone or their actions by spreading rumors or malicious gossip.

and sexually liberal state. His father hoped Laurent would learn tolerance, understanding, and love for *all* people: homosexual, bisexual, heterosexual, omnisexual,[132] or whatever "sexual" they might be. The hope was, he would get over his homophobia[133] and accept his father for who he was. But, more practically, he wanted Laurent to learn how to make wine, get a taste of the wine business, learn to love wine, and therefore want, and be able, to take over Château Bonheur one day.

Laurent enjoyed working in the cellar at Supercilious Cellars, but the tasting room was beginning to get on his nerves. Well, it wasn't the tasting room per se; it was the tourists *in* the tasting room. Laurent could not get over how conceited, pompous, condescending, stupid, and patronizing they all were. He was tired of answering their inane questions while pretending they were good and insightful. He was even more sick and tired of keeping a smile on his face and pretending to be interested in whatever they were saying. Acting like that did tend to sell more wine, but it was driving him batty.

The tourists that came into the tasting room late that afternoon were the last straw. It was a group of four (two couples) and it was obvious the men were tying to impress the women. They were acting like they knew a great deal about wine and they were being quit loud and obnoxious. The final straw was pulled when one of the men asked Laurent what percentage of the wine was Cabernet and what percentage was Sauvignon?

---

132   A person who will have sex anything that moves. If it doesn't move, they will give it a push.

133   Dislike, fear, hatred, and/or disapproval of homosexuality, often for religious reasons or because of insecurity about one's own sexual orientation. Laurent had recently been having erotic dreams starring a very naked Albert Einstein because he thought Einstein's famous formula ($E = mc2$) was: He = I'm so hard.

As soon as he was asked that question, Laurent LaFlamer found himself thinking of his only hobby: hunting. Laurent was an avid wild boar and red deer hunter back home in France and he wanted to try hunting black-tail deer in California.

Laurent thought about this because he suddenly had the urge to buy a couple of tourist tags and do some tourist hunting. It was still tourist season in Fiasco Valley after all, and here were some tourists that were probably in the right zone. The only drawback Laurent could see was that it wouldn't be much of a sport because the "wild game" he would be hunting was totally out of shape, a bit tipsy, and not too bright.

Laurent had planned on partaking in his hunting hobby while in California by going after those black-tail deer. However, it was looking as though the U.S. and California governments weren't going to let him. Unless, of course, he took some sort of class, passed some sort of test, purchased a license, purchased tags, and then somehow got a rifle. He also needed to get bullets because a rifle, or any gun for that matter, is rather useless for killing...anything without bullets. With no bullets, you need to get close enough to whatever you're trying kill to clobber it over the head with your gun and Laurent didn't think he could get that close to a deer.

Thanks to some messed-up kids in Colorado, some nutty Muslims, and some dudes in Boston, it was rather difficult to buy any firearm these days. Even if he did manage to get a weapon, ammunition, and all the required documentation, he still had to find a place to hunt, which apparently was no small task. It all seemed like too much hassle for Laurent. After all, he was French and he shouldn't have to follow these silly American rules.

Amazingly enough, Laurent had recently met a guy who

worked at another winery near Birchwood. That guy knew a guy whose brother had a buddy who knew a guy that had a friend who needed money and so was selling his rifle. Laurent managed to contact the guy and buy the rifle. It was a .30-06 and came with some bullets. Now, if he could just find some land to go hunting on...

On the first Monday after Laurent bought the rifle, he got into his rented SUV and drove around Elviño County looking for a good spot to hunt. Every time Laurent came to an area that looked like an ideal place for black-tail deer to live, it was all fenced and gated, and there were plenty of "Private Property" and "No Trepassing" signs.

Laurent was well aware that in Elviño County there was a good chance the property belonged to a very wealthy American (of course, he thought *all* Americans were wealthy) and he figured there was probably a surveillance system, security guards, someone on patrol, or something that would end-up catching him on the property. If even some of the stories he had heard were true, he might get shot and he certainly didn't want that. Laurent's mantra was: "Americans are quick to shoot and slow to understand," and it was reinforced nearly every time he watched the evening news.

Finally, towards the evening, Laurent gave up and went to the one spot where he had often seen red-neck hunters getting in or out of their Chevy pick-up trucks. Laurent was torn; he was French and didn't want to be anywhere near any of those red-neck American hunters who were probably just quaffing crummy American beer and shooting who-knows-what with their guns. But he *really* wanted to go hunting and here was the only place that it seemed possible.

But try as he might, Laurent couldn't do it. He couldn't

swallow his French pride and put himself on the same hill to do the same thing as those American pigs. He would have to get his hunting fix some other way. So, he drove his rented SUV back to his studio apartment because he had to work tomorrow, as well as return the SUV. Laurent's first attempt at hunting been a complete failure; well that is not entirely true. He did learn that there was no place to hunt in Fiasco Valley unless he wanted to be around a bunch of American rednecks drinking American made swill.

The only solace he had was that he worked in the cellar tomorrow and so wouldn't have to deal with the seemingly infinite number of pretentious American tourists that came into the tasting room.

Chapter 35

A Hunting He Will Go

Laurent was not a happy camper when he arrived for work on Tuesday morning. He hadn't gotten his hunting fix and he was again beginning to feel the onset of the hunting DT's,[134] which was not something he wanted. Laurent was standing in a dark corner at the back of the cellar looking for a hose clamp when he heard people talking. He couldn't hear much, but he did hear a couple of jejune[135] questions and comments regarding wine. Laurent snapped. He couldn't take it anymore. Their ignorance was mind-boggling. Americans were complete idiots but they thought they were superior to everyone else on the planet, when everyone knew it was the French who held that distinction.

At that moment a light bulb, albeit a small, dim, one turned-on in Laurent's head. So, he made his way, surreptitiously, out to his pink Bugatti Veyron 16.4 (which his gay father had bought for him) and retrieved his .30-06 rifle from the passenger seat. He then snuck back into the cellar, planning the entire way.

What he planned to do was "hunt" the tourists. It wasn't much of a plan but Laurent wasn't much of a planner; he just did whatever happened to strike his fancy at the moment. He would track this "wild game" by sneaking around the winery, hiding behind barrels, under tanks, behind bottling equipment, or anyplace he could to avoid being noticed so as not to spook the "wild game." When he was afforded a good shot, he would

---

134   Stands for Delirium Tremors which is a withdrawal symptom of many drugs. Especially morphine based drugs. Laurent needed to hunt...something.

135   Naive, simplistic, and superficial.

take it, just as though he was hunting black-tail deer.

He did have one restriction however, and that was he had to shoot the "wild game" when the tour guide was far enough away so that he couldn't possibly shoot her. The reason being: She was an extremely attractive, recently divorced, "mature" woman with an incredible body, who was receiving large alimony payments. Laurent just wanted to...use your imagination here. However, this plan seemed a little too complex, tricky, and time-consuming for Laurent. So, he said to himself, "Aww, the hell with it, I'll just find a good spot, be careful, try to be quiet, and hopefully she won't notice me or get in the way."

Once he was back in the cellar, Laurent did find a spot amongst the barrel stacks, hoses, forklifts, and everything else cluttering-up the cellar that was well hidden but would afford a good view of the people on the tour. He would have an unobstructed view of the tourists but they wouldn't be able to see him. Then, to make the spot even better, a nearby door led outside and onto the wooded hill that was directly behind the winery so Laurent figured he would easily be able to disappear.

Laurent situated himself comfortably and waited for his tourists to appear. He didn't have to wait long. The attractive tour guide (Laurent couldn't remember her name) came into view but was left alone because he had other "plans" for that mademoiselle. Then came the tourists, or "wild game" as Laurent had been referring to them ever since his ill-fated hunting trip.

He took a deep breath, tried to relax, raised his rifle, aimed at the first head, and shot. He quickly re-loaded and shot at the head of the second tourist. He then repeated the procedure with the third tourist. This wasn't really hunting, but it was all he could get in this godforsaken country, so it would have to do.

Actually, that did not happen; it was just Laurent fantasizing as he lay in bed unable to fall asleep one night. Chances are, Laurent could never shoot anyone in the head because he was such a poor shot. He would most likely miss if he tried to shoot himself in the head (either the small one or the large one) let alone someone else's.

What *did* happen was that when Laurent arrived for work on the Tuesday morning after his ill-fated hunting trip, he was told he had to work in the tasting room as the person scheduled to work had been arrested and thrown in jail for yet another DUI. So, Laurent dejectedly went to the tasting room and began mentally preparing himself for the hordes of tourists that would undoubtedly come for a visit and a tour.

No hordes of tourists came, just four. But those four were enough to convince Laurent to somehow make his fantasy a reality. He was still having bouts of the hunting DT's, he *did* have his .30-06 rifle on the back seat of his Bugatti, and he was disgusted and fed-up with these idiotic Americans. On a whim, during his afternoon break, Laurent went out to his car, retrieved his rifle, and hid it in the tasting room.

Late that afternoon, as Laurent was preparing to leave, another group of tourist's arrived in an SUV and demanded a tasting and a tour. Laurent was about to rebuff them when he saw his rifle and remembered his fantasy. *Maybe now I'll make my fantasy a reality. That'd be peachy.* He thought all this in French, of course.

"D' accord," said Laurent. "We tour first and then taste?"

The group agreed and off they went. Laurent knew these tourists would not live, but he wasn't quit sure how to make them dead.

All during the tour, Laurent was thinking of how to dispatch the tourists. He couldn't think of anything and so convinced himself that his fantasy had actually been a set of instructions, from some Higher Authority, on how to rid the world of tourists who were not French.

Following his divine instructions, Laurent steered the tourist's to the spot in the winery that was the scene of his fantasy. Once the tourists were in the proper spot, Laurent excused himself by saying he had a special treat for them.

"I go see if it ready. Don't move until I back," and with that, Laurent left the tourists in order to prepare himself to fulfill his fantasy. As soon as Laurent was out of sight, he sprinted to the tasting room, retrieved his rifle and some bullets, and made his way back to his fantastical spot.

There they were. He could see them well. Those idiotic American tourists that Laurent would put out of the misery that they *must* be in because...they weren't French. Laurent got comfortable, steadied the rifle against his shoulder, aimed, and fired.

"Aww foock!" exclaimed Laurent. He couldn't believe he had missed. He quickly re-loaded and fired again. He missed again. *Well, third times a charm.* Laurent re-loaded, aimed and fired once more. He missed a tourist, but he did hit a stainless steel tank full of wine...for the third straight time. His targets did not know what was going on. All they knew was that whenever they heard what sounded like a gunshot, a steady stream of wonderful smelling liquid would start shooting out of a small hole in one of the tanks. They rightly assumed the liquid was wine, so they began gulping it down as fast as they could. Laurent had hit three separate tanks, so there was plenty of wine flowing for all of the gulping that the tourists could possibly do.

Laurent just stood in his spot totally perplexed as to how he could have missed the "wild game" three times in a row. He was ashamed, while at the same time stupefied as to how those people could be guzzling so much of that swill they called wine.

After what seemed like an eternity, but was just enough time for the tourists to become blotto, Laurent came to his senses and ran through the nearby doorway that led to the wooded hill directly behind the winery. While running up the wooded hill, he tried to figure out how he could have possibly missed what he was aiming at three times straight. He was French, after all, and that shouldn't happen. He decided the problem must lie with this American made rifle that he had bought from that dude; it was the only conceivable explanation. *If only I had my MAS-49 rifle, those American tourists would all be dead and I'd be running up this hill with the tour guide.* Laurent also had trouble with reality.

Laurent had adrenaline coursing through his veins in incredible amounts at an incredible speed and so was able to run up the wooded hill, reach the top, and run down the other side without even slowing down. He would have kept going but he came upon another winery, which happened to be Pebble Hill Vineyards. He stopped running and hid behind a tree where he had a good view of the winery. As he caught his breath and rested, he saw a limousine pull up and a few people get out.

Oh boy, more game. Laurent thought it must be his lucky day, and was now doubly sure his dream had been a set of instructions from a Higher Being. He cocked his rifle, brought it to bear, aimed at the people who had just gotten out of the limo, and shot at each one sequentially. Miraculously, he hit

244

two of the six tourists that had piled out. Well, "hit" is a strong word; he barely *grazed* them. After he shot, Laurent didn't stick around to admire his work. He ran out from behind the tree and back up the hill, all the while gleefully assuming he had permanently ended those cocky, American tourists lives.

Laurent didn't stop running until he was over the top of the hill and could see Supercilious Cellars again. At the winery, there were a lot of vehicles with flashing lights and people running about. Laurent hid his rifle in some bushes and casually walked down to the winery.

"What go on?" Laurent asked with a thick French accent as he watched bodies that were covered with white sheets being hurriedly shoved into waiting ambulances. *Wow! I thought I had missed but I guess I did kill those American idiots.*

"It seems some tourists got into your wine and drank a bit to much," said the EMT who was nearest to him.

What? Drank too much? I couldn't have missed, could I? I'm French.

"That's impossible," stated Laurent quietly in French and a voice that was bereft of any emotion because he didn't really give a piece of fecal matter how they had died, just as long as they were dead.

He then asked, in English with his thick French accent, where and how the tourists had gotten so much wine to drink. He was told that there were three tanks with holes in them (no one knew how they had gotten there) and the tourists had tried to drink all the wine that was shooting out. They had gotten so tanked that they passed-out, fell face down on the cellar floor, and then drowned in all wine that had pooled there because it couldn't flow out of the cellar, as all the drains were clogged with spooge. Now, the tourons were being taken to the morgue.

After Laurent was told what a morgue was, he could barely contain his delight, but he realized that he needed to so as not to let on how thrilled he was that the planet contained a few less American tourons. Laurent now knew he had finally been successful...at something and that made him feel good.

"Where the hell have you been?" yelled the winemaker as he approached Laurent as soon as he saw him. "The four people you took on the tour are all dead. Why weren't you there? What the hell happened?"

Laurent replied in his thick French accent, "I had excuse myself and go on hill and throw-up. Then I run for the bathroom because I had uh...how you say...diarrhea? I sick." *Probably from all the American crap I've had to eat.* I sorry I become sick."

The winemaker gave Laurent a long, hard, cold stare, but then relaxed and said, "Well, they died happy anyway. At least they sure shoulda been happy, they drank enough of our Cab. But if you had been here, you coulda saved their lives. You woulda been a hero and chics dig heroes." *Even though everyone is a Goddamn hero nowadays.*

Oh yeah thought Laurent *that would have been great. Bummer. I really missed out there.* Laurent did not want to be a hero to any American chics; they repulsed him. He thought all American women were grossly overweight from pure laziness and/or over-eating, or too skinny because of under-eating and and/or an obsession with exercising.

Laurent had lost count the number of times he had seen grossly obese women wearing extremely tight and revealing clothes. Just the sight of them made him want to puke. He had seen women on beaches who had rolls of fat so large that you could not see their bikini bottoms. The fact that they were in bikinis to begin with made him wonder about

246

their mental capacity.

He had also seen countless women who were so skinny they looked as though they would break if you had sex with them. They were so thin, that he swore he could see through a couple of them. They had no figure whatsoever and looked like they belonged in a fagot.[136]

They had no fashion sense either. On more than one occasion, he had gone to dinner and seen American women wearing sweatpants with something written across the butt, and their butt was so large that an entire comedy by Molière[137] could have been written across it. They would waddle over to their table, plunk down, and shovel food into their mouths at an alarming rate.

To top it all off, American women were so staggeringly stupid that Laurent would rather shoot himself than listen to them talk for more than five minutes. He had talked to a couple of women at the local cantina one night, and swore he was dumber as a result.

---

136   Bundle of sticks for firewood. It's different than "faggot" which is a derogatory term for homosexual men. It takes two to tango, so a "faggot" with 2 "g's" is the one meaning homosexual men; that's how I remember.

137   French playwright and actor who is considered to be one of the greatest masters of comedy in Western literature. January 15, 1622–February 17, 1673.

Death Número Nueve

Chapter 36

Tourist Season

Laurent broke away from all the pother at Supercilious Cellars, retrieved his rifle, got in his Bugatti Veyron 16.4, and drove back to his apartment in the low-income housing complex near the edge of Birchwood. Even though he drove a Bugatti, his car did not stand out in the housing complex parking lot, it fit right in...except for the color. Laurent wondered what the hell the American definition of "low-income" was because it sure as hell wasn't his.

He parked next to a four-door, black Mercedes with tinted windows, and went into his apartment for some rest and relaxation and to bask in the glow of a job well done. Problem was: His joie de vivre, or joy of living, was so intense now that he couldn't sit still. He was so pumped-up on adrenaline and so thrilled that he had killed some stupid American tourists that he had to do something...anything. He decided to do more hunting, but he would do it "right" from now on.

He *could* actually hunt properly now (not just on a whim at the spur of the moment in a wine cellar) because of the custom-made hunting license and tags that he now possessed. He had known for a while that he would need a hunting license to go hunting and a tag for each of his kills, and he had tried to follow all of the laws and procure those legally, but it had been such a bureaucratic nightmare that he just gave up and decided he would just make his own. To that end, he had gone to the local public library, gone on-line, and managed to find a picture of, and some information on, a California Hunting License and a

251

black-tail deer tag. He then used all the resources available in the library to make himself a California hunting license and some deer tags...with some minor alterations.

By the time he left the public library, Laurent had a custom made "Touron Hunting License," a handful of custom made "Touron Tags," and he was ready to have some fun; not only by ridding the world of some stupid American tourists, but also by "stickin' it to the man."[138]

For the next couple of months Laurent worked at Supercilious Cellars during the week, but on weekends, he would hunt tourons in the valley. "Hunt" is the key word because the only things he managed to kill were the two opossums he ran over with his pink Bugatti.

Aside from being an incredibly poor shot, every time Laurent got a touron in his gun sights anyone who saw him would know that he hadn't forgotten to take his Cialis or whatever Erectile Dysfunction medication he was on; hunting excited him that much. It's hard to take a slow, deep breath, relax, remain calm, and shoot straight when you're excited enough to pitch a tent,[139] even if it is a rather small tent.

Despite this, Laurent did manage to shoot one rather large female touron in a winery parking lot. After she had been shot, she tried to run but fell over and ended-up lying face down on the pavement. Laurent assumed he had his first kill and so went to her in order to attach his "Touron Tag." To his dismay, however, she was not dead; she had just fallen and couldn't get up. Still, he hurriedly stuck his "Touron Tag" to

---

138   He wasn't going to follow the law and buy a license or tag from the government.

139   "Pitch a tent" – get an erection, a boner, a hard-on, a chubby, the list goes on and on.

the back of her head because he was very optimistic that she would die sooner or later. He then ran and hid in some bushes until the coast was clear.

It turned out that this touron was so well-upholstered[140] that the bullet had been unable to penetrate anything vital; it just became lodged in the copious amounts of blubber the woman possessed. The touron did not even realize she had been shot, she thought a bee had stung her and so freaked-out because she was allergic to bees. She turned and started to waddle back to her car as fast as she could but tripped, fell, and couldn't get up. She couldn't even roll over because she was so large. She just lay face-down, struggling to move, and moaning until she became so weak from lack of nourishment (which only took a couple of minutes) that she shut-up and quit even trying to move; all in an effort to conserve what little energy she had left.

She lay there motionless for a few more minutes until a tour bus full of tourons arrived and found her blocking their reserved parking spot. The bus driver got out, dragged her into the shade, propped her against a tree, gave her some bottled water, and then parked his bus to let the tourists disembark.

Laurent observed all this from his hiding spot in the bushes and became increasingly upset as he watched his first "kill" sitting comfortably in the shade and drinking a bottle of Evian[141] mineral water. He did have a slight snigger, however, as he watched the touron struggle to get up and start waddling back to her car with the "Touron Tag" still stuck to the back of her head.

Laurent's snigger, however, quickly turned to perturbation when he realized that his signature and personal information

---

140   She was...uh...just a tad overweight.
141   Is anyone else troubled by the fact that Evian is "naive" spelled backwords?

were on the "Touron Tag." He jumped out of his hiding spot, sprinted past the woman, and yanked the tag off the back of her head. He never slowed down. He kept sprinting until he was in the middle of some vineyard and all he could see around him were grapevines. He stayed there for a few minutes (it seemed like about five hours) and then carefully made his way back to where he had left his car.

Chapter 37

Burning Vines

Todd awakened after having dozed off on the couch while watching...he couldn't even remember what. He looked out the window, and became sick to his stomach. For there was a haze so thick that the sun looked to be a fiery reddish-orange circle and the visibility was about one-eighth of a mile, at most. He hadn't seen a haze so thick and the sun that color since that weekend he had spent in LA.

He opened the door to go outside and was greeted with the smell of smoke that was somewhat pleasant, but quite strong and couldn't possibly do anything but be the fountainhead[142] of his lung cancer, were he to get it. Every second Todd spent in this smoky haze just made him more furious. *What he hell is causing this? Whatever, or whoever, is doing it must be stopped.* He pulled his t-shirt up over his nose, stalked out of the apartment complex, and went down the street a couple of blocks where he saw the source of the haze. What used to be a large, beautiful vineyard was now just a dirt field, in the middle of which were three large piles of burning grapevines belching enormous amounts of smoke. Todd was stupefied by what he saw and just kept walking. He saw four more large, dirt fields that used to be vineyards but now just had piles of burning, dead grapevines in them.

Todd stopped walking, stood there with his eyes wide-open, mouth agape, and just stared all around. All he could see were big, dark, burning piles that were emitting slow, but

---

142 An original source of something.

certain death. It seemed the whole valley was on fire and all picturesque views of this lovely valley, not to mention the air quality, were being destroyed. He was not only dumbfounded, but furious. *What the hell is going on? What are these people doing? Are they idiots? Haven't they ever heard of air pollution? Apparently not.*

Todd began walking towards the next ex-vineyard he could see. He was going to get to the bottom of this and make someone pay. After a few minutes of walking, he encountered a couple of Mexican dudes sitting in their truck that was parked alongside one of the ex-vineyards.

"What the hell is going on?" asked Todd. "Don't you people know about air pollution?"

The Mexican dudes turned slowly to look at Todd, then at each other, and one of them said, "We burn vines."

"Who told you to burn them, and why? Where the hell are they? I want to talk to them right now because this is total bullshit!" screamed Todd as little gobs of spit were discharged from his mouth and he flailed his arms about.

All during Todd's polemic,[143] the two vatos just sat in their truck drinking coffee from a thermos and looking rather amused at the whole situation. Then they both pointed towards the house down the road and said, "Mister Vabelli tell us. He there now."

Todd didn't say a word. He just started to briskly walk down the road towards the house and Mr. Vabelli. Once he arrived at the house, he sought Mr. Vabelli and found him in the garage petting a dog.

"Are you Mister Vabelli?" asked Todd in an accusatory tone of voice.

---

143   A strong verbal or written attack on someone or something.

"Yes, that's me," replied Tony Vabelli with a mild Italian accent. "And you are...?"

"What the hell are you doing burning all these grapevines?" asked Todd loudly as he approached Tony and ignored his question.

"Relax, paisano. We have burn them. They have *phylloxera* and that's all can be done," answered Tony Vabelli calmly.

"But you're totally polluting the air," countered Todd. "I mean that's terrible. Everyone will breathe it, it stinks, and you can barely see your hand in front of your face. We will all get lung cancer and die." Todd was exaggerating a wee bit, as he was prone to do.

"Aww come on," said Tony, "it not that bad and it go away after a bit. Most people say it smell good."

Todd stared at Tony and Tony stared right back. Todd realized this conversation was going nowhere, so he just gave Tony a condescending look, turned around, and began walking back to his apartment; feeling as though he was much more intelligent and superior to this wop[144] in every possible way. People like him had to be taken care of so, Todd formulated a plan to do that on his smoky trek back home. Once he arrived home, Todd began implementing his plan.

---

144   A racist term used towards Italians. Comes from the Neapolitan (Italian dialect in Southern Italy) word "guappo" (pronounced Wah-Po) meaning thug, bully, braggart.

eLiberals

The first step in his plan to eliminate ignorant, old polluters was to get in his Audi R8 and hightail it to Verkapely, California, which was about an hour and a half away and the site of a major California university. Not surprisingly, the town was full of environmentalist liberals (referred to as eLiberals henceforth in this book) who wanted nothing more than to protest anything and everything people did that *they* deemed harmful to the planet and/or made money that wasn't given to, or at least shared with, them.

Once he arrived in Verkapely, Todd parked his Audi in an out of the way spot because he didn't want to be seen in an expensive sports car, as that would brand him as an evil Republican. He then found a public restroom gave himself a slovenly appearance by tousling his hair and disheveling his clothes. He was now ready for the next step in implementing his plan.

He walked through Verkapely and went into every café he came across, which was quite a few. In each café, there was at least one table with people sitting around it that looked more slovenly than he did. He would head straight for that table and introduce himself. After all the niceties, Todd would say he hated rich people, that all rich people were Republicans, the only thing rich people cared about was money, and they would pollute and destroy Mother Earth in order to make a quick buck. He was instantly accepted at each table and asked if he would like to join them. He always said, "Yes" and would sit down and proceed to tell everyone about what was happening in Birchwood.

When everyone sitting at the table learned of the grapevine-burning environmental travesty, they became incensed and were determined to put an end to it. They figured it had to be a bunch of evil Republican capitalists trying to make themselves richer by destroying Mother Earth and they must be stopped. By the end of the day, Todd had thirty-four college eLiberals so worked-up into a "hate ignorant, rich, white, racist, Republican Americans" frenzy, that they agreed to come to Fiasco Valley the very next day and put a stop to the happenings in the ostentatious[145] town.

The next morning six VW Busses, each spewing copious amounts of black exhaust smoke (they were causing as much, if not more, air pollution than the burnings they were going to protest) pulled into the Birchwood Safeway parking lot after having followed the map Todd had drawn for them the previous day. All of the thirty-four "well-educated" college eLiberals piled out of their particular VW Bus and found Todd waiting for them. His car was nowhere in sight.

Fortunately, as far as Todd was concerned, the valley was still enveloped in a thick, smoky, haze and there was still the strange, albeit somewhat pleasant, odor.

"See?" asked Todd. "Didn't I tell you? This is awful and it was even worse yesterday. You can hardly see the hills and it's hard to breathe this shit. We've got to do something!" Todd, who had put himself in charge, jumped behind the wheel of the lead van, which was still running and spewing exhaust, and shouted, "Here, follow me! I'll show you what's causing this disaster!"

---

145 Characterized by vulgar or pretentious display; designed to impress or attract notice.

With that, everyone piled back into a VW Bus, none of which had been shut down, and followed Todd to the first ex-vineyard he had seen yesterday. The huge piles of burning grapevines were now just smoldering piles of ashes but were still producing enough smoke to get all the eLiberals dander up.[146] But Todd wanted it to go higher, so he herded all the slovenly, Verkapely eLiberals back into the VW Busses, which were *still* running and spewing exhaust, and led them towards another large plume of smoke rising into the sky.

As they drove towards the next plume of smoke, Todd realized they were headed right for Vine Cliff Vineyard and, before long, he saw see that Vine Cliff Vineyard was where the smoke was originating. The protesters suddenly let out a shriek and all the VW Busses began honking their horns. Not because of the smoke, but because just across the road from the now dirt field with the burning piles of grapevines, was some heavy operating equipment that was being used to clear land for they knew not what.

There was a large mulcher, a tree saw, a bulldozer, a tractor with a root grapple attachment, a tractor with a brush cutting attachment, and guys with chainsaws. The busses screeched to a halt, (but were kept running and therefore, spewing exhaust) the eLiberals jumped out, and ran towards a guy wearing a suit and a hard-hat who looked to be in charge. Todd got right in his face and demanded to see his, and everyone else's, Erosion Control Certification, or CPESC.[147]

---

146 "Dander up" – become agitated or angry. When anyone asks me, "What's up?" I always answer, "My dander." I've gotten some rather amusing looks.

147 Certified Professional in Erosion and Sediment Control (CPESC) is a qualification indicating the holder has educational training, expertise, and experience in controlling erosion and sedimentation, and has met certification standards – Todd couldn't care less if the guy had a CPESC. He was just trying to impress a cute eLiberal chic.

The guy in charge gave Todd, and all the other Verkapely eLiberals, a contemptuous glance, shook his head while ignoring them, and then said something into his hand-held radio. This raised the dander level of the protesters even higher and they vowed to be heard and to put a stop to this. The only way they knew how to stop these types of evil folks from doing these evil things was to go live in the trees that were to be cut down. So, they returned to their VW Busses, actually shut them off, and started to unload everything they would need to carry out a long and visible protest.

The protestors, who had brought all of the necessary equipment to live up in tree branches, gathered their equipment and moved right in. Other protester, those afraid of heights, had brought all the necessary equipment to affix themselves to the trunks of trees. They too, gathered their equipment and started affixing. The remaining protesters, which included Todd, who weren't nearly as dumb...I mean devoted, set-up camp on the ground next to the trees that the other protesters were occupying. These protesters planned on camping among their tree dwelling buddies to offer support and encouragement so they would be a strong, undivided group. They had to be strong and united because only *they* knew that once a tree is gone, it can never, ever, *ever* be replaced and that whoever was having this done, would destroy every tree on Mother Earth in order to make a quick buck. So they, the more enlightened ones, had to take stance and put a stop to it.

Before long, there were thirty-four eLiberals living, in various configurations, together amongst the trees that were to be cut down. Todd was not among them. Once he had seen the eLiberals equipment (torn, moldy, smelly tents; torn, moldy, smelly, dirty sleeping bags; moldy, fungus covered cooking utensils; dirty, smelly, bongs[148]) he made an excuse for going to town, got in a VW Bus, and went home. He needed a shower, a good meal, a glass of wine, a comfy bed, and American Idol was on that night.

Although all of the protesting eLiberals had attended the university in Verkapely at one time, none of the thirty-four that were protesting were currently enrolled, and it became glaringly obvious as to why as soon as the sun went down. The protesters that were camping amongst their tree-dwelling buddies, started campfires using wood that had undoubtedly come from all the clearing that had been done that day. The campfires gave off a lot of smoke that went straight up to the protesters living in the branches. When those protesters complained, the protesters on the ground started moving the logs in the campfire with sticks hoping to make them burn better, thus reducing the amount of smoke.

However, this caused embers to be released and they gently floated up and caught fire to all the paraphernalia belonging to the protesters living in the tree branches. Out of dire necessity, those protesters began climbing down the trees as fast as they could, which wasn't very fast because they were stoned and could not think clearly or move quickly in any way. Then, to make matters worse, when they reached a protestor attached to the trunk of their tree, they couldn't figure out a way around them and so ended-up standing on their head or shoulders for prolonged periods.

The protesters attached to the trunks did not like this at all, but they were also baked and all they could do was plead with the tree climbers, between laughing fits, to either knock it off

---

148 A water pipe used for smoking marijuana or other drugs. It unites all four elements: earth, wind, fire, and water.

or speed things up a bit. This, in turn, caused the tree climbers to laugh so hard that they wet their pants; that's not good if you are directly below. Eventually, all of the climbers did get down and were able to detach the protestors on which they had been standing. They dried them off as best they could and tried to make amends.

The eLiberals, who had caused this whole mess by fooling with the campfire and who were also baked, just sat there, laughed, and stuffed their faces with a gooey mixture of burnt marshmallows, sour cream Pringles, and warm, flat Coke. They thought it was the best meal they had ever eaten.

Once all the eLiberals were back together and sitting around the campfire, which was still emitting an occasional ember, they heard a strange, roaring sound which they immediately took to be thunder. They looked up to see the rain clouds, but instead saw that the tree branches had burst into flames.

"Whoa...dude...that's trippy," was all they could say. As they lay laughing and admiring the "trippy scene" the fire, which was being fed by what the protesters had left in the trees and was being pushed by a gentle breeze that had arisen, spread to more trees and then to the ground. Since the ground was covered with logs, branches, and all sorts of dry vegetation that was in the process of being removed, there was no shortage of fuel for the fire.

The protesters saw this and miraculously realized that the fire should probably be extinguished. So, they all gathered around (remember they're totally baked) and began spraying the fire with water from their 22-ounce water bottles and kicking dirt on it. A couple male protestors even "whipped it out" and tried to pee on the flames, but it quickly became too hot to handle...the fire that is. Needless to say, they did not extinguish much of the fire and it rapidly grew in size.

Amazingly, the protestors had enough sense to realize they had better vacate the area while they still had the chance. They ran to the remaining five VW Busses, piled in, and took off down the only access road. However, they didn't get far because the two VW Busses in the lead broke down on the narrow, single lane road and the remaining three busses had to stop. All of the eLiberals piled out of their VW but no one had a clue as to what they should do. As they stood on the road giggling, toking,[149] and looking utterly bewildered, they heard a cacophony[150] of sirens that were rapidly approaching.

The stoned eLiberals thought it was help coming to fix their VW Busses but, to their dismay, the sirens belonged to the fire trucks that were coming to fight the fire. When the fire trucks reached the broken down VW Busses they could go no further and so just sat there while the surrounding area became ablaze. This fire was emitting fiftyfold (that means 50 times) the amount of smoke that the burning grapevines had been so, thanks to the eLiberals, the air quality of Fiasco Valley became even worse.

Meanwhile, back in Birchwood Todd, who was sipping an extraordinary Cabernet Sauvignon (he pronounced it Kab-Her-Net Sav-Hig-Non) while sitting on his veranda after calling in his choice to be the next American Idol, saw an orange glow off in the direction he had come from. The glow seemed to be getting bigger and brighter. *Hmm, I wonder what an orange glow coming from where a bunch of stoned kids were camping could be?* Todd had never been accused of being a genius either.

---

149   The drawing of a puff from a cigarette or pipe, typically one containing marijuana.

150   A harsh, discordant mixture of sounds

Pretty quick, Todd noticed that there was so much traffic on the road going out of town that it was at a standstill. He could hear horns honking, people yelling and cussing at each other, and he thought he saw a fist fight. To sum it all up: Everyone seemed panicked. *Now, what in the hell...?*

There was a strong smell of smoke in the air. In fact, it was becoming so strong that it made breathing uncomfortable and Todd decided he should probably turn on the radio, or TV, or look on his iPhone to try and find out what was going on. As he got up to go inside, Todd could heard someone screaming, "¡Corre! ¡Fuego! ¡El pueblo está en llamas!" He did not know what that meant, but apparently it had something to do with running and fire because just then the fire whistle went off and he saw a lot of people start to run; and run they did until they reached the road.

Once they reached the road, they not only had to stop running, but moving all together. The roads were so clogged with vehicles and panicking people that nothing could move, not even a mouse. A few of the apartment complex residents, the ones that had been educated in the Elviño County School System, decided to get in their cars and drive to safety. They didn't even get out of the parking lot. All during this failed exodus, the fire was gaining strength as it approached Birchwood.

Todd figured the fire was headed straight for the low-income housing and that was where it would do the most damage; that was always the case. The good news was that it was not a trailer park, so he had a fighting chance. To save himself, he did the only thing he could do at that particular moment: He ran out to the middle of a vineyard. Many people saw him, figured he had the right idea, and joined him.

Before long, there were hundreds of people stinkin' up acres of vineyard. While in the vineyards, the people watched helicopters and air tankers drop water and other fire retardants on the fire. But after a couple hours they got bored watching this and so did a few other things...just use your imagination, dear reader, as to what.

The fire trucks that had been blocked by the eLiberals did manage to turn around, eventually, and get back to Birchwood in order to help fight the fire. On the way back into town one of the firemen, who just happened to be the son-in-law of the Fire Chief, radioed his father-in-law, gave him the coordinates of the eLiberals, and told him to have a load of their secret stash of Borate dropped on them. It was done. He hoped the Borate salts, which were once used to fight wildfires but have been found to sterilize the soil and be toxic to animals and are now prohibited, would sterilize the eLiberals, who he thought were just dirt, or at least make them extremely sick.

Chapter 39

Killer Tofu

Tony Vabelli shook his head and sat down in his porch rocking chair. He let out an audible sigh, patted his dog on the head, and then took a deep breath followed by another sip of wine. The recent fire that had swept through the valley burned most of the low-income housing units but spared all of the large homes and quaint downtown shops. It did not damage anything that Tony Vabelli owned, but the people escaping the fire were a different story altogether. His vineyard just outside of Birchwood sustained nearly twenty thousand dollars in damage from the hundreds of town escapees that had stayed in it for the few, tense hours the fire had raged.

As Tony sat on his porch enjoying his glass of Sangiovese, which had been made from grapes that had come from his damaged vineyard, a VW Bus emitting profuse amounts of smoke and filled with a few of the same greasy, smelly, young, eLiberals that had caused this whole mess, pulled up next to Tony's porch. The protestors in the VW Bus alighted and ran onto the porch.

The protestors got right in Tony's face and berated him for burning all those grapevines. They blamed him for all of the air pollution and the all problems it would cause: irritated eyes, nose, and throats, headaches, respiratory problems, and ultimately lung cancer.

"You look fine to me," stated Tony when he was at last given chance to get a word in.

"Well, we are all fine. It's everyone else that your pollution is harming."

"I no see anyone else. Who is everyone else?" asked Tony innocently, but he was clearly mocking them.

The protestors then went on a tirade about how Tony, and the other vineyard owners, was putting fine particulate matters into the air, via the smoke from the burning of grapevines, and it would cause all sorts of health problems for people.

"What people? I no see sick people," said Tony derisively.[151] He was growing weary of these young, little whippersnappers who showed no respect for their elders and were upsetting his relaxing, afternoon glass of wine, and *that* was a mortal sin.

"All you silly Americans worry much of polluting and hurting Earth," he said. "Man could not hurt Earth if he wanted to. Earth destroy man before man destroy Earth. The Earth big; man small."

The protestors did not miss Tony's derisive tone of voice and realized he was showing his contempt for them. They were greatly insulted and offended.

These "all-knowing, all-caring, peaceful, love-everyone-including-Mother-Earth, holier-than-thou" Verkapely eLiberal protestors decided that Tony Vabelli wasn't worth the polluted air he was breathing. Since he was the one polluting the air, they came to the only conclusion they were able to: Tony must die for the greater good...well for their good, anyway.

The biggest, strongest protestor, who wasn't all that strong, pushed the back of Tony's rocking chair forward so that Tony fell out of his chair and onto the porch. Then he, along with two other white, pasty, un-healthy looking protestors, secured his arms and legs so he could not move or free himself.

A fourth protestor pinched Tony's nose closed and forced

---

151 Expressing contempt or ridicule.

his mouth open while a fifth protestor stuffed it full of Tofu she had found in the back of one of the VW Busses. The only reason any of this could be done was the fact that Tony Vabelli was rather old and more than a bit tipsy from drinking wine all morning.

Tony began to gag and choke, not only because he couldn't breathe, but also because the Tofu tasted so ghastly. He struggled for what seemed to him an eternity but was only a couple of minutes, and then he died from lack of oxygen, or maybe it was simply because the Tofu was so...ah...well...Tofu-ish.

To be fair to the protestors, they weren't completely bad. After they murdered Tony, they took his dog with them so they could take care of him, or her, and give him, or her, a good home. They didn't know if the dog was a "he" or "she." The Verkapely eLiberals, who were so much more enlightened and intelligent than everyone else, didn't know how tell a bitch[152] from a male dog, not that they cared. They just knew it was a helpless animal that had undoubtedly been mistreated and abused by this ignorant, old man who was polluting the air we all breathe.

---

152   Relax people; it's in the dictionary. A "bitch" is defined as a female dog, wolf, otter, or fox.

Chapter 40

Peace, Dude

Meanwhile, David Knight was at an expensive restaurant having a nice lunch with a "mature," un-happily married woman he had met via the Ashley Madison Website.[153] As he sat charming his date, a waiter came over to him and said he had a phone call. David excused himself and followed the waiter to the telephone. He returned shortly and explained that he had to leave as there had been another murder in Birchwood and he was wanted at the scene.

He didn't feel bad about leaving his date because she turned out to be good from far, but far from good. He also found out that he knew who her husband was, and he was not a fellow you wanted to upset.

Detective Knight enthusiastically hopped in his 4Runner and drove out to the address he had been given. When he arrived, Officer McMillan and Officer Kendry filled him in on what little they knew.

"Tony Vabelli was murdered with what...Tofu? You've got to be kidding me," exclaimed David.

"We never kid about a murder," stated Officer McMillan flatly.

"But you've got to admit," chimed in Officer Kendry, "that's pretty darn funny."

Detective Knight, being followed by the two officers, was walking up to see Tony on the porch when he noticed

---

153   "The Original Extramarital Affairs Site. 100% Free For Women!" I'm not making this up. Their Motto is: "Life is short, have an affair." But, what they don't tell you is that your life could be even shorter if you get caught having said affair.

something shiny in the gravel. He picked it up and saw that it was a bracelet with a Peace Symbol attached. He turned and showed it to Officer Kendry and Officer McMillan and they were both as curious as he was.

As they were discussing the bracelet, the two vatos who Todd had yelled at about the burning piles of grapevines, drove up and asked to see Tony Vabelli because they needed to know what work needed to be done. Detective Knight pointed to the porch and Tony, and conveyed to the vatos that they had a few days off. He then showed the two vatos the bracelet he had just found and asked if they knew anything about it. They whispered something to each other, laughed, and said. "Sí. We see hombre wearing that morning we burn vines. He no happy about smoke."

"You saw someone wearing *this* bracelet?" asked Detective Knight incredulously.

The two vatos snickered and said, "El hombre es mucho gay." As they said this, they held their arms close to their sides, bent their arms up at the elbows, but kept their wrists limp, signifying he was a homosexual man. They were clearly mocking him. "He no happy too. He act muy mad."

"Did he ask, or do anything else?" demanded Officer McMillan.

The two vatos decided they didn't like this whole scene and conveniently went into "No speaka da Inglis" mode and just stared blankly into space. Detective Knight almost lost it. Here, he had a dead guy with no leads as to why, and two people who had information that could provide a lead, or leads, as to the reason for his death and who may be responsible. Yet, conveniently, and for the time being, they couldn't understand English. Detective Knight stood and stared straight at the two vatos, took some deep breaths, closed his eyes, gritted his teeth, and slowly asked Officer McMillan to contact Officer Ruiz to come and act as a translator. Officer McMillan did and within a few minutes, Officer Ruiz was questioning the two vatos.

All he was able to ascertain was that they had seen a guy who was driving a beat-up, old VW Bus full of people who didn't like smoke. Officer Kendry heard Officer Ruiz impart what little he had learned to Detective Knight and couldn't help but think about his ex-girlfriend.

She was a total wannabe hippie, liberal bitch (not the female dog, wolf, or otter version...although, she *was* a fox) who had gone to the University in Verkapely, but just for a year or two. She was an eLiberal who often rode around in a VW Bus with other wannabe hippies and who wore a lot of jewelry depicting the Peace Symbol. They protested anything and everything that would allow them the opportunity smoke dope and play their bongo drums along with their old, beat-up, out-of-tune guitars.

He conveyed these inescapable thoughts to Detective Knight because he thought that maybe, just maybe, his ex-girlfriend had something to do with this and he would be able to "get her back" for the way she dumped him.

"Interesting," said Detective Knight as he was ruminating about what he had just been told. "Very interesting."

Detective Knight knew Officer Kendry's ex-girlfriend, knew that she still lived in Verkapely, and knew that she leaned so far left that she could not even stand-up straight. In fact, she leaned left so far that her blood flow was completely out of whack and did not flow to and from her brain as it should. As a result, she still believed in the possibility of a utopian[154]

---

154 An imagined place or state of things in which everything is perfect. The key word is "imagined" because such a place, or state does not, and will not ever exist. It is the typical view of pseudo-intelligent, liberal Democrats who believe they can make everything perfect—as long as you do what they tell you to do and not what they actually do.

society, and achieving one was her mission in life. She believed the only thing preventing her from completing her mission was rich, old, ignorant, white men. The fact that her father, whom she couldn't stand, was very wealthy, white, and rather old, had absolutely nothing to do with it.

Something about the look in Officer Kendry's eyes and on his face as he repeated what Officer Ruiz had told him, gave Detective Knight a sudden flash of insight: The Peace Symbol bracelet probably belonged to some Verkapely pseudo-hippie who was mad at all the smoke being produced by the burning of grapevines and had come to Fiasco Valley to put a stop to it. They somehow found Tony Vabelli, decided he was killing Mother Earth, and so killed him. Like all liberals, they didn't think their undertakings through too well; they just knew what would make them feel better at that particular moment.

Detective Knight, who worked alone because he didn't really like people, decided he should to do some research on any groups from Verkapely whose main issue was pollution, or the environment, or some such thing.

To do this, he went to the local public library, sat himself in front of a computer, and started looking for anything in the library or on the World Wide Web that mentioned any groups that dealt with pollution; air-pollution specifically. There was no shortage of groups. So, to narrow his results, he only looked at groups founded or headquartered in Verkapely near the university. The results weren't much different. *What the hell is it about universities? Why do the people there think they are so much smarter than the rest of us? Do they think they are so learned that whatever they believe about the Earth, the environment, or pollution is the only good, or correct belief? If they were truly smart, they would hold opinions the exact opposite of those they do hold; they would agree with me.*

Detective Knight decided that researching environmental-whacko groups from Verkapely on the web was going to be a fruitless—*mmm fruit*—endeavor so he decided to take a more direct approach. He went straight to Officer Kendry and grilled —*mmm grilled*—him about his ex-girlfriend.

Officer Kendry was more than happy to answer any, and all, questions that Detective Knight threw at him. After only two or three minutes, Detective Knight had a good idea as to where to start looking for the owner of the Peace Symbol bracelet.

He drove his gas-guzzling, environment-polluting, child-killing, SUV to Verkapely and found, right next to a Starbucks, the very small headquarters of the group: Smog Holds Intolerable Truths, or S.H.I.T. The group's founder, who was Officer Kendry's ex-girlfriend, was sitting on the only chair in the "office." There was no desk, just an old Frigidaire refrigerator box turned on its side to serve as one. There were also three very unkempt individuals lying on dirty, old beanbags that had been patched with duct tape numerous times. Detective Knight wasn't sure which individuals were male and which ones were female assuming, of course, there were both.

Detective Knight noticed that they were all wearing bracelets depicting the Peace Symbol. *So much for non-conformity, they are just a flock of sheep.*

The room smelt strongly of pot and Detective Knight figured that would explain the empty potato chip bags and Hostess Ho-Ho wrappers strewn about. He sauntered over to the refrigerator box...I mean desk, introduced himself, pulled the Peace Symbol bracelet from his pocket, and asked Officer Kendry's ex-girlfriend if she knew to whom it belonged.

"Oh yeah that's mine. Well it *was* mine until I loaned it to a friend, but he lost it...you know how guys are. But, by golly, you found it!" she rejoiced. "Awesome! Awesome! Where was it?"

"It was found at a murder scene in Birchwood. Any idea how it would have gotten there?"

"Uh hmm...well...um...no...haven't a clue," she stated flatly, as she became rigid and darted her eyes constantly about. It had finally dawned on her that if a homicide detective asks you if you know to whom something belongs you should probably just say "no." But she never thought anything bad could ever happen to a girl as cute, happy, and perky as her and a homicide detective asking about evidence from a murder was more than she could comprehend at a moments notice.

"So, who is your friend?"

"Um well, he's not friend really. He's just a guy I know."

"Well, great. But *who* is he?"

"He's nobody really. Just a guy I had drinks with one night."

"Where did you have the drinks?"

"In a bar."

This back and forth went on for a few minutes when Officer Kendry's ex-girlfriend, who was looking hotter and hotter...I mean tenser and tenser, finally said, "Okay, okay. We were mad at this guy who was polluting the air and we were just going to talk to him but he wouldn't listen to anything we were saying and just kept insulting us. He said we had no manners, no respect for older people, and said we would protest anything or anybody we *thought* was polluting the environment because that's all we *could* do. He said we were complete idiots that probably couldn't figure out a 15 percent tip, let alone the cause of air pollution.

"He said we had no respect for our bodies because we put vulgar tattoos all over them and pierced our noses, lips, belly buttons, and God-only-knows what else. That all we could do was gossip on our cell phones, smoke pot, shovel food into our mouths, and we had never done an honest days work in our lives."

"And *that* drove you to murder?" asked Detective Knight in amazement.

"Well, there was a little more actually. The old guy...uh what was his name again?"

"Tony Vabelli."

"Yeah right. Well good ol' Tony had wandering hands, eyes, and lips if you know what I mean. He kept grabbing my ass and trying to kiss me, he was always looking down my shirt, and I wasn't the only one. He was also trying to 'feel-up' Betsy the whole time."

"Who is Betsy?" asked Detective Knight.

"She was the other girl with us," answered the ex-girlfriend. "And you know how guys are. Todd and a couple of the other guys didn't like Tony trying to 'feel-up' Betsy or me, so they went into 'protect mode,' I guess. They only did what they thought was best...and probably what they thought would most-likely help them get in our pants later on."

Detective Knight ignored that last comment and asked, "They thought it best to kill Tony...with Tofu, no less?

"Well, like I said, they *are* typical guys and so do have a tendency to do stupid stuff."

"Yeah, I'd say murder with pressed bean curds qualifies as 'stupid stuff,'" concurred Detective Knight. "Did *you* help at all? I mean someone had to help hold Tony down."

"No. I never even got out of the van. I would never solve a problem with violence," she said in a deeply offended voice.

Detective Knight was gravely disappointed because it didn't look like he had cause to arrest her. Therefore, he would not get the thrill of frisking her (completely and thoroughly) and putting her in 'cuffs. Of course, she could be lying and be an accessory, so he might still get the chance. Anything is possible.

"Okay, well thanks. Um, do you mind if I look around a bit?"

"No. No. Be my guest."

Detective Knight stood there and literally just looked around, for that's all he had room to do. A couple of walls were in his way and he didn't want to step on the three individuals laying the floor on beanbags. Well, to be honest, he would have loved to step on them but he had become extremely good at controlling those types of urges, and he *was* a professional.

While looking around, he saw a cooler behind the chair the girl was sitting on and asked, "What's in the cooler?"

The girl suddenly became visibly nervous and said, "Ahh, nothing really. It's just for trips we take and we aren't taking any trips."

"So, do you mind if I have a look inside?"

Before she could answer, Detective Knight took the one step needed to reach the ice chest, opened it, and looked inside. He saw three glass jars full of water along with a white, solid substance that he had no clue as to what it was. Some sort of new-fangled drug he assumed.

"What's in the jars?" he asked.

"You don't know?" she replied somewhat astonished.

"No. That's why I'm asking," he said, clearly annoyed. "You said there was nothing in here."

"I didn't know it was still in there, it was supposed to have been cleaned out."

Oh, I see. And why would you want it cleaned out? I bet one of these dudes or dudines[155] on the floor was in charge of getting that done.

"Well, what is it?"

She sighed and said, "It's Tofu." She didn't realize that not everyone recognized Tofu in a jar full of water. "We take it on all of our trips. It's what we eat."

Yuck! "Oh, I'm sorry," said Detective Knight sarcastically. As he closed the lid and turned, he stepped on a half-empty bag of chips and quipped, "Was the floor supposed to be cleaned too?"

He got no response, just a tired expression on the face of the girl behind the "desk" as she sat there without moving a muscle. Detective Knight soon realized that she was not going to volunteer any more information, so he asked, "Where are all the other people who were on the bus with you? The ones who *did* snuff Tony?"

"Beats me," she said.

"What do they beat you with?" asked Detective Knight lightheartedly because he was trying to put her at ease. It didn't seem to work. "Sorry, I couldn't resist saying that. But seriously, where are they?" He stood still for a couple of minutes and waited for some sort of answer; but none came. Detective Knight, who hated conversational lulls then asked, "You do know what 'Obstruction of Justice' means, don't you?" So much for putting her at ease.

When she was asked that question, her eyes became really

---

155   A female dude. This came from the Merriam-Webster Dictionary and that's about as official as it gets. The word "dudette" can also be used but it is considered a slang term and isn't in the Dictionary. Who knew? Not me.

big and she quietly said, "Oh, they're probably down at The Vainglorious Demitasse."[156]

"The what?"

"The Vainglorious Demitasse. It's a coffee shop just outside of town. That's not its real name, but that's what we call it. Its real name is 'The Bay Area of Northern California Coffee Roasting and Grinding Company' or something ridiculously long like that. It's full of young, wealthy adults who think they are each the greatest thing to ever walk the face of the earth. They do have awesome Lattes though, and big tables where we can hang out and talk. It's on the main road, you can't miss it."

"Don't be so sure," warned Detective Knight. "I've amazed a lot of people."

With that, Todd left S.H.I.T. Headquarters, got in his 4Runner, and went to find The Vainglorious Demitasse. He got on to the main road through town and drove until he saw the sign for "The Bay Area of Northern California Coffee Roasting and Grinding Company." He parked his evil SUV and walked into the coffee shop.

---

156   "Vainglorious" – unusually or disproportionately large pride in oneself or one's achievements; excessive vanity. "Demitasse" – a small coffe cup. There are a lot of vainglorius people in Fiasco Valley.

Chapter 41

The Vainglorious Demitasse

Upon entering "The Bay Area of Northern California Coffee Roasting and Grinding Company," Detective Knight spotted Todd right away. He was sitting at the head of a large table right in the middle of the coffee shop, and he looked the same as he did when Detective Knight had first talked with him in the Big Goose Cellars Tasting Room the day Ted was killed. Joining him at the table were two other dudes, a white girl, and a black girl, none of whom Todd recognized.

Also entering the Vainglorious Demitasse were three of Verkapely's finest. Detective Knight had called them to help with any arrests because he had no a clue as to how Todd, or any of the others would react. He only knew that "peaceful protestors" could be some of the most violent and vicious people you'd ever come across. He didn't know if these protestors considered themselves "peaceful" but they had already killed one guy and Detective Knight didn't want to become the second.

Detective Knight went to the head of the table and asked, "Are you Todd Milksop?" even though he knew the answer.

"Who wants to know?" asked Todd very pugnaciously.[157]

"I'm Homicide Detective David Knight and I've got to bring you in."

"What? Bring me in? Where and what the hell for?" asked Todd in surprised innocence.

---

157   Eager or quick to argue, quarrel, or fight.

"The Police Station for the murder of Tony Vabelli."

"Tony Va...who? I don't know any Tony Va...whatever. I don't know what the hell you're talking about."

"Oh yeah sure, of course you don't. Tony Vabelli is the vineyard owner that you and your pals here," Detective Knight gestured to the other people sitting at the table, "choked with Tofu."

"Choked with Tofu? Are you serious? You gotta be kidding."

"I am dead serious," said Detective Knight. "Pun intended." He looked around the table and noticed the two girls look at each other, take deep breaths, and become wide-eyed and fidgety. *Hmm. That tells me all I need to know thought* Detective Knight.

The three of Verkapely's finest that were with David took up positions so that no one could escape...I mean leave the coffee shop. Detective Knight then resolutely walked next to Todd and told him to stand-up and put his hands on his head. Todd did so, for he saw that resistance would be futile, he was chicken to disobey, *and* he was kind of a wuss. Detective Knight got behind him and put the 'cuffs on him. He didn't bother reciting the required "You have the right to remain silent" codswallop[158] because he could never remember that whole thing. The only time he had ever said the entire Miranda Warning was during his training, and that had taken a couple of tries.

As Todd was being 'cuffed, he nodded at all the people seated at the table and said in a whiny voice, "Well, they were all there too and there was someone else who is not even here."

Detective Knight motioned for the police officers to arrest the others at the table as he said, "Oh yeah? Who would that be? And where are they now?"

---

158   Nonsense – wish this word was used more often.

"Grefa Bambalacha[159] and she would be at S.H.I.T. Head-quarters," stated Todd.

"Grefa Bambalacha?" repeated Detective Knight. "Okay, great. We'll go get her." And with that Detective Knight asked two of the police officers, who were done handcuffing the remaining people at the table, to go over to S.H.I.T. Headquarters and arrest Grefa Bambalacha.

---

159   Both "Grefa" and "Bambalacha" are slang words for marijuana. So, if you hear your kid, or kids, say either of those words...look out.

Chapter 42

Depressed Maria

Maria got in line to go to the cafeteria because it was dinnertime. She was sure dinner would be some form of chicken, some dish of what was supposed to be vegetables, and most likely jell-o for dessert. That's what lunch had been and the only difference between lunch and dinner was the time on the clock.

The food really wasn't that bad and she didn't have Ernesto yelling and asking her what was for dinner and when it would be ready. There were no dishes for her to wash or anything else to clean up. All in all, mealtime wasn't that bad in prison, once she learned to sit only with other Latino prisoners and not with black or white ones. That had been a rough and painful lesson.

She stood in line to receive her meal and then sat down with the other Latino prisoners. Pretty soon, a woman who seemed to be very popular among the inmates for reasons Maria hadn't been on the inside long enough to know, sat down at the table next to Maria. It soon became clear as to why this woman was so popular.

Maria had just begun to choke down her dinner when she felt a hand rubbing the inside of her thigh. She looked at the popular woman, Sofía, next her and was rewarded with a wink and the passage of a torn piece of paper. On the paper was some barely legible writing that told Maria to meet her at a certain spot in the exercise yard tomorrow afternoon. Maria turned to Sofía with a questioning glance and saw that she was walking away.

The next afternoon, Maria went to the spot mentioned in the note and was surprised to see a gang of about thirty women, all of whom were surrounding Sofía. Maria was absorbed into the group and quickly found herself face-to-face with the popular woman. Now that the two were together, the games could begin.

Sofía, who was quite buff, grabbed Maria, threw her down, tore off her clothes, and proceeded to rape her. All the other women just watched, whooped, and hollerd. The prison guards, both male and female, knew what was going on and also just stood there and watched, as best they could, hoping they would get a chance to see Maria nude. They got what they hoped for and let out a loud cheer. When it was over everyone, except Maria, just walked away.

After everyone had left, Maria just lay on the grass nude and sobbing until a relatively new female prison guard felt a twang of guilt and ran out to help her. She helped Maria up and took her to the infirmary. A physician checked her and no permanent physical damage had been done, but she did have what appeared to be two small punctures on her neck and she had certainly been emotionally traumatized.

Maria quickly fell into a deep depression. She wasn't eating and during her exercise period, she would just curl up against the wall and cry. The prison psychologist prescribed her some anti-depressants but Maria wouldn't take them because she felt as though she would be betraying her faith in God every time she swallowed the little pill.

Maria would only come out of her cell for meals or when prison officials forced her to. She never went outdoors, unless she could go out at night or on a rainy day, and that rarely happened. Strangely, she would become visibly shaken if a she saw a guard strike a match or generate a flame with their cigarette lighter. She was moved to a solitary cell because whomever she roomed with would be awakened multiple times during the night only to find Maria on top of them attempting to bite their neck.

One day, Maria called her mother in Mexico to hear a familiar voice and to say how miserable she was. Her mother listened and then told her to go to the prison chapel and pray, for God loved her, would comfort her, and everything would be muy bueno. Maria said a lachrymose[160] goodbye, hung-up the phone, and then headed straight for the prison chapel to pray.

As she approached the chapel, she started to feel weird. She couldn't explain it except that she felt hot...extremely hot. It seemed that with each step Maria took towards the chapel she felt more and more like she was burning-up inside. Just as she was about to enter the chapel, she noticed smoke coming out of her nose. Not surprisingly, she freaked-out. She turned and ran, screaming at the top of her lungs, straight back to the safety of her cell. When she got back into her cell, she lay down on her old, squeaky, rusty, cot, buried her face in her pillow, and yowled away for an hour or so. When Maria had cried herself out, she rolled on to her back and just lay there staring at the ceiling and thinking.

The good news was: There was no longer any smoke coming out of her nose and she didn't feel as though she was burning up inside. The bad news was: She was lying on a cot in prison, she couldn't get into the chapel to pray, and everything was certainly not muy bueno.

While lying on her cot thinking, Maria convinced herself that

---

160   Tearful or given to weeping. It would have been much too simple to just say "a tearful goodbye."

her soul was burning as punishment for what she had done. She became very scared and decided she needed to talk to someone. As part of her punishment, she believed God would not allow her in the church, let alone allow her to talk with the prison chaplain, so the chaplain was out. She didn't want to talk to any of her fellow inmates, as she was sure they wouldn't be of any help. She felt the only person who she could talk to, or possibly the only person who could talk to her, was the prison psychologist. She got up, left her maximum-security cell, and found the psychologist alone in his dark office sitting at his desk and in front his laptop computer. Maria cleared her throat and said. "Dr. I need talk to you. It muy importante."

The doctor jumped up from behind his desk with a start while closing his laptop and zipping-up his pants and said, "Oh my! You gave me a start! Uhh...what can I do you for?"

Maria proceeded to tell him about what had happened when she tried to go to the chapel. The psychologist listened to Maria intently but couldn't believe what he was hearing. When Maria finished her yarn, the prison shrink stood-up, took a deep breath, and excused himself so that he could retrieve Maria's file.

With her file, he confirmed that Maria wasn't eating, that she wouldn't go outside unless it was dark or raining, and that a cigarette lighter in use or a lit match caused her to become visibly shaken. Lastly, he confirmed that she had repeatedly tried to suck on the neck of any roommate she had.

"Doctor, what wrong with me? God mad at me? I be punished?"

The psychologist didn't say anything. He just sat at his desk staring at his notes and the reports in Maria's file.

"Doctor...? You okay?"

The psychologist remained quiet.

"Doctor? Doctor?"

After an excruciatingly couple of minutes, the psychologist asked, "Maria, have you been bitten by a bat, or anything recently?"

She quickly said, "No," but was thinking *A bat? What the hell does a bat have to do with anything?*

The prison psychologist, unbeknownst to anyone, was seeing a psychologist himself because he had an acute case of Sanguivoriphobia, which is "fear of blood eaters" and is characterized by specific and isolated fear of vampires. He was the expert on all things vampire and he *always* had garlic in his pants pocket. He was also afflicted with a myriad of other phobias and that could be one reason he was becoming quite masterly at sitting alone in the dark in front of his computer surfing the Web.

He got up from his desk, walked over to Maria, then slowly and carefully began to inspect her neck for bite marks. The closer he got to her neck, the slower he moved. Finally, Maria could resist no more and with lighting speed, she grabbed him with one arm and held him tight and close.

Unfortunately, the psychologist had spent twenty-five minutes that morning looking for his cell phone and so was in a rush to get to work on time. Therefore, he hadn't had time put garlic in his pants pockets, which he normally does. It was the only time in the last five years that he had gone to work garlic-free. If he had garlic in his pants pockets, Maria may have been so repulsed by it that she wouldn't have even touched him. Just ask Ernesto about the night he came home late after eating garlic pizza and watching fútbol (that'just soccer but I'm trying to sound worldly) with his buddies.

At first, the shrink tried to pull away, but couldn't; she was just too strong. She held him with one arm and tore his and her clothes off with the other. She was exhibiting two traits of vampires. Those traits being: movement with unnatural speed and movement with unnatural strength. Some other traits of vampires are: They are sexual predators, they drink human blood, they can read the thoughts of their potential victim, and they are repelled by garlic. Since he had no garlic, this last trait was irrelevant.

Once they were both naked, he became much easier to manipulate as he thought that this might turn into a good situation for a lonely prison psychologist. He had been trying to overcome his Sanguivoriphobia by looking at pictures of nude female vampires on the web[161] and they had become a big turn-on for him.

Maria desperately needed to satiate[162] her sexual desires and she hoped this psychologist would do the trick; he did. As soon as her desires had been satisfied, she left him lying on the floor of his office in a pool of sweat, and went back to her cell.

On the way back, she thought about what she had just done and all of its potential benefits. She figured it would definitely benefit her to do it again and again, and she knew the shrink wouldn't object. So, Maria and the shrink repeated their little escapade a number of times the following week.

Now, Maria figured it was time to make her exploits pay off. She went to back the shrink and told him that he better get her out of jail and pay her mucho dinero or else she would post on YouTube the videos of the "sessions" they had been having. The

---

161   Just Google "pics of nude female vampires," and you'll get a lot of results... seriously.

162   Satisfied to the full—which means totally satisfied...I guess.

shrink dismissed Maria's threats because he didn't think it was possible for her to have videos of their "sessions" and so there was no way she could get him to meet either of her demands.

Maria knew what the shrink was thinking, so she produced the iPhone that had been smuggled into the prison and that she had used to secretly film their "sessions." The hoosegow shrink did a double take when he saw the iPhone and immediately set up a meeting between him and the warden.

During that meeting, the shrink stated that Maria had no more rage issues, felt nothing but remorse for her actions, was psychologically stable, and posed no threat to society. He suggested that, due to prison over-crowding, she be released.

The warden was dumbfounded, and he looked it. He couldn't believe that the prison psychologist would not only ask him to release a prisoner, but that he thought he had the authority to do so. Apparently, the prison psychologist wasn't a very sharp shrink. The warden explained that he didn't have the authority to release a prisoner; a prison review board was needed for that. The closest he could come to releasing her would be to get her on a "work-release" program, and he would have to meet with Maria in person before he could even begin that whole paperwork nightmare. But begin it he did, and a meeting between him and Maria was set up for the next day.

During the meeting Maria, who believed the warden could release her, used all of her sexual wiles that had previously worked on the shrink—plus a couple new ones—to persuade him to allow her release. Not surprisingly, the warden didn't bother to enlighten her of the fact that he didn't have the authority to just let her go and he just let her persuade...and persuade some more.

After the meeting, Maria went into her cell to await word

regarding her release. The news that came, however, was that the warden required a follow-up meeting the next day because he was not yet convinced that Maria was no longer a threat to society, or anyone else, for that matter. That was fine with Maria because unbeknownst to the warden, she was also secretly filming these meetings with her iPhone and was going to do what she had done to the prison shrink if things didn't go her way.

At the follow-up meeting the warden was expecting, and received, the same treatment he had gotten during the first meeting. When this meeting reached its...uh...conclusion—which didn't take very long—the warden again told Maria to go to her cell and await his decision. Maria still had no clue that he couldn't make the decision she was working towards because vampires can't read the minds of government employees; it has something to do with union contracts and homeland security.

After a couple days, with at least two meetings per day, it finally dawned on Maria that she was probably being used for the warden's enjoyment and that he had no intention of releasing her, or even doing anything to facilitate her release.

Now, she was doubly glad that she had been filming her "meetings" with the warden. He was going to pay.

Chapter 43

English as a
Second Language Confusion

Maria desperately wanted out of jail, so she continued having her "meetings" with the prison shrink and warden with the hope of being released, but she never was. They had never even considered contacting, or forming, a prison review board to review her case.

Fortunately, for Maria anyway, there was a superfluity[163] of illegal immigrants working for the California government (many in the prison system; none of whom spoke English) and because of that, there was much confusion and an inordinate number of mistakes were made. Anything the California Government does requires a surfeit[164] of paperwork and many of the necessary forms were filled out wrong, or not at all, and if they had to be sent somewhere they often went to the wrong recipients. Instructions, prisoner movements, statutes, safety procedures, etc. were not carried out properly, if at all. Supervisors were unable to communicate with their workers so mistakes were not caught and problems didn't get solved.

The most troubling result of all this was that a number of prisoners were released that shouldn't have been, Maria being one of them. When she got the news that she was being released, she assumed it was because she had performed so well during

---

163 An unnecessarily or excessively large amount or number of something.

164 An excessive number or quantity of something. There was so much paperwork, that people become sickened, repelled, and bored by it. Which in turn, led to a multitude of errors. Can you tell I'm using my Thesaurus?

her "meetings" with the warden and the shrink. It wasn't, but she was going home and that's all that mattered. Unfortunately, for Maria, the error was miraculously discovered a couple of days later and she was again taken into custody and thrown back in the slammer.

The warden, because of this little snafu, thought his days working for the state, along with his $105,000 a year salary, were over. It turns out, however, that being an employee of the State of California and a member of California Correctional Peace Officer's Association Union, or the CCPOA, makes it virtually impossible to be fired. His days working for the state were not only *not* over but, as you will see, would soon become much more lucrative.

He did, however, become known amongst the vast majority of the prison system employees as someone not to associate, or even be seen with. He felt like a leper and not surprisingly, his job became miserable. So much so, that he was about to quit even if that meant he would lose his salary. He figured he would go on disability because he was afflicted with Caffeine Withdrawal Syndrome and it was included in the latest edition of the DSM, or the *Diagnostic and Statistical Manual of Mental Disorders*. In addition, his condition was included in The World Health Organization's: *The International Statistical Classification of Diseases and Related Health Problems*. Because of these listings, his ailment was officially considered a mental disorder and it made him eligible to receive disability payments. His only hesitation was the disability payments wouldn't be enough to cover even a third of his bills.

The warden, like countless other Americans, had bought, and continued to buy, all sorts of "you just have to have" items on his various credit cards. Because he couldn't afford any of those items he was now receiving threatening letters and phone calls demanding payment or else legal, or possibly even physical, action would be taken.

In addition to his creditors hounding him, he had insurance payments for his car and home, various utility bills, and since the newly passed Affordable Care Act was anything but, he would need to buy health insurance. Not to mention food, prescription drugs, and certainly coffee since he was medically and officially addicted to caffeine...through no fault of his own, of course. Therefore, he decided that he would keep his job and $105,000 a year salary and just learn to grin and bear it.

It just so happened, that the prison psychologist's problems with Sanguivoriphobia, not to mention his other phobias, had just come to light. He also did not lose his job and $200,000 a year salary because he was a state employee and he belonged to the International Association for Correctional and Forensic Psychology, or IACFP, and the unions called the shots in the state. After all of his phobias came to light, the psychological community shunned him even more than they had before. This particular shrink had never been a popular fellow, and now, well...it was unbearable for him. So, like the warden, his job at the prison became miserable. Problem was, he also couldn't quit and so he too, just decided to grin and bear it.

Chapter 44

Filmed Sessions

Maria gingerly walked back to her cell after her latest session with the prison shrink and she had to recover quickly for she had a meeting with the warden later that day. As Maria lay on her cot awaiting the meeting, at which she would learn her punishment for escaping and also be required to do her usual "meeting activities," she thought of her iPhone and decided that it *might* be her ticket out of here, and she really wanted to get out of here.

She would do a Google search and contact someone...anyone that may be able to help her. She knew it was a long shot, but it was a shot and she had to shoot *something*. All she had to do was get her iPhone, find a concealed location, and access one of the many websites that helped people "get out of prison early."[165] She looked high and low for her iPhone, but it was nowhere to be found. What Maria did not know was that her iPhone had been "confiscated" by the prison shrink after their last session.

He had informed the warden of Maria's little undertaking and they had devised a plan to make use of the situation. They transferred all of the data on Maria's iPhone to the shrink's office computer's hard drive; they also saved it to disk because it was too valuable to risk losing.

The hoosegow shrink had then uploaded the hours of film to the adult website he had also recently developed. It was easy for millions, possibly billions, of people to access the site

---

165   There really are some.

because all one had to do in order to be considered an "adult," was to click on a big, red, flashing button that read, "I am over 18" and he, or she, was in like Flynn. It was a supremely stringent system to shelter our striplings[166] from any sort of sexual curiosity and satisfaction. Then, as long as the users credit card was accepted, they could watch hours of Maria performing all sorts of interesting...uh "feats" with the warden and psychologist. There was undoubtedly a number of teenage boys that spent hours of school computer time watching Maria perform these amazing "feats."

---

166   A young man. I am assuming not many young girls visited the site.

Chapter 45

We're in the Money

The white Aston Martin One-77 screeched to a halt in the prison warden's parking spot and the warden stepped out. He loved his new car and wanted to flaunt it as much as possible. Who wouldn't? Right behind him came a red Lamborghini Veneno that screeched to a halt in the prison psychologist's parking spot, and out came the prison psychologist, surprisingly enough. The two men had gotten over the embarrassment and shame they had brought upon themselves and were now flaunting the loads of cash they were making. They loved going to work these days because they felt superior to any person they encountered. Loads of money will do that to some...uh most people.

The warden's Aston Martin One-77 has a price tag of only $1.85 million—buy two they're small. The prison psychologist's Lamborghini Veneno, of which only three were made, has a price tag of $3.9 million. These weren't the Manufacturer's *Suggested* Retail Prices these were the actual prices. If someone buys a car to which the manufacturer has to suggest a price it won't impress people very much, which is the whole point of buying a ridiculously expensive car. The two men high-fived each other and took turns admiring one another's car.

The two men hadn't gotten outrageously rich doing their jobs for the state. No, no, no. They had gotten outrageously rich from the website that the prison psychologist made. It turned out that every ex-con that had been sentenced to this particular prison during this particular warden's tenure, was willing to pay to watch him and the prison psychologist have their "meetings" and "sessions" with Maria. The fact that Maria was rather arresting[167] and a spectacular "performer" certainly did not hurt the number of subscriptions.

The ex-cons, and everyone they knew, were only a small fraction of the people who were willing to fork over good money to see a white, balding, fat man and nerdy, skinny guy with glasses have sex with a young, sexy, beautiful Mexican chic locked-up in prison. Talk about a turn-on for the "average Joe" or "medio José." Not surprisingly, millions of "average Joe's" and "medio José's" subscribed to the site.

In addition to the subscribers of the site, there were also large companies, from those that made Viagra to those that made taco shells, willing to advertise on the website. That is where the real money, and *a lot* of it, was made.

The warden and prison psychologist had become so rich and successful with their porn site, that they became very powerful in, not only the justice system, but the entire state. They also realized that to keep the money coming in, and their power wieldable, they needed fresh material on their website and therefore, they needed Maria.

To ensure that Maria was never transferred to a different facility or her prisoner status changed, they bought meetings with the right people and "greased" any, and all the right palms until they were sure Maria would be their "moneymaker" for a long time to come. Well, at least until the judicial system sent them another moneymaker.

To make sure that that they would be sent another moneymaker in the not-so-distant future, they "greased" the

---

167 Striking; eye-catching. Clever how I used "arresting" as an adjective here, don't' ya think?

hands, arms, and feet of the local sheriff and the local police. The "grease" encouraged them to detain good-looking Mexican women as often as they could.

They also "greased" the hands of the District Attorney and the local judges to make sure that any, and every, good-looking Mexican woman that was arrested ended-up in their jail. The justice system in the county and state was so covered in "grease" that it was hard to walk into a courtroom without slipping and falling down. The "grease" didn't stop there, however. It went international.

Their "grease" encouraged the Mexican Government to form some sort service that would help migrants cross the border into the United States. So, Mexico's Interior Ministry formed a number "Grupo Betas,"[168] whose purpose was: "not to detain migrants, but to help them." They would "provide vital assistance to hundreds of thousands of human beings trying to survive the vicious world of human migration." In other words: "If you want to leave Mexico and let some other country deal with you great; we'll even help you get there."

The guys who worked for any of the Grupo Betas also had their hands and entire bodies "greased" to make sure they gave extra assistance to young, attractive, female migrants. These Grupo Beta's were so successful that the Mexican Government greatly increased their funding.

This of course, was all to the extreme delight of the warden, the shrink, and Maria; even though she absolutely loathed being with these two men and making these "movies." She was delighted because the site had become such a worldwide

---

168 There really are Grupo Betas that were formed by the Mexican Government. I'm not making this up.

phenomenon that her lilliputian[169] cut of the profits was becoming a Brobdingnagian[170] amount of money. Even though her cut was extremely small compared to what the shrink and the warden were pulling in, it was more money than she had ever seen and she would send a large chunk of it back to her mother in Mexico.

Maria was blissfully unaware that her mother was using that money to buy the music and attend the concerts, all over the world, of bands that the church not only frowned upon but spit upon, also. Maria's mother had become a groupie of such notoriety that various hard rock bands not only wrote songs about her, but also had her enshrined on their tour busses and planes. Maria's mother was presently much happier (and more sexually satisfied) than she had ever been.

When Maria's mother was not traveling with some band, she was tormenting Ernesto's mother by buying nice clothes, expensive and unnecessary accoutrements,[171] and whatever else she could buy that she didn't need but that would make her look like a rich American. She would then flaunt her purchases in front of Ernesto's mother, not only to annoy her, but to act like a rich American and hopefully make Ernesto's mother envious.

---

169   Trivial or very small. Another word that only authors use.

170   Enormous; extraordinarily large. One of the lamest looking words I've ever seen. It looks like a dyslexic person with a severe case of ADD came up with it—no offense to anyone.

171   Additional items of dress or equipment, or other items carried or worn by a person or used for a particular activity.

Chapter 46

Ernesto Comes Back

Ernesto was sitting in the shade of a tree with an ice-cold Dos XX cerveza. Ernesto only drank Dos XX because he considered himself pretty darn interesting. As he drank his cerveza, he surfed the web on the iPhone that he had "borrowed" from an incredibly rude, American tourist with a major superiority complex.

He was just tapping on any link to any porn site that he came across and looked to be different from the countless others on the WWW. He was able to access any website that struck his fancy because he had also "borrowed" the credit card of a different rude tourist and used it to pay, and verify his age, for whatever site he chose to peruse.

After an hour or so of surfing the web he came across a site that intrigued him, for it was not like all the others. All the others featured females and males with perfect bodies having all kinds of great sex. This one didn't. It was a balding, fat man having forced sex with a beautiful, young, Latino woman. Other times, there was a nerdy looking guy with glasses having sex with what looked to Ernesto to be the same beautiful, Latino woman.

Ernesto entered all the credit card information so that he could have unlimited access to the site, got comfortable, took a swig of his Dos XX, and began to watch the first full-length "encounter" between the fat man and the hot Latino woman. After a few minutes of moans, squeals of pleasure, and breathtaking body positions, he got a look at the hot Latino woman's face and almost passed-out. For looking at him from between the balding, old, fat man's feet was his wife! *Holy shit! That is my wife! What the hell is she doing down there? I have to go back there! Right now!*

He immediately went back to his mother's (where he was living) and got everything he would need for his trip north to put an end Maria's burgeoning[172] film career. When he arrived at his mother's house, he found her sitting on the couch in tears.

Ernesto sat down with his mother and asked why she was crying. She proceeded to tell him how Maria's mother had all kinds of money now, from she knew not where, and she was flaunting it every chance she got. She told Ernesto about all of the nice clothes, the new car, the flatscreen TV, the DVD player, the Apple computer, and other things that she had recently bought.

She went on to say how Fernando (Ernesto's father) had left her soon after Ernesto was born and had never been heard from again. But, she had just found out that he had become a very wealthy Coyote and lived in a swanky[173] palace just outside of Tijuana.

A Coyote is someone who smuggles Latin Americans, Mexicans in Fernando's case, across the border for a high fee. Fernando had the highest fees of any Coyote...ever because he had the highest success rate—37%—of any coyote...ever. She was thinking about how it should be her with all of the nice things, and more, that Maria's mother had. Ernesto gave his mother a big hug and a small kiss and told her everything would be muy bueno soon.

---

172   Begin to grow or increase rapidly; flourish. Other things were burgeoning for Ernesto but I won't mention what.

173   Stylishly luxurious and expensive. He had an indoor and an outdoor pool, three hot tubs, a game room, a movie theater, a five car garage, horses, and his own taco stand complete with a Budweiser fountain.

He then left her in the house and made his way back to Birchwood, by stowing away on the back of a turnip truck, in order to get ahold of his wife and put a stop to all her frolicking about. When Ernesto arrived in Birchwood he just fell off the back of the turnip truck and immediately went to the police station to inquire about his wife, Maria Gonzalez-Escobar-Garcia-Gutierrez-Cruz-Chavez de Martinez.

He was told that she was in prison but there were visiting hours in which he could probably see her. After getting directions to the prison, Ernesto went to the restroom of the local gas station and cleaned himself up as best he could, which wasn't very good, and then hitchhiked to as close to the prison as he could. He didn't get very close as not many people are voluntarily going to a prison, and those who are, aren't normally in an eleemosynary[174] mood.

After walking the near mile from where he was dropped off to the actual prison, Ernesto stormed into the prison reception area and demanded to see his wife, the warden, and the prison psychologist, but not necessarily in that order. After the prison officials stopped laughing, they said none of those people were available, but if he were to come back during visiting hours he could see Maria.

"Well, I want see warden and shrink first," bellowed Ernesto.

"Well, *the* warden and *the* shrink are tied up at the moment and visiting hours for the prisoners are later, so–" came the reply.

"So...what?" interrupted Ernesto.

"Well, you can't see anyone right now and you will have to see Maria before you see the warden or the 'shrink,' as you call

---

174 Pronounced: el-uh-**mos**-uh-ner-ee and means relating to, or dependent on charity; charitable. People voluntarily going to a prison aren't normally in the mood to pick-up strangers and give them a lift.

302

him. Provided of course, that you have completed a Visitor Questionnaire, or CDCR Form 106."

"Well, where I get Form 106?" asked Ernesto.

"You obtain the California Department of Corrections and Rehabilitation Form 106 by having the prisoner you wish to visit send it to you and the prisoner must sign the questionnaire *before* sending it to the prospective visitor, which would be you in this case," stated the official.

Ernesto thought this was all totally pointless rigmarole and was becoming quite upset. So, he just stood there, took a deep breath, relaxed as best he could, closed and opened his fists, thought of his poor madre, and somewhat calmly asked when visiting hours were.

"Oh, they start in about three hours," came the reply.

Chapter 47

Visiting Hours

Ernesto left the prison reception area, went outside, and sat under a tree to reflect on how complicated and un-fun his life had gotten since the day he had arrived at that warehouse in Los Angeles. After nearly three hours of reflecting (Ernesto's mind didn't work too fast) he saw two guys come out of the prison and walk to the parking lot high-fiving each other, laughing, and rubbing their necks the entire way. He watched as they each got into an exotic, expensive-looking sports car peeled out, and drove away.

Ernesto saw that it was now visiting hours so, he got up and marched into the reception area of the prison and demanded to see Maria, even though he didn't have CDCR Form 106. The prison officials were tired of dealing with him, so they briskly showed him into the visitation area, said Maria would be out shortly, and just left him there.

When Maria entered the visitation area, anger welled up in Ernesto to volcanic proportions, for Maria's hair was a total mess, she had hickeys all over her neck, and she had a roguish[175] smile on her face. She also had the look of satisfaction that Ernesto recognized as the look she would always have after they had done the Tempurpedic Tango.

Maria sat down on the other side of the clear partition and picked-up the "phone." Ernesto did the same thing on his side of the partition and was infuriated by what he heard.

---

175 Playfully mischievous, especially in a way that is sexually attractive. Guys don't normally give roguish smiles.

Maria said in Spanish, "Hi honey, how's it going?" She spoke in a cheerful but tired voice; the same voice she used with Ernesto after their lovemaking to ask him how he felt.

Ernesto was pissed. Another man, well *men* actually, was satisfying his wife and he, well they, was a stupid American cracker. He clenched his "phone" and got right to the point: "So whose foreskin are you rumpling?" Before he got an answer he said, "Your damn Mom is torturing my Mom. It has to stop or else..." He spoke rapidly in Spanish, of course.

"Or else what?" snapped Maria with a look of contentment and defiance on her face. She also spoke rapidly in Spanish.

"Uh well, I don't know yet but it won't be good. And, uh your Mom, what's up with her? She's all rich now. She's buying all kinds of stuff and then shows it all off in front of mi mamá. She brags about everything she buys and she's been going on tour with American rock bands;" both of which were unforgiveable offenses in Ernesto's mind. He did not let Maria respond and continued with his tirade: "So, why *are* you screwing a balding, white man and a nerdy cracker? They're both stupid Americans, I mean it's gross."

Maria just sat and listened to Ernesto with a provocative smile and a look of contentment on her face. Once he finished his diatribe she said, "I'm a vampire now. I just bit the warden and shrink. I control them now."

"What?" said Ernesto in utter disbelief. "Vampire? Are you crazy?" He was trying not to laugh.

"No. No. I'm not crazy. In fact, I just made a really good investment."

"Investment? What the hell are you talking about?"

"I just made two more Vampires. They don't realize it yet, but they will."

"You did? You made vampires?" Ernesto was losing his battle not to laugh. "And it's an investment? How is that an investment?" he asked skeptically while chuckling.

"Well, during our last...uh meeting, I bit them and so I will soon have a brood that I control," answered Maria. "And since I am their Sire,[176] I will take all of the profits from our little film venture, and *that*, my dear husband, is a good investment. Not only that, but I can run the whole operation and won't have to be in the films unless I want to."

You are a vampire? You bit them? Your brood? Under my control? You are their Sire? What the hell is she talking about? I know about the films, but...a Vampire? Come on! At first, he wondered if he was talking to the right Maria, and if so, what drugs was she on because he wanted some. He was fairly certain that if, by some chance, what she was saying was actually true, it was good news. But he didn't think any of this could *possibly* be true.

Not surprisingly, he didn't have much experience talking with, or even knowing a vampire so, he didn't know what to say or do. He just sat with his mouth agape and stared at Maria; she stared right back. He was making a rather feeble attempt at processing all the information he had just been given.

Finally, he asked, "Are you serious? You want to take over the filthy, old crackers dirty movie business?" *Hmm, that could be muy bueno.* Making money was Ernesto's top priority. The fact that his wife said she was a vampire and had cheated on him was only an afterthought.

"Yeah. Why not?" replied Maria. "They now drive very fast, very nice, very expensive sports cars and so could we." She

---

176   A vampire who turns humans into vampires.

knew that would excite and probably titillate[177] her husband. "It must be easy because they are not too bright and they've made a lot of money."

"I know. I saw them," said Ernesto with a far-off, glazed look in his eyes. He was thinking now, that didn't happen very often but when it did, devious plans were always the result. "What would happen if the crackers suddenly disappeared?"

Maria immediately put her middle finger in front of her lips and said, "Shhh, not here. I'll send you a letter. Will you be at your Mom's house?"

"Yes."

---

177 Stimulate or excite especially in a sexual way. I wonder if that is where the slang term "tits" for female breast originted. I bet it is.

Chapter 48

Laurent Keeps Quiet

Laurent arrived at 7:52 A.M. for his first day of work at Big Goose Cellars. Laurent had been hired to replace Todd Milksop, on account he was in jail awaiting trial. Laurent had also been hired because William Strong thought a French-speaking employee in the cellar would make him and his winery more respected. He wanted there to be no doubt as to the bona fidety of Big Goose Cellars on the world's premium wine producer's stage.

Those were the "official" reasons he had been hired. However, neither of those were the actual reason Laurent had been hired. The actual reason was that William Strong wanted to keep him quiet about the homosexual trysts he would have with Laurent's father whenever he went to France, and he went often.

Secrets were nearly impossible to keep in Fiasco Valley, but William figured that if he managed to keep Laurent quiet, his secret would stay a secret, even though he wasn't sure Laurent even knew. If word got out in the valley that he was having a long-distance homosexual affair, his standing in the Valley would be lost and his life, as he knew it, would be over. William did not want that, as he had spent his entire life building an image of himself, not only as a rough-and-tough businessman, but also as a tender-hearted ladies man. That is the man his wife had married and he worried of the devastating effects his secret would have on her, not to mention on his career.

William needn't have worried, because Mrs. Strong was already aware of his trysts and was secretly hoping they would not only continue, but occur more often, as she was having her own homosexual trysts with Laurent's mother. Whenever William went to France, Laurent's mother would come to Fiasco Valley and spend quality time with Mrs. Strong. It worked out quit well for everyone involved...especially the airlines.

As soon as Laurent arrived at the winery, he was tasked with pumping wine from one tank to another; but first he had to clean and sterilize the recipient tank. While he was doing that, Tim Tauscher came by to see how things were coming along. Laurent immediately went into his spiel about how the wineries in France did these tasks, and all others, much better than any American winery did.

Tim just looked at Laurent and shook his head. He had worked with, and for, French people in the past and was well aware of their insufferable chauvinism and attitudes toward the American wine industry. However, Laurent, as well as the other French people Tim had worked with and for, did seem to know what he was doing, had a passion for wine, was a good worker, and did as he was told.

So, Tim took a deep breath and said, "We can discuss that at a later time. But right now, we have to get that tank ready and the wine moved."

With one last comment under his breath about the superiority of French wine, Laurent got back to cleaning and sterilizing the tank. When he finished (he had done a good job) he pumped it full of the wine from the source tank.

While the tank was being filled, a group of tourists came by on a tour (Gee, imagine *tourists* being on a tour.) They heard Laurent speak with his French accent and the women on the tour thought he was just adorable. One lady tried to ask him a question about wine in French, but she butchered the language and actually asked Laurent how old his horse was. *Oh man, I wish was hunting right now. Humph, well maybe I'll hunt them later.* Laurent just smiled with alacrity[178] and took in the whole group.

They had put him in a surly mood and his hunting DT's were beginning to rear their ugly heads. He remembered he had his 30.06 rifle and some ammo in his car so, there was a definite possibility he *could* do some hunting later on and that made him feel better. He had a couple touron tags left over from his earlier hunting excursion so he figured he would be hunting legally, according to his laws anyway.

When Laurent had finished moving the wine, cleaning all of the equipment he had used—pumps, clamps, hoses, gaskets, the source tank, the floor—and putting everything back in its proper place, he noticed the tourons were still at the winery. They, along with Tim and William, were having a wine tasting with food out on the patio by the tasting room. Laurent smiled to himself, went to his car, and then snuck up the hill behind the winery.

---

178   Brisk and cheerful readiness. I want to punch people with those smiles at 7:00 a.m.

Chapter 49

Shots Fired

Detective Knight was disappointed that he had seen the website featuring Maria, the warden, and the shrink. He had "stumbled" across it while doing research on immigrants being sold into slavery for the sex industry, and now the mystique and charisma that added to Maria's desirability were gone. To make matters worse, he couldn't get the images of the naked and obviously sexually aroused warden and shrink out of his head.

Still striving to banish those images from his mind, he drove up the drive leading to Big Goose Cellars. He knew that he shouldn't be doing what he was doing but try as he might, he couldn't help himself. He had heard, through the grapevine, that good 'ol William had hired another young, beautiful, Mexican secretary that made Maria look like an ugly duckling. Detective Knight didn't believe it, but he had to make sure.

As he neared the winery, he glanced out his window and thought he saw somebody sneaking up the hill with what looked to be a rifle. *Now what the...? Was that a dude? Did he have a rifle?* Detective Knight slowed his 4Runner and stopped next to a large Elm tree and scrutinized the hillside hoping to get a better look at what he thought he had seen. He hadn't been looking for long when he saw some movement behind a big tree next to a large rock. He couldn't be sure, but it sure looked like the dude he had just seen sneaking up the hill with what looked to be a rifle. Detective Knight had no idea what was going on, but he knew one of the first rules to being a detective was that if you saw someone sneaking around with a gun, you kept watching; but only if the person with the gun was going away from you.

While he sat there watching and drinking the Mocha he had gotten from the local coffee shop, he studied everyone on the tasting room patio having a wine tasting. There were three obvious couples, but only one woman. After about twenty minutes of chitchat in which Tim and William tried to make the tourons feel as though they were semi-versed in wine, they excused themselves and walked into the wine cellar in order to laugh, which they did quite uproariously.

David watched for another few minutes and then got out of his truck and relieved himself behind the large Elm tree as his Mocha was yelling at him. As he was zipping-up and paying close attention to a manly part of himself, he heard the crack of a gunshot and looked-up just in time to see all six of the tourons hit the deck. He heard a hissing sound and saw one of the limousine's tires going flat. One touron then stood-up and said, "Aw relax, a tire just blew."

The remaining five tourons stood-up and began to brush themselves off when a second loud crack was heard. Again, there was a loud hissing noise as another tire went flat. The tourons stood there scratching their heads wondering how cheap these tires must be, when a third gunshot was fired and the limousine's windshield shattered into tiny bits. The tourons stood rooted where they were with eyes wide open and mouths agape. They stared at each for a moment and suddenly, in unison, they all hit the deck. It was the classic "numbskull-delayed" response.

"Someone is shooting at us!" screamed the woman.

"Why would someone be shooting at us?" a guy said.

"I have no idea. Just stay on the ground," answered a different male touron. "That seems the safest thing to do."

312

By the time the third shot was fired, Detective Knight was peering out at the big tree and the large rock. He saw the shooter stand-up, point his rifle at the tourons, shoot, and then sit back down behind the rock in order to be hidden.

Holy frijoles! He's shooting at those people! Geez! I should probably do something. So, David quickly finished zipping-up, (he had quit in mid-motion when the shooting started) jumped in his 4Runner, and drove up to the tourons. As he drove, he kept an eye on the big tree and the large rock. His vigilance paid off, for he knew the shooter was still up there as he didn't see anyone leave. Unless, of course, there was a secret tunnel, or passageway, or something, allowing the shooter to escape unseen, but Detective Knight didn't think there was much chance of that. Why? No one knows, he just didn't. Detective Knight reasoned he could sneak up there and arrest him...hopefully.

When he reached the tourons, he looked at them and they looked okay, so he didn't stop; he just drove straight to the base of the hill from where the shots had been fired. He carefully parked his 4Runner, quietly got out, and then stealthily walked up the hill towards the big tree and large rock, as he certainly did not want the dude with the gun to notice him.

Detective Knight knew there was someone up there with a gun shooting at people and he didn't want to get himself shot, but he *did* want to catch the sucker. What he didn't know was that it was Laurent up there and, during this shooting spree, he had begun to wear sackcloth and ashes[179] for having killed people.

---

179   If you "wear sackcloth and ashes," you show that you are very sorry for something you did wrong. In the past, clothes made of sackcloth (a rough cloth) were worn by the Jews in religious activities to show that they were sad or sorry for the things they had done wrong. Laurent had begun to feel small pangs of guilt. Pang: a sudden sharp pain or painful emotion.

Laurent needn't have felt that way because unbeknownst to him (but not to you, dear reader) he hadn't actually killed *anyone*. Sure, people had died but Laurent hadn't killed them.

Anyhow, Detective Knight snuck up the hill until he saw the shooter sitting on a fallen tree branch holding his rifle.

"Don't move or I'll shoot!" shouted Detective Knight, even though he didn't have a gun. Laurent heard this command and decided he would definitely move. He stood up, still holding his rifle, and took off running. He didn't know where he was going; he just knew he had to get away. If caught, he figured he would get the death sentence because Americans, unlike the enlightened French, are ignorant buffoons and would kill you to teach others not to kill.

In his infinite wisdom, Laurent decided he would run back to his car and just drive away unbelievably fast. He didn't take into account that there aren't too many 1.5 million dollar, pink, sports cars driving around and so he would be rather conspicuous and that's certainly not the way to be if one is trying to get away from the cops.

As he approached his car, he noticed something odd. His car looked different. It wasn't setting right, or at least not how he had left it. When he reached the car, Laurent discovered the problem: It was sitting on blocks because all of the wheels had been stolen. His beloved Bugatti Veyron 16.4 had been rendered useless when he needed it most. He slowly sank to his knees, cursing the U.S. the whole way. As he sank, he noticed that scratched into the paint were the words: "Deth to 1%ers!!!" Laurent didn't know what that meant or referred to (he wasn't familiar with the word "Deth" or what 1% had to do with anything). All he knew was that his car had been greatly devalued and he was not happy. He looked back and and saw that Detective Knight was still following him so, he stood up and took off running through the vineyards in the direction of the hills.

Chapter 50

No Mayberry Here

Laurent's self-preservation instinct led him back into the hills that formed Fiasco Valley. Detective Knight was right behind Laurent and determined to apprehend him when he happened to spot a couple of girls sunbathing nude in a little hidden meadow near the creek. Detective Knight stopped running and immediately forgot about Laurent.

Now, Laurent on the other hand, either didn't see the girls, had too much on his mind to take advantage of the situation, his procreation instinct did not override his self-preservation instinct, or he was simply more like his father than he wanted to be, so he had just kept running. This was fine with David because American women seemed to dig foreigners; especially ones with a sultry French accent, and David wanted as little competition in this situation as possible.

David Knight stopped and just watched the girls until his gallantry forced him to approach the girls and ask if he could be of any assistance. He offered to rub suntan lotion all over them or to sit and watch for bears, or coyotes, or lions, or elephants, or...anything at all. He was a paragon of gallantry.

Meanwhile, Laurent found a well-hidden spot on the hill near a creek that would provide shelter and water, so he set-up camp, so to speak. He planned on laying low for awhile to give him a chance to think and figure out what to do next. He figured he could live for at least a month just by drinking water, although it *was* American water so, who knows? However, after only a couple of days, Laurent was so hungry he was willing to risk going to town and looking in dumpsters for food. What he did, however, turned out to be much better.

Laurent had a French buddy, Pierre, who worked at a restaurant in Birchwood and he often complained to Laurent about how Americans wasted so much food that he could at least partially solve world hunger just by saving the leftovers. On a nightly basis, he threw out ten or eleven meals in which only a few bites had been taken since the patrons refused to take the leftovers home (wealthy people dining in Birchwood would never stoop that low.)

Laurent made his way to the alley behind the restaurant and waited for Pierre to come out on his smoking break. When he appeared, Laurent asked him if he would bring any leftovers outside and give them to him. He agreed, and so Laurent ate better that night than he had in months.

After filling his stomach, Laurent went back to his mountain hideaway feeling very confident that everything would turn out alright. Problem was, Laurent failed to take into account that Pierre only worked on Friday and Saturday nights and was not a very good employee to boot.

By the time Thursday night rolled around, Laurent was hungry again but couldn't get ahold of Pierre to alert him that he was coming for leftovers. With his tummy growling, Laurent decided to go with his original plan and just look for food in *any* dumpster behind *any* restaurant.

There was a large dumpster behind the fancy French restaurant in town, The French Laundromat (It had a yearlong waiting list just for reservations.) and he settled down in the bushes behind it and waited for someone to toss out food. It was a short wait but he needn't have waited at all, for there was already plenty of food in the dumpster, as food had been tossed out continually the entire day.

After this "freshest" food had been tossed, Laurent ran to the dumpster and dove in head first. Once in the dumpster, Laurent dove into the food (apparently, Laurent liked to dive.) *I no realize how hungry I was. This food effing good!*

It wasn't really, but as my mother always says, "Hunger is a wonderful sauce" and Laurent thought he was eating the most wonderful sauce of his life. The sauce made the food taste so good that he ate until he thought he would pop. When he could physically eat no more, he managed to get out of the dumpster and stumble back to his mountain hideaway.

Laurent was bilious[180] when he got back to his hideaway and just fell into "bed," but not before he had puked all over it. His "bed" was just a pile of leaves, weeds, sticks, really small rocks, and now, fresh vomit. He stayed in his "bed," all of Friday and most of Saturday. About dinnertime on Saturday Laurent, who hadn't eaten anything since Thursday and was feeling more than a bit peckish, got out of his "bed," cleaned-up as best he could (which wasn't very good) and went back to the restaurant where Pierre worked in the hopes getting a bit of edible food.

Laurent waited for three hours hoping to catch Pierre on a smoking break but he never came out for one. However, a different worker did come out with leftovers to be thrown away, so Laurent approached him.

"You know Pierre?" he asked.

"Pierre?"

---

180   1. Unsettled in the stomach, as if about to vomit. 2. Extremely unpleasant to look at. 3. Bad-tempered and irritable. By the time Laurent reached his mountain hideaway, he was three for three as far as biliousness goes.

"Oui, Pierre. You know him? You know where is?"

"Pierre no here anymore. Got fired," answered the worker.

"Fired?" said Laurent in a surprised voice. "You sure?"

"Oui. Oui"

Now what the hell am I supposed to do? I am sick and need food. I have no money. Laurent left the restaurant feeling discouraged, hungry, and nauseous. So, he tottered back to his beloved hideaway to lie down. By the time he got home, he felt worse than he had on Thursday night. In fact, he was beginning to feel so bad that he wasn't sure if he would survive until morning. He spent the entire night sweating, smelling his own bad breath, his own bodily emissions, and trying to figure out his next move. As he lay there thinking about what he should, or more likely *could* do, his mind kept wandering back to his life in France and how he longed for it. He thought about his favorite TV show, "The Andy Griffith Show," that he watched each and every morning, as his father had an extremely good satellite television system that got television stations from anywhere in the world that aired programs tailored to homosexual men.

On "The Andy Griffith Show," which takes place in the town of Mayberry, a character named Otis, who was the town drunk, would put himself in jail on weekend nights after he had gotten drunk on illegal moonshine. He did this in order to sober-up safely and not cause any problems. Laurent, however, didn't buy that explanation. He figured Otis did it because he didn't want to go home and see the old lady or maybe he just felt guilty because he wasn't French. Whatever the reason, Otis would sleep off his drunkenness and let himself out of jail (the key for the jail was hanging on the wall at arms reach) in the morning and go home to his lovely wife, well as lovely as she could be without being French.

Neither the Sheriff nor his deputy ever arrested Otis or gave him any trouble for partaking in the excessive consumption of moonshine. In fact, they encouraged this behavior...at least the part about putting himself in jail, sleeping off the drunkenness, and then letting himself out in the morning.

Laurent, who was delirious from something he had eaten, decided to get up, find the police station in Birchwood, put himself in jail, and then everything would be better in the morning. Much to Laurent's surprise, however, the police Station in Birchwood was nothing like the police station in Mayberry.

There was no jail cell with steel bars in the same room as the police chief and his deputies. The jail cell in Birchwood was out behind the police station and was more like a 7' x 7' closet than a jail cell in Mayberry. It had a small toilet with no lid or back, a small drinking fountain, and some sort of pad on a small frame that was supposed to be a bed; at least that's what Laurent figured it to be. There was no comfy chair, no pitcher of water or iced tea, no flowers or reading materials, and there were no windows.

He couldn't talk to the Sheriff or his deputy. He couldn't even *see* the Sheriff or his deputy, much less anything else. The only things he could see were the grey cement walls, but he did have a good look at those.

It was a good thing Laurent is only about 5' 6" otherwise, he would not have fit on the pad and so couldn't have lain down and gotten comfortable. Laurent was used to luxury and wouldn't do anything unless he could be relaxed and comfortable. He had been lying there for what seemed like an eternity, just staring at the ceiling thinking about Otis and

Aunt Bea and waiting for Barney or the Sheriff to appear, when he heard a noise and the door flew open. A hot female police officer, accompanying a gentleman in handcuffs, came in, saw Laurent, and did a double take for she had been told the jail cell was empty.

"Who the hell are you and why the hell are you in here?" she blurted in surprise. But before Laurent could answer she asked, "And how the hell did you get in here...and when in the hell?" She liked the word "hell" apparently.

Laurent stood-up and calmly said, "I kill people and so, I put me in jail. The door open and I come in Saturday night and sleep."

The hot female police officer, Kaitlin, stood there astounded, as she had no idea what to do or say. All she knew was she wanted to get away from this ferocious frog, at least she assumed he was French because of his French accent.

As she stood staring at Laurent and trying not to breathe through her nose, for the cell had an undefineable and unsavory bouquet, she remembered hearing talk of how the handsome and sexy Detective Knight was working on the recent, unprecedented killings in the valley and she thought this guy might somehow be involved. So, without a word and with thoughts of Detective Knight wearing a Speedo racing through what passed for her mind, she abruptly turned around with her handcuffed companion and returned to the police station. Once there, she asked what the hell was going on.

"What? There is someone in the jail?" asked a macho officer with incredulity. "It's probably one of those damn Yankzee kids. They are a real pain in the posterior."

"Well, whoever it is, he gave someone more than a pain in

the posterior. He said he killed someone and so put himself in jail last night. But I don't know, I think he's probably on some type of drug or something," said Kaitlin.

This macho male officer didn't believe the only female cop in Birchwood, so he got up from his desk and marched out to the jail cell to see for himself. The officer opened the cell door and saw, to his shock, that there *was* someone in there. He spoke with the captive for a moment, recognized his accent as being French, and decided it wasn't a damn Yankzee kid after all. He marched back into the office and told everyone what he had learned.

"But I have no idea who the hell it is," he said. "Some French dude who's pissed-off about something"

The female officer had gotten on the radio and tracked down Detective Knight. She told him that a French guy had thrown himself in jail because he had killed someone.

"What? He killed someone? Did he say who?" asked a surprised Detective Knight, for he had taken care of all the murders he had been apprised of and was unaware of any new ones. However, that's not saying much as Detective Knight was often unaware of happenings around him, except when it came to nude sunbathers.

"No," the hot female officer stated, "Why don't you come down and have a look?" *And I can get good look your nice derrière.*

"Okay. I'll be there shortly." With that, Detective Knight got in his 4Runner and drove straight to the police station. Well, he did stop at the nearest coffee shop and got a Mocha, but other than that he went straight there; he didn't spare the horses.[181]

---

181 "don't spare the horses" – expresses the importance of doing something as fast as possible. It comes from the days when people used to travel about in horse drawn carriages.

When he arrived at the police station, Kaitlin filled him in on the situation and took him out to the jail cell to show him the guy confessing to murder. As soon as Kaitlin opened the cell door and entered, Laurent, who thought she was pretty hot, jumped up in order to accost[182] her. Detective Knight, being the gallant guy he was, stepped forward, pushed Laurent away from Kaitlin, and told him to go back and sit down. When he turned his back to go sit down, Detective Knight recognized him as the man he had chased through the hills for shooting at the tourists. He grabbed the female officer and hurriedly ushered her back out of the cell.

"That's the guy I was chasing through the hills the other day because he was shooting at people," detective Knight informed the officer. "He's a nut case. Don't go near him alone because who knows what the little croissant will do."

"So, he *did* kill people," she stated.

"No. Not a one. He's a really bad shot."

"Well then, he must *think* he killed people. I wonder..." her voice trailed off as she thought. Then she said, "Does he know he's a bad shot?"

"Uh, what do you mean?" asked David.

"Well, he confessed to killing people but you said there have been no murders except the ones you were dealing with, and those have all been solved. Maybe he *thinks* he shot and killed people but didn't because he a missed them."

Kaitlin had dated French guys in the past and they were the most arrogant and egotistical guys she had ever been out with.

---

182   Approach and address someone with sexual intent. *This* particular definition should be used because it has a sexual component and not all of them do.

They were complete narcissists.[183] They thought they were God's gift to humanity and could do no wrong. If something did actually go wrong, it was never their fault,[184] and they could have prevented it in the first place. She didn't know it, but she had just perfectly pegged Laurent's personality.

"It sounds like he could be a non compos mentis narcissist," she said hoping David would be impressed with her mind and take notice, as she was tired of guys just noticing her body, which they always did because she always wore tight, revealing clothes.

"What the hell does 'non compos mentis' mean?" asked an annoyed David.

"It means he's insane."

"An insane narcissist? Hmm, that would be new one, but it doesn't really mattter, I mean it's pretty obvious he's not mentally stable." David said this as he was standing there trying to avoid having the hot female officer notice he was staring at her chest and wondering what it would be like to play with it.

"So, who was he shooting at? Is that why you were chasing him?"

"Well, yeah. I saw him shoot at some tourists, so I went to arrest him and he ignored my demands and ran away. That's why I was chasing him, but–"

"He got away from you?" interrupted Kaitlin.

Detective Knight was in good physical condition, was very athletic, and had the reputation that no one he chased ever got away.

---

183 A narcissist has excessive self-admiration and self-centeredness. It is a personality disorder in which the afflicted (the person with the disorder) overestimates his own abilities and has an excessive need for admiration. Barack Obama is the poster child for this condition.

184 Listen to any of Obama's speeches. He's the king narcissist. Nothing is his fault.

"Yes, I was...ah...distracted, you might say by uh... unanticipated events." David would not say another word because the "unanticipated events" had resulted in him getting yet another case of blue balls and that is something guys never, ever, *ever* mention.

Fortunately, this conversation was forcing David to concentrate on Laurent because he didn't want one brain cell tasked with thinking of how and why he had gotten his most recent case of bolas azules.[185] Having all of his brainpower now focused on Laurent, Detective Knight was able to put one and one together.

"He's the guy who shot the tanks," David exclaimed suddenly, "and at the tourists at Stone Mountain." It was an epiphany.

"Huh? Tanks? Tourists at Pebble Hill? He thinks he shot people there?"

"Apparently," said David. "I bet he thinks he killed them and his conscience was beginning to bother him. To bad more criminals don't end-up having a conscience that bothers them. My job would be so much easier."

"Then you'd be out of a job," stated the female officer. *And you'd end up with a permanent case of blue balls because no woman wants to be with a man unless he's making money...and the more the better.*

"Oh, I'd figure something out," and with that, David went to the jail cell to talk with Laurent.

---

185   "Blue balls" in Spanish.

Chapter 51

"I Take Fifth"

Detective Knight heard strange noises coming from the cell holding Laurent. For personal safety reasons and since he didn't know what the noises were, he didn't just barge right in. He lightly knocked and then timidly, some might say cautiously, opened the door and slowly, some might say carefully, stepped inside. What he saw was Laurent keeping himself busy and he showed no signs of stopping.

Detective Knight just stood in the doorway with his eyes closed and waited for Laurent to finish "getting the job done." What else could he do? Except leave for a time, watch him, or join in. Detective Knight certainly wasn't going to join in, there wasn't much to watch and/or see, and he wasn't going to leave thereby giving Laurent some sort of small victory.

When Detective Knight heard Laurent squeal in pleasure and breathe a sigh of relief, he opened his eyes, told Laurent to clean himself up, put on some clothes, and get ready to answer some questions.

After Laurent had cleaned-up and dressed, he asked, "Okay, what you want know?"

"Did you shoot at people at Supercilious Cellars?" asked Detective Knight. Detective Knight always got straight to the point because he hated "beating around the bush."

"I take Fifth," answered Laurent because he had watched enough American television and seen enough American movies to know that was the correct answer when a lawyer, a cop, or anyone asked you a question you didn't like or might cause you problems in the future.

"Okay. Sure. Whatever. Then, did you shoot at people at Pebble Hill Vineyards?"

"I take Fifth."

Detective Knight hoped he wouldn't get that answer but it didn't surprise him, so he remained calm...well pretty calm.

"Now Laurent, I know you shot at people at Big Goose Cellars because I saw you do it," said David Knight through clenched teeth. "You then resisted arrest and I had to chase you through the hills. Why were you running from me?"

"I want lawyer present and I take Fifth," answered Laurent contemptuously.

Detective Knight sighed because Laurent had every right to "take the Fifth" and to have a "lawyer present." It didn't make much sense to David, but then not much did nowadays. *I can't believe that someone who is just standing on U.S. dirt has the same rights and protections as someone who was pushed out of a womb here. They haven't paid the price of admission* (taxes) *so they shouldn't be allowed to enjoy the show. It makes no sense to me but...it's in our Constitution so I guess I'll have to live with it. What they were thinking when they wrote that thing?*

Detective Knight left Laurent, returned to the police station, and told everyone what Laurent had said; it didn't take long. As luck would have it, in the police station was a male, fledgling[186] lawyer who had never been in court and was there just to hit on the hot female police officer, as she was well known to the entire male populace of Birchwood, if not all of Fiasco Valley.

---

186 A person or organization that is immature, inexperienced, or underdeveloped. I'm a fledgling...everything.

"I'll be his lawyer," he said hoping to impress Kaitlin. "Let me talk to him."

It sounded okay to David so, he took him out to the jail cell and introduced him to Laurent.

Chapter 52

Answer Me Truthfully

The greenhorn lawyer entered the cell with Detective Knight, who made introductions and then promptly left. As soon as he was gone, the lawyer explained to Laurent toot sweet[187] that he needed to answer all questions asked of him truthfully and completely in order to be helped effectively, or in other words: To get off scot-free.

"My job is to get you out of here," said the lawyer. "It doesn't matter to me if you are guilty or not, but I do need to know what I'm working with. So, tell me, did you shoot at the tourists visiting Supercilious Cellars?"

"Oui. I kill them," said Laurent cheerfully and matter-of-factly.

The lawyer raised his eyebrows and wrote something in his notebook.

"Okay. Did you then shoot the tourists at Pebble Hill Vineyards?"

"Oui. I kill them too."

The lawyer again raised his eyebrows and wrote in his notebook. He was glad Laurent was answering these questions truthfully, but he seemed a little too cavalier[188] in his answers. He wondered why because his answers could land him prison for the rest of his life or even get him put to death.

He left the cell and went back into the police station posthaste[189] to get some more information that might explain

---

187   Immediately

188   Showing a lack of proper concern; offhand.

189   With great speed or immediacy.

why Laurent was being so cavalier with his answers, vis-à-vis[190] these murders.

"Well, he just freely admitted to shooting and killing those people," said the lawyer.

"What?" asked an astonished Detective Knight. "He didn't take the Fifth?"

"No, he seemed kind of proud actually. Like he wanted to tell me."

"Proud?" said Detective Knight, the hot female officer, and the other officer in surprised unison. "But he didn't *kill* anybody," added Detective Knight.

"What? He didn't?" asked the lawyer whose turn it was to be surprised.

"No. He shot *at* them, but that's all. He missed," stated David. He then thought about Laurent, and his kind, for a moment, and suddenly got a got big grin on his face, for he had another epiphany. He yelled, "Oh man! Let me tell him he didn't kill anyone. I can't wait to see the look on his face!"

David had realized that Laurent was trying to kill Americans, tourists of Fiasco Valley anyway, because he felt they were so inferior to the French and were complete wine ignoramuses. David couldn't wait to see how Laurent looked when he was informed that he failed miserably in his quest to kill the "Inferior Americans."

The lawyer and the hot female police officer looked at each other with confused looks but didn't say anything.

"Okay, whatever," said the lawyer. "That's fine by me."

"Great, I'll go right now. You want to join me Kaitlin?"

---

190   In relation to; with regard to. Are you thinking I'm a well-educated, world traveler? I hope so, because that's what I want you to think.

Detective Knight used the first name of the hot female officer and asked her in such a way that he hoped it would annoy the lawyer and make him envious because he simply liked to annoy lawyers and did so at any, and every, possible opportunity.

Detective David Knight and Kaitlin then went into the jail cell to give Laurent the good news, depending on your point of view, of course. Detective Knight could not wait to see Laurent's reaction.

"It turns out you didn't kill anybody," stated Detective Knight gleefully.

What? thought a shocked and disappointed Laurent as he lay on the pad. *I didn't kill anybody? Impossible!*

Detective Knight continued, "You missed the tourists at Supercilious Cellars but you did hit the tanks. Therefore, you *are* an accomplice to their murders because they died from all the wine they drank that came out of the holes you shot in the tanks." David paused, stared at Laurent for a long moment while smiling, and continued. "You are not very good shot, are you? I mean my ninety year-old grandma with cataracts can shoot better than you," added Detective Knight because he couldn't resist that slight slur. He carried on, "Then you shot at the tourists at Pebble Hill Vineyards, but fortunately for them, you barely grazed them. That means your bullet just gave them a little scratch."

"I know what mean," said an annoyed Laurent. "It because I use American rifle and it no good."

Detective Knight ignored that last comment and said, "Oh, but that's not all, not by a long shot...pun intended. At Big Goose Cellars, I *saw* you shoot at and miss, amazingly enough, more tourists. You did hit their limousine though, and that'll cost ya, and not just money but jail-time as well."

"It because American rifle no good."

"No. It's because the shooter can't shoot. Now, speaking of cost, Supercilious Cellars estimates you cost them a total of 1.75 million dollars in wine lost down the drain, future wine sales, loss of tourism, and bad press in general. They want restitution." Detective Knight said this with gritted teeth and his mouth right next to the ear of Laurent as he lay on his stomach on the bed.

Laurent didn't hear any of this however, as he was trying to comprehend how he had missed those pathetic, American tourists. He rolled over, his lips nearly coming into contact with Detective Knight's lips, and asked, "What about fat lady in parking lot? I kill her?"

Detective David Knight didn't answer. He just stood there and stared at Laurent balefully[191] because he did not like Laurent and thought he was just arrogantly messing with his mind, for he had no clue who Laurent was talking about.

"What about her? I kill her?" asked Laurent again, insistently.

After a few seconds, Detective Knight looked over at Kaitlin hoping to get some help but she just shrugged her shoulders and shook her head; she had lots of practice doing that. Detective Knight needed to know about this "fat lady in parking lot" business, so he went back into the police station to find out about this person.

Once in the police station, he was directed to a report that had recently been completed and was sitting on the Chief's desk. Detective David Knight grabbed a cup of coffee, sat behind the Chief's desk and put his feet on top of it, opened the report, and began reading.

---

191   Threatening harm; menacing.

According to the report, a morbidly obese woman had been found sitting against a tree in a winery's parking lot. She was not able to stand and was suffering from heat exhaustion, as she had been there all afternoon. When help arrived, she was loaded into the vehicle and driven to the Emergency Room of the local hospital. After numerous lengthy and expensive tests, it was determined that, not only was this woman suffering from heat exhaustion, but she also had a bullet lodged in her body; in the layers of fat on her body to be exact. When the doctors asked her about it, she thought and thought, but couldn't even *imagine* where the bullet had come from.

After signing two handfuls of forms, the hospital released her. But, she had become so distraught over this bullet business that she went to a hypnotist to be hypnotized (imagine that) in order to hopefully bring up memories as to where the bullet had come from. During her hypnosis she remembered that on her recent trip to a winery, she thought a bee had stung her and so had panicked and fallen over. She remembered lying in the parking lot until a big, black dude picked her up, put her in the shade of a tree, and gave her some water.

Detective Knight needed more information, as the report was woefully incomplete. So, he called the tour company to find out who had been driving their bus that went to the winery on that particular day. After a few minutes of listening to a recording of a syrupy sweet female voice tell him to stay on the line because his call was important, a male employee came on the line and was able to tell Detective Knight that their driver that day did not work there anymore because he had recently become disabled and couldn't work.

"Disabled?" asked a surprised Detective Knight. "How and when did that happen?"

It was explained to him that the driver, on his last job, had to "move some fat Honkie" (those were his exact words) out of his parking space at the winery and, during that move, had injured his back and neck, and also done permanent damage to his psyche. The employee on the phone continued by telling Detective Knight, in a voice of awe, that the bus driver was now receiving Unemployment checks, SSDI (Social Security Disability Insurance), SSI (Supplemental Security Income), Workman's Comp. payments, a pension, Welfare checks, and a few others that he couldn't remember off the top of his head.

The former bus driver was, in fact, making more money now than when he had been working. Detective Knight rightly guessed that the retired worker had used a fair amount of BS on the applications for all of these benefits because he could not imagine how someone could honestly and legally be eligible for all of them.

Detective Knight was then told that the former driver also had the NAACP (National Association for the Advancement of Colored People) suing the winery on Semillon Circle because it had no black employees. If it had, this would never have happened.

"What? It would never have happened?" asked Detective Knight incredulously. "How does he figure?"

"Because according to our driver, well our *former* driver, if the winery had any black people working on the premises at the time, they could and would have helped the driver move the fat Honkie, and therefore, he wouldn't have hurt himself. Brothers always look out for brothers."

During the remainder of his time on the phone with whomever he was talking to, Detective Knight learned that the "brothers" who should have been working for the winery would surely have insisted that there be warning signs against moving fat, white trash around without qualified personnel (meaning additional brothers) to assist them in order to prevent just these sorts of injuries. There weren't any "qualified personnel," so the winery was, and is, clearly full of ignorant, hate-filled, Republican, white supremacists, and certainly culpable for any injuries sustained by a brother while taking out the trash.

Detective Knight marveled at this logic, or lack thereof, but he also knew the guy was probably right. He shook his head in disbelief, said his good-bye, hung-up the phone, and finished reading the report.

He read that the touring company was, in turn suing the winery to get money to help pay all the benefits they were legally obligated to give their former driver. He learned the "fat Honkie" was also collecting SSDI, SSI, Unemployment checks, Welfare checks, and Medicare was paying all of her medical bills. To complicate matters even further, both the state and federal governments were suing the winery *and* the touring company because they were low on cash and couldn't afford to pay all the benefits the people involved were entitled to.

To make matters worse, for the wineries anyway, a couple of their legal documents required by the County and State had not been filled-out exactly as required and so they were being punished by having an enormous amercement[192] imposed on them.

To Detective Knight, this whole situation seemed to have turned into a lawsuit free-for-all; it was the legal kerfuffle[193] to end all legal kerfuffles. It would turn out to be good for him

---

192   How intelligent people say "fee." That's why I've never said the word.

193   A commotion or fuss, especially one caused by conflicting views. I just like saying the word.

however, as his buddy, who was a Tort Lawyer[194] and whose wife had just left him, was handling a large part of this legal free-for-all and when it was over, he and David would have the time and money to go to a baseball game at Fenway Park, Yankee Stadium, Wrigley Field, Camden Yards, and AT&T Park. He would be able to pay for any, and all, beer that was to be consumed and all private viewings at strip clubs they just happened upon.

---

194   A tort lawyer is one who specializes in bringing personal injury lawsuits.

Chapter 53

Technicality

Detective David Knight awoke and got out of bed on this beautiful but hot summer morning. He didn't have care in the world and so slept like a baby, sans diapers and everything else, for that matter. Detective Knight could never decide what to sleep in so, he slept in nothing, although he did think adult diapers would come in handy after long nights spent in the local watering hole or on cold mornings. Thankfully, contemplation was as far, or as close,[195] as he had gotten to wearing them.

He got out of bed and made his way into his kitchen to have breakfast while thinking that his life was pretty darn good. As he sat at the kitchen table eating his breakfast which, that morning, consisted a bowl of Kellogg's Cracklin' Oat Bran followed by a bowl of Cap'n Crunch's Peanut Butter Crunch, David Knight thought about how great a success he had become as a detective. He thought about Laurent who had simply put himself in jail and was now serving time for attempted murder and general buffoonery. Detective Knight figured that he was so feared by criminals on the lam, that they would put themselves in jail rather than face his spleen;[196] at least that is how he saw it.

Detective Knight, who had not done much of anything since Laurent had been "captured," except go to baseball

---

195   I couldn't decide if I should say, "Contemplation was as far as he had gotten..." or "Contemplation was as close as he had gotten..." Since I am wishy-washy and they essentially mean the same thing, I figured I'd write 'em both and let you, dear reader, decide.

196   Bad temper; desire to hurt, annoy, or offend someone. As far as I know, it has nothing to do with the internal organ.

parks around the country, continued to sit at the kitchen table slurping down his cereal. At the same time (he was multi-tasking) he thumbed through the paper that was sitting on the table because he wanted to see what was going on in Fiasco Valley and hopefully get some idea as to what he could do that day, as he was getting rather restless.

The first headline he saw was: "Prisoner released to go back home." He began reading with interest and nearly choked on his Captain Crunch, for the story was about the recently convicted Laurent LaFlamer who had just been released to his father and taken back to France. *How can this be? You can't just release a prisoner to his father to take him back home to France. There's something fishy going on here.*

David stood-up, still nude mind you, and got on the phone. He called a few of his connections in law-enforcement and the judicial system to get some answers. He found out that Laurent's father had threatened to go public with the DA's secret homosexual affairs with a number of political figures and to expose the three term, very liberal State Governor's secret life as a gay-bashing, (especially gay immigrants) communist sympathizer, and general all around kook; for all of which he had irrefutable proof. David also learned that the top law enforcement official in France, the Interior Minister, was an outrésexual[197] in that he was only attracted to gay or lesbian hermaphrodites.[198] He too, was afraid Laurent's father might somehow expose him. *Well, so long as Laurent's there and not here, we're all safe...I guess, anyway.* That thought only gave David small solace, however,

---

197   "Outré" means unusual and startling – It's a French word. I'll let you, the reader, provide your own definition of "outrésexual."

198   A person having both male and female sex organs. I don't know if a hermaphrodite can be a homosexual or heterosexual. Maybe they are both. A homterosexual maybe?

and he needed to collect himself and relax.

To do that, he went to the local café to get a Mocha and think about what he had just learned. As he sat at an outdoor table drinking his espresso drink (he had gotten dressed) and contemplating the French Interior Minister's sexual orientation (or would it be orientations?) he glanced toward the street and saw Maria walking on the sidewalk. *Holy...! What the...? Why isn't she in prison?*

Detective Knight got up and ran back to his pad. Once there, he got on his phone and started making calls and what he found out did not improve his state of mind. In fact, it made it worse because he learned that Maria was out because she had not been read the Miranda Warning in Spanish and therefore, her arrest was illegal. Detective Knight immediately and strongly contended that Maria knew English and had understood every word.

"Well, that's not how the Ninth Circuit Court Judges saw it," came the reply.

Detective David Knight let out a frustrated yell and slammed the phone down as hard as he could. He couldn't apprehend[199] how the judges had been bamboozled into releasing from prison a young, innocent looking, Mexican woman with a great pair of eyes, a nice ass, and a set of protuberant[200] mammary glands. On second thought, maybe he could understand. Rumor had it, the judges on the bench ate Viagra and Cialis like it was candy and with the arrival of Maria before their bench, parts of them that hadn't been awakened for many years, suddenly awoke with a flourish.

---

199   That's the right word. It means "understand or perceive." I purposely did not use "comprehend."

200   Protruding; bulging

Detective Knight went to the fridge, grabbed a beer, sat down, and began thinking about the "technicality" that had let a brutal killer (albeit a very sexy one) walk free. Detective Knight had no idea how the whole "appeal to the Ninth Circuit Court" process worked but he knew that, in the past, they had made a lot of rulings that he couldn't understand. What David figured was that she let the judges get a good look at her party bags during any court recess, court session, or whenever the judges happened to look her way, in exchange for her freedom.

David began to question the whole point of enforcing the law and catching criminals. It seemed to be an exercise in futility. Added to that, he had defense attorneys, court appeals, and the entire judicial system running through his head. He was questioning his whole belief system and becoming rather depressed when he decided he needed a pick-me-up.

So, David Knight did what he always did when life got him down: He watched a Monty Python Movie. Today, he settled on: *Monty Python's: The Meaning of Life* because he needed a fresh outlook on life and what, if anything, it meant. When the movie was over, he felt only marginally better. This was a shock to David because that movie had never before failed to make him feel better about life.

In his second attempt to make himself feel better, David went online and surfed the XXXWWW.[201] It worked for about 47 seconds and then it just made him lonely and depressed.

To combat his loneliness, David logged on to the Ashley Madison Website and, lo and behold, he arranged a dinner date with an unsatisfied housewife in Birchwood. She turned out to be extremely dull and not too bright, but she had a hot body

---

201 That's the Triple X-rated World Wide Web. I've never seen anything X-rated on the web. I'm just assuming it's there based on stories I've heard.

and so was just barely tolerable. At dinner, David's potential extramarital affair ordered a dish that included artichokes, and *that* got David thinking and talking, which was always a bad combination for him on a first date. As his date sat there eating, he told his ineluctable[202] thoughts, rather loudly, about artichokes.

"Now, what the hell is up with artichokes?" he asked. "Who actually ate the first one? How the hell would someone even think to eat one? 'I know, we'll just cook this weird-looking green thing and just eat the part of the leaf, at least I think it's a leaf, that you can scrape off with your teeth. Yeah, that'll work. Boy, it sure is tasty, but I bet it will be even better with mayonnaise.' How would they even think to do *that*? I mean that seems totally effing random to me. Did they eat them with roast dinosaur, or just by themselves? They would have had to eat twenty or thirty of them just to make a snack."

It turns out the grandfather of his date had grown artichokes and his company supplied North America with 91% of the artichokes it consumed. Her family had grown exceedingly rich and everything was honky-dorey until the grandfather was killed in an artichoke planting mishap. Therefore, she did not take kindly to David's thoughts, and as soon as he finished his tirade, she excused herself to go "freshen up." The moment she left, Detective Knight's cell phone vibrated in his front pocket and it was Joanie from the Police Department.

"You're never gonna believe this," she said, "but another dead body has been found."

Yes! thought David while pumping his fist in the air. "Oh man, that's terrible. Where?" he asked with relief in his voice

---

202 Unable to be resisted or avoided; inescapable. I couldn't resist or avoid using this word.

because he now had an excuse to leave the restaurant.

"Over in those new low-income apartments."

"Okay, I'm on my way. I'll be there shortly." With that, David practically ran out of the restaurant, jumped into his 4Runner, and sped away. Shortly thereafter, David's date returned from the bathroom looking fresh but there was no one at the table to see her, which was a great disappointment. There was however, a large bill and within moments a stern looking waiter and restaurant manager who certainly *did* see her.

Later, David found out that she never actually paid the bill. She did, however, get her sought after extramarital affair that night with both the waiter and the restaurant manager; at the same time mind you because those two men were married...to each other *and* they liked to experiment. Apparently, none of them held the belief that "two's company but three's a crowd." They held the belief that, "Two's okay but three's even better."

Deaths Número…uh

Oh man, I lost count…

…and there are plenty more

Bored to Death...Literally

Detective David Knight arrived, without any fanfare, at the new low-income apartments in Birchwood. There, he found Officer's Kendry and McMillan.

"Howdy boys! Long time no see. What seems to be the trouble now?" asked Detective David Knight in a light-hearted tone of voice and with a big smile.

"Well," said Officer McMillan, "we found a young, healthy lad dead on his couch. There seems to be no evidence of a struggle, no forced entry, no one saw or heard anything unusual, and no one saw anyone who didn't belong here. We're at a loss."

Detective Knight turned towards Officer Kendry and said, "Well, anything to add?

"Yeah. I found this stack of *Playboy* Magazines next to his bed, so it probably doesn't have anything to do with a jealous male lover, but that's all I got. I did take some pictures but...what you see here is what I took. I didn't find anything suspicious *and* we haven't touched anything."

What Detective Knight saw was a messy apartment with a dead guy sitting on his couch in front of a TV, which was tuned to DogTV.[203] He went through his normal routine of taking pictures, dusting for fingerprints, and collecting fluids from the deceased. He then bid the officers adieu, and drove back to the crime lab.

---

203   There really is a TV channel called DogTV. It is "television for dogs as a 24/7 digital TV channel with dog–friendly programming scientifically developed to provide the right company for dogs when left alone.The result: a confident, happy dog, who's less likely to develop stress, separation anxiety or other related problems." The end is near.

Once there, he examined the fingerprints but had his assistant examine the blood and other fluids and develop the pictures. The pictures did not shed any light on the cause of death and all the fingerprints belonged to the dead dude.

A coroner, a medical examiner, and a forensic pathologist examined him thoroughly. No poisons or toxins, of any sort, were found in his system. There was no trace of any drugs, legal or illegal; so he hadn't overdosed. He hadn't died of carbon monoxide (CO) poisoning or even carbon dioxide (CO_2) poisoning, which would have been twice as bad. His heart and lungs were in good working order and he looked to be in good physical condition. He had no diseases, no kind of cancer, and no wounds of any kind. The blood work showed his blood type to be 0+ and that his cholesterol levels were fine. All in all, he was in tip-top shape and shouldn't be dead. Everyone was mystified.

As a last, desperate attempt to understand how this person had died, a necrophiliac[204] was brought in to take an intimate look at the corpse and possibly notice something unscientific or unmedical that the tests wouldn't pick-up as the cause of death. The "Necro," as he was called, looked for anything that was gross, strange, unnatural, or just plain wrong with the corpse. No luck. Everyone was at a loss as to why the guy had "bopped his last Betty."

Later that week as Detective Knight was sitting at his kitchen table, rubbing his temples and going over all the information he had on the dead guy found on his couch, his phone rang.

"Yeah?" said David tiredly; for he hadn't slept in days as he was deeply troubled by the fact that a young, healthy, male

---

204   Someone who has an obsession with, and usually erotic interest in, or stimulation by corpses.

346

seemed to have simply died while just sitting on his couch. "What? Uh-huh. Another one? Where?"

"That rental out on Malbec Lane," stated Joanie.

"Malbec Lane? Is that the one on top of the hill?"[205]

"Yep, that's it."

"Okey-dokey. I'll see what I can do," and with that, David hung-up the phone, got in his 4Runner and drove, very slowly (he didn't really want to go there) up to the rental on Malbec Lane. When he arrived, none other than Officer McMillan and Officer Kendry greeted him. They filled him in on what they knew and it sounded eerily familiar to the guy found on his couch in the low-income apartment complex.

Detective Knight did his routine of taking pictures and looking for evidence but he didn't find any. Again, the coroner, the medical examiner, a forensic pathologist, and even the "Necro" (who found this victim very attractive and asked for permission to date him) could not find any cause of death. Another mystery.

This made everyone nervous because they thought it was possible some disease that had never been seen before had shown-up in Fiasco Valley. The CDC, or Center for Disease Control and Prevention,[206] was called in to add their expertise, state-of-the-art equipment, analyses, and leading scientists to hopefully unravel this mystery and maybe find a cure for this new disease, if that's what it was. To the delight of the local coroner, medical examiner, and forensic pathologist, and even the "Necro," the CDC scientists did not come up with any answers or discover anything new, but they sure looked good trying.

---

205   Malbec grapes grown at higher altitudes produce much better and longer-lasting wines.

206   Why isn't it CDCP? Prevention doesn't really count?

Detective David Knight was so distraught over these last two deaths that it caused him to get heavily into online porno. Not only because it kept him from dwelling on the fact that people in Fiasco Valley kept dying and he had no idea as to how...or why, but because so much of it (the aforementioned XXXWWW) was free, and David Knight always took advantage free stuff. He would spend hours sitting naked in front of his home computer ogling the screen with a small trail of spit running from his mouth to his keyboard.

Detective Knight had taken care of, and justice had been served for, the unlikely and unfortunate murders that had previously taken place in the blissful Fiasco Valley. Now, inconceivably, there were two more deaths in Valley and again, he had no idea as to how...or why. There was no evidence of foul play but, the fact was: two young, healthy males had turned-up dead and there seemed to be no natural cause or reason as to why. No one had put themselves in jail or confessed to the crime...assuming there was one. The previous murders, which were rare enough, had all been dealt with and justice had been served, but now... Life in this small town was becoming more than David could handle.

Behind him his phone was ringing, as it had been for the last two or three minutes, but he ignored it. Finally, the phone quieted down and his computer played a simple tune whilst a small pop-up window appeared on the screen telling him that he had an instant message from Joanie at the police station. He clicked on the window and read the message. It did not improve his mood. It said that he was needed at a location outside of town because another dead body had been found.

Now, I have to see Officer Kendry and McMillan and they'll tell me they don't know squat and there won't be a cause of death.

That will be three murders that I have no clue about. Maybe the third time really is a charm and it will be obvious. Yeah right, that'll happen.

Detective Knight turned out to be right on all accounts, except for part about the third time being a charm. Another healthy, young male had been found sitting on his couch in front of the TV, dead as a doornail.[207]

All the same procedures were followed and the same people performed the same analyses and tests that had been performed on the previous dead bodies. Again, no one had any clue as to the cause of death. This was the third death in Fiasco Valley, in a short period, with no known cause and it was becoming quite upsetting to Detective Knight.

Detective Knight, who managed to avoid the relentless lure of the XXXWWW so that he could look into these latest three deaths, began by assuming the deaths involved foul play and so were not simply deaths but murders; otherwise, he wouldn't have much to do.

He studied the test results, wracked his brain, and looked for anything the dead dudes had in common, other than the fact that they were all dead. Here is what he came up with: 1) They were all young, healthy, single, males. 2) They all lived in or near Birchwood. 3) They all worked in the tasting room of a winery in Fiasco Valley. 4) They had all died while sitting on their couches. As far Detective Knight could fathom, they should all be alive and lovin' life, well they should at least be alive.

---

207 "dead as a doornail" – Phrase could come from a standard term in carpentry. If you hammer a nail through two pieces of timber and then flatten the protruding, sharp end over so it can't be removed, the nail is said to be dead because you can't use it again. Doornails would very probably have been subjected to this treatment to give extra strength to the doors in the years before screws were available.

Late one night, while lying awake in bed, David realized there was one more commonality he had previously dismissed: All of the televisions of the deceased had been tuned to DogTV and none of them owned a dog. Detective Knight had dismissed this commonality because he couldn't see how it had anything to do with...anything. However, as he continued to think about the causes of the recent deaths and not come up with any answers, he was incessantly niggled[208] by this DogTV fact. So much so, that it was becoming a hindrance to his deductive reasoning. *Maybe they just died from watching TV. Most shows nowadays will bore you to death.* That thought seemed silly, but the more he thought about it, the more plausible it became. The vast majority of shows on TV were so idiotic, repetitive, and the stories were so tedious, that they required little to no thought. *Can someone really be bored to death? If one does not use their brain, can they actually die?*

David didn't think so, but he decided to do some research and gather some information just to make sure. He began by tuning his television to DogTV one afternoon, and into the evening, just to get a sense of how desperately bored a person would have to be in order to watch it. By 6:00 pm he was suicidal, because A) He was *watching* DogTV and he wasn't a dog, and B) The mere thought that there was a demand for a television station that aired programs to provide "Physical and mental stimulation among dogs when home alone" was more than he could handle.

Not only that, he couldn't comprehend how anyone with a shred of common sense would give birth to the idea that a television station for dogs was good enough to be brought to fruition. Thinking about this, almost made him lose the will

---

208   Cause slight but persistent annoyance, discomfort, or anxiety – Rev. Jesse Jackson would never use this word.

to live. Fortunately, however, he had enough sense to turn the damn TV off and listen to some excruciatingly loud Pantera and Metallica, and *that* renewed his will to go on.

In this process of ending his DogTV induced inanition,[209] David couldn't help but think about death and dying.[210] He didn't think it was possible for someone to literally die of boredom, but he wasn't sure.

To make sure, he called a fraternity brother of his who was as smart as a brain surgeon because he *was* a brain surgeon. To David's shock, his fraternity brother did not dismiss this idea as daft.[211] He explained that boredom can increase the rate of natural brain degeneration that comes with age because people that are chronically bored lack curiosity, and curiosity helps our brains stay young. Each day our curiosity system devotes our efforts toward the pursuit of all the traditional rewards of the world: water, food, warmth or coolness, sexual gratification, and social relationships.

He then explained that bored people have brain degeneration and "age" prematurely because they aren't curious and so have no desire to learn or do anything new. Therefore, they don't build and strengthen existing neuron connections.[212] They just plant themselves in front of the TV and don't heed what their curiosity is trying to tell them because then they would have to get off the couch and miss an episode of some asinine TV show. Therefore, he concluded that extreme boredom could, theoretically, shorten one's life. He even had a name for it:

---

209   Lack of mental or spiritual vigor and enthusiasm.

210   Why isn't it spelled "dieing?" Too many vowels in a row?

211   silly; foolish

212   http://www.huffingtonpost.com/todd-kashdan/science-shows-you-can-die_b_457199.html

torporicide.[213] To put it all in terms David could understand: One *could* possibly be bored to death.

As far as DogTV was concerned, he didn't think it would do much for our curiosity system except possibly make one curious as to who the hell came up with the idea for DogTV, who the hell would actually have their dog watch it, and what kind of dog *would* sit there and watch it. He thought that watching DogTV might have been each of the dead guy's last-ditch effort to save his own life.

When David added this new information to the fact that there was a scarcity of women in Fiasco valley that weren't just looking for a rich husband, and to the fact that there was a total lack of a social scene for younger, not so wealthy, single males, the result he came up with was this spate of torporicides in the Valley.

Detective David Knight was actually thoroughly relieved because he no longer thought of himself as a clueless detective and *that* made him feel better. He, in fact, hadn't missed any clues, or signs, or motives, or anything really because there had been no crime. These latest "victims" had all died because their brains had simply degenerated, from intense boredom, to the point of not being able to run the bodily functions needed to live. He also felt good because his name would be associated with the first recorded case of people literally being bored to death. Wait a second, that didn't sound right. He felt good because his name would be associated with *discovery* of the first people that were literally bored to death. Yeah, that's the ticket.

---

213   Being killed by "torpor." What's "torpor" you ask? It's a state of physical or mental inactivity; lethargy. What's "lethargy" you ask? It's a lack of energy and enthusiasm. There is also a medical definition of "lethargy:" A regular state of sleepiness or deep unresponsiveness and inactivity. Note: "Torporicide" is not really a word; I just made it up, as far as I know.

Chapter 55

Foreign Flare

Ernesto waited behind a car parked in the dark behind the only cantina in town until he saw Maria walking by. He then pounced on her while holding a wooden stake and carrying a mallet, both of which he had gotten out of the "Ye Olde Vampire Slaying Kit" from 1857 that he had purchased on eBay for $3,867.98. Well, he received the kit but had sent a bogus check to the seller and so got it free. Ernesto did not have 3,867.98 dollars or even 3,867.98 cents. All he had was zero sense.

He sprang from behind the car, grabbed Maria, threw her to the ground, and sat on her stomach with the intention of driving the wooden stake through her heart, thereby permanently killing her. If not killed in this manner, vampires can come back to life, and he certainly didn't want that.

He sat on her chest to drive the stake through her heart with the mallet, but hesitated a moment because he couldn't remember what side her heart was on: The left or the right. *I'm pretty sure it's on the left.* He was about to hammer the wooden stake into the left side of her chest but then thought *Wait a minute, is that her left or my left? Her left side would be the right side to me, right?* It's a well-known fact that Ernesto did not think to fast, so while trying to figure out where to stab Maria, she had ample time to regain her composure and recoup her Vampire traits.

With her recouped strength, she threw Ernesto off of her, wrestled with him for a short time, and then tossed him over the car and onto some nearby grass that was being watered by sprinklers. During their short struggle, Maria had torn off her shirt (she wasn't wearing a bra) in order to distract Ernesto and guarantee her victory. When Maria ran over to the grass to finish him off, she saw him lying there wearing a soaking wet t-shirt and tight, cotton pants.

Seeing Ernesto lying there in wet clothes was more than Maria could handle because she was such a horny vampire. He, in turn, became visibly excited because her pants had also become wet, tight, and see-through. He wanted to "jump her bones"[214] and she wanted to "jump his bones" right then and there. They both gave in to temptation and had wild sex on the wet grass and in the mud. *I'm screwing a vampire. I'm screwing a vampire. I'm, screwing a vampire in the mud. God, I love this country! Anything is possible* thought Ernesto.

In their throes of passion, Maria bit him on the neck (Ernesto didn't notice because his mind was occupied with more pressing issues) so he would come under her control, thus adding to her brood. When they were done with their passion throes, they lay on the wet grass and talked about their future. Maria talked slowly because she was just killing time waiting for her bite to take effect. While talking, Maria convinced Ernesto to go back into the cantina with her. On their way into the cantina, the bite took affect and Ernesto was under her control. Maria then expounded[215] her plan to increase her brood, and thus expand her wealth and power. Ernesto liked her plan and agreed to be a part of it which, unbeknownst to him, he already was.

Once they were in the cantina, Maria and Ernesto worked as

---

214   Have sex with. Typically guys trying to be manly and impress their buddies say they would like to "jump her bones" when talking about a woman they have no chance of ever going out on a date with, let alone having sex with.

215   Present and explain – a theory or idea – systematically and in detail.

a "tag team" and took on a group of young, foreign interns who had consumed plenteous amounts of alcohol. Maria managed, throughout the night, to bite the necks of all the male foreign interns and one female, which gave her an unexpected thrill. Ernesto managed to bite the necks of each female, foreign intern and two of the male ones; Ernesto vehemently denied biting those two because he had become aroused while doing so and it threatened his manhood.

All this was done in order to add an international flavor to her website which, she hoped, would significantly increase the paid memberships and thereby increase her profits. One cannot be too rich; it's impossible.

Chapter 56

Jumping Bean Studios

Maria summoned her driver, who just happened to be the ex-prison warden and who was driving *her* white Aston Martin One-77; the one that used to belong to him but had been "given" to her after she had bitten him. As soon as he arrived, Maria ordered him to take Ernesto to her house so that he could get her other car, the red Lamborghini Veneno; the one that used to belong to the prison shrink but had also been "given" to her after she had bitten him. They could then both ferry the newly bitten interns to her house.

The interns loved everything about this. Here they were in a bar in California getting hammered on drinks that were being bought for them. They were about to get a ride in either of two extraordinarly expensive sports cars to the house of an extremely wealthy woman, with an incredible body no less, to do even more drinking and partying; at least that is what they were told. Life couldn't get much better.

When they arrived at Maria's magnificent mansion, they were led down to the basement where they became thoroughly thrilled. For in the basement was a film studio complete with a lot of lighting (including a softbox light,) a couple of HD video camcorders, a makeup table, a computer, a couch, a bed, and there were a number of unlit candles in various places. The room was dark, as none of the lights had been turned on, and it had an anomalous[216] smell to it that wasn't pleasant, but wasn't

---

216   Deviating from what is standard, normal, or expected. They didn't know what expect, but they knew what they smelt was weird.

unpleasant either. The interns just milled about the studio while waiting for what would come next because they had no idea. Maria and Ernesto soon arrived and immediately began stripping. While they were doing so, Maria said, in Spanish, "Welcome to Jumping Bean Studios."

The foreign intern from Spain understood her *and* spoke English, so she told the rest of the interns what Maria had said. They all just stood there and stared at her and Ernesto with mouths agape, for Maria was now flaunting her magnificent mammary glands and Ernesto was right beside her in a fully aroused state.

Finally, they all answered (in their native tongue,) "Thank you. Glad to be here." The male interns simultaneously began pitchin' their own tents. During this time, Maria and Ernesto went around the basement and lit all of the candles in a slow and deliberate manner in order to be certain their bites on the interns had time to take full effect. They did not turn on any lights because they knew that vampires don't react well to bright light.

Over the next seven hours, Jumping Bean Studios produced three hours of movies that were then uploaded to its website. An e-mail was simultaneously sent to all of the subscribers so they would know there was new material to be enjoyed. The website, www.xxxjbs.com, received 1.2 million hits in the first two hours.

The Jumping Bean Studios website, which was the definition of a cash cow,[217] had become such a worldwide phenomenon that people everywhere of all ages, colors, gender, sexual

---

217   A business, investment, or product that provides a steady income or profit. Don't try visiting that site because it doesn't exist...at least not at the time of this writing.

orientations, and beliefs at least took a quick gander at it to see what all the hubbub was about. One of these people was the extremely concupiscent[218] mother of one the interns whose husband kept forgetting to take his Viagra pills.

She recognized her daughter and thought she saw her daughter's best friend in one of the films. She immediately called the mother of her daughter's best friend and invited her over to watch the film and make a positive I.D. It was not necessary however, because the other mother had already seen the film, plus a few others, and it *was* her daughter.

Both of these mothers had thought their wonderful, innocent, delightful daughters were in America learning how to make wine, the nectar of the God's. But no, here they were on the World Wide Web starring in pornographic films...and hard-core ones to boot. Both women exhibited shock, horror, and disappointment. Secretly, however, they were jealous and found the films to be quite titillating. In spite of that, it didn't set well with them and they weren't about to let their recalcitrant[219] daughters get all this action while all they got was what the little bird left on the rock.[220] It just wouldn't be fair. Both of these mothers were abnormally horny, some would say to the level of perversion, and had husbands who were more interested in their fantasy soccer (they called it fútbol) leagues than their wife's fantasies. They needed satisfaction.

Since these two women now believed that their daughters had just taken the first step to becoming famous Hollywood movie stars and they themselves had always wanted to be

---

218   Filled with sexual desire; lustful. She was a horny, old broad

219   Having an obstinately uncooperative attitude toward authority or discipline.

220   A little bird would leave a little shit.

part of that whole "scene," they made a beeline for the U.S. in order to find them. Once in the U.S., they used Google Maps and Google Earth on their phones (which just happened to be quite smart) to locate Jumping Bean Studios. After three days of hitching rides with truckers or anyone else, as long as they were male, they arrived at Maria's mansion and used all of their sexual wiles to get through security and just barged in to the dark house.

They found themselves in a large room, in which all the shades were drawn and was being illuminated by two small candles, and therefore was nearly dark. In the room was the Sire, all dressed-up in an elegant gown, with her Brood surrounding her. The female members of her Brood (the former female interns) were also dressed in elegant gowns, although not as elegant as Maria's. All the male members of her brood (the former male interns) were dressed in black tuxedoes and looking quite sharp.

The intruding mothers were extraordinarily pissed, and I do mean *extraordinarily*. They got to within centimeters (that's reallly close) of each person's face until they found their respective daughter and then grabbed her by the ear and dragged her outside. Unbeknownst to them however, was that vampires transform when exposed to sunlight.

Once outside, both mothers began to yell at their daughters with the hope that their daughters would feel so guilty and ashamed that they would let them join in on the fun. However, as soon as the daughters were dragged into the sunlight, they transformed into a pile of brown...uh...goo, for lack of a better word. Both mothers instantly shut-up and looked at each other in wide-eyed shock and horror because they had absolutely no idea what was going on. Within moments, the two piles of goo began to jiggle and wiggle. Why? Because the vampires had been turned into piles of mosquito-like larvae that were now hatching into small, winged annoyances with a lust for blood.

These newly born winged annoyances, formed into a large, dark, cloud-like mass and instantly flew into the neighbor's yard where a large group of people was out on the grass enjoying their late-evening glass of wine.

Unfortunately, for this particular swarm of blood-lusting mosquitoes, their brains were not very far along the evolutionary scale and a yard full of people, surrounded by electric bug zappers, was more than they could comprehend. They went straight for the zappers instead of the wine drinkers and this particular swarm of *vampiroteous suckalotofbloodfromus annoyeveryoneofus* ceased to exist within moments of it having come into existence, with one exception: their Sire.

She was an extraordinarily horny blood-lust mosquito and so went for flesh rather than the bright, ultraviolet lights. She was drawn to a good-looking fellow in tight, Lycra bicycle shorts and jersey and so made a beeline for him. She landed on his neck, drank her fill of his blood, and then flew away to figure-out and decide what to do next. Unbeknownst to her however, that decision had already been made, for the good-looking fellow she had just sucked blood from was none other than Vance Legweak, the world's best unicycle rider, and he was so doped-up on performance enhancing drugs, or PED's, that his blood was poisonous to her and she died within minutes of leaving his neck.

Hang on...let me clarify that: *Parts* of her died. The human part of Maria was fine. It was the blood-lusting mosquito and the Vampire Sire parts that died. She did feel a bit queasy however, and because of that, decided to go to the emergency room of the local hospital and get a free check-up and, if need be, some free medical care.

After waiting about five hours, she was finally able to see a doctor and he (It could of been a "she" but it just so happened it wasn't) ran a battery of tests and the results were so...unusual that he wouldn't let her leave.

After filling out 37 pages of forms, in which 57 of the questions were repeated 15 times, Maria was officially admitted to the hopelessly overcrowded hospital and shown to her room, which already held three patients. One patient had inconceivably bad gas, one had breath so execrable[221] it was attracting flies, and the third snored so loud he would set off car alarms. Maria was not happy. After sitting in the room (there wasn't enough space for another bed, just a La-Z-Boy chair) for a couple of hours, the stench and the noise were more than she could tolerate and she was feeling fine so she decided to go for a walk (All hail *Monty Python and the Holy Grail*). She left the hospital and walked around Birchwood in a dazed and very confused state. *What the hell just happened? I became a mosquito? We were all mosquitoes? How is that possible? Ernesto is dead? Everyone is dead?*

---

221 Extremely bad or unpleasant. He needed to gargle gallons of mouthwash for hours just to be tolerable.

Chapter 57

Maria and her Knight in Shining Armor

Maria thought about all of the recent, mystifying events while walking aimlessly through and around Birchwood. She did this for hours, until she happened upon a knight in shining armor, literally. Detective Knight, who had gone to a nearby Renaissance Faire, was dressed in a full suit of armor and walking home from a nearby house where he had been drinking some braggots and mead[222] with the wife of a guy who thought Renaissance Faires were a bit silly.

David had met this special wife through the Ashley Madison website and they had gone to the nearby Renaissance Faire together. Everything had gone swimmingly...until now. David got one glimpse of Maria and her glorious glands and forgot all about the wife he had just been with.

Maria saw Detective Knight and immediately got a smile on her face, for Detective Knight had become somewhat of a celebrity since he had played a major role in the discovery that people could literally be bored to death. Of course, he had also become somewhat of a villain to mothers around the world because when their child said he, or she, was bored to death, they had to take action or else it could very well cost them a lot more than money.

Recently, a mother in California had been sentenced to life

---

222   Braggot is made by blending spices and herbs with mead and beer to produce a strong concoction with uncommon flavors. Mead is an alcoholic beverage created by fermenting honey with water. Gee. Sounds yummy!

in prison for the murder of her 12 year-old son because he had complained of being bored to death and she hadn't instantly taken him shopping for the latest video game console, (not even a new video *game* for the two-month old game console he already had) or the new iPhone 15 to replace his five-week old iPhone 14, or a new computer, or even a new flatscreen TV. She had cold-heartedly, purposely, and with malice aforethought[223] said, "Go outside, there's plenty to do out there."

That evening at dinnertime, he was found dead in his room holding a deck of cards with the rubber band still wrapped around it. Apparently, he didn't know what, or couldn't think of anything, to do with a deck of cards and so was not being amused for a length of time; no one knows how long. The jury heard the evidence and unanimously found her guilty of murder by neglect because her son had died of boredom.

"Detective Knight, is that you?" asked Maria as she approached him.

David Knight saw her, showed a look of surprise, and said, "Hi, Maria. Ah...are you sure you want to talk to me? I might use it against you someday. You never know." David Knight was still fuming over her release on the technicality. She stood still and remained silent, so David asked, "You *do* understand me, don't you?"

She rolled her eyes, ignored the question, and asked, "What kind clothes are those?" Maria had never seen a medieval knight's suit of armor before.

Detective Knight stared intently at her chest for a long

---

223 "malice aforethought" – The conscious intent to cause death or great bodily harm to another person *before* causing the death or bodily harm to that person. In other words: you plan on killing or hurting someone *before* you kill or hurt that someone.

moment, shook his head to clear it, and then said with gritted teeth, "I went to a Renaissance Faire and wore this appropriate costume. There *were* knights in armor during the Renaissance, you know."

Maria didn't know. In fact, she had no clue as to what the Renaissance was, let alone a Renaissance Faire, and she had no idea as to what a knight in armor was. So, she just humored him and said, "You look muy handsome and muy strong," all the while inching closer to him.

David complemented her on her appearance as he took a whiff of her perfume...or fragrance. Whatever it was, it awakened David's loins and he asked her what she was doing right now and if she had plans for later. David was actually surprised that he was so "into" this murdering Latina chic. Apparently, his Freudian mind and thoughts[224] had triumphed over every ounce of common sense he had.

She answered by saying she was just out for a walk and had no plans for later. So, David told her that he would change, get cleaned up, and then meet her at the local cantina for a drink, if that was okay with her. Maria said it was, and they agreed to meet shortly. She then walked off provocatively[225] at a slow pace, smiling broadly and humming, while David just stood there, very uncomfortably for few minutes (it can't be comfortable to sport wood in a suit made of metal) and thought, "I just asked a convicted killer to meet me for a drink. What was I thinking? Well, maybe I'll get some action at some point. Wouldn't that be nice?"

---

224 "Freudian mind and thoughts" – Coming from very deeply hidden desires or feelings. All he could think about when it came to Maria was sex.

225 Arousing sexual desire or interest, especially deliberately. She was "hot," she knew it, and she liked to flaunt her assets. She always got what she wanted.

David walked to his house, showered, changed, and went straight to the cantina in town. Maria was already there waiting for him in a tight, black, mini-skirt, and high heels. They had a couple of drinks and then went to dinner (via David's new limo and driver) at the most expensive restaurant in the valley: The Frenchie's Laundromat. After dinner, they returned to the cantina and had more drinks. David paid for everything including twenty-five percent tips for everyone, which did not go unnoticed.

Maria, who always paid attention to guys with money, asked Detective Knight how he could afford all this because she knew that detectives normally couldn't afford to have a limo, a driver, and pay for dinner for two at The Frenchies's Laundromat. She also knew that he liked to ogle her chest at any and every opportunity and would also probably enjoy playing with it.

Taking all this into account, she figured David would be easy pickin's and would give her the things she wanted and she wanted to have babies. She wasn't getting any younger and so now was the time.

"Where get money for this?" Maria asked in her cute, Spanish-accented, broken, English whilst getting very close to him and gazing lovingly into his eyes.

"Well Maria, my dear, the wine business here in California is worth billions of dollars a year. I had a major role in showing that boredom can be a cause of death amongst young people working in a winery and living here in Birchwood. The wineries and the tourist industry don't want that news to get out, for obvious reasons, so they pay me to keep quiet."

"Keep quiet? What you mean?"

"They pay me, quite well I might add, *not* to go on any talk shows or news programs and talk about the health hazards of being bored here in Fiasco Valley."

"Talk shows?"

"Yeah, you know, like Jerry Springer, Oprah Winfrey, Wendy Williams, Maury Povich, Queen Latifah, and others of that ilk.[226] All those daytime shows where couples yell at each other and fight because her husband is sleeping with her sister and he already has two kids with her cousin but he didn't tell you, or summ'in' like that."

Maria just looked at him with a wide eyes and an open mouth and flabbergastedly said, "My sister no do that."

"No. No. Not *your* sister. The sister of whatever poor schmuck is on the show," explained David. "And as far as news programs go, there are a lot of news programs, on both radio and television, and I get paid every time I *don't* grant an interview and just lay-low."

"Lay-low?" All Maria could think of at the moment was getting laid and she was hoping it had something to do with that.

"It means to stay in the background and don't draw attention to yourself," explained David.

"Oh," said a disappointed Maria. "You still get paid now?"

"Yep, sure do. Not only that, I also get paid *not* to talk to newspapers or magazines."

She got a devious smile on her face and began to move even closer to Detective Knight making sure he would have a clear view of her cleavage *and* would get a good whiff of her reproductive pheromones. She moved close enough to him that body-part contact was inevitable.

After a couple more beers, a few tequila shots, a lot of body-part contact, some whiffs of pheromones, and plenty of cleavage

---

226   A type of people or things similar to those already referred to.

sightings, David's limo was summoned so that he and Maria could be whisked-away from this poky pub to his posh palace. They both lusted for each other and wanted to act on that.

You, the reader, can fill-in the ensuing events based on your own life experiences. Keep in mind that you have: A wealthy, drunk, horny, Mexican, woman with a great pair of fun bags (who was turned into a mosquito and then back again) and a drunk, lonely, desperate, wealthy, detective in a small town, who have been taken to *his* nice, big pad in *his* big, black limousine. Whatever you, the reader, filled-in, the result was the same: Maria got knocked-up.

Chapter 58

Mayans

David Knight, formerly known as Detective David Knight, got out of bed to get a drink. He was dead tired because he and his wife, Maria, for the last few hours, had once again, been trying to produce another living being. That sounds like every guys dream, and it probably is, but one does need to hydrate. The couple had been trying to produce a zygote[227] every night for the last few months, no matter what: headache, tummy ache, too tired, that time of the month, it didn't matter. David really enjoyed trying, but it wasn't producing any future people and it was beginning to wear on him and his best friend.

They had produced a very small person back when they lived in Birchwood, but Maria had a miscarriage and that was the end of that kid. As a result, Maria could not deal with living in that particular house. David couldn't deal with living there either because he was embarrassed and ashamed. He couldn't face the fact that poor ol' Ted's killer hadn't been caught, hadn't put themselves in jail, or hadn't just confessed. He, or possibly she, had gotten away with murder and that meant that David was no longer battin' a thousand when it came to catching the ruthless killers that ran amok in Fiasco Valley. He wanted to bat a thousand because that is where the money lied. He would be able to go anywhere in the US, or quite possibly the world, and charge exorbitant fees for his services because he *always* "got his man." Wealthy land barons, or rich software developers, or

---

227 The cell that is formed when egg and sperm combine. It's a fancy, sophisticated way to say "got knocked-up."

famous actresses or actors, or even foreign nobility would hire him to solve cases that the regular police could not crack.

So, to make themselves feel better, Maria and David moved to Zapata, Texas and into a house on the shores of Fir Lake. David even managed to convince himself that Ted had been drunk and simply driven his tractor, that had been full of beer cans and hard alcohol containers, off the cliff and so had not been murdered. Therefore, there was no murderer to catch and he was still battin' a thousand. He dismissed the mechanics findings and explanations as those of a resentful, frustrated man.

David and Maria had originally wanted to move to Nogales, AZ because Maria had some family nearby and it was the one of the best places in Arizona to retire. However, they didn't because it was also the best place in Arizona, hands down, to be murdered by some Mexican drug cartel. Instead, they moved to Zapata, TX which was an even better location than Birchwood, CA and Nogales, AZ. The reason being: The Mayor, the Sheriff, and the City Treasurer were cousins of Maria, as were the County Judge and the County Attorney. So, in essence, Maria's family controlled and owned the town.

One hot summer evening, David and Maria were topless and relaxing on their deck. David was drinking a beer while Maria was having a "Bloody Good Time."[228] They were going over the lab report that showed Maria could not become pregnant because she had the reproductive organs of a mosquito. The doctors were shocked as they had never seen anything quite like

---

228   It's a drink. **Ingredients:** 1 ½ ounce tequila, 1 ounce Triple Sec, 3/4 ounce lime juice, 1 tablespoon and 1 teaspoon puree, sea salt flakes – **Directions:** 1) Mix 1 1/2 ounces sea salt and 1 tablespoon blood orange purée. Spread mixture flat onto a saucer and let dry for at least an hour. 2) Rim a cocktail glass with blood orange salt. In a mixing glass, combine tequila, Triple Sec, lime juice and ice. 3) Shake and strain into the rimmed cocktail glass. Slowly drip the blood orange puree down the side of the glass for a "bloody" effect.

369

this and were, understandably, at a loss. It seemed impossible to them, but they were looking right at it. They had no idea how to proceed, so they just prescribed Maria a slew of drugs from whichever drug company would make them the most money. They were also hoping that they would stumble upon a cure for this "condition" because it could be some sort of plague, and if that were the case, which they secretly hoped it was, the number of people needing the cure would be in the millions, possibly billions. Their cure would make them obscenely rich *and* famous, and then chics from all over the world would dig them and they might actually get some action for free.

Suddenly, David and Maria heard a big commotion out on the lake. They looked and saw a small, homemade raft that didn't look very seaworthy, or even lakeworthy, in this case. They watched as it tipped over, broke apart, and began to sink. Seventeen small children then appeared in the water, and swam towards the shore right below David and Maria's deck.

As soon as all seventeen children were on the shore, they scattered and ran towards any cabin or house they saw. Three of the children (two boys and a girl) ran up the stairs and onto David and Maria's deck.

"Give us something to drink and some dry clothes," one child demanded in Spanish.

Maria immediately replied in her native tongue, "And who the hell are you?"

Once the kids heard Maria speaking Spanish, they looked at her closely, saw that she was a Mexican, and their demeanor instantly changed. They explained that they had left Palenque about three weeks ago and were coming to America with their parents because they had heard about all of the entitlements available to them. Unfortunately, U.S. Drug Enforcement Agents had murdered their parents along the way and they were left on their own.

They then heard about Mexican children entering the U.S. and being taken care of, by whom, they knew not, but that wasn't important. What *was* important was that the American government would pick up the tab for everything...for the rest of their lives.

Maria instantly knew they were fabricating their story because Palenque is not a modern city, or town, or even a small village. It is a popular tourist and archeological destination because it is an ancient Mayan city, the ruins of one at least—no one knows how, or why, Maria knew this, but she did. When Maria pointed out this fact, all three kids stood motionless and silent for an uncomfortably long time and then burst into tears.

When they finally quieted down, they were able to tell their true story: Their parents were involved in the drug cartels in Southern Mexico. The family was on its way to their fields of coca plants, when two rival cartels assailed them. The three children managed to escape unharmed by hiding behind some rocks, covering themselves with leaves, and not making a peep. It was a brilliant plan. The cartel members looked around, didn't see anyone alive, figured they were done, and so went to get high. Over the next three weeks, the three children managed to come all the way North to the shores of Fir Lake by stopping at isolated villages and making deals with some of the parents to take their children with them across the border and into the U.S. Once there, the children could take advantage of any, and all, entitlements in the U.S. that benefited *illegal* immigrants. All the parents had to do was provide food, clothing, shelter for the time being, and possibly some form transportation. By the time they reached Fir Lake, they had fourteen kids with them.

After the three kids had finished their yarn, there was a rapidly spoken exchange between them and Maria, after which they all became very cute and cuddly. They sat down on the deck whilst Maria went into the house and returned with three Cokes and two large bags of potato chips.

The three children were then each given their own room (it was a large cabin) and the next day Maria took them shopping. She bought them new clothes, iphone's, ipad's, ipods, and the newest gaming console, including a few games. She also bought them a superfluity of snacks, soda pop, and a couple gallons of ice cream. All she asked of the three kids was that they call her "Mommy," which they gladly did.

David was not as gung-ho as his lovely wife was about having these three kids around, but he knew from experience that if he said anything, he wouldn't be getting any nookie for the foreseeable future. So, he stayed in the background and kept his mouth shut

Over the next couple of weeks however, the kids voluntarily began calling him "Daddy" and his outlook completely changed. Maria was teaching them English; they were getting better every day and working hard, so David got them a puppy as a reward. The kids were on cloud nine in seventh heaven.

This wonderful life continued for a couple of months when David and Maria had a long, intense, discussion (over margaritas I might add) and decided to make everything permanent. First, they went about starting the adoption process of the three children. Maria's dream of raising a family and giving her Mom grandkids could finally be realized.

However, the adoption "process" turned in to such a long, drawn-out, nightmare that David and Maria just gave up and decided to go with plan B. This plan had been formulated from

372

all the information they had gathered during their attempt, and subsequent failure at executing Plan A.

Plan B was based on the fact that David and Maria had determined it was better, for everyone involved, *not* to adopt the children but just have them live under their roof illegally in Zapata, TX. If they did that, the children would be eligible for all kinds of entitlements that the current Democratic leadership in the U.S. had approved...for some incomprehensible reason. The children could attend the best schools (even colleges) for less than a legal immigrant, or even a U.S. citizen could. In fact, with all the government programs, financial aid, tax credits, and contributions from all the liberal "only we can save the world" groups, David and Maria would be making money by *not* adopting the kids and just raising them in the U.S. Truth was, this new "income" would vault David and Maria into the hated top .5% of wage earners in the United States. They would join Bill and Hillary Clinton who see the top 1% of wage earners in their gold-plated, rear-view mirror.

Maria had to tell her Mom the good news: She was now a grandmother...pretty close, anyway. So, Maria spent the entire day trying to track her mother down, no luck. Then, she spent the next day surfing the web trying to locate her. Finally, she did...sort of. Maria discovered that her Mom was on tour with Justin Bieber somewhere in Canada but that's all the information she could get. Apparently, Justin Bieber likes to keep his exact whereabouts unknown.

The Good Ol' USSI

These three kids, along with the fourteen others that had been with them, had comfortable, financially secure lives now. That, in combination with the new immigration policies put in place by the current U.S. President (who was a bleeding-heart liberal that believed in unicorns) were not only encouraging foreigners to enter the U.S. illegally, but encouraging parents to simply dump their kids into the good ol' U.S. of A. in order for them to take advantage of all the programs and benefits that they were eligible for.

The result was a lot of young, illegal migrants were living in the U.S. and not working (legally anyway) or paying taxes. They were however, taking advantage of all the services and benefits that were intended for U.S. citizens who had paid the price of admission.

The programs being taken advantage of included, but were not limited to: financial aid, free healthcare, and free education. The U.S. Government was actually bringing planeloads, trainloads, busloads, and carloads of *illegal* immigrants *into* the United States, for some incomprehensible reason...votes most likely.

To make matters even better for anyone who was *not* a U.S. citizen and had come, or was coming, here *illegally*, the U.S. Attorney General (with presidential support) sued any state that tried to *stop* people from breaking the immigration laws. Therefore, no state tried to stop them, and thousands upon thousands of people who wanted a piece of the U.S. pie walked, swam, ran, rode, drove, or flew into the U.S. without a legal worry. This was in addition to the illegal immigrants who were brought into the U.S. *by* the government. It all seemed to be a rather schizophrenic[229] policy to David and he felt that his beloved USA was becoming the USSI, or the United Schizophrenic States of Immigration.

This unregulated immigration led to a population explosion, which led to crime, hunger, and disease becoming rampant. Poverty greatly increased, morale greatly decreased, and friendliness and trust amongst the population virtually disappeared. All towns and areas anywhere near the border became like a war zone, *except* on the shores of Fir Lake; life there was Elysian.[230]

The shores of Fir Lake were protected from the drug cartels *by* the drug cartels and became part of a major corridor for drugs coming into the U.S. and cash going out. The cartels went so far as to build a four-lane, paved freeway that only they could use. It went along the shores of Fir Lake and through Zapata, TX and aided in transporting all the drugs and money. This four-lane freeway quickly became an eight-lane freeway and the drug traffic was bumper to bumper, in both directions, at all times. They even had their own helicopter giving traffic reports.

The drug cartels became so rich, powerful, and greedy that they formed their own country which stretched from Monterrey, Mexico up to Monterey, CA, over to Pueblo, CO, and back down to Matamoros, Mexico. The capital of their new country was at Fir Lake because everything around there

---

229 Schizophrenia is a severe brain disorder in which people interpret reality abnormally. Schizophrenia may result in some combination of hallucinations, delusions, and extremely disordered thinking and behavior.

230 Of, relating to, or characteristic of heaven or paradise.

(buildings, land, roads, water system, etc.) was in great shape because it had been protected from all the drug trafficking mayhem. The Presidential Palace of this fledgling country was built on the shores of Fir Lake and, as luck would have it, right next to David and Maria's house.

David Knight had inadvertently given this country its name when he was overheard saying, "...this country is becoming the USSI." The leaders of the new country had no idea what that meant but they liked it so...that is what they called their country. It didn't take long however, for the people to demand to know what the letters stood for. To appease the people, the leader went on TV one night and told the entire nation what the letters stood for: Ultima Senorita Siestas Infeliz, which translates to: "Last Señorita Naps Unhappy." It was pure piffle[231] that he had made up on the spur of the moment while flying high on a new drug the cartel/government was experimenting with.

This new drug caused people to believe that a Utopian society was not only possible, but probable as long as Democrats were always in control and Republicans were ostracized every few years. This drug worked so well that it went into mass production and was widely and expertly distributed throughout the USA, as evidenced by the fact that Barack Obama was re-elected to be President. His election greatly benefitted the drug cartels for they could now freely cross the border (the USA-USSI border) without fear of being captured, prosecuted, or deported. They could write their own rules, and they did.

The leaders of the new USSI elected their own President and made their own laws. One of which stated that if anyone were caught entering *their* country without permission, they would

---

231   Nonsense. I prefer to use "codswallop" but hey, variety is the spice of life...or so I've been told.

THE GOOD OL' USSI

be shot on the spot. They formed their own army, got a spot on the UN, and even started their own space program in an attempt to find new markets for their Utopian drug.

The USSI's Utopian drug had found its way to nearly every nook and cranny of the planet and as a result, the USSI expanded to include major parts of all seven continents, including Antarctica. It was pretty cold there and there weren't many people, but there were *some* and they wanted their Utopia drug. The USSI became the largest, richest, and most populated country on planet Earth, and so set their sights on Mars.

The Elysian shores of Fir Lake had deteriorated so rapidly and completely due to the USSI's rapid expansion, that Maria and David, along with their "adopted" children, just left everything but the clothes on their backs and high-tailed it to Minnesota. Once there, they saw how the U.S. had become a dystopia[232] so, out of desperation, they managed to gather all their wealth they had left behind and make their way to Sainte-Anne-des-Monts, Quebec in Canada, which is located between the Chic-Choc Mountains and the St. Lawrence River estuary.[233] It was one of the few spots on planet Earth that hadn't become tainted by Utopia. With an average high of 69.4° F in July and an average low of 3° F in January, no dealers wanted to traffic their Utopian drug there; it was too damn cold. So, David and Maria built a warm mansion on the St. Lawrence River and had their own drug-free utopia.

David learned how to fish the St. Lawrence River, which

---

232   A bogus utopia run on propaganda; ruled by a repressive government which breaks promises, dashes the hopes of its citizens, and destroys wealth. Thank you Barack Hussein Obama, with help from clueless Democrats—which is all of them.

233   The tidal mouth of a large river, where the "tide meets the stream."

fed into the sea, and Maria became the worlds first exclusive "mammary gland" model and quickly made another fortune as guys high on Utopia loved looking at her boobs, especially after they found out she had been the star of the films on the www. xxxjbs.com website.

Their three kids went through law school on the U.S. taxpayer's dime (even though they lived in Canada) and became immigration lawyers. Problem was there was no need for immigration lawyers. The reason being: The USSI was expanding at an exponential rate and swallowing-up all other countries. There were simply to few remaining countries for people to *emigrate* from and only one country to *immigrate*[234] to. Therefore, everyone just ran around willy-nilly high on Utopia, believing nothing could go wrong.

Eventually, with nothing else to do, the three children moved back in with David and Maria in Sainte-Anne-des-Monts, Quebec in Canada where they lived in bliss, ate a lot of fish, and lived to a ripe, old age.

Even though the drug cartels were extraordinarily rich and powerful, they had recently ceased to exist because of a little incident on the planet Mars, which is the only reason Maria, David, and their three kids were able to live to the aforementioned ripe, old age.

The drug cartels were always looking for new places to sell their product, and since the vast majority of the Earth's population was addicted to their Utopian drug, they wanted new markets. They spent billions of dollars trying to land on, and colonize Mars in order to expand their market for Utopia, and

---

234 Emigrate = leave one's own country in order to settle permanently in another. Immigrate = come to live permanently in a foreign country. So, one can't *immigrate* until one *emigrates*.

believe it or not, they succeeded. However, their new customers didn't react to the Utopian drug the way Earthlings did.

The Martians, who were much more intelligent than even the smartest human,[235] didn't think everything was perfect and wonderful after taking Utopia. In fact, they just became intensely mad, but only at people who had used or dealt the drug. They quickly disposed of all the drug users on their planet and all of the equipment and structures they had brought with them or had built once they arrived.

The Martians, who had their own space program since 1931 and only used it in the search for intelligent life, hadn't bothered visiting planet Earth. Now, however, they were hell bent on getting to Earth and so quickly got in their vehicles and headed out. They knew that Earth was where Utopia was being manufactured, dealt, and ultimately consumed by billions of people. They were all to be punished.

As soon as they landed on Earth, they went about exterminating everyone who had taken, manufactured, sold, or even touched Utopia. Their only concern about landing on Earth and killing billions of people was the nuclear arsenal held by what remained of the United States. A nuclear missile could possibly injure them and would probably hurt.

This concern was allayed however, when they found out that the U.S. Commander in Chief had disappeared after going into the woods to look for his golf ball. This enabled them to move about Earth with impunity[236] and systematically exterminate

---

235 Terrence Tao is one of the smartest, possibly the smartest, people in the world. He has an IQ of 230 and at the age of 24, became the youngest ever full professor at UCLA. However, the Martians made him look like a dunderhead who would try to eat Chinese food with one chopstick.

236 Exemption from punishment or freedom from the injurious consequences of an action. Obama has impunity from the press.

anyone who had anything to do with Utopia. Therefore, Maria, David, and their three kids were untouched.

Now, that Earth was free from the Utopia drug, the Martians had no need to be there and so just left. That is why Maria, David, and their three adopted kids were able to live happily-ever-after and, by extension, to a ripe, old age.

Postlude[237]

Maria never did contact her mother and tell her about her grandkids. She later found out that the tour bus her mother was on had been stopped, because of an anonymous tip, at the U.S.-Canadian border. The Homeland Security Officers, who stopped and searched the bus, reported seeing a woman and Justin Bieber run off into the wilderness hand-in-hand during the search. They were never seen again and it is unlikely that they survived as the temperature was in the low teens (Fahrenheit) and they were both naked.

The anonymous tip was regarding a stash of illegal child pornography, the likes of which would have made Bernie Ward[238] envious, hidden on the bus. The stash was found and confiscated by authorities, who were themselves later implicated (as dealers) in a child pornography ring that stretched from sea to shinning sea.

David and Maria settled into a life that would be the envy of nearly anyone. They didn't have to work because the government was paying them to do nothing, even though they were already quite wealthy. They lived in a nice house, and had three great kids. In addition, the leader of the drug cartel that killed the parents of the three kids was the only person involved with the Utopian drug that managed to escape the

---

237 A final or concluding phrase, chapter, or development—an epilogue, an afterword, a postscript. The ending.

238 He is a former radio talk show host in San Francisco, CA. who is now serving a seven-year prison sentence for the online distribution of child pornography. Ward, once billed as "The Lion of the Left" and "unabashedly liberal," was the host of the daily news talk program, *The Bernie Ward Show*, and the three-hour program, *GodTalk*, on Sunday mornings. I am assuming that he, himself, did not hear what God was talking about...at least I hope not.

Martian cleansing. He did it by hiding in the tunnel that Maria and Ernesto had used to illegally enter the U.S.

He, himself, was a family man who put children above all else (except profits) and when he heard about these three children that had been "adopted" by a Mexican woman and her husband and were now living on the shores of Fir Lake, he offered them protection from anything and everything; no one even bullied the kids at school for fear of being beheaded.

So, Maria, David, and their three "adopted" kids lived to a ripe, old age in comfort, opulence, and security in Zapata, Texas on the shores of Fir Lake.

The End

El final de la historia.

CPSIA information can be obtained at www.ICGtesting.com
Printed in the USA
BVOW08s0455140116

432823BV00001B/15/P